THE ICE QUEEN BILLIONAIRE

ENEMIES TO LOVERS ROMANCE

THE FRAZER FAMILY
BOOK FOUR

ZOE DOD

Edited by
V STRAW

MILKY DOWN PUBLISHING

Copyright © 2025 by Zoe Dod

All rights reserved.

No part of this book may be reproduced in any form or by any electronic or mechanical means, including information storage and retrieval systems, without written permission from the author, except for the use of brief quotations in a book review.

This is a work of fiction. Names, characters, places, incidents and dialogues are products of the author's imagination or are used fictitiously. Any resemblance to actual people, living or dead, or events is entirely coincidental.

The Ice Queen Billionaire is written in British English.

ISBN ebook: 978-1-917413-06-0

ISBN paperback: 978-1-917413-07-7

Editor: Victoria Straw

Cover Design by ChristineCoverDesigns

To wonderful friends
xxx

CHAPTER 1

KAT

"Lottie," Caleb says, the relief in his tone palpable.

My gaze goes to the door as Lottie enters, tucked under Elijah's shoulder. Her head is buried against his chest, his arms locked tightly around her.

I close my eyes and let out a deep breath, sending up a silent prayer of thanks.

"Lottie? Darling."

Darra jumps to her feet, trembling hands reaching towards her daughter, before coming to rest over her chest.

An ache forms in my throat. Despite everything she's put my brother and Pen through, no mother should find out her daughter is missing. God only knows where.

"Mum?" Lottie says, her head coming up. "What are you doing here?"

"You expect me to ignore the fact that you didn't arrive on the plane you were supposed to?" Darra's voice catches, her eyes blinking rapidly. "I know you think I'm the world's worst mother, but—"

"I don't think you're the world's worst mother," she replies, her eyes widening as she takes in the police officers and family members. "I sent you a message telling you I was staying here for my birthday. You didn't get it?" she whispers, her voice cracking.

"Clearly," Darra says, her tone hardening.

My stomach clenches as Darra's mask slips, and Lottie tries to placate her mother.

"Mr Frazer?"

Elijah looks up as the police officer in charge steps forward.

"As Miss Frazer has returned?"

"Yes. Please. If you need a statement, I can bring her to the station later," Elijah says quickly.

His rigid posture tells me he wants to remove all eyewitnesses. As a family, we don't need our dirty laundry aired in public.

The officer nods and motions for his colleagues to clear up and move out.

An awkward silence descends.

Pen steps forward and walks them out. I can hear her talking in the corridor. It's good to see my friend where she's meant to be, standing beside the love of her life.

"Hey, button," Caleb says, stepping forward and giving Lottie a hug. "You had us scared."

"I know, I'm sorry, Uncle Caleb…"

I tune out the rest of their conversation as my eyes come to rest on the man standing in the doorway.

A sudden chill expands deep within my core, and I curl my fingers inward, gripping the chair I'm sitting on.

"What the—" Gabriel hisses.

I sense his gaze move to me, but my focus remains locked on the man in the doorway as I work on schooling my features.

"Zach?" Caleb says, breaking the spell.

Darra moves towards Zach. When she touches his arm,

my lungs constrict, spots flashing in my vision. I clench my jaw, swallowing against the painful tightness in my throat.

Zach shakes his head and steps away. "No." His gaze finally leaves me before landing on my older brother.

My thoughts spin as I question my reality. Our reality.

How the hell did we get here?

"Listen to me." Elijah's words pull me back into the present. "You have every right to know who your biological father is. I just wish you'd spoken to me. You scared me, princess. You going missing—"

My niece throws herself at Elijah. The sound of her heaving sobs echoes around the room, and I pinch my lips together to keep them from trembling.

Elijah pulls Lottie onto his knee and cradles her against his chest, the same way he always has. Tears well up behind my eyelids, but I blink them away. My brother loves his daughter, irrespective of her biology. Lottie is a Frazer. No one will take her away from us, that I vow.

My eyes return to Zach, and our gazes lock.

He flinches and lowers his head. He closes his eyes before opening them again. The look he sends me has a knot forming in my stomach.

"I wanted to marry her," Zach says suddenly, pushing off from the wall and stepping forward.

My heart rate slows at the sound of his voice.

Focus.

"As Darra said, I wasn't good enough," Zach says, stumbling slightly over his words. "Her father threatened Dad. He'd just moved jobs, told me he'd set him up, that he had the power to do it. Showed me footage of... I couldn't."

Zach's eyes are overbright, his voice shaky, as he tries to justify his actions.

My skin crawls, and I fight the urge to scratch it.

Zach is the eldest of five much younger siblings. They'd

often come to stay with us when we lived together. If his dad had lost his job, or worse, it would have had devastating consequences for the family. I should feel pity, but instead the bitter tang in my mouth leaves me cold.

His eyes lock on Lottie. "Then he told me if I interfered and warned you, there'd be no baby."

My hands clench as heat rushes through my body.

No, you bastard, you don't tell a child that!

Lottie buries her head in Elijah's chest at his words.

He kisses the top of her head before tilting her chin up to look at him.

"I told you once before. You may not carry my blood, but you will *always* be the daughter of my heart. Wherever you come from, however you came into this world. You will always be mine. I love you, Lottie Frazer, and I will always be here for you, no matter what."

Her arms fly around Elijah's neck, and I inhale a ragged breath.

"Zach is her father," Darra spits, her nostrils flaring, her lips pulled back. "He was my lover for years, even after you threw me aside."

There's a pounding in my ears as my eyes move back to Zach.

Whatever he sees in my expression has his hands going to the sides of his head, the heels of his palms pressing down hard. Adrenaline rushes through my body, making me grip the cushion tighter as my vision narrows.

Everyone is looking at me. The need to flee is becoming overwhelming.

"Never show your true feelings or insecurities, Kitty Kat. That way, they can't be used against you."

Words from the past hit me hard.

Dad.

Instead of running, I allow the coldness filling my chest to expand outwards, leaving me numb, empty.

My hand goes to the chain I wear around my neck. I grip the pendant tight, and it digs into my skin, the discomfort grounding me.

The buzz of muffled voices continues.

"What was I?" I ask coldly, tilting my head, my eyes never leaving Zach's.

He grimaces, and my lips curl, my eyebrows pinching together.

Why?

"If you continued your affair with Darra, why did you need me?" I ask, my voice surprisingly steady.

His body becomes unnaturally still as his chin drops to his chest.

"Kat," he says, his voice thickening.

I stare at him until his gaze drops to his hands.

"You were sleeping with her while you were living with me?" My voice is distant, flat. "You lied to me. You deceived me."

A dark flush sweeps up his neck and across his face. My eyes track its progress. A sheen of sweat breaks out on his forehead and upper lip. Yet, there's no satisfaction. How can there be? His lies and deceit set in motion a string of events that can never be undone.

"Kat," he whispers, his gaze pleading. "I—"

My stomach contracts.

Darra steps forward.

"You were convenient," her tone is smug. "Enabled him to stay near Lottie."

She cocks her head, her lips twisting in a sneer.

It takes every ounce of self-control to prevent me from slapping the smug look off her face. I'm a Frazer, I won't give her the satisfaction.

She's toxic, always has been, but Elijah was too blind to see the snake he invited into our lives.

The charge in the air changes. Darra thrusts out her chest, not sensing the danger as she continues her rant.

"He should be thanking you," she spits. "You're as frigid as your brother. Is it surprising he looked elsewhere?"

Zach spins to Darra.

"Shut up. Enough of your toxic lies," he hisses. His gaze hardens as he stares at his ex-lover.

Elijah gets up and stalks towards Darra.

"Get out," he snaps.

Her head tilts up as she slowly raises an eyebrow.

My brother stops, inhaling deeply, making her give a short, disgusted snort.

Elijah moves forward, but Caleb grabs his arm. Caleb might be the joker among us all, but he has a fierce sense of loyalty.

"Don't give her the satisfaction," he says, stepping between them, his hands landing hard against Elijah's chest, stopping his forward motion.

Caleb turns his head, his voice cutting through the silence. "Get your toxic arse out of my brother's apartment."

Darra sneers and rolls her eyes.

I grit my teeth harder.

"Do as he says," Elijah hisses. "Before I return us to court and remove everything I agreed to. Believe me, I have more than enough evidence to do it."

Darra freezes. Her eyes lock onto Elijah over Caleb's shoulder. All colour drains from her face.

There's a pause. Darra flicks her hand in front of her face, her mouth tight, as if she has suddenly smelt or tasted something bad.

"Lottie, you're coming back with me," she says, her eyes moving to her daughter, her expression hard.

"No, no, no. I'm sorry. Don't make me leave," Lottie pleads, her arms locking around Pen, her heart-wrenching sobs twisting something inside me.

"She doesn't have to go anywhere with you." Elijah's voice is deadly quiet. "I'm now legally her father. Your threat no longer stands. If you know what's good for you. You'll turn around and leave. Now."

Darra's shoulders go back, and she stares at him, weighing up his words. Whatever she sees, she turns on her heel.

"Zach?" she all but shrieks as she makes her way to the door.

My eyes return to Zach, who is once again watching me.

His gaze drops to the floor. But he remains static.

Darra harrumphs as she storms out, the front door slamming behind her.

I flinch as the sound reverberates around the room.

Gabriel and Caleb drop to the floor in front of me, their hands resting on my knees.

No, no, no, little brothers. Back off. Can't you see I'm hanging on by a thread?

I move my hands and squeeze each of theirs before quickly standing up and making my way towards Lottie. I take my niece's face gently in my hands and drop a kiss on her cheek.

"I'm sorry, Aunty Kat," Lottie sobs, a fresh set of tears running freely down her cheeks.

I incline my head and smile at her, using my thumb to brush away her tears.

"You, my darling girl, have nothing to be sorry for." I swallow past the tightness in my throat. "I'm sorry you got caught up in the games of adults." I cup her face in my hands, my gaze holding her watery one. "All you need to know is that everyone loves you unconditionally, whoever your father and mother are. You're Lottie Brooke Frazer, and you always will be."

I look Lottie in the eye as I inhale. The need to get out of here, to escape, is riding me hard. I move my hands, cupping her chin in one hand and squeezing her shoulder with the other.

"I need to leave right now, but I want you to know that has nothing to do with you. I love you, sweet girl."

Lottie lets go of Pen and wraps her arms around me. I close my eyes and hug her back, allowing this young girl's courage to bolster my own.

How have we got here?

"I love you too, Aunty Kat," Lottie whispers against my shoulder.

I allow my lungs to fill with air as I calm myself. I give her one final squeeze before stepping back, praying my voice remains steady and my legs hold me up.

"I need to go," I tell Lottie. "But we'll get through this. Call me if you need me."

Lottie nods, her eyes still glistening.

Pen's hand comes up and grips my arm, sending me a silent message of support.

I meet her gaze, offering her the slightest nod.

"I need time," I whisper.

I know my friend well. She won't push me now, but she'll need to know I'm okay.

I turn to my siblings and hug each in turn. I suck in a ragged breath before turning and making my way to the door.

A hand lands on my arm.

Zach.

I pause, my eyes dropping to where his hand is encircling my bicep. I curl my lip as I look up, my stare as cold and dead as I can make it.

Don't you fucking dare!

He drops his hand as if burned.

"We need to talk," he says quietly.

"We do," I say. There's no point in denying it. "But not now."

It's like a fog has descended, and my brain has stopped working. I've never felt like this before.

He dips his chin.

I open the door and use that moment to dart out before anyone else can stop me.

I hit the down arrow on the elevator multiple times.

I need to process, take stock, and rebuild my barriers. Escape.

"I'm going after Kat," I hear Gabriel say, close to the door.

The elevator pings, announcing its arrival, and I breathe a sigh of relief.

I step in, the door closing, just as my younger brother makes it out of the door.

I drop my back against the wall, my head thumping slightly against the hard surface. I grip the pendant on the chain around my neck before closing my eyes and focusing on my breath.

In and out, in and out.

It stutters, and I pinch the skin on my wrist, twisting it. My eyes spring open just as the elevator stops. The doors open, and I thrust my shoulders back, running my hands down my clothes before stepping into the car park.

I freeze as Darra's voice echoes across the parking garage.

"We made love in your bed for hours. More than once. But he won't tell you that."

I lift my chin and bite my tongue before heading towards my car.

"You've never been able to keep a man," she shouts, stepping into the light, her expression venomous. "Looks like even your brother's best friends couldn't defrost your icy heart. It certainly wasn't difficult to turn their heads."

I stuff my trembling hands in my pockets.

Ignore her!

"Nothing to say?" Darra goads me but keeps her distance.

As I reach the door. I grip my keys. The car bleeps as it unlocks, and at the same time, the elevator pings behind us. Gabriel and Caleb burst out of the doors.

Gabriel growls as he takes in the situation.

"*Fuck off,* Darra, haven't you done enough damage?"

My quiet, introverted brother takes a step towards Darra, and I use the distraction to get into my car. Switching on the engine, I wait for it to roar to life. It's a sound I need. It's not only Gabriel and Caleb who have a love of cars. This baby, my ice silver McLaren Artura, is my pride and joy.

My hands grip the steering wheel tight to quell the tremors racking my body.

I put her into reverse and pull out, passing the twins who are still next to the elevator door, waiting, watching... my protectors. Darra is nowhere in sight.

I acknowledge them both as I drive past, but don't stop.

I need time and space. I pray they understand my compulsion to flee, to lick my wounds in private. My breathing stutters, and I close my eyes as I'm forced to wait for the barrier to go up. My stomach heaves, my throat burning as I finally put my car into drive and escape the nightmare that has only just begun to unfold.

CHAPTER 2

KAT

It's late when I finally make it back to the apartment. A few hours in the office going over mindless reports, the perfect way to shelve the shit show that became my life this afternoon.

Not that I blame Lottie. No, I blame her bitch of a mother, and my two-timing, back-stabbing ex, who appears to be her biological father.

I roll my neck, trying to ease the tension in my head and shoulders.

When that doesn't work, I massage my temples.

Fuck!

It's not like Zach and I are still together.

Only the two of us were together when he was sleeping with her.

I scrub a hand over my face, letting out a frustrated growl.

"We made love in your bed."

Darra's words echo through my mind.

I thump the back of the sofa, withdrawing my hand quickly as if stung.

Did they make love here, too?

Zach and I lived together for seven years. How many of those was he shagging her too? Here in our home?

My vision blurs, my heartbeat pounding in my ears. I blink rapidly, fending off tears he does not deserve. A sharp pain lances through my palm. I look down to see crescent-shaped welts where my fingernails have broken the skin.

Fuck you, Zachary Greville!

I give myself a mental shake. This is not what I need right now. No distractions.

What I need is sleep.

Everything will be better in the morning.

I walk into our bedroom, my eyes instantly drawn to the bed.

My vision tunnels, an alien sound escapes me as I pick up the first pillow, throwing it across the room, then the second—

Destruction.

I grind my teeth, my muscles quivering, taking in what's left of my bedroom. My heart beats rapidly in my chest, and a trickle of sweat runs down between my shoulder blades.

Blankets and pillows litter the floor, even the mattress is upturned, and the bedhead sits at an awkward angle. Nothing escaped my wrath. There's no way I'll ever be able to sleep on this bed again or even here in this room. Everything is tainted by *them*. My apartment, my sanctuary, is no more.

Bile burns the back of my throat, and the pounding in my head intensifies.

I drop to my knees as knots cramp in my stomach.

Why care? We've been over for three years.

But the whole twelve years we were together were based on a lie.

I crawl forward and grab my overnight bag, thankful I'd

left it next to the wardrobe. Pulling myself up, I thrust my shoulders back before stuffing it with clothes and toiletries.

I pick up my phone. Twenty-four messages and six missed calls.

I scan them. They're all from my siblings, wanting to know if I'm okay.

I listen to the voice messages, my heart aching. I'd disabled the ringer.

Elijah: "Kat, we just need to know you're okay. Please, sis, I'm worried."

Caleb: "Kat, we're worried about you. Please call."

Gabriel: "If you need anything, sis, we're here for you."

I freeze at the next one.

Zach: "Kat, we really need to talk. I'm sorry, I never wanted you to find out—"

I delete the message, letting out a deep, gratifying sigh, before blocking his number.

No, Zach, I'm sure you didn't want me to find out, you two-timing bastard.

I inhale deeply before firing off a message on the family group chat.

ME:
> Please don't worry about me, I'm fine. I'm going to stay with Mum.

I groan at the three dots that appear and disappear rapidly. Finally, a single message comes through.

CALEB:
> Drive safely. We're here if you need us.

I send one more message before hoisting my bag onto my shoulder and turning my back on the chaos I've wrought.

ME:

I'm coming home.

MUM:

See you when you get here. Drive carefully.

* * *

It's late by the time I arrive.

Mum doesn't say a word, simply pulls me into her arms and gives me a fierce hug. I squeeze her back, absorbing her strength. I pull back, her eyes scan my face as she cups my cheeks in her hands.

My throat constricts, and I blink rapidly. She nods at the weak smile I offer her. Her message is loud and clear.

I'm here when you're ready.

I shiver, and she pats my cheek before stepping to one side. I head straight to my childhood room and shut the door, sinking into the comfort of my bed. I run a hand down my face, surprised to find it damp.

I move to my ensuite bathroom, flipping on the shower. Steam fills the room. I strip off and step into the scalding water, scrubbing my skin until it's pink and raw.

When I'm done, I wrap myself in a towel and make my way back into my room.

I stop. A whine followed by scratching. I get up and open the door. Mum's puppy, Diana, darts in and jumps on the bed, curling herself into a ball.

I lie down next to her, my hand going to her short coat. I rub her silky ears, watching as she rolls onto her back, showing me her belly.

"You want to sleep with me?"

She nuzzles my hand, scratching at the duvet. I lift it

slightly only to have her burrow under it before curling herself into a tight ball, her eyes closing.

Zach and I never slept together here. Mum always put us in one of the guest rooms when we came to stay. Unlike Caleb and April, or Gabriel and Leah. Even Elijah and Pen have shared Eli's childhood bedroom.

Did she have an inkling? Knew I would need this space?

I climb in next to her, and Diana moves into my body, curling herself around me, the warmth of her tiny body the comfort I need.

I take several deep shuddering breaths before closing my eyes and forcing the memories of the day away.

THE EARLY MORNING sun lights my way. My feet pound against the ground as I weave my way through the trees. I jump over fallen branches, careful to miss obscured roots. The last thing I need is to trip and break something. Running and running hard is my only escape from my thoughts, from the torment of the images plaguing last night's dreams. For my brothers, it's always been swimming, but for me, I need to run. It was still dark outside when I woke up, with my tense body bathed in sweat, my heart pounding.

The need to get out, to feel the air on my face, and the ground beneath my feet was almost too much, so here I am. In another month, this run will become treacherous as the fallen leaves will mask unseen dangers, but not today. Today I'm granted the solitude of the woods, a release only the peace and tranquillity of being at one with nature can offer.

Sweat temporarily blinds me, and I stumble forward, my hand grazing one of the tree trunks as I work to catch myself. The bite of the wood, therapeutic against my negative thoughts. I rub my eyes to clear my vision and push off.

On and on—just an intense burn in my chest and heavy, quivering limbs.

My muscles begin to spasm.

How long have I been out here?

I reach out and grip the trunk of an old oak tree. I drop my head forward through outstretched arms, my breath coming in loud, noisy pants. I suck in air and wait. Wait for the ringing in my ears to subside, for my racing heartbeat to slow.

When my breathing finally calms, I turn around and drop back against the strength of the trunk, sinking to the ground among the carpet of dry leaves. Tipping my head back, I close my eyes, the heaviness of my limbs immense.

Fuck!

I smack the ground next to me with the flat of my hand. The bite causes my fingers to sink into the dry vegetation. I run my hands through it, allowing its dry, brittle texture to ground me. I open my eyes and stare up into the canopy of branches and leaves.

Our old treehouse, little more than a shell now, rests in the branches. I've run to the far corner of the estate. This was my safe space growing up, somewhere my overactive imagination could run wild. A place I could escape and be whoever I dreamed of being. Not simply a Frazer.

I shrug off my backpack and pull out a bottle of water. I take a long swig, allowing the liquid to quench my parched throat. One shuddering breath follows another. I swallow hard, trying to get my breathing under control. I twist to the side as a wave of nausea hits me. I wretch, but there's nothing left. I haven't eaten since yesterday lunchtime.

I sit up, banging my head back against the tree, before closing my eyes and shutting out the world.

Fuck you, Zach, and fuck you, Darra!

I draw my knees into my chest, wrapping my arms tightly around them before throwing back my head and screaming.

Like a madwoman, I let it all out in the sanctity of my safe place.

The birds in the trees take off, complaining at the noise, trying to escape the lunatic who's invaded their space, the lunatic I've become.

When I'm finished, I suck in a breath, followed by another. I force myself to breathe in and out as I work to calm my racing thoughts. With each inhale, my strength returns.

I pull myself up, brushing off the leaves and dust. My now-cold muscles complain bitterly. As I stretch, I work on rebuilding my mental shields.

I growl at myself.

Kat Frazer, you appear to attract bastards like bees to a honey pot.

I can hear Mum now.

It's not you, it's them.

But I'm the common denominator.

And Zachery Greville was supposed to be my safe option!

Before I leave, I kick dry leaves over the evidence of my weakness before grabbing my backpack and heading home. It's time to work on something I can control.

Jaxson

I STAND SILENTLY in the trees, keeping my presence hidden. I know better than to approach, my being here would probably be seen as an act of war, but watching Kathryn Frazer's icy cold exterior shatter has a bigger impact than even I could have anticipated.

To do nothing is hard, but I've done what was requested. I found her, and she is not physically harmed. Mentally, on the other hand...

I run a hand down my face. We may not see eye-to-eye on many things, haven't for years, but I would never want any harm to befall her. She's my best friends' sister. Has always been tenacious and tough, yet the woman in front of me is none of those things today. It feels wrong to be standing here watching such a personal moment.

I turn away, offering her a semblance of privacy, only turning back when I hear her move. She stands, her shoulders back, her chin up, as if the past thirty minutes were a figment of my imagination.

I smile.

I wait and fire off a message as soon as Kat leaves.

ME:

She's on her way back.

My phone vibrates with a thumbs-up emoji.

I turn around and head back to Caleb and April's house on the neighbouring estate. I did the right thing. Making my presence known would have exacerbated the process. She clearly needed this time. My stomach flips, and I grimace. I know something happened yesterday, but I don't know the details. But whatever it was, her siblings are worried about her. And, Kat wanted to let it out in private, no witnesses. I'm trespassing. But when I received the call this morning to keep an eye out, I couldn't ignore it. The last thing I expected was to find Kat screaming out her anguish in the middle of the woods.

I make my way back to Lofton House. It borders the Frazer estate and will soon become Caleb and April's main residence. But for now, it's my office as I focus on drawing up the plans for its renovation.

CHAPTER 3

KAT

Ten Weeks Later

My jaw clenches as my email pings with yet another notification.

I shrug and roll my shoulders to ease the tension in my back and neck. It reminds me that I need to book a deep-tissue massage with Carla.

I fire off a message, and my phone chimes almost instantly.

CARLA:

See you at eight at the hotel.

I give her message a thumbs up before turning and opening my email. I grimace as fifty new messages from the past ten minutes download.

At least I knew this was coming and have set things in motion.

Not that the board knows this. I'm sworn to secrecy. And looking at the messages, they're the ones blowing up my phone and email.

There's a knock at my door.

"Come in."

Michael, my PA, bursts through the door, waving Sunday's copy of The Edition, the leading UK newspaper.

"Have you seen it?" he asks, approaching my desk. He stops, drawing up short and shaking his head. "Of course you have."

His expression is one of admiration. He seems to think I'm all-knowing and all-powerful. The consummate professional. It would never cross his mind that I might slip up, miss something.

How little he knows me.

He, like so many others, can't see past the persona I've spent years cultivating.

"I'm so dumb," he says, chastising himself.

I frown. That's one thing Michael is not. If he were, he wouldn't be working for me.

His eyes widen suddenly, and he snaps his fingers.

"That's why you've been stonewalling the development," he says, grinning.

I sit back in the chair and rest my hands flat on the desk.

"Not so dumb," I say, and his smile widens.

"How?"

"I can't reveal my source, but in business, it helps to have friends in a variety of places. Always remember that."

It was one of the first pieces of advice my father ever gave me. That and, *"Never show your true feelings or insecurities so they can be used against you, Kitty Kat."*

In this case, it was Quentin Cavendish, head of the country's largest media corporation and best friend of my baby brother, Caleb, who saved the day.

"So, what now?" Michael asks, taking a seat and pulling out his note taker.

I suppress a smile. Always ready to work. His enthusiasm knows no bounds.

"Send a memo to the press department. We'll need to release a statement immediately distancing ourselves from Moorland and Sons. The Frazer Hotel Group is no longer associated with them. Call a meeting with the asset management team, tell Elliot we need to revisit the initial list of architects we compiled, find out who's available, and review their pitches. Arrange an emergency board meeting for Wednesday afternoon."

My heart sinks a little at the thought, but I keep my emotions in check. The original list was short, and Moorland and Sons were by far the best.

"I'm on it. Anything else?" Michael asks, standing up.

"I'll let you know," I say, as he heads towards the door.

As soon as the door closes, I spin my chair towards the window and drop my head back. I close my eyes against the incessant pounding in my head and release a breath, trying to force the rigid muscles in my shoulders to relax. Eight o'clock can't come fast enough.

I open my eyes and head to the coffee machine I had installed in my office, just for moments like these. I lean against the sideboard as it does its thing. My mind races with questions as I rehash all the information I've received.

Come on, Kat, you've got this. You've dealt with setbacks before.

I pick up the coffee mug and cradle it in my hands, taking a sip. My stomach churns at the bitterness, reminding me I skipped breakfast. I move slowly to the window and stare out over the city. I really need to shake the heaviness sitting on my chest.

This is just one more crisis for me to overcome. It's nothing new.

When Quentin called a couple of weeks ago, I wanted to

scream. We'd just signed the contract with Moorland and Sons. He warned me he had a team of reporters investigating them, and that I should be careful.

At the time, it had been one more thing to add to my list of things that could and were going wrong.

Moorland and Sons is one of the few companies within the UK that focus on sustainability in their architectural designs. They appeared perfect on the surface. Behind the scenes, however, it appears they've been paying off planning officers and buying officials. Something Quentin's newspaper uncovered and exposed over the weekend. As a result of the exposé, they're now under investigation, but the scandal is not something I want anywhere near the Frazer Hotel Group or our latest project.

It also means there'll be a delay, something the board and our investors are not going to like. This project is something I've worked hard to sell them, it's my baby, and has been my vision for the FHG since before my father died. But that's me. I'm focused and driven to the point of obsession. As one reporter wrote a couple of years ago.

KATHRYN FRAZER IS the queen of the boardroom. She's unafraid to rise to the challenge of running an international business even at her young age and is single-minded in pursuit of her goals.

THE PHONE on my desk rings, and I move back to my desk.

"Michael," I say, pressing the connect button.

"Caleb is on the line," he says.

Ah, my brother. I shouldn't be surprised. He recently joined the board at my invitation. The FHG is the founding company that built the Frazer fortune. I felt it was important that another family member be present and have input in how it operates. He's pretty silent, letting me run the show, but it's good to know he's there.

"Thank you, put him through." I hear the click as Michael connects us. "Hey, little brother."

"Hey, Kat," Caleb says. "I've just seen the newspaper. Please tell me Quentin gave you the heads up."

I chuckle. "He did, but swore me to secrecy."

As with all exposé pieces, the more people who know, the greater the chance the sting is leaked. As a result, Quentin gave me the heads up as a favour, but made it clear I wasn't to discuss it with anyone, including Caleb.

His sigh of relief comes over loud and clear. I'm not sure why Caleb would doubt his friend, especially after all the help he's given our family recently.

A wave of cold washes over me at the thought of Harper, our baby sister, alone on the other side of the world, all because of some sick bastard's twisted mind games.

"So, what's the plan?" Caleb asks.

I stifle a chuckle at his profound confidence that *I* have a plan.

"We'll release a statement to the press distancing us from Moorland. Luckily, the project is still in its initial stages, so there's minimal damage."

Quentin's heads-up ensured I refrained from handing over too much detail.

That reminds me, I need to send Quentin a box of wine. He saved my bacon on this one.

I write myself a note.

Contact Tristan St John, send Quentin a box of his favourite wine as a thank you.

This project has been years in the making, and will be ground-breaking if we succeed, the first of its kind and will cement the FHG as market leaders. It is therefore not something I want falling into our rivals' hands.

"I'm scheduling a board meeting for Wednesday afternoon if you're free? Michael will be sending out the invites shortly."

"I'll be there," Caleb says. "What about other architects?"

"We have our previous list. I'm having Elliot revisit them with his team. Our biggest issue will be their availability and timeframes. It's something I'll discuss at the board meeting."

There's a pause, and I get the impression he wants to add something.

"Is there anything else?"

There's another pause.

"No, see you on Wednesday, sis."

Caleb disconnects before I can say anything else.

I sit back in my chair, finding my centre as I work to refocus my energy. My muscles tighten in readiness as the caffeine hits, and I prepare for what's to come.

You've got this.

This is, after all, what I'm good at. Circumnavigating obstacles and strategising. Yes, it's been a stressful couple of months, first finding out about Zach and Lottie, the cyberattack on both Elijah's company and the hotel, Harper's scandal, and now this. I'm beginning to wonder if someone is trying to see how far I can be pushed.

I open my drawer and take out some painkillers. Swallowing them down with the leftover coffee.

Leaning back in my chair, I close my eyes and exhale loudly. I'm tired, so bone-wearily tired.

No time for a pity party, there's work to do.

I shake off my fatigue and sit forward, pulling up my ideas sheet for the new hotel development. Moorland were a good fit. He understood my vision, or at least what I'd shared with him. It's a shame he's corrupt. But I'm not going to let that stop me. Where one door closes, another one opens, or so everyone tells me. I just have to be patient and see where and what it is.

CHAPTER 4

JAX

April grips Caleb's arm, her eyes sparkling.

"Jax, I don't know what to say. These plans are amazing."

Caleb pulls April back into his chest before wrapping his arms around her waist, his chin resting on her shoulder. "You really have outdone yourself this time."

A warmth spreads through my body at their response.

"If there's anything you want to change, let me know. I've printed off the plans so you can take them with you this weekend. Walk them through. It's a big project, you need to be one hundred per cent happy with everything I've proposed."

My role as their architect has meant extensive conversations with both of them. I've even lived at Lofton for a time. As such, I have a good understanding of their vision, but there still may be something I've overlooked.

This project has taken me back to where my career began, and I've relished every moment of it.

April leans forward and clasps my forearm.

"Thank you, I mean it, Jax. Everything we talked about. It's all here and more," April says.

She turns to Caleb with a grin. "Our home."

He drops a kiss on her lips. "Our home."

I smile. Seeing these two together and happy after all they've been through gives me faith that love is possible. At least if you are in one place for long enough.

"You're welcome," I say. "The house is beautiful."

Caleb grunts, his face twisting, and I laugh. "It's dated, but its potential is endless. As you can see, I've tried wherever possible to retain the features you both loved, or repurpose where it was an impossibility."

"I can't wait to show Pen when she gets here," April says, grinning. "Speaking of which, I need to check on dinner."

"Your genius is showing again, old man," Caleb says, squeezing my shoulder after April leaves. "You never cease to amaze me. This design is a whole other level, even for you. The old house was functional at best. This is an amazing wedding present, thank you."

Caleb's eyes wander to the kitchen, where April is. His love for her shines bright. I never thought I'd see Caleb Frazer lower his walls and fall so hard, but April knocked him on his arse the moment he met her.

His eyes return to the plans, scanning them as he does with every property we work on together.

He told me about his desire to purchase the old property when he and April got married.

What do you give the billionaire and his bride who have everything as a wedding gift?

I offered to redesign their house.

I also needed to take a step back from the day-to-day running of my firm. Delegation not being my strong point.

As if sensing my thoughts, Caleb turns his head to look at me.

"How's it going? Have you broken out in hives yet?" Caleb asks.

I chuckle. "Not quite, and it's been harder than I anticipated," I admit. "Letting go of the reins after twelve years has not been easy, but with the latest expansion, I don't have a choice. Something had to give."

"You're a workaholic, my friend. I'm just glad you've finally realised jetting backwards and forwards from the US every month is not sustainable."

"You can talk."

I tut. Until April, Caleb was completely driven by work and growing his company. It's why Frazer Developments has expanded at the rate it has.

"Maybe once, but now I have other priorities." He smiles, his eyes darting back to the kitchen. "I'm starting to realise I want to slow down and enjoy life. It's why this house is so important. It's our escape."

I nod. I understand probably more than most.

They say, *Be careful what you wish for.*

Twelve years ago, when I first went out on my own, I wished for success. After specialising in sustainable architectural design, my business took off, making me a very wealthy man.

My reputation and designs have won me and my company more awards than we can physically display. When we moved into our new offices last year, the marketing department dusted them off and set up a room dedicated to past projects and the awards we have received.

Until recently, I have remained involved in every project that passes through our books, but that is no longer feasible. My partnership with Frazer Developments has meant I'm spending more and more time this side of the pond. And I'm getting too old for all the late-night conference calls and early morning meetings.

But I'm the first to admit that taking a step back has not been easy, but I'm starting to see the benefits. I'm more buoyant, energised. I'm no longer waiting for the phone to ring or having heart palpitations when it does.

"What time are Elijah and Pen arriving?"

Caleb checks his watch. "Another couple of hours."

"I may head downstairs for a swim."

"My pool not good enough?" Caleb laughs.

"Your pool is not a swimming pool," I say, rolling my eyes. "It's a plunge pool."

It's twenty metres, but for an ex-swimmer, I like to extend, get lost in my strokes before turning.

Caleb tuts.

"Ignore him, Jax," April says, coming back into the room. She wraps her arm around Caleb's waist, placing a hand on his chest. She grins up at him before returning her attention to me. "He knows that. Elijah tells him all the time. When you get back, we can celebrate. The champagne is on ice."

* * *

MY ARMS CUT through the water. I touch the side and turn, kicking off the wall as I head back the way I've just come. I hit the opposite end and grab the side, pulling myself to standing. I pull off my goggles and lift my head. Two familiar legs, clad in jeans, stand by the pool.

"Hey, stranger," Elijah says. "Feeling better?"

"Much," I say, placing my palms on the side of the pool, before hauling myself out and onto my feet.

Elijah hands me my towel.

"You haven't lost any of your form," he says.

It was something we always critiqued when we were training, any slight deviation could mean seconds on our time.

"I still swim every day, old habits die hard," I say. "You're early."

Elijah chuckles. "Or you're late. You've been down here an hour and a half."

My eyes flash to the clock on the wall. *Shit.* I really was lost in the moment.

"It doesn't matter, but the ladies wanted me to check you hadn't drowned."

"Let me grab a quick shower, and I'll meet you back upstairs."

I love swimming, but the smell of chlorine is not something I enjoy.

"Not a problem. I'll have a cold beer waiting."

Elijah turns.

"It's good to see you," I say.

We only reconnected over the summer, his ex-wife, Darra, having driven a wedge between our friendship. Recent events have highlighted why she had such a major hard-on for ensuring I wasn't part of their lives.

Elijah must read something in my expression, because he smiles and nods.

"You too. We have a lot to catch up on."

I nod and head to the showers.

By the time I make it upstairs, everyone is sitting in the living area.

"Jaxson," Pen says, getting up and giving me a hug.

"Hey, beautiful. How's this old man treating you?"

"Oh, you know," she says with a wink, earning us both an *eh* from Elijah.

Pen returns to his side on the sofa, his arm sliding around her shoulders, her hand resting on his thigh.

"How was your swim?" April asks, appearing next to me, holding out an ice-cold beer.

"Good. Just what the doctor ordered," I say, raising my beer and saluting the others before taking a deep swallow.

We swap pleasantries until April tells us dinner is served.

"Have you heard anything from Zach?" Caleb asks.

Elijah scowls, and Pen places her hand over his clenched fist.

His gaze meets hers, and he sighs.

"He sent me a letter," he says.

"And?" Caleb presses.

"And, it's sat unopened in a drawer. I'm not sure I can deal with any of his pathetic excuses. I might have been able to forgive him if it were only me affected, but he dragged Kat into their sick and twisted game."

My chest tightens. Thoughts of Kat screaming and punching the woodland floor, her pain and frustration palpable.

"How *is* Kat?" I ask.

Silence descends around the table.

"You know Kat," Caleb says. "She tells everyone she's fine, but all she does is work, work and more work. I called around to see her at the apartment, but there was no answer."

"She's not living at the apartment anymore," Pen says quietly. "She's moved into the family suite at the hotel."

"What the *fuck*?" Caleb hisses. "Why am I only hearing about this now?"

"Take a breath, big boy," April says, gripping his forearm tightly. "You can't fix this. Kat has to deal with this in her way. Trying to force her is not going to help her heal any faster. All you can do is be there for her, support her."

Caleb turns to his wife, his expression softening.

"I know—it's just. *Fuck.*" He runs a hand through his hair. "She's being all Kat like, stoic as if nothing bothers her. But she's not invincible, and now there's all the drama with her latest project. I don't know how she's still standing, a lesser person would have crumbled. She needs a break."

"What drama?" Elijah asks, his brows furrowing.

"The architect they contracted for the new hotel project has been involved in a bribery and corruption scandal. Apparently, his company have been paying off officials. There's a press release going out tomorrow."

"What does that mean for the project?" Pen asks.

"It's back to the drawing board, from what I can tell," Caleb says, sighing.

His hand runs through his hair again, highlighting how worried he truly is about Kat. He joined the FHG board six months ago as a consultant.

"They'd only just signed a contract, from what I can gather, when Quentin gave Kat the heads up on their exposé. From what I understand, she stonewalled the project, but the board and investors are not going to be happy with the latest turn of events. There's a board meeting scheduled for Wednesday."

I remain silent, this is a family matter.

"Isn't the project focusing on sustainability?" April asks, her eyes flicking towards me, eyebrows raised.

I hold up my hand. "Best to keep me out of this," I say quietly. "Kat and I, we don't exactly see eye to eye."

April frowns, but her pursed lips tell me she's not happy with my answer.

I may be the number one architect in this field, but there's a reason Kat hasn't approached me or my firm. As she has told me many times over the past sixteen years, she'd rather stick pins in her eyes than be forced to spend any length of time in my company.

"I don't know what you did to piss my sister off, but she really knows how to hold a bloody grudge."

Caleb tuts, his unasked question clear.

I ignore it.

"You used to be such good friends before Kat got together with Zach. I always assumed it would be you she shacked up with, not him," Elijah adds.

I concentrate on the mouthful of food I've just eaten, but it catches in my throat, causing me to choke.

Caleb whacks me on the back.

Across the table, Pen's gaze locks on mine, and for the first time, I wonder what she knows.

"That was a long time ago," I say quietly.

"She could really do with your help," Caleb says, clearly choosing to ignore my previous comment.

I turn to face him. "Cal, I'm the last person Kat would accept help from, or agree to work with, for that matter. You're wasting your breath."

"She wouldn't be working with you. Her team would be," Caleb says, his expression brightening. "This would really get her out of a hole, Jax. She needs some good fortune, and as you said yourself. This is your area of expertise."

"Caleb's right," Elijah says, and I scowl at him.

"Not you as well," I say, running a hand down my face. "Listen to yourselves. This is your sister we're talking about."

I look around the table and grimace inwardly.

"Caleb, have you forgotten about your housing project, the new development we're supposed to be working on?"

"Of course I haven't," he says. "But I know we can shuffle a few things around. The plans for Lofton House are near enough perfect, as for the new project, you were telling me earlier how you're all about delegation these days."

I roll my eyes and groan. Trust Caleb to use my words against me.

"Look, April and I can go through the plans for Lofton this weekend and make notes. As for Frazer Development, this might be the perfect time to bring Simon, your protégé, up to speed. He can take the lead, and I can help him. I've worked on enough of these projects with you over the years."

I scowl at my close friend and business associate, who is quite happily reshuffling my work schedule.

"That frees you up to help Kat."

Problem solved clearly.

I'd love to be a fly on the wall when he broaches his plan with Kat.

"Kat didn't even invite Lockwood Associates to tender for this job. She's not going to want me anywhere near her project."

"What?" Caleb frowns as if this is news to him.

I pinch the bridge of my nose and inhale.

Did Kat tell him something different?

"Okay, how about this?" Caleb says, and I know instantly I'm not going to like it. "If I ask Kat and get her agreement, will you be open to a discussion with her?"

All eyes turn to me.

Fuck! Ground swallow me up.

"She really needs your help. You're the only one *we* trust."

I inwardly cringe at their words, knowing they wouldn't if they only knew.

"Kat's a grown arse woman, gents," Pen says, scowling at both Elijah and Caleb. "She's not going to take too kindly to you sticking your nose into her business, any more than you did Eli when Gabriel got involved in yours."

Elijah turns to Pen.

"Yes, but he was right in the long run. Even I'm man enough to realise that. And look at me now."

The grin Elijah gives Pen has her rolling her eyes, and I chuckle. I've missed seeing these two interact.

"Pipe down, big boy. All I'm saying is, Kat might have this under control. You storming in, and with Jax of all people." She shoots me a look. "No offence, Jax."

"None taken," I say quickly, glad someone is finally speaking some sense. "I'm with you, Pen."

"I'm worried about her." Caleb's brow wrinkles as he runs a jerky hand through his hair. "She's not Kat. She looks and sounds like Kat, but there's something missing. It's like—" He sighs. "It's not like the board goes easy on her. They've been after her blood since Dad died."

I've known Caleb a long time. This is the first time I've seen him like this about one of his siblings.

"What do you mean?"

Caleb and Elijah drop their chins to their chests.

What the hell?

Caleb looks up. "After Dad died, several of the board members came to see Mum. They wanted Gabriel or me to take over from Dad."

I frown.

What?

"But Kat had been working with your dad for six years, worked her way through the various departments learning the ropes, attended all the board meetings," I say.

We may not have been on speaking terms, but I listened when Kat's name was mentioned.

"She had. Dad was training her to be his successor, and that's why Mum told them to turn around and walk away before she said or did something that, as the majority shareholder, they would seriously regret. Unfortunately, Kat wasn't born with a penis and, therefore, in their eyes, was incapable of running the Frazer Hotel Group. Mum might only be small, but she will fight tooth and nail for her children. You really don't want to cross her if she feels any of us have been wronged."

Go Francesca!

Pen growls. This is clearly the first time she's heard this.

"Kat knew about this?"

"She did. Our sister is no pushover, but she's had to fight to both claim and maintain her position. Why do you think she's been so driven to take the company further than any of her predecessors?"

I swallow, knowing I'm probably going to regret my next words.

"Fine," I say. "If Kat agrees, I'll speak with her about the project. But Caleb, only if she agrees."

Caleb grins like the Cheshire Cat, while Pen tilts her head, her eyes locking on mine.

I shrug.

There's no way in hell Kat will agree to this, so why am I worried?

CHAPTER 5

KAT

When Elliot Granger, the head of my asset management team walks into my office, his pinched expression tells me everything I need to know.

"When?" I ask.

"Six months at the earliest."

Fuck!

My hand grips my pendant, sliding it backwards and forwards.

Think Kat.

"And that's all of them?"

"Everyone we approached before. Donovan and Jones have said they can put one of their other teams on it to begin with, but they were low on our list of preferred contractors."

My hand pauses mid-slide.

Will someone give me a break! Please!

I hold my voice calm and steady. "No, this is too important," I say honestly, earning myself a nod. At least someone is on my page. "Fine, we'll go with Highcliffe and Partners. I'll just have to sell the delay to the board."

I stand up and run a hand down my trouser suit.

"Thank you, Elliot."

He pauses as he reaches the door. "Good luck. Let me know the outcome so I can begin drawing up the relevant contracts."

"There's no such thing as luck," I tell him truthfully.

"You make your own luck, Kitty Kat."

Dad's words echo in my mind.

I often ask myself what he would do or say.

Where have the past seven years gone?

One thing I know for sure. He would tell me to be confident.

"This is a hiccup, Kitty Kat, not a disaster. Focus on the positives. You're the boss, they'll follow your lead. Never show your insecurities, or the vultures will swoop in."

After Elliot leaves, I move to my private bathroom, checking my hair and makeup. I pull on my tailored suit jacket, my eyes meeting in the mirror.

It's showtime.

I grab my laptop and move to the door.

I close my eyes briefly as I wait for the elevator. The board and our investors are going to have to suck it up. Since taking over as CEO, I've managed some pretty amazing feats, but on this occasion, I can't *bloody well* magic an architect firm out of thin air, especially one with the knowledge and skill set we require.

I open my eyes as Michael appears at my side. "Caleb called earlier."

The elevator arrives, and I step in, Michael following.

"Did he say what he wanted?"

"Nothing urgent, he said he'd see you in the board meeting."

"And that's all he said?"

Michael looks confused.

"Outside of *good morning* and *how are you*, yes."

My gut roils, and my muscles twitch.

Caleb never rings to tell me he'll see me later.

He's a chip off the old block in terms of our father. I love him dearly, but… I frown.

"Is everything okay?" Michael asks.

I give myself a mental shake. He's learning to read me too well. I suppose that's what happens when you work closely with someone every day for a year, mentoring them. I replace my metaphorical mask.

But the butterflies don't leave as we make our way to the boardroom. Several of the board members are already in their seats, and tea and coffee are being served.

"Morning, everyone," I say, making my way to the head of the table.

"Morning, Kat," Lewis says, entering and making his way around the table.

He's one of the longest-standing members of the board and was a close friend and ally of my father's.

I place my laptop down and plug it in, just as Sadie Tripp and Douglas Chapman enter.

Only Caleb's seat remains empty.

The door opens as soon as I think of his name.

"Morning, everyone," he says. "Sorry, I'm late. London traffic."

He takes his seat and turns to face me.

I meet the gaze of every member of the board individually, and set my jaw.

"I'd like to thank you all for coming at such short notice." I hold my voice steady as I was taught. "As you are all probably aware, both through the press and my email, the architects we hired, Moorland and Sons, are currently under investigation for bribery and corruption practices. A press release has been sent out detailing the termination of their contract with the FHG."

Sadie drops back in her chair, her arms folded over her chest.

"So what happens next?" Sadie asks. "You've asked us to have a lot of faith in this project, invest a lot of resources, time and money."

I push my shoulders back and lean in. Sadie and I don't see eye to eye, and I know she'd like nothing more than to see me fail. Being five years older, she was my father's protégé before I decided to join the company. Being sidelined has made her more of a foe than a friend.

"Give Kathryn a chance," Lewis says.

His fatherly nature shines through, but I don't need him fighting my battles.

"Highcliffe and Partners are available. They were our second choice."

"But," she says, her eyes never leaving my face.

I set my jaw, my muscles tightening.

Breathe Kat.

"There will be a delay of six months."

Conversations erupt around the table.

"May I say something?"

My eyes dart to my brother.

He takes that as his, *go.*

"I missed updating you this morning," he says, his eyes telling me to go with whatever bomb he's about to drop.

I clench my jaw.

Oh no, he wouldn't!

"Kat and I have spoken to Jaxson Lockwood."

My stomach hardens, and I bite the inside of my cheek as I work on schooling my features.

What the bloody hell?

I shoot him a look, but he ignores me and continues on, addressing the table.

"We spoke to Jaxson yesterday, but he needed to check his

schedule and speak to his New York office." Caleb's eyes meet mine. "He got back to me this morning to say he's been able to move a few things around, and would love to come on board."

I swallow sharply, almost choking on my saliva.

What the fuck, baby brother?

"Really?" Douglas says excitedly, his eyes flashing back and forth between Caleb and me. "Kat, why on earth didn't you say anything?"

Doug is always raving about Lockwood's designs, and has begged me to get him involved in one project or another. At nearly sixty, you'd think he was too old for a boy-crush!

I clench my jaw before turning and smiling.

"As Caleb said, there were no guarantees. When I hadn't heard anything, I assumed it was a no."

I shoot my snake of a baby brother a smile, and watch him swallow. His own slipping ever so slightly.

"I was under the impression Mr Lockwood's company wasn't available," Sadie says, shooting me a look of disbelief.

"You're correct," I say. "But like with most things, schedules can change."

I turn to my brother, whose eyes are now sparkling at my comeback.

Hold up, little brother, you're not getting off that bloody lightly.

"Perfect, perfect," Lewis says, almost bouncing in his seat. "Looks like fortune favours the Frazers once more. It will be good to have Jaxson Lockwood onboard, I'm sure the investors will be happy too, and I know Robert would have been thrilled."

I refrain from rolling my eyes, but watch as several other board members are not so subtle.

"Is he willing to come in and speak to us?" Douglas asks. "Discuss his ideas for the project?"

I turn to Caleb and raise an eyebrow.

Your moment of truth, little bro.

Caleb grins at me, and I square my shoulders.

"When would you like him?" he says, not breaking his stride.

What on earth? Jaxson is really on board with this?

More conversation erupts, and I stand, chin up, watching on. Eventually, when a date has been set, I close the meeting and watch everyone file out.

"Caleb, a word," I say, as my brother slopes off, deep in conversation with Lewis.

He comes upright as if I've grabbed him by the collar. A common occurrence when we were younger and he'd steal my toys.

He turns on his heel, offering me his brightest, kilowatt smile.

I fold my arms over my chest and raise an eyebrow.

I wait until the last person has left.

"My office. Now."

CHAPTER 6

KAT

Caleb and I walk back to my office in silence, apart from the meet and greets that seem to happen the whole way there.

My personable and charming brother.

I want to roll my eyes but refrain.

When we finally get there, Michael jumps to his feet.

"Michael, why don't you grab yourself a coffee?" I say.

His brows furrow, and he stares at the kitchen, which houses another state-of-the-art coffee machine. "Or cake," I say, more firmly when he doesn't move.

He nods and grabs his coat, making a quick exit.

We enter my office, and I close the door.

I walk around my desk.

"Poor guy," Caleb says, chuckling.

"I wouldn't feel too sorry for him."

Not by the time I'm finished with you.

Cal smirks, and the tenuous thread I'm holding on my temper finally snaps.

I slam my palms flat down on my desk, the reverberating bang makes Caleb flinch.

He walks further into the room and drops himself down into the chair opposite me, cool as a cucumber.

I lean forward and glare at my brother.

"Do you want to explain what the hell that was all about? And why you felt the need to lie to my fucking board? And what's worse is, you forced me to lie to the board."

He shrugs. "I didn't force you to do anything," he says, brushing invisible lint from his trousers. "And I didn't lie."

I grind my teeth together, my hands curling into fists on top of my desk.

"I'm beginning to see what Gabe's problem is," I snap.

Caleb chuckles. I mean, chuckles.

Does he take nothing seriously or realise what he's just done?

"Oh, don't be fooled. Gabriel loves me dropping in. It's the highlight of his day, or at least it was until Leah and Callum came on the scene. As for you, you'll be thanking me."

He smirks as I drop into my chair. I lean back, gripping the arms.

I eyeball him over the top of my desk.

Sadly, with Caleb being my brother, it doesn't have the same effect as it does on those who work for me.

"Is this your *best* icy stare?" he asks, and I swallow my growl.

I take several deep, slow breaths to slow my racing heart.

"What are you going to do to rectify this mess?" I ask, as calmly as I can. "As I said before, you just lied to the board. Made *me* lie to the board."

"Absolutely nothing," he says, the glee in his voice clear and obvious.

"And why not?" I ask, counting to ten. But instead of calming my racing pulse, it quickens.

"For fuck's sake, Caleb. Can you be serious for once in your life?"

His expression hardens.

"I didn't lie to the board, only you did that," he says, his eyes narrowing. "And technically, you didn't lie either. You just weren't in possession of all the facts."

I close my eyes and inhale deeply.

"You better start talking and fast, before I call security and have you thrown out."

Caleb leans forward, resting his elbows on his knees.

"Such gratitude," he says, rolling his eyes. "I didn't lie, because Jaxson has, in actual fact, agreed to work on the project."

"Impossible," I say, before I can stop myself.

He wouldn't.

Tension builds in my muscles, and my head begins to pound. At this rate, I'm going to be calling Carla again.

"Not impossible. I spoke to him. We reorganised his schedule, and now he's free to work on this."

I pinch the bridge of my nose and inhale.

"Look, you need him."

"No, I don't."

Actually, that is technically not true, but we're talking about Jaxson Lockwood. We can barely stand being in the same airspace, let alone working on a project of this magnitude together.

"I beg to differ, and you were the one who invited me to be a member of the board." He runs a hand through his hair. "Jaxson and his firm are the best qualified for this job, and you bloody know it."

I open and close my mouth.

"And what's this I hear that you never even approached his firm?" Caleb tuts. "I'm sure Sadie Tripp would have had a field day with that little nugget of information, if it ever came out."

"Are you blackmailing me, little brother?" I ask quietly.

"Would I steep that low?" he says.

I harrumph, and he chuckles.

The fact is, Caleb is telling the truth, Jaxson is the best qualified.

"I can't work with him," I tell him sharply.

"Then don't. He can deal with the team running the project."

I harrumph again.

"That's the problem, you idiot. I *am* the one running the project. This is my baby."

It's Caleb's turn to look surprised, as the colour leaches from his face.

"But you're the CEO," he says.

"Yes, and so are you. You're also hands-on with all your projects."

"That's because I'm a property developer. I have to be." He runs a hand down his face. "You run a chain of hotels. Don't you have your fingers in enough pies to keep you busy?"

I straighten the pile of papers on my desk. Caleb's eyes track the movement.

"This is my vision…"

"Delegation. Ever heard of it? Vision or not." His brows come together. "I know you're a workaholic, sis, but this is too much, even for you."

I sigh and drop back in my chair.

"I won't run it forever. Only until the initial designs have been finalised, then it will be handed over to Elliot and a team, I will handpick."

We stare at each other.

"Shit," he says. "You're serious."

I ignore him.

"Now, back to what I said before. You caused this problem. How are you going to fix it?"

"I can't. You saw the board, they're thrilled Jax is on

board. I thought Doug was going to hyperventilate with excitement."

I shake my head as my brother once again fails, or chooses to ignore the enormity of what he's done.

"What part of *we can't work together* are you missing?" I snap. "We can't even be in the same room as one another." Then I'm hit by a thought. "How the hell did you get Jaxson to agree to this fiasco?"

Caleb leans back and crosses his arms, his left ankle resting on his right thigh, the picture of calm.

"Elijah and I were having dinner with him…"

"Elijah's in on this?" I say open-mouthed, my body temperature rising suddenly. "Does Pen know, April?"

"Er… they heard the conversation about Moorland, but not the rest."

Caleb's eyes shift away from mine, and I smirk.

Oh, you're in so much shit when your wife finds out what you've done.

"That still doesn't explain how you got Jaxson to agree?"

Caleb's shoulders slump slightly, and he looks at me sheepishly.

He sighs, suddenly dejected.

"I lied," he admits.

"You lied?" I raise an eyebrow. "So Jaxson hasn't agreed?"

I almost sigh in relief.

"Oh no, he's agreed to work on the project. That isn't a lie." His throat bobs, and he swallows. "The lie I told was that you were on board with the whole thing. You were desperate, and he wouldn't be working with you directly, just your team."

Well, that explains the whiter shade of pale he turned when I said I was running it.

I drop back hard in my chair, the back flexing underneath me, making my heart race.

"You told Jax I was desperate? I should—" I seethe.

"Look," Caleb says, sitting forward, both feet now firmly on the ground, his elbows braced on his knees. "Jax is the best person for this job. I know it, you know it." He raises an eyebrow, and I want to smack the smug look from his face. "If it wasn't for that enormous Jaxson-sized stick you have wedged up your arse, you'd be thanking me."

I freeze. "Thanking you?" My voice drops to a hiss. "Watch it, little brother, you're very close to overstepping and really pissing me off."

"Bullshit," Caleb gets up and starts pacing the room. "If you weren't so pig-headed."

"Insults…nice. Keep digging," I say, sitting back and folding my arms over my chest, watching him pace.

"As I was saying, if you weren't so bloody pig-headed, you'd agree with me. You need to get over yourself and suck it up. If it were me sitting in the chair, you'd be telling me the exact same thing. Jax is perfect for this job."

He sinks back down into his chair, panting as if he's just run a marathon.

"Have you quite finished?"

Caleb's eyes lock on mine, and I'm surprised when he refuses to drop his gaze.

He's right, not that I'll ever admit it.

Jaxson Lockwood *is* the perfect architect for this project. I do know this. His firm is world-renowned, having won an obscene amount of awards. His speciality is in line with what I'm trying to create with the new hotel complex. However, working with him… My visceral reaction to the man is not normal. He rubs me up the wrong way. Just looking at him has my body temperature rising, breathing the same air as him makes me want to up-sticks and leave.

I close my eyes and draw in a deep and steady breath.

My biggest problem. My family bloody adore him.

If only they knew.

Then Jaxson Lockwood might not be quite as cocky and confident. Walking around with his playful, flirty grin and that mischievous glint in his eye.

But they don't, and it's a secret I'll take with me to the grave.

I drop my head back and close my eyes. I have a choice to make.

If I want this project to go ahead, I'm going to have to *suck it up*, as my brother so beautifully put it. If not, it could be years before I get the board's approval again. Sadie will see to that.

Opening my eyes, I lock them on my brother.

"Fine," I say. "But don't think you've won." All credit to my brother, he keeps his expression neutral. "But you can deal with Jaxson. Collect the brief from Michael on your way out, he should be back by now. And let's see what Jaxson's got. He still has to convince the board."

"Fair enough," Caleb says, offering me a genuine smile. "You know, you won't regret it."

"Let's just hope I don't, little brother. Let's hope I don't."

* * *

CALEB LETS HIMSELF OUT, and I sink back into my chair.

I stare blankly ahead, my limbs heavy, my head pounding.

I'm exhausted.

The past couple of months have left me drained. I'm struggling to sleep despite being physically exhausted, my usual mental sharpness has dulled, and I'm regretting past choices.

I pick up my phone and dial.

"Hey, Harp," I say.

"Hey, Kat."

I hear her moving around.

"What are you doing?"

"Just getting ready for work."

I look at the clock. It's seven thirty in the morning in New York.

"How's the new job going?"

"It's good... however, my boss is an arse, but which bosses aren't?"

I chuckle. "I'm sure my employees say the same thing."

"Never." Harper laughs.

"But you're enjoying it?"

"It's okay. I've been assigned grunt work, but I'm the newbie, so I suppose that's to be expected."

"Has anyone..."

The question hangs open.

"No, no one has twigged I'm *The Infamous Frazer*." She laughs, but the sound is hollow. "At least not since I spoke to you yesterday morning."

"Sorry, it's just I hate you being so far away," I admit.

Growing up, Harper was my baby sister, prize pain in my arse, like the twins. But in recent years, the gap has closed.

Harper is silent. "I miss you too. How's Mum?"

"Haven't you spoken to her?"

"Yes, just before you," she laughs. "But what she tells me, and what's the truth, are two different things."

"She's doing okay. We all miss you, little rebel."

"I miss you too, I really do." Harper pauses. "But Kat. I think this is going to be good for me. Teach me to stand on my own two feet. Here, I'm Brooke Feldmann, a small-town nobody. For the first time ever, I can be whoever I want to be. I'm not constantly worrying about letting anyone else down, of never measuring up." She sighs. "I've never truly known who I am, only what I was expected to be. I've spent most of my adult life rebelling, especially after Dad..." She pauses. "I know it's probably difficult for you to understand."

I wipe a tear as it tracks its way down my cheek. Goosebumps rising on my arms.

It's like hearing my inner thoughts all those years ago.

"No, I get it," I say, forcing my voice to remain steady.

Probably better than most.

"Harps, you have never let us down. This is not your fault, but I get wanting to find yourself. Being a Frazer... We're all hard on ourselves." I exhale. "It seems to go with the name, it's why we stick together, look out for each other."

It is, after all, what Elijah and Caleb have just tried to do for me.

"Kat, are you okay?" Harper asks suddenly. "You spend all your time worrying about us. What about you?"

"You know me," I say, chuckling, although the sound is flat.

"You need a break," she says. "After everything you've been through."

"I wish I could," I admit. "But work—"

My eyes catch an incoming message.

Maldives Report - potential issues.

"Hold that thought," I say, suddenly. "I may check out our new acquisition in the Maldives."

I make a split-second decision.

"Really?" Harper laughs. "Not quite the break I had in mind, but a working holiday... that's a start. Make sure you send me plenty of photos. It sounded amazing when you were telling me about it before. Wish I could come with you."

We both fall silent. "I do too. Next time, rebel." I say, closing my eyes.

"I'll hold you to that."

I smile because, knowing Harper, she will.

"I love you, sis, but I really need to go. As I said, I'm working for a grumpy old fart. He really needs to lighten up."

"Well, if he's working with you, I'm sure he will. Love you, little sis."

"Love you, big sis."

We disconnect, but the hollow feeling in my chest remains. If Leonard Crawley wasn't dead, I'd murder him myself for what he's done to Harper. But I can't.

"Michael," I say, picking up my mainline.

"What can I do for you?"

"I've decided to make a semi-surprise visit to our new acquisition in the Maldives. Can I leave you to organise it?"

There's a pause.

"Of course, I'll get straight on it," he says, always Mr Efficient. "And just so you know, I gave your brother the brief he requested."

"Perfect. Thank you."

There's another pause.

"You're welcome."

I disconnect the call and open the email that's just landed in my inbox.

CHAPTER 7

KAT

*P*enelope Dawson is glowing as I walk across the restaurant towards her.

If her beaming smile is any indication of how well her relationship with my brother is going, it's clearly having a positive effect on them both.

She gets up as I reach the table and pulls me in for a hug.

"How are you doing?" she says, stepping back, but holding onto my upper arms.

Her eyes scan my face, making me shift uncomfortably. Pen has always been able to read me.

"Oh, you know," I say with a shrug.

A frown mars her brow, and I instantly regret my words.

Shit! What's wrong with me?

I grab her hand in mine and squeeze. Our waitress hovers nearby, before jumping forward to pull out my seat. I plaster on my *everything is fine* mask as I sit down, waiting for my napkin to be settled across my lap.

I look up. "Thank you," I say. "Can we have a moment?"

She nods and smiles in response. "Of course. I'll be back to take your orders."

My hands move to my cutlery, then drop back into my lap. My eyes meet Pen's.

I'm usually positive, but the last couple of months, it's become harder to maintain that persona. It's like a weight is pressing down on me constantly. That and the fact that sleep has not been my friend for far too long.

"How are you?" I say, redirecting the conversation with a smile. "Is that brother of mine treating you well?"

Pen scowls slightly, but lets it slide. I'm not stupid enough to think she'll drop it. This is but a momentary reprieve. My hands drift back to my knife and fork, straightening them. When I look up again, I'm fascinated by the pink flush that's spreading over her cheeks.

I quirk a brow, and her hands go to cover them. I laugh.

"I don't think I've seen you blush in all the years I've known you," I rib her.

"I'm pregnant," she blurts out, her hand slamming against her mouth, her eyes darting around the area in case anyone has overheard.

My jaw drops, but I close it quickly, my hand snaking across the table and grabbing hers.

"That's wonderful news," I say excitedly, before taking in her expression. "Isn't it?"

Pen bites her lip, a habit of old, one she reverts to when she's feeling less than confident.

"It's just so soon. Elijah and I are only just finding our way back to one another."

"Is that a problem?" I ask, wondering if I need to slap my elder brother upside the head for making my friend feel unsure.

Pen shakes her head. "Heavens, no. Elijah is thrilled. He wants us to elope and get married. And Lottie. She's over the moon at the idea of being a *big* sister."

I grip her hand tightly until her gaze meets mine.

"Pen, my brother loves you. He's loved you for so long… even when he couldn't be with you."

I pick up my glass of water, taking a sip.

"That's the problem. I don't want us to get married because I'm pregnant. He's already done that once."

I choke.

What?

"Um, you and Elijah are nothing like the first time around," I say. "Believe me, there was never any love between Darra and my brother. Lust, yes, at least in the beginning. Convenience, in the middle, but by the end, it was pure necessity as far as he was concerned. But it definitely was *not* love."

I should know.

Zach and I spent enough time around them in the early days of their marriage, and then Darra was always bringing Lottie around.

Now I know why.

A sudden tightness grips my chest, my body growing hot.

I choke down some more of my water as a distraction to my wayward thoughts.

Pen sighs. "I've told him he can propose after the baby is born, if that's what he still wants."

I place my glass down, pleased that my hand is steady.

"You think Elijah, of all people, is going to change his mind?"

Pen grins. "No, but it gives me some time to breathe."

"Then the question really is, do *you* want to marry Elijah?"

My heart stalls as I ask the question. I think I know the answer, but with everything that's going on, I'm struggling to trust my judgement.

Pen stares at me wide-eyed. "Really?" she says.

"I had to ask," I reply, expelling the breath I'm holding.

She chuckles. "Don't tell him, but I'd marry him in a heartbeat," she says, the honesty of her words shining through.

"Then, I better keep my eyes open for the perfect wedding outfit," I say with a wink. "When are you due?"

"June."

I squeeze her hand again, only this time she flips it, grasping mine in hers.

I smile. "I couldn't be happier for you both. You and Eli were made for each other. I'm glad fate has finally stepped in."

Our waitress reappears, and we order our usual. When she leaves, Pen inclines her head.

"Enough deflecting. How are you?" she asks. "And I mean, *really*? Not the bullshit you've been feeding everyone else."

I chuckle, although the sound is flat. Pen's one of the few people who really understands me.

"So, so," I tell her honestly.

She's known me for too many years to accept any lies, and I know better than to feed her any.

She leans forward and waits patiently.

I screw up my face and earn myself a *look*.

"Fine," I say. "Zach has written me a letter." I sigh. "Before you ask, I haven't read it, and I'm not sure I'm going to. Do I want to hear his feeble excuses? No." Pen remains silent, so I continue. "The hotel has recovered from the cyberattack, thanks to you," I say, smiling. "Now, I just want to string my younger brother up for sticking his nose into my business affairs."

Pen doesn't look surprised, so I'm taking it she's heard of Caleb's meddling.

We sit and stare at each other.

"What?" I ask.

"I asked how you were, and you told me about a letter, a

recovered cyberattack and Caleb. What I want to know is how *you're* doing?"

My vision blurs as pain engulfs my throat. I swallow against the growing pressure.

Shaking my head, Pen tilts hers, her eyebrows coming together. She opens her mouth, but closes it again, as if she decides better of whatever she was about to say.

How to articulate the monumental mist of anger, frustration, hurt and betrayal, to name but a few of the intense emotions, that are swamping my every waking moment.

"I'm here when you're ready," she says, and I nod my appreciation.

Pen understands my need to process. She locked herself away for weeks after she and Kris split up.

"If it helps, I had words with both Caleb and Eli when I heard what they'd done."

"But—"

She smiles. "They aren't wrong, you know. Jax is the best qualified for the job, even you have to admit that."

I take my time resetting my napkin on my lap. When I look up, I rest my hands on the table.

"I can't deny he has the perfect skill set. But Pen, working with him? We can barely stand to be in the same room together—" I growl, unable to find the words to describe how frustrated he makes me.

Pen remains silent.

"There's a lot of animosity between us. It's not something we can simply ignore."

"You're both professionals."

I pinch the bridge of my nose, trying to stem the headache that's been festering since Caleb dropped his latest bombshell.

"We are, and I know you're right," I sigh. "But I didn't take kindly to being ambushed in my boardroom, especially by my own brother."

"I can understand that."

Silence descends between us.

"I need a break," I say suddenly. "I'm thinking of visiting our new acquisition in the Maldives. There are a few issues that need ironing out. But then I might take a short break."

Pen's face lights up. "That's a wonderful idea."

Our waitress arrives with our food, so we pause until she's gone.

"How long are you going for?"

"I thought five to seven days. There's nothing urgent that can't survive without me, apart from the new project."

Jaxson wants to schedule a time to run through the brief, but I don't have the energy or brainpower to meet with him right now.

Pen takes a mouthful of food, closing her eyes as she chews.

"Yum," she says, swallowing before opening her eyes and catching mine in her gaze.

"Why do you dislike Jax so much?" she asks suddenly. "I saw your face at Eli's."

I look down at my plate, pushing the food around with my fork.

"Did you think Jax was Lottie's dad?"

Her question comes out of the blue, leaving me reeling.

"I suspected he might be," I admit honestly.

Pleased she made that connection and not another.

Pen squints at me, as if trying to read my mind.

"But it's more than that," she says slowly.

The look on Pen's face lets me know she's not going to let this drop. I inhale a shuddery breath.

Sixteen years I've held my secret, kept Jaxson Lockwood at arm's length.

Pen continues to stare at me.

"You're not going to drop it, are you?" I say, already knowing the answer.

"Not when I can see what all this is doing to you," she says. "I wouldn't be much of a friend if I did."

I look down at the table and push my salad from side to side.

"Come on, Kat. This is me you're talking to. You've lost weight and are sitting here playing with your food. Not to mention the dark circles under your eyes, which tells me you aren't sleeping. You're my best friend, woman." There's pain in her voice. "Let me be there for you, like you were for me."

I run a hand down my face, my hand gripping my pendant.

"Jax and me—" as soon as the words leave my mouth, I realise I've given too much away.

"What do you mean, Jax and you? What am I missing, or more rightly, *what did* I miss?" Her eyes widen as her fingers spread out over her breastbone.

I squeeze my pendant, enjoying its bite against my skin. I chuckle.

"Hard to believe, huh? The stud and—"

She cuts me off with a grunt.

"Not hard to believe, no. Very bloody obvious, now I think back. I just can't believe I missed it," She does a double take, her eyes scanning my face. "You two were thick as thieves one moment, and then…" A furrow appears between her brows. "Did he hurt you? If he did—" By the time she has finished her monologue, she is practically growling.

"No, Jax didn't hurt me. Only my pride," I say.

He simply stamped all over my heart.

I don't say that aloud, although my heartbeat slows momentarily at the memory.

"Do you want to tell me what happened?"

"What's to tell?" I shrug. "I fell for the Lockwood charm, then found out he was using the same line on all of his other women."

"Women?" Pen asks, her brows furrowing. "What women? Kat, when was all this?"

I sigh. "Your last year of uni."

It's why I've never talked to her about it. It wasn't fair. Everyone had so much going on.

I put my cutlery down, my appetite gone.

Pen waits patiently.

"Jax and I got together. We had a thing for a couple of months until I overheard one of Darra's friends repeating the exact same line he'd used on me. They were laughing about how it seemed to work for him. How, by using it, he was able to keep all his lady friends in the dark about one another."

Pen frowns. "What line? I'm really confused. Jax was the most celibate one of the group. He was focusing on his studies in that final year. I'm certainly not aware of a harem of women he had dancing to his tune."

I sigh. "When we were together, he told me we should keep our relationship between the two of us, at least until after graduation." My gaze drops to the table, zeroing in on a crumb next to my plate. "He said, it was no one else's business but our own. His reasoning was Elijah, that it would complicate things as they were living together. But when I heard them talking, I could see how it would work in other scenarios too."

"What did Jax say when you confronted him?"

I love that Pen knows I would not have let that ride, would have faced it head-on.

"He denied it, of course."

Pen's frown deepens.

"But you didn't believe him?"

"He'd been secretive about a couple of things, and I had

proof they'd been at the hotel together." I take a deep breath, hating the need to rehash the past. "So, I asked Zach and Elijah about Jax's love life—"

Pen tilts her head, her eyebrows squishing together as she purses her lips.

"What on earth did *they* say? Surely they set the record straight?" She pauses as her words sink in. "But they didn't, did they?"

I shake my head.

"Zach confirmed everything I'd heard. He laughed and said he was considering trying it, as it had been so successful. Elijah told me about the harem of women who would follow Jax around. His fan club he called them."

Pen's fingers curl into a fist on the table top, and she takes a deep breath before meeting my gaze.

"I don't know what happened between you. All I can give is my perspective, and I'm a pretty good judge of character." Her gaze locks on mine. "Jax was never a player, Kat." She grips my forearm. "Yes, he certainly had the looks to be. And what Eli said was true, he did have a fan club who would follow him around." She sighs. "But it embarrassed him, especially when the boys would rib him about it." She shakes her head. "Kat, listen to me when I say Jaxson Lockwood was all about bettering himself. Like me, he was there to build a solid future for himself. He certainly wouldn't have wasted his energy, juggling more than one relationship." She moves her head, ensuring I'm watching her. "And I can promise you, Jax would not have been messing around with any of Darra's friends. He hated her and everything she and her stuck-up group stood for. He knew she was manipulating Eli, but he could never prove it."

I shake my head, loving her loyalty to her friend.

"But Pen, you don't understand. When I overheard them, Darra and her friends, they didn't even know I was there."

Pen raises an eyebrow. "Are you sure?"

I press my fingers into my temples.

Of course, this is Darra we're talking about. Anything is possible.

Manipulation and cunning should have been her middle names.

"No one knew we were together."

My pitch rises as my heart rate increases.

We made sure of it.

Or so we thought, not wanting Elijah or anyone else sticking their noses into our business. It had been exciting, all the sneaking around.

"I'm not saying you're wrong." She squeezes my arm again. "Just think about where your confirmation came from."

My empty stomach rebels, the water swashing around.

"The last thing I'll say on this is, I can't believe Jax would have risked his friendship with Elijah, messed around with his sister if you didn't mean anything to him."

My chest constricts. I'd thought the same, but then, when Zach backed up what I heard. At the time, there'd been no reason to doubt him. Suddenly... the pressure behind my eyes intensifies. I close them as a wave of dizziness overwhelms me.

Pen's grip on my arm increases. I focus on the pressure, breathing in and out. When I open my eyes, I raise my chin and square my shoulders. Pen withdraws her hand, but I can't miss the concern radiating from her.

I smile, albeit a weak one.

"It doesn't matter now. It's all water under the bridge."

Pen doesn't call me out on my bullshit, but her expression says it all.

"After everything that's happened, do you think maybe you should talk to Jax?"

I shake my head.

"I'm not sure what that would achieve, or even what we would say."

Pen looks like she wants to say more, but holds her counsel, for which I'm grateful.

We spend time eating our food. She fills me in on Lottie, Darra and the latest Frazer family dramas.

When we're done, I look at my watch.

"I better get back, especially as I'm heading out on Monday. There are a few things I need to finalise."

Pen gets up and pulls me in for a hug. I pull back and grip her upper arms.

"Pen, please don't say anything to Elijah. I didn't rock the boat back then, there's no reason to now, especially when he and Jaxson are rebuilding their friendship."

Jaxson was always the best of friends to my brother, had his back. Elijah needs that in his life.

"I won't say a word," she promises. "But I think you and Jax are long overdue for a conversation."

I shrug. "Maybe, but we're very different people now. I'm not sure what raking up the past would achieve."

"Sometimes it's simply about putting your demons to rest."

We hug goodbye, and I make my way back to the office.

* * *

MICHAEL LOOKS up as I approach my office and smiles.

"Any messages?" I ask.

"Your two-thirty has called to apologise and say they'll be five minutes late. Mr Chapman called and asked for a meeting. I told him you were in back-to-back meetings for the next couple of days, but he insisted it was important."

I nod, everything always is, with Douglas Chapman.

"I've scheduled him in for seven this evening?"

"That's fine," I say. He no doubt wants a rundown on Jaxson and the project.

I step towards my office.

"Mr Lockwood called," Michael says.

I pause, turning to face him. "He'd like to schedule an appointment to go over the project brief with you."

I'm not sure I have the mental capacity to deal with Jaxson before I leave. Plus, my schedule is packed between now and Monday.

"That's fine," I say. "Arrange a meeting for when I get back."

"Already done." I begin moving again. "He sent across a list of questions he would like answered. I've sent them to your inbox."

"Thank you, Michael, I'll take a look," I say. "Is everything finalised for Monday?"

He nods. "The jet and flight plan are set. The hotel is expecting you. I've arranged meetings with the manager and relevant staff for you to go over the issues that were raised in the report."

The problems are more a funding issue than a staffing problem. They need money invested, something the previous owners had withheld. This could all be done over the phone or via video link, but the need to get away, escape is riding me hard. A week out of the office will do me good, allow me to reset. Allow me to face Jaxson Lockwood.

"Perfect. Can you forward me the itinerary?" I say.

"In your inbox."

"Thank you," I say, disappearing into my office and waiting for my next meeting to start.

CHAPTER 8

KAT

"Ms Kathryn, welcome on board," Claudia says.

"Thank you, Claudia. It's good to see you again."

I make my way into the family jet and place my laptop on the table. I'm glad, for once, we have a bedroom. I hope I can finish up what I need to do, and then get some much-needed sleep.

"I'll leave you to it," she says. "Captain says we'll be ready for take-off in a few minutes. Can I get you anything?"

I drag my water bottle out of my bag and shake it.

"I'm good."

I need to keep my wits about me. I have too much to do, however tempting several gin and tonics sound right about now.

I take my seat and strap in as the engines begin to whirl. It's a good thing I don't mind flying. This job certainly has me racking up air miles.

I lean back and close my eyes as we take to the sky. The change in pressure makes my ears pop, and my stomach sink.

As the plane rights itself, the door at the back of the cabin opens. I sit up sharply, my heart rate increasing.

I turn my head sharply.

"What the hell are you doing here?" I say, my voice sharp.

"You've refused to take my calls."

He folds his arms over his chest before dropping into the seat opposite me.

"Now I have your undivided attention."

"You know it's illegal to stow away."

"I'm on the manifesto," he says. "If only you'd checked."

My hackles rise at his smug tone.

"You always did think you were clever," I hiss, staring at the man in front of me, my body tingling, as the ache in my chest intensifies.

"There was a time when you liked that," he says.

"That was a lifetime ago, and before I knew better."

I cringe inwardly. Everything I thought was true has turned out to be a lie.

"You've wasted your time. I've nothing to say to you," I add.

If it wasn't time-critical for me to be at my destination, I'd have the pilot turn us around. Land at the nearest airport and order him off, but I can't. Somehow, I have a sneaky suspicion he knows that.

"Well then, it's a good thing I have plenty to say to you. We do have a project to discuss after all."

Fuck! I'm going to kill Caleb the next time I see him.

I lock eyes with the man opposite me.

"Fine," I say, sitting back and crossing my arms over my chest, the plane suddenly becoming very warm.

His open gaze meets mine, and the usual fluttering in my belly begins, as it always does when we're in the same space.

Jax lowers his chin to his chest and rubs at his eyes. When he lowers his hand, his words surprise me.

"Look, can we start again?" The rich timber of his voice startles me, making me catch my breath.

Our eyes lock, and the air almost crackles at the connection.

I clear my throat, curling my fingernails into my palm, but remain silent.

"I was surprised when Caleb told me you'd agreed to me working on the project."

I inhale, locking my jaw.

I exhale, unfolding my arms and placing my hands flat on the table.

"Let me make one thing perfectly clear," I say slowly. "This is *all* my brother. He lied to you and then set me up. I never agreed to this, I was coerced."

Jax's posture doesn't change.

"I know."

I incline my head, my brows furrowing.

"If you knew, I—"

"Don't understand?" he fills in. "Caleb admitted, after the event, that he'd been a little free and easy with the truth about your agreement. But he also told me he's put you in an untenable position with your board and felt bad about it."

Felt bad, my ass. He'd played us both.

"That's an understatement," I say. "If I don't work with you, the project is likely to be shelved indefinitely. There are certain members of the board who are less than favourable to what I'm trying to do."

Why am I telling him this?

Because you're out of options!

Jaxson inclines his head slightly, his expression thoughtful. "That's what he said. At least we know that was the truth."

He smiles, and my heart does a flip.

He holds out the palms of his hands. "Anyway, I'm here."

I stare at him, my eyes squinting.

"Stowing away on a private plane to the Maldives?"

He shrugs, as if it's nothing. "Not stowing away, hitching a ride on a friend's plane." He shrugs. "I'm here on a working holiday. I have a large project to prepare for, and there are worse places to be. I hear the Maldives are beautiful at this time of year.

The hair stiffens at the nape of my neck.

"You can't just turn up somewhere and hope they'll be able to find space for you."

"Oh, that's all been sorted," he grins.

I narrow my eyes, pressing my lips together.

Which sibling do I murder now?

I bite back the growl that threatens. My heart rate is elevated.

"What's in it for you?" I ask, after getting my heart rate under control. "It's not like you're beholden to my board. You could just walk away."

Jax sits back in the chair, his broad shoulders filling the back, his posture relaxed.

"That's very true, I could. However, I've seen the brief and in the true spirit of transparency," he says. "I want in." As if it's that simple. He inclines his head, his eyes never leaving my face. "Kat, what you're trying to do is groundbreaking. I want Lockwood and Associates to be part of that."

It's my turn to sit back. I cross my arms over my chest. I search his face for anything, anything that can explain what the hell is going on here.

We sit in silence. Staring openly at each other.

Claudia takes that moment to reappear. Her face breaks out into a smile.

"Mr Lockwood. Can I get you anything?"

Great, Claudia thinks he's a welcome guest.

"An Americano would be lovely, thank you, Claudia. And it's Jaxson."

The smile he offers her has my hackles rising again.

Thank you, Claudia, and it's Jaxson. Who the hell does he think he is?

"Kathryn, can I get you anything?"

My name pulls me back into the present with a jump.

"Sorry, Claudia, I was miles away. Can I have a latte, please?"

Claudia grins at us, her eyes sparkling before turning away.

Heaven only knows what she thinks is going on here.

After Claudia leaves, I turn to Jax.

"So, I take it I have Caleb to thank for this little fiasco?"

Jax chuckles, running a finger over his lips. My eyes track the movement, butterflies dancing in my stomach.

I sigh.

Not that it matters. The damage is done.

I stare out of the window, out into the wispy white cloud surrounding us.

Claudia returns with our coffees, placing them down on the table.

"Can I get you anything to eat?"

Jaxson holds up his hand. My stomach rumbles. I skipped breakfast, but there's no way I'm going to sit here eating in front of him.

Claudia nods and withdraws.

Jaxson picks up his coffee, and I watch his throat bob as he swallows.

"How? How's this going to work?"

He shrugs. "Like any project, I presume. I'll ask you questions, you'll give me the answers I need. I'll go away and write up my proposal. I'm sure we can be professional," he says, taking another sip of his coffee.

I growl before I can stop myself, making the pretentious prick laugh.

My breathing picks up, and a hot flush spreads throughout my body.

"But we're not *any* people, Jaxson," I say, folding my arms over my chest. "This project could take months, if not years."

How am I not going to throttle him?

He shrugs again, the movement setting my teeth on edge.

"Well, I can, if you can," he says, throwing down the proverbial gauntlet, making me want to scream.

"Are you serious? Just like that. Sixteen years of animosity, simply pushed to one side?"

His face hardens. "You seem to be the one with the problem here, Kat. As I said, I can be professional. Can you?"

"Fuck you, Jax," I say, before I can stop myself.

"You already did that, and isn't that part of the problem?"

Don't rise to the bait! Don't rise to the bait!

"I think we're done here."

I move to stand up.

Jax stays put. He runs a hand down his face, stopping at his mouth. When he pulls it away, he sighs.

"I'm sorry, that was completely uncalled for."

"You say?" I'm unable to hide the sarcasm in my tone.

I grimace. He always brings out the worst in me. I close my eyes for a second, and when I open them, he leans forward.

"Caleb has stitched us both up. For what purpose, I don't know. What I do know is, it's in both our best interests to make this work." He leans away again. "I know I can help the FHG and you with this project. It's my main area of expertise after all."

He sucks his top lip between his teeth. I zoom in on the movement, flipping back to his eyes when he continues. "I also know you're a consummate professional, and you always want and do the best for your company. I'm the best, Kat, whether you like it or not."

I unfold my arms and place them in my lap.

He's not wrong.

If it were anyone but Jax, I would be selling this project to them, trying to win them over.

Can I ignore the fact that it's him?

"You're right," I say, watching for any smugness. Credit to him, his expression remains impassive. "I'm not going to blow smoke up your arse. As you said, Caleb stitched us both up, me especially with the board. I can't back out, not without serious consequences. I've worked too hard to get this project through to walk away now, and I'm not prepared to go back to the drawing board." I lift my chin and square my shoulders. "But let me make myself *very* clear. I don't trust you. I want to sign off on everything. Do you understand? *Everything.* This is *my* project."

"Crystal," he says, sending a flush of adrenaline tingling through my body. "But remember, Kat. My reputation and that of my firm are at stake here, too. I will not let you do anything to damage that. Do *I* make *myself* clear?"

Our eyes clash.

"Crystal," I say, repeating his word back at him.

"Good, then I think we have a deal."

He swallows the rest of his coffee. When he puts down the cup, he holds out a hand.

Our hands meet, his head lifts, his eyebrows drawing down, as if he's trying to read me.

I school my features, ignoring the sparks shooting up my arm and into my chest.

His lips curl up, and I swallow a snarl.

He withdraws his hand, and it's then I realise we were all but holding hands.

Ahhhhhhh! That man!

"Did you receive my answers to the list of questions you sent over?"

Jaxson looks at me, a frown marring his brow.

"No, I…" He picks up his phone and begins scrolling through his emails. I sit back and wait.

Jaxson looks up, startled. "Two-thirty this morning?"

"I wanted to send them over before I left. Did you think I wouldn't look at them?"

He taps his screen and opens the document on his phone. All fifty pages of it. I may have gone a little overboard with some of my answers.

I'd spent every free moment of the weekend going over them. They were good questions, well thought out. Had got my creative juices flowing, as they say.

"In all honesty, I wasn't sure," he admits, his eyes scanning the document. "This is detailed," he adds, sounding surprised.

"As I said before. I need this project to be a success. I don't want any additional delays."

Jaxson's eyes meet mine.

"When you refused to see me. I assumed," he runs a hand through his hair. "That you were stonewalling me. I apologise."

I bite the inside of my cheek. *Not entirely incorrectly*, but I don't tell him that.

"I do run a company. Being out of the country means meetings had to be brought forward."

"Touché."

I grip my pendant in my hand. A gift from Mum and Dad for my twenty-first. The boys got watches, we girls each got a necklace.

We stare at one another.

"We have ten hours to kill," I say. "Do you want to go through some of it now?"

Jaxson inclines his head. "Are you sure?"

"As I just said, we may as well make the most of a ten-hour flight."

At least I might get some peace on the other end.

CHAPTER 9

JAX

When I stepped out of the cabin, I took one look at Kat and wondered if Cal was right in setting this up.

Yes, I'd complained she wasn't returning my calls. I'm set to meet with the board to discuss my proposal in two and a half weeks. Her lapdog, Michael, arranged a meeting for over a week and a half's time, telling me she was going to be out of the country. This is my reputation on the line.

I saw red.

That timeframe was going to stretch even my talents, and I don't take kindly to being messed around. But now it seems like I jumped the gun. I scan the document Kat sent me. It's detailed. Her answers are clear and well thought out.

Fuck, now I feel stupid.

I don't know what Caleb did to get me on board, or what he told Claudia and the pilot, to prevent them from tipping Kat off. However, looking at the woman before me, she's a shell of the woman I've spent the past sixteen years jousting with.

Her face is drawn, and she has dark circles under her

eyes. Even her *fighting* voice sounds exhausted, and it's not surprising if she was still up at two-thirty this morning.

Cal's words come back to haunt me.

"She needs you. Do this as a favour for me."

I just hope he knows what he's doing.

"Shall we get to work?"

Kat's voice pulls me back into the present.

"Let me get my laptop."

I head back into the cabin, grabbing my bag. My phone pings.

CALEB:
Are you in the air?

ME:
Yes. You have one very pissed off sister.

CALEB:
I'll deal with that when you both return. Happy working.

I shake my head. My eyes drift towards the door. My phone pings again.

PEN:
Please tell me you're not where I think you are.

ME:
Depends where you think I am.

PEN:
She doesn't need this.

I stare at the message. This is not like Pen. Three dots keep appearing and disappearing as if she's trying to decide what to say.

ME:

I need answers.

Surely Pen gets that. She's a businesswoman after all.

PEN:

Don't push her. Give her time.

ME:

I don't have time Pen, I'm on a deadline. This is my reputation at stake.

PEN:

You're there for the project?

ME:

What else would I be here for?

ME:

Pen?

PEN:

Ignore me, pregnancy hormones.

ME:

I call BS.

PEN:

Kat has been through enough recently.

PEN:

She doesn't need you giving her any grief.

ME:

I'm here to work.

ME:

Once I have the info I need, I'll stay out of her way.

PEN:

For your sake, I would.

The phone goes silent. Pen, like everyone else, is clearly worried about Kat. The bombshell that Darra and Zach dropped over two months ago has had far-reaching consequences for the entire family. And Kat held a ringside seat.

My stomach turns over when I think of Zach and what he's done to Kat.

I don't get it.

She chose him, yet he threw her away.

I jump as Kat appears at the door.

"Are you coming?"

"Just answering some messages."

"My brother?"

I chuckle. "Who else? He's on warning, but I think he assumes he's safe, at least for the next week."

She smirks, and I breathe a sigh of relief.

"He is, then all bets are off. In the meantime, I've messaged Pen, April and Leah."

"Ouch, low blow," I say, chuckling, knowing that the Frazer women, born and married-in, stick together like glue. It also explains how Pen knew where I was.

I should feel sympathy for Cal, but he knew what he was doing when he set this train in motion.

"Shall we do this?" Kat says, sweeping her arm back towards the main cabin.

"Let's."

Kat turns and heads back, her long, glossy hair flowing loose down her back, her trim waist and tight arse are clearly visible in the leggings she's wearing for the flight. I swallow at the sight. It's obvious she wasn't expecting company. I haven't seen Kat this casual in over sixteen years. My cock begins to harden, and I close my eyes, counting to ten. This is my problem. She's always had this effect on me, although these days, it's purely physical, there was a time when it was mental as well.

When I re-enter the cabin, Kat is sitting back in her seat, her laptop open in front of her. She ignores me as I take my seat, setting myself up. When I'm finally ready, she looks up.

"This is what I have so far."

* * *

For the next couple of hours, we work our way through the brief. When I said I wanted to be involved in this project, I wasn't joking. Speaking to Kat, going into more detail, I'm hooked.

Kat exhales loudly and stretches her arms above her head. Her top outlines her perfect breasts. I force my eyes upwards, pleased to find Kat's closed, so she did not see my slip-up. I'm going to need to be more careful.

When Claudia appears with some food and drink, we place our laptops on the seats next to us. Kat continues to drink water. Some of the exhaustion I saw in her eyes earlier has been replaced by sparks of excitement. She clearly meant it when she admitted she's invested a lot of time and energy into this project.

We've spent time bouncing ideas back and forth. Not just going through my questions, but also discussing possibilities and what is currently available on the market. Kat appears to be impressed by my knowledge and insight. As the leader in this field, I have more contacts than even Kat is aware of and am privy to a lot of new and upcoming technology.

Claudia places our food in front of us.

I tuck into the beef stew Cal had requested for me, while Kat pushes her salad leaves around her plate.

"You really should try this," I say.

She looks up, a little startled as if she was lost in her own thoughts.

"It's fine."

"Doesn't Leah say, people who say they're fine, never are?"

Kat rolls her eyes, but her lips turn up at the edges.

"She does," she says, surprising me.

I put my knife and fork down and sit back.

Kat looks up again.

"What?"

"You just said you're fine. Then agreed with me that people who say *they're fine* usually aren't."

"Are you trying to be obtuse?"

"Are you trying to dodge the question?"

Kat shakes her head and looks down, repositioning the napkin in her lap.

"Kat?"

My muscles tighten, and a dullness spreads through my chest as I watch her.

She screws the napkin up before changing her mind and folding it neatly. She places it on the table.

"If you don't mind, I'm going to try to get some sleep. It's been a crazy week."

I kick myself mentally as she closes down before my eyes. Her famous icy facade slips neatly into place.

You idiot! Why did you push her?

Kat gives me her best professional smile before sliding herself out of the chair and making her way to the back of the plane and into the bedroom.

She stops and turns, her voice subdued. "Do you need anything from your bag?"

"No, I'm good. I'll continue working on the brief with the information you've given me."

She nods and disappears into the room, her limbs appearing heavy as though she's carrying the weight of the world. The door clicks shut softly behind her.

I lean in, cupping my chin in my hand. This is not what I

expected to find. Part of me can understand why Caleb pushed for me to help. He knows I only have his best interests at heart, and therefore, by default, Kat's. What he doesn't understand is that I've always had her best interests at heart, even when she's hated me.

CHAPTER 10

JAX

Kat still hasn't reappeared when the pilot announces we're about to land.

I should have kept my mouth shut.

I've spent the past seven hours working through Kat's answers and making notes on the project. I wasn't wrong, Kat's responses are both thorough and well thought out. The only problem is that they've created a thousand more in my head as I've begun to dig deeper.

I drop my head back against the seat and stare out of the window.

I wasn't lying when I said I wanted in. The project she's attempting is both innovative and brave. If she pulls it off, her position as queen of the hotel industry will be well and truly cemented.

"Jaxson, we'll be landing shortly. Can I get you anything?" Claudia says, appearing in the cabin.

"No, I'm fine. Thank you," I say, wincing at my turn of phrase as she collects the remnants of my last meal.

I switch off my computer and stow it on the chair next to me. I glance at the bedroom door. There's been no sound from inside since Kat disappeared. She must be hungry. Guilt niggles me.

Why did I have to provoke her?
It's too late now.

* * *

Kat retakes her seat opposite me, fastening her seat belt as the plane's engines roar and whine as we begin to make our descent. She's clearly showered and changed. Gone are her leggings. Instead, they've been replaced by a full-length maxi-dress. It may not be her usual tailored business suit, but it leaves no doubt of her power and position. The perfect combination of casual yet professional. Her hair and makeup have also been reapplied.

"Kat," I say.

She looks up, her eyes locking with mine.

"I'm sorry."

"For what?" she says, as if our earlier conversation never occurred.

Okay, so we're playing that game.

"Look, I promise to stay out of your way," I add. "But if you have any spare time, I'd love to discuss some additional points with you."

The enthusiasm in my tone must spark her interest.

"I'm sure I can find some time," she says, before busying herself with something in her bag.

The engines roar as the plane's wheels touch down, and the ever-efficient Claudia reappears as we taxi towards the hangar.

"Thank you, Claudia," Kat says as she passes. "Enjoy your break."

"Thank you. I will."

I thank her too, and follow Kat down the steps to the waiting golf cart and hotel host.

"Welcome to the Maldives and Valena International Airport, Ms Frazer and Mr Lockwood. I'm Em. I'll be with you until you depart for the island. Please." She motions with her hand for us to climb onto the cart.

Kat greets her with an unexpected warmth, but I notice the shift instantly. Her chin is high, her shoulders back. This is pure *business* Kat.

Kat gets on first, and I climb in next to her. Our thighs touch in the confined space. She shifts in her seat, but it appears that in the limited space, there's nowhere to escape. I stifle a grin as she angles her body away from mine. When she sighs, I turn my head to look the other way. The pressure of her leg against mine, suddenly all I can focus on.

Our host continues talking as the golf cart begins to move, telling us about the history and structure of the Maldives.

"This building houses the hotel lounges. The Frazer Hotel lounge is on the second floor. It offers our guests a space where they can freshen up and rest after their flights, as they wait for their seaplane transfer."

"Sounds perfect," I say, earning myself a smile from Em. I don't miss Kat's eye roll.

What's her problem?

The chance to freshen up after a long flight is ideal. With Kat using the bedroom, and my bag being inside with her, I haven't had an opportunity until now.

Em smiles again. "There's a buffet offering a range of savoury snacks, fresh fruit and pastries. As well as a selection of hot and cold drinks."

"Thank you, Em," Kat says. "What time will our seaplane be departing?"

I half-listen as Em explains there was a storm the

previous evening that continued into this morning. I look up at the blue sky above us.

"Unfortunately, it means there will be a slight delay to your departure. Hopefully, we can get you in the air and on the island in the next couple of hours."

Our host continues to smile, but Kat's shoulders drop ever so slightly.

The thought of spending another couple of hours in my company is clearly not to her taste.

We are led into the lobby and up to the lounge. Em wasn't kidding when she said it was a wide area filled with daybeds and large, comfortable seating. There's even a balcony, overlooking the landing and take-off port for the seaplanes. A buffet of delicious-looking pastries, fresh fruit and savoury snacks sits on one side, with a deluxe coffee machine and a number of fully stocked fridges.

"Help yourself," Em says. "And if you need anything, please don't hesitate to ask."

Several couples of varying ages are sitting in the lounge. They all look like they've been here a while.

Kat moves to the far corner of the room by the window. She drops her handbag onto one of the sofas before sinking down next to it. The seat she's chosen overlooks the water, her back to everyone else, but despite not seeing her face, I can sense the exhaustion radiating off her.

What the hell is going on?

I move to the buffet, my eyes never leaving Kat.

"Mr Lockwood, can I get you anything?"

Em appears by my side.

"Is it possible to get Ms Frazer a chicken salad?"

Her face lights up. "Of course. Anything else?"

"That's all."

I move to the opposite corner of the room and pull out my laptop, keeping Kat in full view.

Em reappears ten minutes later, holding an enormous chicken salad fit for a king or queen. She makes her way over to Kat.

Kat looks up. When Em says something, her gaze darts towards me. I focus on the screen in front of me, although my body is aware of every move she makes.

As she moves away, Kat turns back to the window. Her arm moves, and I see her place food in her mouth.

My shoulders relax as I watch her take another mouthful.

Job done.

Time to freshen up and head for the showers.

CHAPTER 11

KAT

I drop down onto one of the sofas in the corner and stare out of the window. The speed with which the storms pass is unbelievable. It's the catch-up that takes time.

My head begins to spin, my muscles heavy. I want nothing more than to fall into a comfortable bed and sleep for the next twenty-four hours.

Despite leaving Jax and going into the bedroom, I failed to get any sleep. The tightness in my chest and throbbing heartbeat make it impossible to wind down.

So much for a relaxing work break. I'm going to kill Cal when I get home.

"Here you go, Ms Frazer."

I look up to find Em standing next to my chair. In her hand, a plate of food. Not from the buffet, but what looks like a fresh chicken salad.

"Mr Lockwood said you would like some food," she says, placing it and a chilled bottle of water down on the table in front of me.

I stare at the plate, and back up at the woman who delivered it.

"Thank you, Em."

She smiles before walking away.

My eyes search out Jaxson. He's done as he promised and has made himself scarce, sitting on the opposite side of the room. He appears engrossed in something on his computer.

The man calls me a workaholic.

My stomach grumbles. I pick up the salad and take a mouthful. I bite back a moan, my body screaming in delight, at finally receiving sustenance. The chicken is warm and lightly spiced, the salad fresh and crisp with a variety of different greens and vegetables. If this is a taste of the food to come, I may find my appetite returns.

I sit back, salad in hand, and eat it while watching the seaplanes land and take off. I finish the plate of food in record time, the dizziness from before slowly dissipating as my blood sugars rise. I open my laptop, turning my attention to the screen, reading the latest updates from Michael, and a number of reports from some of the other managers.

I'm lost in work when Em finally reappears.

"Ms Frazer, the seaplane is ready. We'll be heading down to the boarding gate in five minutes," she says.

"Thank you, Em. And thank you for the salad, it was delicious."

Her face lights up at the use of her name.

"Take the time to memorise names, Kat. Use them whenever possible, goes a long way in building relationships with your staff."

Dad's voice, once again, echoes through my mind, as it has been doing a lot recently.

I close down my laptop and return it to its sleeve.

I stand up as Jaxson appears silently by my side.

"Thank you for the food," I say.

His gaze meets mine before softening.

"You're welcome."

I nod before turning my attention to Em, who has returned.

"If you'd like to follow me."

We make our way down to the boarding gate, where she bids us farewell and a happy break.

The seaplane is busy. Jax offers for me to board first. I get on board and take one of the single seats, trying to ignore the roar of the engines.

Jaxson drops into the seat behind me, but I keep my eyes forward.

The pilot comes over the tannoy as we take off, the plane bouncing and accelerating before soaring up and over the water.

It's forty minutes to the island.

A new acquisition to the FHG's portfolio. There've been a few issues, which is why I'm here. A working holiday. The report says they need a large influx of cash. It's my responsibility to decide if that's true.

The past ten weeks have been a rollercoaster, and I feel like I'm holding on by my fingertips. I needed an escape, time to decompress. My attention has been wandering, and my judgement is definitely impaired. My agreeing to work with Jaxson is evidence of that. My icy, calm demeanour is cracking.

This was my chance to reset, and my bloody brother has seen to it that I now have to deal with Jaxson.

I stare out of the window at the crystal waters and islands below.

Jaxson Lockwood is not going to derail my plans.

This trip will be on my terms. I will work with him for the good of the project. His input on the plane was impressive for someone who's just come on board. But other than that, I'm demanding my own space.

* * *

WE FINALLY COME INTO LAND. The seaplane bounces over the waves as it pulls into the island's jetty. A team of representatives from the hotel are waiting to greet us individually.

Nice touch.

"Ms Frazer, Mr Lockwood. My name is Bethany. If you have any questions or need anything, I'll be your representative during your stay with us."

"Thank you, Bethany," I say, ignoring the fact that Jaxson and I have been grouped together.

Jaxson follows silently behind as we make our way down the jetty and onto the island itself.

Bethany motions us to enter a covered seating area. A server appears with a warm smile, a facecloth to freshen up, and a long, ice-cold, fruity drink.

We sit and listen as we're given the standard welcome and explanation. Some is as I would expect at any FHG hotel, the rest is island-specific.

Other guests drift off one by one with their representatives.

"Ms Frazer, welcome." A man approaches, his hand outstretched. "It's lovely to have you with us. I'm Don Baskin, the general manager. I hope you had a pleasant flight."

My professional persona locks back in place as I accept his hand.

"Mr Baskin," I say, trying to infuse some enthusiasm into my tone.

"Don, please."

I don't return the offer, not yet. We'll see by the end of the visit whether he earns the position of trusted staff member. Until then, it's all professional.

"Is there anything I can get you while you wait?" he asks.

My scalp prickles. Something is off.

"Mr Baskin, I don't mean to be rude, but it's been a long trip. I'm sure Mr Lockwood, like myself, would appreciate being shown to our rooms."

The colour drains from his face, and I swallow my groan.

What now?

Mr Baskin turns to Bethany. "Bethany, can you show Mr Lockwood to his water villa?"

"Of course."

She plasters on a smile, but I don't miss the lack of eye contact as she leaves.

"I'll catch you later?" Jaxson says, his brows furrowing.

He's also sensing something is off.

"I'll drop you a message," I say, wanting to get whatever Mr Baskin needs to say over and done with.

Jax and Bethany disappear.

Don's body language changes as soon as they are out of sight. The man almost shrinks into himself.

"What is it, Mr Baskin?" I say, as my extremities start to twitch from a combination of impatience and exhaustion.

"There's been a slight issue. I'm working with our maintenance team to get it rectified as soon as possible."

His words come out thick and fast.

I close my eyes briefly and count to ten.

Of course there is.

"What's the problem?"

His shoulders drop.

"Last night's storm has damaged your villa. Flooded it."

I sigh.

Is that all?

I force a smile. "That's okay," I say. "I'm happy to stay in one of the guest villas."

His colour drains further.

"Er, Erm," he stutters.

"Mr Baskin, please. It's been a long flight, I don't have the time or the patience for a thousand questions and answers. Tell me what the problem is."

"We're fully booked," he blurts out. "There are no spare villas."

I rub my temples.

"Let me get this straight. What you're saying is, there's nowhere on the island for *me* to stay?"

He wrings his hands, and I want to scream.

I get that this is not what you want to tell the CEO of the company that just bought your hotel. But as the general manager, you need to handle a crisis without drama.

"Can you take me to the villa?"

He jumps up. "Of course."

He grabs one of the golf carts and drives us to the villa. Pointing out the various parts of the island as we pass. Restaurants, tennis courts, staff quarters, and spa.

I half listen, the travel catching up to me. My muscles twitch and scream in protest.

He pulls up at the villa and unlocks the gate, walking us through. The outside shows remnants of the storm and seawater damage. The plunge pool is full of debris, and the furniture is filthy. But it's on the inside, the staff are busy working. Water-damaged furniture is being carried out, while another team is replacing the smashed glass door. This is not good if a guest had been staying here.

"What happened?" I ask, adrenaline burning through my exhaustion.

Mr Baskin leads me to the beach, pointing out the barrier circling this side of the island. I look out over the now calm sea.

"It's washed away. Part of the money we've requested is to rebuild the breakwaters. The previous owners let them go. With global warming, the storms are getting more frequent. They help reduce the energy of the incoming waves. We're already being forced to rebuild the beaches in places where they've been washed away."

Five PM.

I pull out my phone and dial the UK office.

"Michael," I say.

"Ms Frazer," the surprise in his voice is unmistakable. "Is everything okay? Have you arrived?"

"Yes. Although there's an issue. I want you to call James Lawson. The breakwaters need to be repaired ASAP. It's all in the report. I'll send him an email with details as soon as I have somewhere to park myself. Until then, I want you to start the ball rolling."

Luckily, the team are aware of my initial orders coming from Michael.

"On it," he says.

I disconnect and turn back to Mr Baskin.

His eyes are wide as he stares at me. "Thank you," he says.

"There's still the issue of me needing somewhere to stay," I say.

He nods. "I'm having my quarters prepared for you as we speak. I'll move into the staff quarters. The renovations should be complete within forty-eight hours."

"Aren't you worried it'll happen again?"

"It's the first time it's happened. As part of the renovation, another team will be fixing the breakwater, with a temporary fix, but it won't last."

I nod. "My team will get this resolved properly, Mr Baskin. If you can find me somewhere to work, I'll send off the relevant requests."

"You can either work from my office or the library. The library is probably more comfortable. I can also send someone to bring you food and drink."

"Kat?"

I look up at the sound of Jaxson's voice.

"Oh hell," he says, taking in the destruction of the villa.

Mr Baskin moves away, giving us space.

"What are you doing here?" I ask.

"I gathered something was wrong when Bethany spirited me away, so I asked her. She told me what happened."

"It's a bit of a wreck, at least for the next forty-eight hours."

"Where are you staying? According to Bethany, the island's fully booked."

"It is. Mr Baskin is having his living quarters prepared for me," I admit.

I walk back towards the villa, my ankle catching on the sand, making me stumble. Jax reaches out, catching me, his hand wrapping around my bicep, sending sparks of awareness up my arm.

He speaks close to my ear, his breath making my stomach somersault despite my exhaustion. "You take my villa, I'll take the manager's room."

I shake my head, turning to face him.

"For goodness sake, Kat. Why not? You look like you're on the verge of collapse."

I scowl at him.

"Is that what you say to charm all the girls?" I ask.

He scowls, his forehead furrowing.

"I know you, Kat, even if you'd rather I didn't."

I wrap my arms around my stomach and concentrate on placing one foot in front of the other.

"That's kind of you. However, guests can't stay in staff quarters. It's against company policy. It's also not fair on the staff, as it's their space," I say.

Jax steps back and shakes his head.

"Fine, then we share. My villa is more than big enough."

I let out a bark of laughter, which draws the eyes of the staff.

"Share? We'd kill each other in hours."

"Would we?" he says, his voice dropping, making my stomach contract. "We didn't the weekend we snuck away."

Heat rises in my cheeks.

"That was different," I hiss, looking around.

"Why? Because we were lovers?"

"Exactly," I say, wishing instantly I could take the words back.

"Well, the offer is there," he says with a shrug.

Mr Baskin takes that moment to return.

"My rooms are ready for you," he says, ushering us towards the gate. "The villa should be ready within the next forty-eight hours, but until then, my rooms are at your disposal."

He drives us to the staff quarters, pulling up outside one of the larger buildings. The place is alive with off-duty staff. All greet us with a welcoming smile. It's a private community, with its own general store, cafe, and gym, all hidden from view, in the centre of the island.

My head pounds at the noise.

"Last chance," Jax whispers, his breath tickling my ear, causing goosebumps to erupt over my body.

I bite the inside of my mouth.

Can I?

There's a crash from the kitchen. My body flinches as my tired muscles twitch.

I stare at Jaxson for a moment.

"Mr Baskin," I say. "Mr Lockwood has offered for me to stay at his villa with him."

Mr Baskin spins around in his seat, his eyes wide.

"He's a long-standing family friend," I say, wanting to make it abundantly clear that there's no romantic entanglement going on. "We were wondering if it's possible to have a second bed installed in the villa?"

A smile spreads over his face. "Of course, of course. That can be done immediately."

He ushers us back to the golf cart and practically races us out of the staffing area, pulling up instead at the beach bar.

"Please," he says, jumping out. "Let me get you both settled while I get it organised."

Staff jump at the sight of us. Mr Baskin disappears as drinks and snacks are delivered to our table.

When we're alone, I turn to Jax.

"Thank you," I say. "I'm not sure how much sleep I would have got."

"I promise not to snore," Jaxson says with a smirk, making my lips twitch.

His eyes sparkle in response.

"Look, I know this is a working holiday, but you also want some private downtime," he says. "We can stay out of each other's way. I'll be out of the villa for most of the day, so it will be all yours."

"That doesn't seem fair."

He shrugs and takes a sip of his ice-cold beer, the condensation running down the outside of the glass.

"It's for forty-eight hours. We can make it work. What can go wrong?"

CHAPTER 12

KAT

We sit in silence and sip on our drinks.

I fire off an email to James and his team. This is not something that can wait. I'm sure there'll be additional items that will need to be addressed. The report told me as much, but this is the most urgent by far.

Bethany appears a little while later to deliver us to Jax's water villa. I'm not sure what possessed me to agree to stay with him. The only thing I can think of is that exhaustion has stolen my sense of self-preservation and impaired my judgement. That and the guilt of displacing the general manager, even for forty-eight hours. It simply seemed wrong when we got there. The staff would also have felt ill at ease. The CEO living amongst them.

I listen in fascination as Jax questions Bethany about the sustainability factors the hotel has in place. She's surprisingly knowledgeable and offers him a behind-the-scenes tour should he want one.

His enthusiasm is contagious, and I find myself looking forward to learning more about how this hotel operates. At the end of the day, it has to sustain itself. It's an island, so water, electricity, and sewage disposal all have to be dealt with on-site.

Bethany turns off the main island and drives us along another jetty. This one houses all the water villas. Individual buildings, mounted on stilts, sit in the shallow waters of the reef that surround the island. Fish, reef sharks and manta rays circle beneath us.

Several maintenance men are working on the thatched roofs of some of the buildings.

"Storm damage?" I ask, making a mental note to speak to Mr Baskin about how often this happens.

"Sadly, yes," Bethany says. "But they'll all be fixed by nightfall."

She pulls up outside one of the villas.

"Here we are again," she says, smiling at Jax, before taking out a keycard and opening the door.

I follow her into a hallway with a floor-to-ceiling glass window at the opposite end. The crystal clear water of the Indian Ocean spreads out as far as the eye can see, stealing my breath.

"To the left is the bedroom, the right, the bathroom. There's plenty of storage for clothes here. On the balcony, you have your plunge pool, sun loungers and steps leading down into the sea."

I leave Jax with Bethany, and step into the main bedroom.

A small, single bed has been added to the space.

"If you have any questions?"

"I think that will be all," I hear Jax say.

I turn and look towards the hallway. "Thank you, Bethany."

She smiles before letting herself out.

"It's a beautiful location," Jax says, entering the room and throwing his bag down into one of the chairs near the window. "The water looks tempting, I might go for a swim."

His presence and accommodating attitude are doing strange things to my equilibrium. I need to put some space between us.

"I'll leave you to unpack," I say, suddenly. "I'm going to explore."

"Are you sure? I can leave if you want me to."

I shake my head and hold up a hand, stopping him.

"I'm fine," I say before cringing at my words.

Jax chuckles.

"I'll rephrase that. I could do with a walk. If I stop now, I'm likely to fall asleep, and it's too early."

I turn and leave before he can say anything else, or worse, offer to come with me. Jax has always had a profound effect on me, almost from the beginning. It's not just his looks. He is, by anyone's standards, beautiful. His chiselled jaw and high cheekbones have caught the eye of both men and women. I'm surprised he was never approached to model. His swimmer's physique, broad shoulders and trim waist make his frame perfect for modelling.

But I don't need to think about him, and certainly not in that way.

That ship sailed a long time ago.

I make my way along the jetty, passing the other water bungalows. It's hot despite the time of day, and it's not long before I have an uncomfortable stream of sweat trickling down my spine. I curse myself for not thinking of changing before I left. My need to put space between myself and my old nemesis was stronger than my common sense in that moment.

I hit the island itself and kick off my shoes. The pathways are sand. I make my way to the bar we were in earlier.

There are a number of guests, couples sitting in seats, sipping on cocktails.

Several look up as I pass and smile.

"Hi," I say, moving towards one of the empty tables.

I take a seat, and a bartender appears almost instantly with a menu.

"Welcome to The Frazer Hotel. Can I get you anything, or would you like to see our menu?"

"I'll have a Mai Tai and a water, if I can."

"Perfect."

He disappears. I close my eyes and allow my senses to roam. Something I always do when I arrive at one of our hotels. The gentle roll of the waves on the sand, the murmur of guests talking, laughter, birds, a splash and a squeal of delight from a guest.

I open my eyes and take in the view.

The enclosed bar sits at the top of the beach. Its sides are open, but can be closed if a storm comes in. Outside, there are a variety of seats, doubles and singles, some with shade and others for those guests who prefer to sit in the sun.

The bartender returns, carrying my drinks and a selection of nibbles.

"Here you are," he says, placing them down on coasters in front of me. "If there is anything else?"

"This is perfect, thank you."

Once he's left, I sit back and soak in the rest of the atmosphere. For the first time in months, I can feel the stress beginning to ebb away, despite my exhaustion and knowing I'll be sharing a living space with Jax for the next two days.

My phone pings.

CALEB:

I'm sorry. This is on me. Please don't blame Jax.

I clench my jaw as I stare at the message. I draw in a long and ragged breath.

> ME:
>
> What the fuck were you thinking, Cal? I told you to stay out of it.

I reply, trying to keep a lid on my rising temper. My stress levels are rising exponentially.

Three dots appear and disappear several times as my baby brother decides which excuse to come up with.

> CALEB:
>
> You actually told me to deal with Jaxson.

> ME:
>
> How is sending him on my business trip, you dealing with Jaxson?

> CALEB:
>
> I thought it would help. He needed answers to write the proposal.

> ME:
>
> So you decided to blindside me?

I take a deep breath as more dots appear and disappear. I've half finished my Mai Tai by the time his reply finally lands.

> CALEB:
>
> I'm really sorry, Kat.

> CALEB:
>
> Believe me when I say, April, Pen, and Leah have shown me the error of my ways.

I choke on my Mai Tai.

I just bet they have!

Knowing my best friend and sister-in-laws, he's been raked over the coals and back, and as a minimum, been read the riot act.

. . .

> **CALEB:**
> In my defence, meeting him away from the office seemed like a good idea.

> **CALEB:**
> At the time.

> **CALEB:**
> He needed answers.

> **CALEB:**
> You've always approached things head on. With Jax you don't. I didn't want you to derail yourself or this project, just because I forced you to work with him.

HIS WORDS SURPRISE ME, insightful for Caleb.

When it comes to Jaxson, I do have a mental block. I just never dreamed Caleb would take it this far. Gatecrash my trip.

> **ME:**
> I'd sent him answers. Fifty plus pages. You were out of line.

> **CALEB:**
> Oh shit. How was I to know?

> **CALEB:**
> Just don't kill him. Jax is a good guy.

> **ME:**
> I won't kill him. You, on the other hand. All bets are off when I get back.

I smile as I hit send. Let him stew. Cal knows better than to mess with me.

CALEB:

> I deserve it. Try to enjoy your break. And I mean it. Please don't kill Jax.

My mind returns to my discussion with Pen. It's been playing on my mind since our lunch, waking me up in a bath of sweat. Was I really that naïve? Did Zach, Darra and her friends really play me like a fiddle? Did I accuse Jax of something he was innocent of? Does it really matter anymore? Some things have been said that can never be taken back.

I keep our sleeping arrangement to myself. No one at home needs to know that.

I know Caleb meant well with his plan. He loves both me and Jax, of that I have no doubt. I know after everything that went down with Zach, he and the rest of the family are worried about me. It makes sense that he wants to help fix my problems, but he doesn't know what inviting Jax in means. None of them do.

I take another sip of my Mai Tai.

It will be fine. You're older and wiser now.

Jax said we can both be professional, and we can. *Professional* is my middle name after all.

I finish my drink and make my way back to the villa, hoping that Jax has done what he said and gone for a swim.

CHAPTER 13

JAX

I watch Kat leave and run a hand through my hair, tugging it slightly.

Fuck, this is not what I anticipated when I agreed to Caleb's harebrained scheme to get the answers I needed. Answers she actually provided.

What an idiot!

Not only have I invaded her break, but we're quite literally stuck, living together for the next forty-eight hours. The only person she has an actual physical aversion to.

I sink down onto the sofa.

Caleb says he's worried about her, and I'm beginning to see what he means. Kat's mask is slipping. The Kathryn Frazer I know has always been reserved. Was never overly keen on outward, public shows of emotion. When we were together, our relationship was a secret, so all emotions were kept behind locked doors. After that, she just became short and direct, letting me know my presence was unwelcome.

Her animosity towards me was initially seen as a joke by her brothers. They thought she disliked me because I slept with one of Darra's friends, someone she didn't approve of. It all happened as Elijah's life descended into turmoil, with Darra announcing she was pregnant. No one questioned Kat's emotional switch. Typical siblings, they laughed it off, blaming me for being a babe magnet. Kat never corrected them. Instead, she allowed my friendship with her brothers to flourish, despite her own misgivings about me.

Now we are here... I stand up and begin to pace. When Kat picked up that bloody chicken salad and ate it in the lounge, I'd felt an unexpected lightness. I'd all but flopped back into my chair as I'd pretended to be engrossed in my computer. When she thanked me, I thought we might be getting somewhere. Instead, she has run, like her dress is on fire, when I know she's exhausted.

Shit!

I run a hand down my face.

Maybe we can come up with a rota? I'll speak to Bethany, find out if there's somewhere I can work with internet access. Somewhere far, far away from this villa. Give Kat the space I've promised her.

My eyes move to the bed, and the single bed that's been erected. It's a child's bed and certainly not designed for an adult male or female. I groan. There I was, hoping to get some sleep. The main bed is vast. Not that I think Kat will be keen on the idea of sharing.

My phone pings.

ELIJAH:

What the hell? Do you have a death wish?

ME:

Ha Ha. It seemed like a good idea at the time.

ELIJAH:

In what universe?

ME:

I needed answers for the project. Kat was not cooperating.

ELIJAH:

So you stowed away? You're a braver man than me.

If only you knew. You'd have hung me out to dry years ago.

ME:

I'm a big boy. Kat has agreed to work with me. Plus, I didn't stow away. Cal got me on the plane manifesto.

ELIJAH:

Cal clearly has a death wish too.

I can sense the incredulity of Elijah's message.

My phone rings, and I answer immediately.

"How did she take it?"

"About as well as you'd expect. I take it she messaged you all?"

"I'd say my sister is royally pissed. I'm surprised you're still breathing."

I am too, if I'm honest, and that's what concerns me most.

There's a pregnant pause.

"Try not to piss her off any more than necessary. From what Cal told me, the board are happy. Kat needs you on this project, don't force her to do anything she'll regret."

I bite my tongue. Kat's brothers are treating her like she's a child, not a grown arse woman who runs one of the world's largest hotel groups. A CEO who is both revered and feared in equal measures by her competitors.

"Don't worry, I want to keep all appendages intact. I'm not going to mess with Kat."

I decide not to tell him about our living arrangements for the next forty-eight hours, or the fact that his sister had sent me the information before I left. It will fuel the fire, and not something Kat or I need to deal with.

"We've already discussed keeping our relationship purely professional," I say.

Elijah chuckles, and I groan.

"You know what I mean. We've agreed to act like professionals around one another for the sake of the project."

"Oh, for a moment… don't mind me. It's being with Pen. The thought of you and Kat—"

He begins to laugh even harder.

I force out my own laugh.

Elijah probably wouldn't be my friend, and I certainly wouldn't have spent years working with Cal if they knew my true history with their sister.

"Sorry," he says, getting control of himself. "On a serious note, we're all worried about her. She's not been herself since Zach and Darra's revelation. She's thrown herself even further into work. Pen told me she was using this time as a working break. Now you're there. No offence, my friend, but you're not my sister's favourite person."

"Look, don't worry. I'm a big boy, and your sister is more than capable of holding her own. Kat's fine."

I cross my fingers as I lie to my friend, but I'm going to do my utmost to ensure Kat gets what she needs this trip.

"Elijah, Kat's not known as the queen of the hotel industry because she's seen as a pushover. I'm here to do my job, she understands that, and appreciates it," I say.

"I hear you," Elijah replies with a sigh. "What you're telling us is to back off and let Kat fight her own battles. That we are being overbearing brothers and should butt out."

"If that's how you want to phrase it."

Elijah laughs, and it's good to hear that sound. It reminds me of times long gone, when we both used to laugh a lot.

"Now we've sorted that, I'm going for a swim to clear my head before dinner."

"Enjoy."

Elijah ends the call, and I throw my phone down on the side.

Kat and I may not see eye to eye, but her siblings are the brothers I never had. If they are worried about her. I will look after her, even if it's from a distance.

I open my case and hang up the few clothes I brought with me in the bathroom wardrobe.

When I'm done, I grab my swim shorts and pull them on, heading out onto the terrace and down the steps leading onto the reef and into the sea.

The fish dart away from me as I move towards the edge of the reef. I launch myself off, diving beneath the surface, using my arms to propel myself forward, cutting a path through the crystal water. The sea is at a beautiful temperature, and the sun is still hot despite the time of day. I swim out but keep track of the shoreline.

I reach some of the larger buildings and start to slow my stroke. I spot Kat sitting in the bar alone, and my chest tightens.

I give myself a mental shake and press on, my arms cutting through the water at speed again, as I try to push all thoughts of Kat Frazer from my mind and the first time I saw her.

* * *

Eighteen Years Ago

The rich and luminous tone of the piano drifts down the hallway. I recognise the piece. Whoever is playing is effortlessly navigating the most challenging passage. Captivated, I find myself standing behind the door of what must be a music room. The pianist is out of sight. I wonder if it's Elijah's mum, whoever it is, is masterful, the passage they're playing appearing effortless.

Dad plays, he has since boyhood. He tried to teach me, but I was much more interested in drawing. I close my eyes and listen. Dad has the technical skill, but this is heartfelt, soulful. I'm drawn in.

"Are you just going to lurk, or are you going to come in?" a female voice says from inside the room.

I step around the door. My eyes instantly lock on the young woman sitting at a grand piano.

"Oh, sorry. I thought you were Caleb or Gabriel."

I know I'm staring. The woman in front of me is definitely related to Elijah. She is the feminine version of my best friend, only her features are more petite, softer. Where my friend is handsome, she's breathtaking. Her long, almost black hair trails midway down her back, and her enormous dark brown eyes stare back at me. I drag my gaze away, knowing I must look like a creep. I use the time to centre myself and look around the room. This is a library, not just a music room. Thousands of books line the wall. My gaze returns to the beautiful woman in front of me.

She inclines her head, a furrow appearing between her dark eyebrows.

"Do you speak?"

"Sorry," I say, rubbing my hand awkwardly down my trouser leg before stepping forward and holding it out to her. "Jaxson Lockwood."

She looks at the outstretched hand and draws her lips between her teeth, smothering her grin. Eventually she places a smaller, more delicate hand in mine.

"I'm a friend of Elijah. I just arrived. I'm here for the summer to train with him."

The words spill out of me like verbal diarrhoea, and I wish the ground would open up and swallow me whole.

Why the hell did I stop outside this room?

I'm making a complete tit of myself.

Way to go, Mr Cool!

I hold her gaze, more because I can't drag my eyes away from hers.

"Pleased to meet you, Jaxson Lockwood, friend of Elijah," she says, her dark eyes twinkling. "I'm Kathryn Frazer, Kat to my friends. Welcome to our home."

"Thank you," I say. "Your playing is amazing. I'm sorry I disturbed you."

"You didn't, I—"

"There you are. I know the house is big, but bloody hell, Jax, only you'd get lost!" Elijah says, bursting through the doorway. "Hey, Kitty Kat."

I spin to face my friend with a grin, but I don't miss the hiss from the woman behind me.

"I see you've met my little sister."

This time, Kat growls, and Elijah laughs.

So, this is what it's like to have siblings.

As an only child with no cousins, my friends have always been important to me.

"Come on," Elijah says. "Zach is out by the pool. If we don't hurry up, he'll have fallen asleep in one of the inflatables."

He turns and heads for the door. "Are you ready to train?"

"Always," I say.

Since I started training with Elijah at the beginning of the year, I have continued to beat every personal best. The guy is a machine. I don't think I've ever met anyone as driven.

I follow Elijah to the door, turning back, mouth open. I close it quickly when I find Kat has already turned her back to us and is rearranging her music on the piano.

Elijah claps me on the back, and I stumble forward. I'm not small at six foot two, but he has at least four inches on me.

"Come on," he says. "Let's go and leave Kat to her music."

CHAPTER 14

KAT

Jax is nowhere to be found when I re-enter the villa. The balcony door is unlocked, and a beach towel is sitting on one of the sun loungers, so I'm taking it he's gone for a swim.

I grab my case and unpack. I may only be here for forty-eight hours, but my clothes need hanging, or I'll require the ironing service.

I go to the wardrobe and pull open the door. Jax's clothes hang neatly on one side of the space.

I grab a hanger and turn away, slipping one of my dresses onto it, before sliding it back onto the rail. I bend down to pick up the next item, doing the same. When I'm finished, I move to stow my case in the bottom, my eyes locking on our clothes hanging side-by-side. My breath catches at the fluttering deep in my stomach. I slide the door closed and turn away.

I take in the bedroom, groaning at the sight of the tiny child-sized bed they've added.

There's no way Jax is going to be able to sleep on that, and this is his villa after all.

I throw down my nightdress to stake my claim, hoping to stem off an argument later.

The internal phone rings, and I move to the bedside table. "Hello?"

"Ms Frazer, it's Bethany. I was wondering if you and Mr Lockwood had a preference for which restaurant you would like to dine in tonight?"

Oh shit!

That was not something I'd thought about.

"Do you have a recommendation?" I ask.

"I would suggest The Jetty. The sunset is beautiful, and you can watch the sharks and fish swimming beneath you while you're eating."

"Sounds lovely," I reply.

Too tired to really care, but knowing I need to eat something. The Mai Tai I drank has made my head swim.

"Seven thirty?"

"Perfect," I tell her.

She ends the call, and I sink down onto the bed.

After I made a song and dance about him being a family friend. There's no way I can be seen to be eating alone. Friends dine together, and I don't intend to set tongues wagging.

It's six thirty now. Hopefully, Jax won't be too long.

I head to the bathroom, undress, and step into the shower.

The warm jets soothe the aches of the journey, easing the tension in my back and shoulders. I drop my head back and let the spray soak my hair. Picking up my shampoo, I pour some into my palms, running my hands over my hair before digging my fingers into the pressure points on my scalp, the way my stylist showed me. I almost moan at the sensation, the tender spots releasing.

Opening my eyes, I draw in a breath as I look out of the bathroom window. Jax emerges from the water and steps onto the terrace. His eyes lock on mine, the towel he's just grabbed frozen halfway to his head.

My gaze drops to his broad chest and tribal tattoo, moisture flooding my mouth.

That's new!

I close my eyes and drop my head back, placing my face under the water, before turning around and leaving my back exposed.

Shit! We're going to need a rota. Everything in this place is fucking glass!

I finish up and turn off the water, grabbing one of the towels off the rack. I dry myself, then unwrap one of the hotel robes and slide it on.

Jax has disappeared, so I select the dress I'm going to wear and grab my makeup bag, before heading into the bedroom.

"All yours," I say, popping my head out onto the terrace, after I spot two hairy, toned legs on one of the sun loungers.

Jax gets up, his towel wrapped tightly around his waist. My eyes drop, not missing the tent ballooning the front.

Jax follows my gaze and grins.

"Really?"

Although my heart skips a beat.

"Don't take it personally, princess."

I turn away, not wanting him to see my heated cheeks.

"Don't worry, I won't."

I storm back into the bedroom, before remembering about our dinner reservation.

I turn almost having Jax walk into the back of me. He holds out a hand, steadying me. The tiny hairs on my arm standing up, as if I've been shocked.

"Careful," Jax says, his boyish grin still present.

"Dinner's at seven thirty. We're eating at The Jetty," I say, before spinning away and moving further into the bedroom.

Jax stays surprisingly silent. When I turn around, he's gone.

As soon as I hear the shower start, I drop the robe and get dressed in record time. I place product in my hair before scooping it up.

I open my makeup bag and place it on the dressing table, beginning my regimented skin care routine. My mind wanders to Jax standing on the terrace. I may not like the man, but I'm not blind. His broad shoulders and narrow hips. His height, dark hair. The addition of the tattoo adds further intrigue. I'm not usually a fan, but even I have to admit the dark lines swirling over his shoulder, chest and bicep. I swallow hard.

Pipe down, hormones!

It's definitely been far too long since I've seen any action, if I'm fantasising about Jaxson and his tattoo!

I finish applying my makeup and style my hair. Having straight hair has its benefits. Jax still hasn't appeared by the time I'm done, so I open my laptop as a distraction, flicking through emails, firing off answers and requesting more information where necessary.

Like my father and grandfather, I'm not a CEO who sits in her ivory tower. I get down and dirty with the day-to-day running of the chain. The FHG has continued to go from strength to strength over the past couple of years, and with this new project, it will cement our name in history.

I close my laptop as Jaxson reappears. My breath catches in my throat, and I swallow hard. Fitted jeans accentuate his long, toned legs and arse, paired with a dark navy polo shirt that hugs his chest and shoulders.

"Ready?" he asks, ignoring my gaze, if he noticed.

"Let's do this," I say, dragging my eyes away and pulling on my Louboutin's.

I stand up, my sundress floating around my legs, hugging my figure.

Jaxson moves to the door, holding it open so I can step through. The heat hits me instantly, a stark contrast to the air-conditioned bedroom.

We walk in silence along the wooden walkway. The restaurant itself is situated at the end of the jetty. The sun is starting to go down, and I have to admit, Bethany wasn't lying. The sunset is beautiful.

We're greeted at the door of the bar area by one of the staff.

"Welcome," he says, ushering us to a table. "Can I get you something to drink before your meal?"

Jax looks at me questioningly.

Act normal.

"A drink would be lovely. A Mai Tai, please," I say, knowing I'll need to take it slowly until I consume some food.

"A beer," Jax says. "Thank you."

We take a seat opposite one another. I gaze out at the sunset, the orange, peach and blue against the now dark water is stunning.

"This is a surprise," Jax said.

I shift my gaze to his. "Anything else would set tongues wagging," I say, my tone matter-of-fact.

He nods before staring out over the water.

"It's very beautiful."

"It is," I say. "I'll ensure the marketing department uses it as a selling point. Maybe offer a photographer for honeymooners and couples."

"Do you ever switch off? Just enjoy the moment?"

His words take me by surprise.

"This is a working break," I say.

"There's no such thing."

"If that's the case, why would I switch off?"

"Everyone needs a break."

"Worried about my well-being?" I ask, my tone sarcastic, but my stomach does somersaults.

He grunts, but remains quiet.

We sit in silence until our drinks arrive.

The shower has offered me a new lease of life, chased away some of the exhaustion, at least for the time being. I pick up my cocktail and take a sip, closing my eyes briefly enjoying the explosion of flavours on my tongue. Perfect. Strong and flavoursome, but not ridiculously overpowering.

I always test the cocktails when I visit our hotels. There's nothing worse than a poorly made cocktail when you're paying top prices.

Jax watches me as I return the cocktail to the table.

"Does it pass?" he asks.

"It does."

"Everyone has to have downtime, Kat, even you. You can't be *on* twenty-four-seven."

I laugh, and he raises an eyebrow.

"It's not a healthy mindset," he says, making my hackles rise.

"I love my job," I say, unsure why I'm feeling the need to defend myself.

"There has to be balance."

"I have balance," I snap, but stop myself from expanding as my temper flares.

I'm known for my cool, calm head with everyone else, but this man turns any conversation into a battle.

More couples enter the bar area. Jax acknowledges one who smiles as they pass.

I recognise another, older couple from my visit to the bar this afternoon.

"I have a few more questions on the project," Jax says.

"You're giving me whiplash, Jaxson."

I want to laugh at the irony, but he shrugs as if reading my mind.

"If you've got some free time tomorrow," he adds.

Our waiter reappears before I can say anything else.

"Your table is ready, if you'd like to follow me."

He collects our barely touched drinks, and we follow him into the dining area. It's a wraparound balcony overlooking the sea. Lights illuminate the water, which is filled with reef sharks and other aquatic life.

I make another mental note to pass this on to the marketing team as well.

Our waiter pulls out first mine, then Jax's chair, placing our drinks down and opening our menus.

"Thank you," I say.

When he disappears to get our preference in water, I look across at Jax.

"Any questions, send them across, or we can find some time to go over them tomorrow afternoon. I have a meeting with the general manager and his team in the morning, but after that, I'm free."

Jax nods, his attention returning to his menu.

The guests around us chat, the low murmur of their conversations lightens the atmosphere.

I sip my drink and watch the fish in their carefree world, swimming beneath us, the waves gently lapping against the stilts.

"Are you ready to order?"

"I'll have the prawns, followed by the fish," I say.

"I'll have the salmon, followed by the steak, rare," Jax adds.

Predictable. Still a steak man.

Our waiter leaves.

"Your questions?" I ask, unable to take the intolerable silence when everyone around us is talking.

Jax leans forward and smiles.

My chest aches at the sight.

"Hobbies. What do you do to relax?"

CHAPTER 15

JAX

"Hobbies?"

She stares at me like I've asked her an alien concept.

"Yes, you know, the things you do to unwind, relax?"

She grunts, but I see the moment she realises I'm serious.

"I run," she says eventually.

"You always liked to run."

I think about the morning almost three months ago, when I saw her running through the estate. She's skinnier than she was then. The stress is not something she's handling.

"Anything else?"

"I read magazines," she says, her tone becoming defensive.

I chuckle. "Hospitality Design and Boutique Hotelier are not magazines."

"I beg to differ," she says, raising an eyebrow in challenge.

"They're linked to your job."

"Are you saying I'm boring? That I'm a workaholic?"

"If the shoe fits," I say.

"Guilty as charged," she admits, with a smile. "I love my job, what I do."

"Do you still play the piano?"

Her smile fades, her hand dropping to her cutlery. She straightens it.

"Do you?"

"I haven't played in a while."

"Isn't there a piano in the suite at the hotel?"

"What is this, twenty ... questions?" She pauses, clearly trying not to swear.

I've touched a raw nerve.

Her eyes narrow. "What about you? What do you do as a hobby?"

"I swim, read crime novels, watch documentaries on the planet."

"Ah, that could be classed as work," she says, raising an eyebrow.

"Touché. But learning about whales and their mating habits is not really linked to my job. Only understanding the need to protect them from the human race."

Her cheeks darken at the word mating, and I bite the inside of my lip to stop myself from smiling. My heart aches that Kat no longer plays piano, that she has shelved her talent.

"Anything else?" she asks.

"I ride, go out with friends, watch the football."

"I'm surprised you have any time to work."

"I make time for the things I enjoy. I think it makes me better at my job."

"Each to their own," she says, shrugging.

"There was a time when I'd stopped doing anything else," I admit. "Then someone close to me had a health scare, it was enough to make me stop and take note of what I was doing to myself."

Her eyes clash with mine. Whatever she sees there, has her sucking in a breath.

"I'm sorry, I didn't know."

"Cal's the only one who does. My old mentor, Dillon, was diagnosed with cancer last year. He was told to reduce his stress levels. His wife, Susie, stepped in and demanded it," I say, with a smile. "When I went to visit, she told me I needed to enjoy life, stop being a slave to my work. I decided to give it a go."

"You're still close to them?"

"You sound surprised," I say.

"You were engaged to their daughter and broke it off. I just assumed—"

"Emma and I are still friends. She's married now with a gaggle of kids. She got her happily-ever-after."

"How's Dillon now?"

"He's in remission, but he said it was the wake-up call he needed."

"If you're all about relaxing and less work, why get involved in my project?"

I sit back.

"Because it intrigues me," I admit. "And I didn't say I don't love my job, only I've cut back on the day-to-day running. Learned to delegate. It also means I can get involved in projects that really interest me, rather than being locked in mundane tasks."

She sits back and inclines her head as if processing everything I've just said.

"I can see that," she says, surprising me. "It's why I've fought so hard for this project. It's something I'm passionate about."

"Tell me," I say.

Kat comes alive as we discuss more of her ideas and thoughts on the project. She was beautiful before, but animated, as she is now, she's ethereal. For someone not as heavily involved in the sustainability industry, she's done her homework. Some of the ideas she wants to integrate are cutting-edge. I realise we barely scratched the surface on the plane.

Her eyes sparkle, her voice slightly breathy as she answers every question, her intentions are well thought out.

Our starters arrive, then the main course.

If she…we can pull this off, it really will be groundbreaking. Hotels that are not only self-sufficient but also fully sustainable. For countries where tourism is high but resources are scarce, these resorts will no longer simply take, but instead give back to their communities. The possibilities are endless.

We're still talking when the waiter finally arrives to clear our dessert plates.

"Any coffee, tea?" he asks.

"I'm fine," Kat says, looking at me.

"I'm okay, thanks," I say.

He turns and leaves.

"Are you ready to head back?" I ask. "Or do you want another drink?"

"I'm good," she says, pushing her chair back and standing.

I'm pleased to see she ate tonight.

Note to self, don't wind Kat up at meal times.

I follow suit. We bid the staff goodnight before making our way back to the villa.

I step forward and use our key card. Another couple from the restaurant have followed us down.

"Goodnight," they say.

Kat automatically turns around. "Goodnight, enjoy your evening."

They grin, their hands clasped together. "You too."

"Newlyweds," I say, as we enter the room.

"What?" Kat says.

"That couple. They're newlyweds."

"How do you know that?"

I chuckle. "I'm a details man. They both have incredibly shiny rings on."

Kat smacks her forehead. "And I just wished them an enjoyable evening."

"They offered you the same," I chuckle, and Kat groans. "At least they look happy. Obviously enjoying their stay."

Kat pulls off her shoes and tosses them into the corner of the room. She sits down on the tiny bed and begins rubbing her feet.

"You okay?" I ask.

"Heat and heels don't go well together," she says. "I'm in mules from now on."

I chuckle.

"Do you want to use the bathroom first, or shall I?"

"You can go first," I say, taking a seat at the small table where Kat was sitting earlier.

I remove my shoes before getting up and placing them on the shoe rack next to the door. Old habits die hard. Mum never let us wear our shoes in the house.

When Kat disappears, I grab her shoes from the corner and place them next to mine.

However tempting, I don't venture onto the balcony.

Once was enough. I don't need to see Kathryn Frazer, wet and naked, while we're sharing a room.

It took a long time, under the icy cold spray of the shower, to get my cock to calm down. Despite our mental battles over the years, my body still responds to hers physically, and always has. I didn't think Kat or her brothers would appreciate me relieving my sexual frustration with her in the room next door.

I run a hand down my face at the memory. It took all my

willpower to turn away. I didn't think it was possible that Kat could become more beautiful, as she's got older.

I look up as she enters the bedroom, wrapped once more in one of the hotel dressing gowns. Her hair is tied up in a messy bun, her face is shining, and makeup-free.

"All yours," she says.

"Thanks."

I grab my sleep shorts and t-shirt and head to the bathroom.

Tonight was not what I expected. Kat could have knocked me over with a feather when she said we were having dinner together. I was thinking of room service, but it makes sense. She needs to experience the hotel if she's to put the FHG stamp on it.

More importantly, it looks like Kat meant it when she said we could be professional. Tonight was informative and surprisingly enjoyable, even if it was all work.

I take my time getting ready. When I return to the room, Kat is already in the tiny bed.

"Kat," I say. "You should take the main bed."

She looks up from her phone. "It's okay. Besides, there's no way you can sleep on this. Your legs would be hanging over the edge."

"That's not the point. You need to get a good night's sleep."

She frowns, and I kick myself.

"You do too," she says. "I'm more likely to sleep on here than you are. Besides, I won't get any sleep if you spend the entire night tossing and turning."

I scowl, and she smiles.

"Thanks for the offer," she says. "But honestly, I'm fine where I am."

I look over at what is little more than a child's bed. Kat is five feet ten, and her legs are hitting the end. She's correct in her assumption. Mine would be hanging off.

"Besides, I've put an order in for full-sized single beds and mattresses. I've already sent off an email. We can't be the first to have this problem."

"Always super-efficient," I murmur under my breath.

"It's what keeps the cogs turning."

I let out a huff of air, making my way to the luxurious bed I'm going to be sleeping in, alone.

I pull back the cover and sit down. The mattress gives beneath me, and I know this is going to provide one of the best nights' sleep I've had in a while.

"Okay, goodnight then," I say, putting on my headphones and connecting to my favourite podcast on my phone.

"Goodnight."

I turn off the lights and settle down, my body relaxing as sleep takes me.

I'm not sure what disturbs me, but I find myself drawn out of my slumber.

I remove my headphones.

Damn, I fell asleep while listening.

Something woke me.

I lie still and listen.

It's then I hear it. Kat moving. Turning one way, and then the other. Eventually, she gives a harrumph. I sense her move in the dark and watch as she grabs her duvet and blanket.

She makes her way to the door, stopping to look over at me. I lay still, wondering what she's doing.

She sighs before opening the terrace door and slipping outside, closing it behind her.

What the?

I sit up and watch as Kat moves to one of the plush sun loungers. She sits down before pulling the covers over herself.

No way.

I get up and pad towards the door.

I open it, and she yelps, twisting to face me.

"Shit, you scared me!" Kat says, her hand going to her chest.

"What the hell are you doing?" I ask.

She turns and faces me, one eyebrow cocked. "What does it look like? I'm taking in the view."

I fold my arms over my chest. "In the middle of the night? In the pitch black?"

She pinches her lips, but remains silent.

"You'll be eaten alive," I tell her, leaning against the door frame.

Her face sinks, she obviously hadn't thought of that.

"I can't sleep. This is comfier," Kat says, spinning her legs back up and onto the sun lounger.

It's then that the first drop of rain hits.

"You've got to be kidding me," she says, dropping her head back and closing her eyes.

The wind picks up, and the heavens open. The joys of a tropical storm.

I race forward and grab Kat's bedding before heading back through the open door.

Kat remains on the sun lounger.

I watch on from the doorway as she lifts her face towards the sky, her hair and nightdress clinging to her. She stands up and holds out her arms, spinning in the rain, her laugh filled with wonder and delight.

Her eyes sparkle as she turns towards me. I shake my head and smile. She always enjoyed the rain.

How had I forgotten that?

I carry her semi-damp duvet into the bathroom, draping it over the bath to allow it to dry.

I look out of the window. Kat has moved to the edge of the terrace and is staring out over the sea.

She tilts her head back again, her eyes closed. Her nipples protrude against the soaked material of her nightgown. The outline of her panties is clearly visible. She has swept her hair off her face, and it cascades down her back.

Lightning cracks overhead, lighting up the deck. She flinches at the sound before turning and making her way back inside.

I grab a towel and a robe and meet her by the door.

"Here, get inside," I say, as another flash lights up the sky, followed instantly by a crack of thunder.

"Thank you. I love the rain," Kat says, half talking to herself.

Kat grabs the towel and uses it to squeeze out her hair.

"You always did."

I remember finding her in the pool after everyone had gone to bed. She was swimming laps in the rain. Kat, like all the Frazers, is an amazing swimmer, though, like Caleb, she has always preferred to run.

Kat peels her nightdress over her head, before I have a chance to look away, taking the robe I'm holding out.

"Thank you," she says.

I open my mouth and close it again, as her body is enveloped in the white material.

"What?" she says. "It's not like you didn't get an eyeful earlier."

This woman will be the death of me.

I glance at the clock. It's three thirty.

There's another clap of thunder, and Kat turns to face the window, the lightning illuminating her face and the sky. My breath catches in my throat at the sight, my body becoming warm despite the air con.

"You need to get dry," I say.

"Yes, Dad," she says automatically and with extra sass.

She draws up short when she remembers who she's speaking to.

I move back towards her bed and grab the pillows.

"What are you doing?"

"I'm not going to argue with you," I say, putting the pillows down the centre of the large bed, creating a barrier.

"I will not sleep in a bed with you," she says.

I sigh.

"You won't be, you'll be sleeping on your side of an enormous mattress, and I'll be sleeping on mine. Now, if you don't mind, I want to get some sleep. Yesterday was a long day, and I'm tired."

I get back into bed and roll over so I'm facing away from her.

I hear her sigh and head for the bathroom. Two minutes later, the hairdryer goes on as she dries her hair.

When she returns, I stay silent, closing my eyes, slowing my breathing.

I sense her stop at the end of the bed. I can almost hear the indecision swirling in her brain. After a couple of minutes, common sense kicks in, and she moves to the other side. I bite the inside of my cheek. The covers move, and I grin into the darkness as Kat slides into bed on the other side of the pillow barricade.

I lie still and wait for Kat's breathing to even out before finally letting myself drift off.

CHAPTER 16

KAT

I wake up dazed, and it takes me a moment to remember where I am.

Shit, what time is it?

Reaching for my phone, I realise it's by the other bed.

I roll onto my back, staring up at the ceiling before pressing my thumb and forefinger into my eye sockets.

Inhaling deeply, I turn my head. Jax's side of our pillow barricade is empty, the duvet pulled up and into place.

Lying still, I listen intently to my surroundings. The villa is silent, no sign of the man himself.

My muscles begin to relax, until memories of the night before come flooding back.

Not being able to get comfortable on the bed, deciding to move outside onto a sun lounger, the rain, and me stripping off my nightdress, standing there naked. Him handing me a robe.

My heart rate picks up.

What the hell was I thinking!

Bolting upright on the bed, I look around, my skin tingles

at the realisation, Jax managed to sneak out without waking me.

I'm not sure how to feel about that!

I must have been dead to the world, although I'll admit, I haven't slept this soundly in what feels like forever!

Pushing back the duvet, I swing my legs off the bed before moving to throw open the curtains, allowing the morning sunlight to flood the room.

I take in the cloudless sky and sunlight shimmering off the calm waters of the ocean surrounding us. It's then I hear the gentle lap of the waves against the jetty, the sound soothing, almost hypnotising.

Snapping myself out of a trance, I collect my phone from the cot bed, before making my way to the bathroom.

It's just past eight.

My stomach grumbles, letting me know it's time for breakfast

I shower in record time, pulling on one of my sundresses and sandals. Stopping by the door, I check my reflection in the floor-to-ceiling mirror. Perfect. Summer chic, with a professional twist.

There's still no sign of Jax, but I need to eat. My body doesn't mind fasting, but when I start to eat again, it lets me know.

Grabbing the lone keycard from the side, I head towards the main restaurant where breakfast is served.

One of the waiters greets me at the door.

"Good morning, Ms Frazer. Can I show you to your table?"

"Thank you," I say.

I follow him in silence, taking in the atmosphere. The restaurant is alive. The gentle hum of conversations and the hotel team working to meet everyone's needs.

My eyes and ears are on full alert as I take my seat.

"Can I get you a tea or coffee?"

I focus back on the moment.

"Coffee, would be lovely, thank you. A strong latte."

My server smiles. "I'll be right back. Please help yourself to whatever you'd like at the buffet."

I take in my surroundings. The buffet is split into different areas. Fresh, hot, chilled, fruit, cereals, and pastries. There's something for everyone.

I get up and move towards each section, eavesdropping on guest conversations as they discuss the food and their rooms, and listen to see if anything is off. The FHG has built its reputation on customer excellence. We've only just acquired this hotel, and although a team has been on site for the transition, I want to check everything is in order.

"Still in CEO mode?"

I jump slightly at the voice next to my ear. I turn my head to see a very refreshed and smiling Jax.

"I told you yesterday, I'm here to work."

"You're going to make yourself ill."

He tuts.

My mind wanders back to one of my last GP appointments, where they said the same thing after my blood pressure was elevated.

I shrug.

"Have you eaten?" I ask.

"No," he says.

"Would you care to join me?" I ask, before I can stop myself.

Jax's eyes light up as a smile breaks.

"Thank you," he says, grabbing himself a plate and piling on a number of the delicious-looking fresh pastries.

My mouth waters at the sight, but instead I move to the fresh fruit counter. Piling up on pineapple, melon, and dragon fruit. I grab a Greek yoghurt from the chill counter and make my way back to the table.

Jax arrives at the same time as my waiter with my drink.

"An iced coffee, please," Jax says when asked.

"Certainly, sir."

"How did you sleep?" Jax asks when we're finally alone.

I look up, "Very well, thank you. You?"

"Like the dead," he says.

It takes me back to another time and a place. It was Jax's favourite saying. He always slept like the dead. It's why I was so surprised he woke up last night while I was moving.

"What are your plans for today?" I ask.

"I've been for a swim, the water around here is amazing, definitely a selling point for swimmers."

I make another mental note.

"Once I've finished breakfast, I'm going to go through everything we discussed at dinner. I had some additional ideas while I was swimming that I'd like to run through with you. But, before I do that, I want to be able to show you something concrete."

He places a small slice of each of the pastries onto a side plate and pushes it towards me.

"Kat, you really have to try these," he says, leaning forward, his eyes glowing. "I've never tasted anything like them."

My mouth waters at the sight.

I take a small bite and smother my groan. Jax isn't wrong. The pastry flakes off, and the filling is like an explosion on the tongue.

"Good, right?" he says with a grin, motioning to the rest of the plate.

I nod, trying to downplay my love for all things sweet.

"Let me know when you're ready, and we can meet this afternoon to go through your ideas."

I want, no need to get us back onto the topic of business. Our conversation last night was surprising. Jax appeared as passionate about my ideas for the new resort as I was. It was refreshing after spending months battling certain members of the board.

"Yourself? Do you have anything planned?"

"I'm meeting with the general manager, Mr Baskin, after breakfast," I say. "Then I'm hoping to meet with his management team. The FHG transition task force was on site for over a month, working with the current team. I'm hoping to gain an understanding of any outstanding issues. The team we sent in raised a few concerns. I need to know if they're still valid."

Jax nods.

His iced coffee arrives, and he disappears off to get more food, returning this time with a mixture of Asian and British food.

"Where do you put it all?" I say, before I can stop myself. "You're like Elijah."

Jax grins. "I'm a growing lad."

I shake my head and raise an eyebrow.

"Hey," he says, holding up his hands. "I swam, the equivalent of one hundred lengths this morning, in open water."

He taps the watch on his wrist.

"I'll let you off," I say sarcastically, his smile widening.

It reminds me that I need to head to the gym. I could run laps of the island, but I prefer the idea of a treadmill. Less chance of twisting my ankle on the sand.

I don't say anything, just return to eating my fruit and yoghurt.

We continue in silence, but it's not the awkward silence I feared. Instead, it's comforting. Like being around an old friend.

When we're done, I bid Jax goodbye and head to the

manager's office, situated inside the staff compound. This is the hub, at the centre of the island. It includes staff living quarters, the island's filtration and sanitation units, water purification, a staff restaurant, and a shop. It has everything, or appears to have everything, that the staff may want. There's even an undercover area where plants and vegetables are growing.

I pass the staff gym, where members of last night's serving team are working out. Tam, our server, waves and smiles.

I return his greeting.

The general manager's office is on the outskirts of the staff area. Still, I wanted an unfiltered look behind the scenes.

I knock on the office door.

It opens, and I'm greeted by a much less flustered Don Baskin.

"Good morning, Ms Frazer," he says, with a bright smile, although it does not quite reach his eyes.

I don't take it personally. I have that effect on people, it goes with the territory.

"Mr Baskin. Shall we get started?"

CHAPTER 17

JAX

I lied. It was a *long* night.

Lying next to Kat, listening to her breathing... for the first time, sleep eluded me. Thoughts of Kat naked in the shower, talking passionately over dinner, laughing in the rain, sleeping a mere arm's length away.

At daybreak, I gave up and went for a walk around the island, followed by a gruelling swim. Everyone else was asleep, only hotel maintenance was busy cleaning up after last night's storm, getting the island ready for the guests when they awoke.

I look down the beach to see Kat walking along the shoreline. I stop what I'm doing, my gaze locking on her. Kathryn Frazer has no idea how beautiful she is, which is something that has always amazed me. Her sandals dangle from her fingertips, swinging as she walks, her mid-length sundress floating around her legs. She's the epitome of poise and grace. A light breeze gently caresses and lifts her hair.

She turns and stares out over the water. Her meeting with the general manager and his team must have ended. She tilts her face up towards the sun, and I can picture her eyes closed as she absorbs its power.

This morning, when I saw her at breakfast, she looked as tempting as the pastries she was staring at. Our waiter could have knocked me down with a feather when she invited me to join her. As for the plate of pastries I consumed, I usually don't eat them. I'm more of a savoury man, but when the opportunity arose, offering her little tasters was too good to miss. When she'd accepted them, a pressure had built within my chest.

Last night, in the rain, was the first time I've seen Kat that relaxed in a very long time.

Elijah always used to joke that his sister took life far too seriously, needed to loosen up and remove the stick from her arse. At least he had, until his own life became a complete *shit* show.

I never saw that in Kat. It's true, she's not as carefree as Elijah or Caleb. Instead, she's quieter, more reserved, like Gabriel. One thing is certain, she has the same steely determination and inner drive as her brothers.

She's known to analyse any situation before jumping in. Her decisions are always well-informed.

It's something I should've remembered sixteen years ago. When faced with all the facts, my simple denial had been weak at best. With no alibi, nothing to back up my truth. I just wanted Kat to have faith in us, to trust in me and in what we had. But I'd been asking too much.

* * *

Sixteen Years Ago

"Where were you?"

"What do you mean?"

"Answer the question, Jax. Where were you?"

"You're asking me a question from two months ago."

"You weren't with me. Do I need to jog your memory?"

My heart starts to race. What the hell is going on here?

"There are lots of nights I'm not with you. I'm hoping we can rectify that soon."

"Really?" Her tone is one of disbelief. *"After graduation?"*

"We've discussed this," I say, stepping forward and placing my hands on her upper arms. She flinches, and a shiver runs down my spine as she shrugs me off.

"Kat, what's going on?"

I frown, my pulse rate kicking up. Something is seriously wrong. I've never seen Kat like this.

"Sasha Dennison," she spits. *"Remember her?"*

"Sasha? Darra's friend?" I ask. *"What the hell has Sasha got to do with anything, with us?"*

"You tell me? Apparently, you and she..."

I laugh, a full belly laugh, before Kat can finish.

"Kat, you can't be serious? Sasha?"

My laughter dies in my throat as I take in Kat's expression, a line of sweat breaking out along my spine.

"What the hell? Kat, where is this coming from?"

"I heard her. She was telling Darra and their friends. She repeated the exact words you used on me. About keeping our relationship quiet, at least until after graduation."

"She's lying."

"If she's lying and it's not true, then how did she know to use those exact words?"

Kat raises an eyebrow, her chin high. The challenge is there.

A wave of dizziness hits, as adrenaline floods my system.

"I don't know." I run a hand down my face. *"Believe me, she's the last person I would touch. You know that."*

"Do I? Why would she say it? She didn't even know I could hear

them. They were laughing, how it's your standard line, allows you to play the field."

I shrug, my mind racing, searching for answers to things I'm struggling to understand.

"I don't know, but I promise you. It's not true. You're the only woman in my life."

"She's not the only one. Other people have confirmed it."

"Who?" Pressure builds in my chest. "They're lying."

She shakes her head. I can see from her expression. Her mind has already been convinced by these mysterious people.

"Kat."

Her eyes won't meet mine.

"Kat, look at me."

Our gazes clash, and I reach for her, only to have her step back. The pain radiating from her eyes steals my breath.

"I love you. There's nothing between me and Sasha. I promise you," I whisper. "I don't have time to mess around. Not between swimming practice and focusing on my studies."

"I saw you together, at the hotel. I checked the security footage. You were both there."

Her eyes swim with tears, and a crushing pain forms in my chest.

She shakes her head, her arms wrapping around her waist as she says the words that shatter my world.

"I'm sorry, Jax, I don't believe you."

Kat's expression tells me she's serious.

That day, my stupid pride and insecurities had me turn and walk away.

I'd wandered for hours, wracking my brains, trying to understand what had happened. Yes, I'd seen Sasha at the hotel that day. It was the same day I'd met Dillon Myers for my apprenticeship interview. Robert had arranged the meeting and sworn me to secrecy.

Sasha had already been there when I arrived. She was an old friend of Emma, Dillon's daughter. They'd gone to boarding school together. But why would Kat think we were together? Apart from overhearing Sasha's affirmation.

Shit!

I'd returned to our apartment in a daze, half expecting Elijah to burst into my room, beat me senseless, and then throw me out onto the street. Instead, he returned home, striking up conversation as if nothing had happened.

I realised then, Kat hadn't said anything to him. Zach looked at me and asked if everything was okay. I'd simply shrugged it off, while inside I was broken. Kat had not believed me.

* * *

OFF THE BACK of that one conversation, and bad timing, sixteen years of animosity have ensued.

I sigh heavily and rub the back of my neck.

An older woman walks up to Kat, and they begin talking.

"You should tell her how you feel, you know."

I look up to find an older man standing next to my table, his eyes following my gaze.

"Pardon me?"

He looks down and smiles. "The woman you're staring at so intensely. You need to tell her how you feel."

I chuckle.

I'd probably end up minus my balls if I tried.

"Our relationship isn't like that," I say instead.

"No?" he says, sounding totally unconvinced. "Because I used to look at Mary that same way. Thought she wasn't interested." His eyes lose focus, disappearing into a memory. "It was fifty years ago today, we tied the knot."

"Congratulations," I say, motioning for him to take a seat.

He chuckles, pulling out a chair.

"It's not all been plain sailing, lad. Mary's as stubborn as they come. She was married to her career when I met her, world-renowned heart surgeon, one of the first females in her field," he says, his pride clear. He must see something in my expression because he smiles. "But then nothing that's worthwhile is ever easy. Remember that."

"Thank you. But take it from me, you've got it all wrong. I'm her brothers' best friend, we're working together on a project."

I motion to my laptop and watch as his face crumples as he openly laughs.

"I was Mary's brother's best friend. When he found out I had feelings for his sister, he threatened to castrate me."

I chuckle.

I wonder what Caleb and Elijah would think?

I'm not sure I'd be as lucky as this gentleman. If they truly knew what had gone down between us, I'd already be missing my balls.

He looks at me and inclines his head. His tone softens.

"Don't give up, son. All good things are worth fighting for, makes the experience so much better when you finally get there." He laughs again. "Listen to me, I sound like a talking cliché."

Before I can say anything, he gets up and leaves, making his way down the beach towards Kat.

He holds out his hand, and Kat takes it. Her smile is more relaxed now. He pulls the older woman, who is talking to Kat, into his side.

Ah, Mary.

They talk for a few minutes more, and I pray he doesn't say anything. Our truce is tentative. The last thing we need is a couple of old romantics rocking the boat.

Kat says goodbye and begins her journey back up the beach.

I force myself to concentrate on my laptop as she draws closer.

I sense her stop and know she's seen me. I frown at my screen, the words blurring under the scrutiny.

Part of me hopes she'll stop and come over; the other wants her to keep going. I'm not sure of the rules, but I know I'm playing with fire, and if I'm not careful, one of us runs the risk of getting burned.

I need to keep my head down and in the game.

Kat is and always will be, the one who got away. When Elijah said that about Pen, I knew what he meant. Understood his pain. No one else has come close to what we had in the past sixteen years. She ruined me for everyone else, despite our young age. I've tried everything to forget her. I moved away, even got engaged, thinking moving on would help. Instead, I almost ended up ruining someone else's life in the process. Luckily for both of us, I came to my senses.

I suck in a breath as she turns and moves away, my eyes trailing after her. I rub a hand over my jaw and try to focus on the notes in front of me, but it doesn't take me long to realise I'm fighting a losing battle. I close my laptop and drop back in my chair, signalling to one of the waiters. I order a beer and wonder if I'll get any sleep tonight, with Kat lying only a few feet away.

CHAPTER 18

KAT

I leave Mr Baskin and his team and decide to take a walk along the sand.

I check on the progress at my waterlogged villa, finding the island's maintenance team hard at work. At sea, another team is working to fix the breakwater.

I kick off my shoes and pick them up, letting my feet sink into the sand. It really is as beautiful as the photographs make it seem. Crystal blue waters and bright white sand.

I move further down towards the water, walking where the sea and shore meet, as the sand grows hot beneath my feet. The breakwaters mean the water is calm, the waves barely lapping at the sand.

I sigh and stop, enjoying the peace and tranquillity of the moment. Turning towards the sun, I close my eyes and tilt my head back, letting its warmth envelop me.

"Beautiful, isn't it?"

I open my eyes and turn to find an older woman walking towards me.

She smiles, and I find myself returning it.

"Make sure you stay hydrated, love," she adds. "It's very

easy to get dehydrated this close to the equator." She holds up a hand. "Sorry, I was a doctor, old habits die hard. I can't help myself."

She comes to stand next to me, staring out over the water.

"Thanks for the reminder," I say.

"All inclusive, we enjoy a good cocktail or three," she says, with a wink. "They serve beautiful coffees, but it's easy to forget to drink water."

"That's very true," I say, making a mental note to add it to the welcome speech. "Are you enjoying your stay?"

She turns her head and grins. "It's been wonderful. My husband and I are celebrating our fiftieth wedding anniversary. Today, actually."

"Congratulations. That's amazing."

Knowing it really is in today's society, where divorce is prevalent.

She laughs, and the sound warms my heart.

"It is. We have stickability." She chuckles. "Poor man, would have been out by now for good behaviour." She winks, making me laugh. "It's not been all plain sailing, I don't know a marriage that is. We argue, of course. But we love each other, and we're always there, supporting and encouraging one another."

She reminds me of Mum and Dad before… they would argue, but their love for one another was evident in everything they did.

"How did you know?" I find myself asking. "He was *the one*?"

She smiles. "One day he laughed, and I knew from that moment, I wanted to hear that sound for the rest of my life."

My throat constricts at her words.

"How about you?" she asks.

"I'm here on business," I say, before I can stop myself. "I'm Kathryn Frazer."

The woman inclines her head.

"Ah, the CEO of the Frazer Hotel Group," she says, her eyes twinkling. "A successful businesswoman. If I have any complaints—" She trails off.

"I try," I say, laughing. "Do you have any complaints?"

"No, it's been absolutely fantastic," she says. "We came a few years ago. I loved it then, but it wasn't a patch on how it is today."

I smile. "Thank you."

"Are you here alone?" she asks, inclining her head.

I get the impression she's fishing. I recognise her from the restaurant last night.

"I'm here with a family friend," I say, with a smile. "We're working on a project together."

"Ah, that incredibly handsome young man I saw you with last night."

"That would be Jaxson," I say, harrumphing, before I realise what I've said.

Her eyes sparkle as they meet mine.

"Oh no," I say quickly, when I see where her mind has gone.

"Why not? He's very attentive. Is he single?"

She winks, and it's my turn to chuckle.

"He is, but our relationship is most definitely not like that," I say. "We're strictly business."

She turns to face me, her hand reaching out and landing on my arm. I meet her gaze.

"A piece of advice from someone who knows. Don't be married to your job," she says, her voice suddenly serious. "I nearly made that mistake. Philip saw what I didn't. He made me realise that being with someone wasn't me giving up part of myself, it was gaining something more."

"You really have the wrong impression of Jaxson. He's my brother's best friend. Two of my brothers, in fact."

"Even better. You know he's been well vetted."

I gasp, choking on the air I inhale.

She pats my arm. "There's a reason there are so many romance books containing *brother's best friend*," she says, raising a knowing eyebrow.

"Reality can be very different to fiction," I tell her truthfully, thinking about Jax and my tumultuous past.

She looks at me, her gaze speculative. She opens her mouth.

"There you are."

An older man approaches us.

"Hello," he says.

"Philip, this is Kathryn Frazer. The CEO of the Frazer Hotel Group."

"Hello, Kathryn," he says, holding out his hand. "Is my wife interrogating you?"

I shake his hand and smile.

"No, not at all. I hear congratulations are in order. Fifty years, that is quite something. Happy golden anniversary."

"Thank you."

His arm slides around his wife's shoulder, pulling her into his side. She rests her head against it. The gesture makes me want to sigh.

"I better get going," I say. "Enjoy the rest of your stay."

"You too, and remember what I said."

Philip pulls her away. "Please tell me you weren't giving her the third degree," I hear him say.

"Of course not, but we working women sometimes need a push in the right direction."

I hear him chuckle, but I miss his reply as they walk out of hearing range.

I make my way back to the villa, passing the bar I was in the day before. Jax is set up in the corner. Glasses perched on his nose, his forehead furrowed in concentration.

I'm tempted to approach, but decide against it.

He promised professional. I need to do the same, keep to my side of the bargain.

* * *

The villa is lovely and cool when I enter. A refreshing change to the midday sun.

The maid service has been. My duvet returned to the cot bed. They must have wondered what the hell happened.

I gaze out onto the terrace at the now dry sun loungers.

I make a quick call to the guest relations team and order a bottle of champagne and a fruit platter for the couple I met. I only have his name, but that's all I need.

Stripping out of my dress, I grab a bikini and lather on more sunscreen.

I pick up my phone and headphones and move outside. Maybe Jax is right, I do need to take it easy. Enjoy the sunshine while I can. We're heading into winter at home and one of the busiest times of year, the Christmas holidays. Maybe some rest and relaxation is just what the doctor ordered.

Was the lady on the beach right, about the need to compartmentalise?

Who knows? It's not something I'm going to think about now.

Instead, I'm going to focus on getting a tan and relaxing, putting my feet up, and clearing my mind.

I stretch out on the sun lounger and close my eyes, starting one of the audiobooks Pen and Harper recommended.

CHAPTER 19

KAT

I listen to the audiobook, or at least try, but my mind keeps wandering, refusing to shut off.

My conversations with Jax, with the woman and her husband on the beach, and even my meeting with Mr Baskin and his team.

I take out my headphones and lie back, enjoying the warmth of the sun on my skin. I listen to the distant chatter of the other guests and the waves lapping against the reef and jetty.

It's no use.

After five minutes, I get up and walk into the villa, heading for the minibar. I pull it open.

It's impressive, as it should be.

A range of chilled confectionery and a selection of both alcoholic and non-alcoholic beverages fill the fridge. I grab an iced peach tea and head for the balcony door. My handbag sits open on the chair, the paperback I picked up at the airport poking out.

I grab it as I pass, knocking the bag onto the floor.

Shit!

I scoop up my purse and keys.

I unzip the pocket inside, set to lock my keys away.

A white envelope, my name neatly scrawled on the front.

Crap!

I yank it out, the corner tears on the zip, exposing a portion of the paper inside.

Zach's letter.

When the concierge handed it to me, my heart had almost beaten its way out of my chest. I'd stuffed it in the side pocket, zipping it away as fast as humanly possible, not wanting to think about it.

I press my lips together and massage the middle of my forehead, closing my eyes.

When I open them again, it's still there, although the envelope is slightly more crumpled.

Why didn't I put it straight in the bin, shred it?

I sink down onto the side of the bed, placing the book next to me, and clasping the envelope in both hands.

I know why. It was to allow myself time to digest. I've never been one to make rash decisions, and this is no different. I wanted options.

Well, now you have some.

Option one, stuff it back into my bag and forget I've even seen it.

Option two, stuff it back in my bag and dispose of it when I get home.

Option three, throw it into the sea.

Not, option three, knowing my luck, it'll wash up on shore intact, and someone would find it and share all our family's dirty secrets.

Option four, I grow a backbone and read the thing. Then destroy it!

But then I've given Zach airtime. What he did was despicable. He stitched up his best friend and played me like a fiddle.

My stomach clenches at the familiar scrawl.

Kathryn Frazer.

I drop back on the bed and stare up at the ceiling.

With a growl, I slam it onto the mattress and sit up. Grabbing my book and iced tea, I head back outside returning to the sun-lounger.

I open my book and begin reading, the words bouncing around on the page, as my mind drifts.

I look back at the door, the bed and the letter is visible.

Shit, shit, shit!

I get up and head to the edge of the terrace, staring out at sea.

Come on, Kat. What's the worst that can happen? You know he slept with Darra and fathered Lottie.

Pen's words come back to haunt me.

No, I'd seen the proof of Jaxson with my eyes. He was at the hotel with Sasha. They'd both gone into the same room.

I head back into the villa, snatching up the letter, before tearing open the envelope.

I close my eyes briefly, sucking in an uneven breath.

When I open them again, I roll my shoulders and lift my chin.

You've got this!

A tightness spreads through my chest as I unfold the sheet and begin to focus on the words.

Dear Kat,

I close my eyes, blocking out the words, shoving it down onto the bed next to me.

For goodness sake, woman, grow a pair! It's all in the past. His words can only hurt you if you let them. Isn't it better to know? To understand?

I open my eyes again, grabbing the paper.

> Dear Kat,
> I'm sorry.
> More sorry than you'll ever know. I always hoped my part in Lottie's conception would remain a secret. Not because I don't love her, I do. But Lottie is not, and never has been mine. Darra and her father saw to that, but I knew, if the truth came out, the pain and suffering it would cause you and your family.

No shit, Sherlock! You duped your best friend into allowing his psycho girlfriend to trap him into marriage, practically hold him hostage while raising your child.

My vision clouds, blood pounding in my ears. I close my eyes and steady my breathing.

It's only words.
You know this story, and how it ends.

> Not long after Darra and Elijah split up, we bumped into one another on a night out. We drank too much, I'm not sure how it happened. I never meant to hurt anyone, and we were both single. Elijah was about to move on with Pen, we all knew it, even if he hadn't asked her at that point.
> Later, when Darra announced she was preg-

nant, I confronted her. She laughed, thanked me for my generous donation. I realised nothing about that night was an accident. I'd been played.

I tried to do the right thing, but her father's threat towards my family was real. He's a dangerous and ruthless man who was determined to win, whatever the cost. Destroying my family to get to yours would have meant nothing to him.

Darra was distraught. She pleaded with me to stay quiet. She believed her father would terminate her pregnancy, and despite everything, I genuinely believe she wanted and loved our baby. Whichever way I turned, there was no winner, so I remained silent.

Adrenaline rushes through my body. Although we didn't officially date until years later, the knowledge of what he'd done should have been enough to make him stay away from our family. I scan ahead.

Despite what you must think. I did love you, and my marriage proposal was genuine.

I'd told Darra we were over, that I wanted to make a future with you. But I'm starting to understand, you can't force something that isn't there.

I spent years admiring you from afar, wanting you to notice me, and then you finally did. Although I can see now it was for all the wrong reasons, and this is the hardest thing for me to write.

I knew about you and Jaxson. That you'd started seeing each other in secret. I came back to the house when you and he were there. I overheard you talking about how you were going to keep your relationship a secret until after graduation.

My mind returns to that time. Zach had started behaving differently towards Jax and me. Elijah put it down to final year nerves. Zach had been struggling, and his grades were down.

I was gutted and more than a little jealous. Elijah had told me to stay away from you, had told us both to. And there was Jax, Mr Smooth, with everything I wanted. He'd grown closer to Elijah over the years, and now he had you. It seemed I was always the consolation prize.

Elijah and Jax have always shared the same drive. It's why they gravitated to one another so strongly, despite their difference in social standing. Firstly, through their competitive nature with swimming, and then their ambition to succeed in their chosen fields. Zach was missing that, happier to party and follow in their shadows.

> Somehow, Darra knew about my feelings for you and tried to help me win you. At first, I was grateful. I couldn't see past my own wants and needs. However, as with everything, Darra's help came with a price. Having me around, the biological father of her child, was for her benefit, not mine.
>
> This is me coming clean.
>
> Darra set up Jaxson. You may have already realised this, and I'm praying you do. That your animosity towards him stems from something other than what we did. Sasha and Jax were never in a relationship. You overhearing Sasha and Darra's conversation was a set-up, orchestrated by Darra. They knew you were listening because I told her you were there. I'm sorry.
>
> I shared what I'd overheard that night, between you and Jax. They knew what to say, for maximum effect, because of me.
>
> Darra sold it to me, that she was paving the way for me to step in and mend your broken heart.

My stomach churns, bile burning the back of my throat. *Zach had backed up Sasha's words. It's why I believed them.*

Zach was Jax's friend, he wouldn't have lied. Why would he have?

I screw up the letter.

But I saw them together at the hotel!

I smooth out the paper. My head spinning, trying to focus.

> Sasha was at the hotel that day to meet Emma Myers, Dillon's daughter. They went to school together. Jax just happened to be meeting Dillon. It was his first interview for his internship. When Darra heard, it cemented her plans. She knew you'd check the cameras.

My breathing becomes rapid and erratic. I slap a hand over my mouth and run to the bathroom, violently losing what's left of my breakfast.

Jax denied it. He'd looked shocked when I confronted him. I can still picture his face. That look. It's never left me.

I wretch again, my hands gripping the toilet seat, as my stomach dry heaves over and over.

I'd thought it was the guilt of being caught.

But I fell for it. Hook, line and fucking sinker!

I lean against the toilet cubicle wall. My head back, eyes closed. I wait for the swirling in my stomach to subside.

Fucking Zach, fucking Darra!

I wrap an arm around my waist and swipe at a tear tracking its way down my cheek.

And you thought you knew the worst of it!

Pushing myself up the wall, I wash my face and brush my teeth, careful not to catch sight of myself in the mirror.

I drop my head, gripping the edge of the sink unit, drawing in several shuddering breaths. My throat is raw.

You're stronger than this, Kathryn Frazer! He's gone from your life. Don't let his words hurt you.

The problem is, they do.

Worse still, he caused me to hurt someone I cared about... loved.

I lift my head, my eyes locking in the mirror, my body suddenly numb.

What the hell do I say to Jax?

Sorry? Just doesn't cut it.

Pushing off, unable to face my reflection, I head back into the bedroom and sink down onto the bed. My eyes lock on the now screwed up letter beside me.

It was bad enough knowing Zach slept with Darra and fathered a child. If I'm honest, I've struggled with the fact that he continued sleeping with her while in a relationship with me.

That I wasn't enough for him.

But to know he manipulated me, they both had, for their own sick gains...

My empty stomach twists again, and I suck in a breath, trying to ease the pressure building in my chest.

It takes a lot for me to trust someone.

I trusted Jax, loved Jax. His betrayal... supposed betrayal.

I drop my head into my hands and squeeze.

Believing he betrayed me, almost broke me. But it's shaped the woman I am today. Taught me to portray a strong image, despite being damaged on the inside. It's how I survived Dad's death, and I could step into his shoes.

But then maybe I hadn't trusted Jax enough. Was that why I was so quick to believe their lies? Deep down, I never truly believed he loved me, not like I loved him. How could he? He was gorgeous and had all the women chasing him. He was athletic and smart. Who was I? The nerdy, desperate sister of his best friend.

As for Zach, I had no reason not to trust him. He was far from perfect. Would never have hurt my brother, or me.

I scoop up my hair, ignoring the numbness spreading through my limbs and walk onto the terrace, sinking into the cool water of the plunge infinity pool. I lie back, allowing my body to float, trying to clear my mind. When that fails, I move to the edge and stare out over the water, the letter and all conscious thought abandoned.

CHAPTER 20

JAX

Kat doesn't reappear for lunch, and I wonder if she's decided to order room service. As promised yesterday, I've left her alone, but after a morning of working on the proposal and the rising temperature, I want to change. Tomorrow, I'll bring my swim shorts with me and use the gym facilities, but until then.

I enter the villa.

Silence.

Is Kat actually here?

The balcony door is slightly ajar, the air-conditioning off. I'm not sure what makes me decide to look. I could just collect my shorts and leave, but as always, I'm drawn to Kathryn Frazer.

I open the door. Kat's in the infinity pool, with her back to me, and her arms resting on the side.

I step out onto the terrace, closing the door behind me. A bottle of iced tea sits untouched by the side of the sun lounger, along with a paperback and her phone.

I look across, still no movement. The hairs on my arms rise. Something is off.

"Hey, Kat," I say cheerfully.

Nothing.

Does she have her headphones in?

I walk to the side of the pool. Her hair is piled up on top of her head, no headphones visible.

I try again. "Hey, Kat."

Still nothing.

It's then I see it, her lips pressed tightly together, her hand gripping her chain. Her chest rises and falls, as if she's struggling to catch her breath.

"Kat?"

I repeat, this time more gently.

Shit, something is wrong.

She turns to face me with a start, her gaze distant, her skin flushed.

I drop over the edge and into the pool, ignoring the fact that I'm in my clothes.

"Hey, princess," I say, approaching carefully.

Kat gives herself a shake, as if pulling herself out of the trance she's in.

"Jax?" she says, taking in my wet t-shirt and shorts. "What are you doing?"

I smile, letting out a little huff of relief.

"Taking a swim in my clothes," I say, with a shrug.

Her brows draw together as she takes in my floating t-shirt.

Her fingers whiten around her pendant.

"Kat. Are you okay?"

This time, when her eyes lock on mine, there's a fire burning deep inside.

"I'm fine," she says, her expression closing down.

I want to roll my eyes.

Sure, you are!

"As long as you're *fine*," I say, unable to hide the sarcasm in my tone.

I move away and climb the steps, the weight of the water in my clothes dragging them down. I strip, leaving them on the decking.

I open the door and head inside to the bathroom.

I step into the shower and rest my hands on the wall, dropping my head, letting the water cascade over my shoulders, back and head.

I close my eyes and count. Breathing in and out, calming the pressure in my chest. Kat is the only woman who leaves my stomach in knots.

The woman is beyond frustrating.

But then, why would Kat confide in me? It's not like we have that kind of relationship. Once, maybe, but not anymore. That ship has long sailed.

I switch off the shower, I stand up, my heart skipping a beat as I find Kat standing there watching me.

She holds out a towel, and I take it. Our eyes lock.

I rub myself dry, wrapping the towel around my waist.

"I'm sorry," she says.

I incline my head, my heart rate picking up, but I wait.

Kat looks down at her hand, and it's then that I notice the paper she's holding.

A letter?

"You need to read this."

She extends her arm, but I notice her gaze looks away from the paper.

Confusion ensues.

"What is it?"

She shakes her hand slightly, as if encouraging me to take it.

"It's a letter. From Zach."

My stomach sinks. I'm not sure I want to read about their relationship.

She moves to the sink and places it down on the top, as if it has suddenly burned her.

"The choice is yours," she says, her expression grave. "I'm sorry, Jax, truly. For everything. Not that those words can ever make up for all I've said and done over the years."

My breath catches.

"What's in the letter, Kat?"

She rests her hand on it, staring down, before her eyes meet mine, her demeanour sad.

"The truth." Kat opens her mouth and closes it again, swallowing. "It contains the truth, sixteen years of lies."

She turns and leaves the bathroom, heading back onto the terrace, leaving me staring after her.

My gaze drops to the paper, resting on the marble top.

CHAPTER 21

KAT

The door of the villa closes. An unprecedented heaviness sits in my body.

He caught me at a weak point, and typical Jax, was trying to help. Has always been there to help.

Despite the heat, a coldness spreads through my limbs. I close my eyes, begging the sun to warm my frozen soul.

I've been such an idiot.

They say, *"Sorry is the hardest word."*

But to me, it's not sorry. That's the easy part. It's the other words that go with it. The words that make a true apology, not a lame excuse.

Played. I was played, like the Steinway grand piano I loved so much as a child.

I look back at the door.

Jax has gone.

Gone with the letter that vindicates him.

My chest constricts, pain crushing my heart and lungs. I suck in a breath, then another. Sobs wrack my body.

I bite down on my wrist to stifle the sound, but the usual confident and controlled me, has gone.

All the anguish of the past sixteen years. Jax, Elijah and Darra, Pen, Lottie, Zach… Dad, rise to the surface. Everything I've ever suppressed. And I'm the queen of suppressing my feelings.

* * *

Sixteen Years Ago

"Oh. My. God. Is that Danny?" Carol hisses, next to me.

I follow her gaze, stopping short.

"The bastard," she says, turning to face me, her hand gripping my arm.

What the hell? He said he was studying.

Danny called me two hours ago to cancel our date.

"Sorry, babe, but I'm going to have to bail. I really need to get this proposal done. If not, Mr Kick-My-Ass is going to fail me, and my parents are going to freak."

"Do you need any help? I can come over."

"No, no, it's fine," Danny says, a little too quickly. "I'll just get distracted. You do that to me, babes. You're just so beautiful."

"Okay," I say, barely able to keep the relief from my voice.

We've been dating for a couple of months. I was hoping it would get better, but Danny is more brawn than brain, and his lack of conversational skills is getting a little tiring.

"What will you do now?" he asks.

"I'll have an early night, read that book I bought the other day."

"I'm sorry, babes, I really am. Anyway, I better go, this assignment won't write itself."

Carol had called two minutes later, and I decided to be spontaneous and go out with the girls, let my hair down.

"Is that?"

I watch my flatmate Cleo walk up to Danny. I freeze as she wraps her arms around his neck and pulls his face to hers. I expect him to pull away, but instead, he grabs her arse and hauls her against him, smashing his lips to hers.

"Do you want to leave?" Carol asks quietly, placing a gentle hand on my arm.

I shake my head and lift my chin. I turn to face her.

"I'll be back in a minute," I say.

I square my shoulders and walk over to where Danny and Cleo are still sucking face. Two of Danny's mates look up, the colour draining from their cheeks as they spot me.

"Er, Danny," Ed says.

"Fuck off, mate, can't you see I'm busy?"

"He can, but he's trying to warn you I'm standing behind you."

Danny jumps back from Cleo like she's on fire, almost sending himself flying over the stool behind his knees.

"What? I thought you were—"

"Like I thought you were working on an assignment for Mr Kitterman."

Danny bites his lip.

Cleo's hand comes up, but he shrugs it off with a grunt.

"Not now, Clo," he says, with a little too much familiarity.

"What the hell, Dan?" she says, stepping up next to him. "I'm not just here for you to fuck." *She turns to me and gives me the once-over.* "I thought you said you were going to dump the frigid bitch."

Wow, I know Cleo isn't a close friend, but we still live in the same house. So much for the girl code I keep hearing so much about!

"Clo, don't be daft. He's never going to do that, she's worth billions."

Terry, Danny's other friend, laughs, nudging Ed.

"Shut up Ter," Danny hisses, reaching for me. "Kat, baby," he whines.

A twitchy feeling starts in my extremities, and I shrug him off.

I turn to my housemate. "Cleo, honestly. You're welcome to him," I say, turning and walking away. "Goodbye, Danny."

"Kat, no. She doesn't mean anything to me. It's just, a guy has needs, and you keep saying no—"

I spin around, putting up a hand to prevent him from smashing into me. Instead, it ends up flat against his chest. Danny clasps it in both his hands.

"Kat, listen, I'm sorry."

A roiling heat fills my belly, and I pull my hand away, using all my willpower to refrain from wiping it down my jeans.

"Ever think the reason I didn't jump into bed with you is more to do with you than me? Go back to Cleo, Danny."

I look over his shoulder, but Cleo has disappeared. Maybe she only wanted him because she thought he was mine.

Call dibs on stealing Kathryn Frazer's boyfriend.

I stop the grimace that threatens.

Oh joy, living together now is going to be so much fun!

I turn to walk away, only this time he grabs my arm.

"Don't walk away from me, Miss High and Mighty Frazer," he snarls.

I glare down at his hand curled around my bicep.

"Remove your hand, Danny," I say quietly.

"Or what?"

I don't say anything, instead I grab his hand and twist, the way my self-defence coach taught me years ago. Danny spins, and I press him down onto the nearest table.

"That's what, Danny. Don't fucking touch a woman when she doesn't want to be touched," I say next to his ear, shoving down hard before I let go.

A camera flash goes off, and I grimace.

Great, just what I need.

Mum and Dad are going to love that headline.

He slides off the table onto the beer-soaked floor, grabbing at his shoulder.

"You're a fucking psycho," he yells.

I raise an eyebrow, but say nothing, turning on my heel and walking back towards my friends.

Carol runs up. "Are you okay? Where the hell did you learn to do that?"

I smile at her. "Dad made sure we all had self-defence lessons growing up. Glad I'm not rusty."

"It was really cool, can you teach me?" she asks.

"Of course."

Every girl/woman should know some form of self-defence. The other girls gather around. Danny has clearly sloped off somewhere to lick his wounds. He's Mr Popular, he won't appreciate having been put in his place by me, not so publicly.

"I don't know what you ever saw in him," Rach says, coming up and giving me a spontaneous hug.

"If I'm honest, I don't either," I say.

At the time, I thought it would be the quickest way to fit in. I've been here two years, and my social life was non-existent until I started dating Danny. When he invited me out, I decided to throw caution to the wind and go. I met these lovely ladies at one of the house parties we attended together. Danny got so drunk that he passed out. I made friends. No regrets.

"Good riddance," Claire says, stepping forward and pulling us all in for a group hug. "Are you going to be okay? You share a flat with that backstabbing bitch, don't you?"

I shrug. I can't say I'm looking forward to coming face-to-face with Cleo, but I refuse to be intimidated.

"I'll be fine. I'll call Eli."

The girls nod, and Carol fans herself, making the others laugh. She has a huge crush on my older brother.

"There's no accounting for taste."

I chuckle at my friend.

I pull out my phone and dial Eli's flat. I put my finger in one ear to hear over the music.

"Hey, Stud Central. How may I be of service?"

I roll my eyes.

"Hey Jax, is Eli there?"

"Kat? Shit, sorry about that. It was a dare."

I pick up the embarrassment in his tone.

"Where are you?" he asks. "It sounds like you're in a club."

"I am. Is Eli there?"

"No, he's out with Darra."

There's disapproval in his voice. I know he doesn't like her, he's told me as much.

"Damn," I say, before I can stop myself. "It's fine, I'll try his mobile."

"What's up? Can I help? I can come and get you if you need a lift."

My heart speeds up, as it always does at the thought of seeing or spending time with Jaxson Lockwood.

"It's okay," I say.

"Kat," he warns. "What's going on?"

Rach steals my phone and gives him the rundown of what's happened.

She smirks, before handing it back to me, mouthing, "You can thank me later."

Jax's deep voice comes over the line.

"Kat, stay where you are. I'm on my way."

CHAPTER 22

JAX

I wander the island, aware of the paper burning a hole in my pocket.

Leaving Kat was not easy, but I needed to put some space between us. Whatever Zach has divulged…

The look on her face tells me I'm not going to like it.

I find myself outside her villa. The maintenance team have finished for the day, so I make my way into the garden, sitting down on the new plush daybed beside the plunge pool.

In for a penny, in for a pound.

I pull out the letter and begin.

When I finish, I clench my fists and have the strongest desire to punch something.

The letter crumples in my hand.

One phrase keeps swirling around and around in my brain.

You never loved me, it was always him. I'm sorry I ruined that for you.

Sorry! He's fucking sorry!

He took what wasn't his on a bed of lies and deceit.

My stomach churns. No wonder Kat looked green.

Between them, he and Darra have made a career of ruining people's lives. Elijah and Pen, Lottie and now I find, Kat and I.

I rest my elbows on my knees, pressing the palms into my eye sockets. I've not cried since that day. I look up at the canopy of trees above me, blinking rapidly. I cough, working to clear the lump in my throat as emotions I thought I'd let go, resurface.

When Kat walked away sixteen years ago, it was like someone taking my heart in their hand and squeezing with all their might. The pain was unbearable.

I throw back my head and laugh. The memory of Mum and Dad telling me, "There are plenty more fish in the sea."

How wrong they were.

Kathryn Frazer ruined me for all other women. From the moment I met her to the moment she told me she felt something too, I was lost.

* * *

Sixteen years ago

"Kat, stay where you are. I'm on my way."

I disconnect before she can argue, and knowing Kat, she'll definitely try. The details her friend gave me are enough to have me moving quickly.

I grab Elijah's keys, glad I decided against the beer earlier. I need to finish my assignment, but there's no way I'm leaving Kat in that club with that dickhead.

I drive across London, pleased it's late, so I don't have to navigate the traffic. Eli put Zach and me on his insurance when we all moved in together, as much for convenience as anything else. I don't think he'll mind me borrowing it for his sister.

I make it to the club in record time. I pull up into one of the spaces outside, reserved for VIPs. I chuckle. The monster Land Rover Discovery with its custom trim and Frazer personalised number plate fits in perfectly.

I get out and make my way to the door. The bouncer looks at the car, then looks at me, removing the barrier instantly.

I make my way inside. It's packed. I pull out my phone.

ME:

Where are you?

KAT:

You didn't need to come, I'm fine.

ME:

Well I'm here now.

KAT:

Far corner near the fire exit.

I look up and spot the fire exit notice, pushing my way through the crowd of drunk students.

I catch sight of Kat immediately. She stands out in the crowd. She always has.

A guy is trying to talk to her, but her friend is giving him a hard time.

I walk up and sling my arm over Kat's shoulder.

"Hey, gorgeous," *I say.* "Ready to get out of here?"

Kat doesn't jump, instead, she sinks into my touch. The guy in front of her frowns, he's definitely had too much to drink.

"Who the fuck are you? Why have you got your hand on my girlfriend?"

"I think that's ex-girlfriend," *Kat says.* "I don't share."

"I told you, she means nothing to me. Clo was just a—"

"What? An easy lay while you waited for me to come around," *Kat says, rolling her eyes.*

I want to chuckle, but bite my tongue. Kat was always quick, probably being raised with brothers.

"Sloppy seconds aren't my style," she adds.

She turns to me and gives me a wide smile.

"Shall we get out of here?"

I nod.

"'Bye, ladies, I'll see you tomorrow."

"Do any of your friends need a lift?" *I ask Kat.*

She shakes her head. "They all live together and have a taxi booked."

We turn.

A hand closes around my arm.

"I asked you a question. Who the fuck are you?" *the dickhead asks again.*

"I'm Kat's new boyfriend," *I say, before I can stop myself.*

"I'm her boyfriend," *he says, his eyebrows coming together.*

I chuckle. "You were her boyfriend, dickhead, but I think you blew that this evening. A woman like Kat isn't alone for long."

He snarls and pulls back an arm, but his friend catches it.

He shakes him off.

"Good luck, she's a frigid bitch," *he hisses, snarling at Kat.* "You're a total prick tease."

I step in front of Kat and glare at the dickhead. What the hell did Kat see in this guy? I feel her hand on my bicep, her voice close to my ear.

"Jax, he's not worth it, believe me," *Kat says, her breath triggering a fluttery sensation deep in my chest.*

I give him a withering look and turn toward Kat.

"Let's go," *I say, wrapping my arm around her shoulder and navigating us both towards the door.*

When we finally make it outside, I breathe a sigh of relief.

"Thanks," *Kat says.*

"Is he always such a dick?"

Kat shrugs.

"Kat, I seriously thought you had better taste," I say.

She bites her lip, her nose wrinkling.

"He's popular," she says, with a shrug, as if that explains everything.

"You went out with him because he's popular? Why on earth would you do that?"

Kat puts her hands on her hips and glares at me.

"Because I'm not," she says, her eyes flashing. "I'm a nerd, or a geek or whatever else you want to call me. I've spent the past two years in my room, with no friends. It seemed like a good way to gain a social life."

I stare at her for a moment, amazed. How am I only just hearing this? Does Eli know?

"Was it worth it?"

She sighs.

"No," she admits. "It's been awful! I realised quite quickly, his brains are in his balls, and he can only talk about rugby. He's failing in all his subjects and will probably get kicked out at the end of this semester."

She sighs again.

"But you hate rugby," I say with a smirk.

"I really do." She laughs, her eyes now sparkling. "On the plus side, I met the girls I was with tonight. They're fabulous."

I sling an arm over her shoulder.

"I'm glad," I say. "Come on, let's get you home."

Kat groans.

"What?"

"Cleo... Clo as he keeps calling her. I live with her."

"The girl he was kissing and sleeping with behind your back is one of your housemates?"

"Yes,"

"That's fucked up, Kat."

"I agree," she says with a sigh. "But it is what it is."

"I'll come back with you."

No way am I letting her walk into the lion's den without backup. I don't know who this Cleo is, but sleeping with someone's boyfriend, especially someone you live with. She's not a person I want Kat around.

Kat stops and turns to face me.

"Jax, you really don't have to. If you could just drop me home, that's fine."

I shake my head. "Kat, stop arguing and get in the car."

"Eli's?"

Kat chuckles.

"It was an emergency, he wasn't using it, and he's insured Zach and me on it."

Kat smiles and touches my arm. The tiny hairs, standing upright at the contact, send a shiver down my spine. "I know he did. You're a good friend to my brother."

I place a hand over hers and squeeze gently. "I'm your friend, too."

"I know. Thank you."

I unlock the car and hold the door open while Kat jumps in. I move around to the other side and reverse out of the space.

"The girls you were with, they seem nice."

"They are. They're lovely," *Kat says.*

"I thought you said you didn't have any friends."

Kat turns her head to look at me. "I didn't. I met them after I started dating Danny. We went to a house party. Danny got drunk with his mates, Carol, Claire and Rach were there, we got talking, and as they say, the rest is history."

"You hit it off. Why did you stay with him if you'd achieved your goal?"

Kat's nose wrinkles, making her look super cute and incredibly sexy.

"I couldn't get rid of him, he was like superglue. Tonight, I found out why. He's a Frazer money hound."

"I've heard you guys use that term before."

"I'm sure you have. It's girls and guys who see our parents' bank balance, not us," Kat explains.

My heart lurches at the thought.

"It's not just potential lovers, it's also friends. People befriend us for who we are and what they think they can get."

"I'm sorry, I never realised."

Kat places her hand on my leg.

"You wouldn't." The look she shoots me tells me I should know this. *"You're not like them. You befriended Eli because you're similar, share the same drive to succeed."*

I cough, she couldn't be further from the truth. Eli and I are polar worlds apart. My parents are divorced, and I'm up to my neck in student loans. Even Elijah doesn't know by how much.

"I don't mean in terms of money," Kat says, as if reading my mind. *"I'm talking in terms of your ambition, determination to succeed. You're both relentless. You'll keep going, fight on, until you get to your destination. Eli admires that in you."*

Elijah Frazer was not what I imagined when I first met him. I'd expected some wealthy, privileged prick. But then, when I saw him train in the pool and how much effort he puts into his studies, our friendship grew.

Kat rubs her hands together and shoots me a smile. *"Well, at least I'm rid of him now,"* she says.

"You think he'll drop it?"

Looking at the guy, I'm not sure it will be that easy. He seemed to have a major hard-on for Kat.

"I can hope," she says, but her tone lets me know she's not convinced.

We pull up outside the large Victorian house, which she and her fellow students are renting.

"Thanks, Jax, I really appreciate you coming to my rescue."

"Anytime."

The front door opens, and music blares out.

Kat groans. *"Just what I need,"* she hisses under her breath.

"I'm coming in," I say before I can stop myself. "Check everything is okay. Once I know you're safe in your room, then I'll leave."

I walk into the house. The base has the walls pulsing, it's that loud.

I follow Kat past the stairs and into the kitchen. It has been extended into a large living, dining, and kitchen area. It's packed with drunk students.

"Great," I hear Kat hiss.

A young woman is standing by the kitchen sink, her face a mess, mascara smudged down her face.

Her eyes lock on Kat, and her face crumples again. One of the other women pulls her into her arms, while the girls around her turn and glare at Kat.

What the fuck?

My arm slides protectively around Kat's shoulders, and I pull her into my side. She stiffens before the tension begins to ebb.

"Hope you're proud of yourself," one of the girls says, coming up to Kat.

"Pardon?" Kat says.

"You, Miss High and Fucking Mighty. You think you're too fucking good for all of us. See what you've done to Cleo?"

"Cleo?" Kat says, her eyes wide. "She was sleeping with my boyfriend. Behind my back. How is this my fault?"

Even I can't wait to see how they can justify this one.

"She's loved him since she was a little girl. They grew up together."

"And that's my problem, how? I didn't ask him out, he asked me."

"He would, you're a fucking Frazer. Mummy and Daddy's bank balance is enough to turn anyone like Danny's head," she sneers.

"Then she's better off without him if he's that shallow. I know I am."

I catch the girl's hand before it connects with Kat's cheek.

The girl stares at me wide-eyed, as if suddenly realising I'm there. I would step in, but Kat appears to have this covered, only I'm not going to allow physical violence towards her.

"Back off," I say, shoving her hand away. "You're directing your anger in the wrong direction."

She lifts her chin and glares.

"And who are you?" *she says, her tone changes as her eyes travel up and down my body.*

Really?

"I'm a friend of Kat's."

She wrinkles her nose as if I've just dumped rubbish all over the floor. She turns to Kat.

"I want you out," *she spits.* "By the end of the day tomorrow."

"Not a problem," *Kat says, turning around and heading towards the stairs.*

"And don't think I'll be refunding your rent," *she shouts after her.*

I stop and turn around.

"You might want to rethink that. Legally, she's done nothing wrong."

She stamps her foot like a spoiled little princess, and I grin.

I turn and follow Kat up the stairs.

I enter Kat's room and find her on the bed with her head in her hands.

"Hey," *I say quietly.* "You okay?"

She looks up, squares her shoulders before inhaling deeply. The smile she plasters on her face makes me want to storm downstairs and tell those bitches exactly what I think.

"I'm fine, Jax. It's been a long time coming. It's been a mismatch since the beginning. I thought moving in here..."

She stops, and I think back to what she said earlier.

"Hey, you can always crash at ours."

She raises an eyebrow.

"No offence, but your apartment needs a health warning attached."

I grimace.

She's not wrong. I've been onto Elijah and Zach about cleaning up their shit, but neither is particularly bothered.

Someone crashes into the door with a loud bang.

Kat jumps.

I look around her room. It's pretty sparse. She hasn't got many personal items. A few books, some fairy lights and her computer. The TV is attached to the wall, so I'm taking it's part of the room.

I wrap an arm around Kat's shoulder and pull her into my side. She comes willingly. I inhale her scent, resting my head on top of hers.

"We'll get onto the letting agents in the morning," I say.

It's not like rent is an issue.

"It's okay," Kat says. "Rach just messaged to say one of their roommates has dropped out. The room is small, but it's mine if I want it."

"You sure?"

She looks up at me, her face millimetres from mine.

"Positive," she says breathlessly. "They're more my kind of people."

Her gaze drops to her knees.

"He's an idiot," I hear myself say.

"He is— He is?" she says, her eyes locked on mine.

"He is. If you were mine, I'd treat you like a princess."

Kat flinches.

"What?" I ask, knowing I've said something wrong.

She shakes her head. "He called me an ice princess."

I think back to all the conversations we've had, how Kat jumped in and rescued Pen from drowning, tearing shreds off us all for not noticing. The way she keeps her younger brothers in check with love and devotion. How she adores her parents and is hoping to follow her father into the hotel business once her degree is complete. Kat Frazer is far from cold.

Before I can stop myself, my lips touch hers. Tentatively at first, Kat lets out a slight moan, and I find myself pulling her close, deepening the kiss. She yields beneath me, her mouth opening, when her tongue meets mine, it's my turn to groan.

I pull her into my lap, her hands sinking into my hair, pulling me closer. I'm not sure how long we sit there tasting and teasing. My body is alive, my breathing uneven. I pull my lips away, trailing them across her cheek and down her neck, burying my head in her shoulder.

We're both breathing hard.

I pull back, my eyes scouring her face.

"Shit, Kat, I'm sorry," I say.

She bites her lip, her gaze not quite meeting mine.

"I'm sorry," she says, her tone serious.

Her hand goes to her hair, straightening it.

"What?" I ask.

Her eyes clash with mine.

"I'm sorry?"

"But I kissed you," I say, frowning.

"Oh, I thought I kissed you. I was thinking about it and then—"

"You were thinking about kissing me?"

Her cheeks darken, and my chest swells.

"Elijah is going to kill me," I say, running a hand through my hair.

Fuck, what was I thinking!

"My brother can do one," Kat says, in a very un-Kat-like way, her tone completely serious.

My eyes clash with hers.

Kat moves suddenly, straddling my hips, pushing me back onto her bed. I lie back, her hands resting on my chest, her hips cradling my throbbing cock between her thighs.

Eli would kill me if he saw us.

"I don't care what my brother thinks. I'm a grown woman with her own mind."

My hands move to her hips, holding her still. If she moves, I'm going to blow my load. Fuck, I've never been as turned on by anyone as I am by Kathryn Frazer.

Kat lowers her face towards mine.

"I want to kiss you again, Jaxson Lockwood."

I moan as she leans forward and nips at my bottom lip. Sucking it into her mouth. My hips buck, and she presses down against me.

"Fuck Kat," I say, closing my eyes and counting to ten.

"You see me, Jax. You always have. Being around you makes me feel alive. I want to feel alive."

I moan again, but this time I roll us, so I'm on top.

I drop my forehead to hers.

"You've had a shock tonight. I'm not going to take advantage of you."

Kat's fingers find the short hair at the nape of my neck, the sensation sending shivers down my spine.

I drop a kiss on the tip of her nose.

"Kiss me," she says, her tone almost pleading.

Eli really is going to kill me, but the look in Kat's eyes makes something in my chest lock.

I place my mouth over hers. Kat's legs wrap around my hips, her fingers gripping my shoulder and head, holding me in place. Our tongues duel, a throbbing, tingling warmth spreads out through my body, until I'm overcome with a sense of completeness, and I forget this is my best friend's sister and let myself go.

CHAPTER 23

KAT

I swipe angrily at my damp cheeks before rubbing the back of my hand over my eyes.

Looking down, I see mascara smeared across my skin.

I draw in a shuddering breath and stand up. I don't want anyone to see me like this... broken, damaged.

You don't want Jax to see you like this. Be honest.

I glance down at the soaking wet pile of clothes Jax left behind, memories of his naked arse as he walked into the villa, then again as he stood in the shower. I close my eyes at the fluttering sensation low in my stomach. The man's body is a work of art, it always was.

I bend down and scoop them up. As I pass, I drop them on the floor of the outside shower. I turn it on, rinsing the saltwater from the pool.

He got into the water in his clothes.

He did that for you... was worried about you.

I drop my head against the wall and sigh.

Just wait until he reads the letter.

What will he think then? What the hell do I say to him?

I switch off the water and pick up each item, squeezing out the excess water, before shaking them vigorously, as Betsy, our cook/housekeeper, showed me. I hang them over the railing to dry.

I enter the villa and stop, my eyes finding the entrance.

He left, and he hasn't come back.

I move to the bathroom, my eyes are bloodshot, my face puffy from the tears. I wash away the evidence of my meltdown. Time to see if these thousand-pound eyedrops do what they claim. I blink rapidly, before throwing them back into my wash bag.

Back in the bedroom, I open the minibar, grabbing myself a bottle of red wine.

I remove the cork, and pour myself a glass.

I hold it up to the light, swirling it around, then place my nose to the top of the glass and inhale its bouquet. The fruity aroma invades my senses. Taking a sip, I allow it to coat my palate before swallowing. I close my eyes, letting its flavour linger. I pick up the bottle, filling the glass to the rim, before emptying it in three swallows. I refill and head outside, taking a seat under the large umbrella.

Sitting back, I close my eyes and raise my glass to my mouth.

When I open them again, something in the water catches my eye. I watch as muscular arms cut through the waves like someone possessed.

Jax.

I raise my glass again, only my throat burns with the next swallow, and my eyes water.

How did life get so complicated?

I put down my glass and close my eyes, allowing memories of the past to overwhelm me.

* * *

Sixteen Years Ago

My hand snakes under Jax's t-shirt and across the smooth, taut skin of his back. I pull him closer. I can feel his rock-hard cock between my legs, rubbing against my throbbing, swollen core.

I suck in a breath. Jaxson Lockwood wants me.

He moans, and I tighten my grip, my body temperature rising, my pussy pulsing with need.

I rock against him, adding pressure where I need it most.

My body is humming.

Jax groans against my mouth. I suck on his tongue, something I heard one of the other girls say drove her man crazy with lust.

He thrusts against me, his cock hitting my clit, sending shockwaves of pleasure dancing through my body, making my stomach clench with need.

I rake my fingernails along his spine, making his hips flex, pressing me further into the bed. I moan and lift my hips, trying to get more friction. I've never wanted anyone the way I want Jaxson. It's why I never went very far with Danny. He left me cold, whereas with Jaxson, my whole body is tingling, and my pussy seems to have a life of its own.

His hand moves to my breast, kneading it through the material of my top.

I yank his t-shirt up, and he pulls back.

He looks down at me, his dark eyes smouldering.

"Kat?"

"I want to touch you," I say, unsure where my spark of confidence has come from.

It's not like I haven't seen Jaxson topless. He's spent the past three summers at our house by the pool.

He opens his mouth, but I place a hand on his chest.

"I've seen you in a lot less," I say, raising an eyebrow.

He grabs the back of his t-shirt and, using one hand, pulls it over his head, before throwing it to one side.

My hands go to my top, and before he can stop me, it joins his on the floor.

"Kat, you're killing me," he says almost painfully, a flush darkening his cheekbones as his eyes roam over my exposed breasts and hard pebbled nipples.

"Do you want to stop?" I ask, my confidence suddenly waning.

He drops his forehead to mine and closes his eyes briefly. When he opens them again, his expression is pained.

"We should," he says honestly, before rolling off me and flopping onto his back. He uses his forearm to cover his eyes.

I drop back and stare at the ceiling, swallowing against the tears building in my throat.

Way to go, Kat! What were you thinking? Jaxson Lockwood is a superstar, a heart-throb. He's not going to be interested in a silly little nerd like you.

I let out a whimper, surprised when Jaxson's hand finds mine, interlocking our fingers.

"There are so many reasons I should get up and walk out of here," he says quietly.

I turn my head and find him staring at me. I bite my lip as I drown in his gaze.

"You should be telling me to go, Kat." His eyes are pleading.

"We should forget this ever happened," he says.

"Is that what you want?" I ask, my hand coming up and covering my breasts, suddenly aware of how exposed I am.

I drop my gaze, breaking eye contact.

Jax's finger lifts my chin, raising it until I'm looking deep into his dark eyes.

"Kat, do you have any idea how long I've fantasised about kissing you? Your brother would have drowned me a long time ago if he knew."

My pulse thunders in my ears. This can't be real. I must be dreaming.

Jax has fantasised about kissing me?

"You have?" I say, the disbelief in my tone making him chuckle.

He cups my jaw, his thumb sliding up and down my cheek.

He nods, a smile playing on his lips. "Since the day I saw you playing piano. You were so beautiful, the sun shining through the window. You were lost in the music. You captivated me."

I gasp. That was three years ago.

Jax closes the distance between us, his lips once again finding mine. His finger and thumb holding my chin.

I move my hands to his chest, sliding them up and over his shoulders, pulling him towards me. His mouth leaves mine, trailing its way down my throat. He cups my breasts, his thumbs sliding over my nipples. They pebble against his hands, aching with need.

"Beautiful, so perfect."

Jax takes one nipple deep into his mouth, my hands clasping his head. My body swells with desire, my hips rocking, as my body pulses.

He kneads my other breast with his hand, tweaking and tormenting my nipple. My thighs spread, demanding more.

Jax's mouth returns to mine, his hand grasping my thigh. He rolls us onto our sides, until we're facing one another, lifting one of my legs, and sliding it up and over his hip, pulling me hard against him.

When he rocks into me, I gasp as stars explode behind my eyes.

He pulls back slightly, his mouth still locked on mine. His fingers glide down my stomach, my muscles quivering beneath his touch. I moan into his mouth. He turns his hand, sliding it between us.

I suck in a ragged breath as his hand cups my core, massaging the sensitive skin through my clothes.

"Oh," I squeak, as he rubs it back and forth.

My body swells and pulses under his touch, my muscles contracting deep inside.

Jax deepens our kiss, each kiss and touch becoming more frantic. His fingers breach my panties, and I almost fly off the bed when he touches my swollen, sensitised skin.

"Kat...You're so responsive."

He deepens our kiss, as if trying to devour me. I meet him stroke for stroke.

His finger finds my clit, and lights flash behind my eyes. I lift my thigh higher, wanting, no demanding more.

"Yes," *I say, my hips thrusting back and forth against his skilful fingers.*

When his hand moves lower, I all but wail.

He moans as he trails a finger through my soaking wet centre, before pressing forward, and sinking it into me. My body contracts sharply, making me hiss, and I almost come on the spot.

I drop onto my back and spread my legs, giving him greater access. I pull him with me, his mouth returning to my breast as his finger slides in and out. He withdraws his finger, coating my lips and clit with my desire. He teases and torments me until I'm a moaning mess.

"Please, Jax."

"Please, what?"

"I need—"

He reinserts his finger, while his thumb draws lazy circles around my clit, driving me higher. He increases the pressure, his mouth returning to my nipple. I drop my head back against the bed, holding his head in place. My hips are rising and falling. He withdraws his finger slightly, only to add a second, holding them both just inside my entrance. He gently opens and closes them, stretching the sensitive muscles, until I'm left panting.

"Oh," *I whisper.* "Oh yes, just like that. Oh Jax."

He moves, pressing them deep into my body. I groan, biting my lip to stop myself from screaming when he twists his hand, continuing to open and close them against my side walls, creating the most exquisite pressure.

"That's it," he says, his thumb still circling my clit.

When he suddenly presses both fingers against my front wall in rapid succession, my chest rises up. His mouth slams down on mine to capture my scream as my body detonates around him. A thousand fireworks go off, as my body pulses, my muscles clenching hard around his fingers.

He thrusts them in and out gently, dragging my orgasm on and on.

I grab his hand, stilling the movement, unable to take any more.

I open my eyes, forcing them to focus on the most stunning man I've ever seen.

He drops his mouth to mine.

"Beautiful," he whispers against my lips.

I sink into his kiss, my muscles weak, my body still shuddering from the aftershocks. I press my chest against his, my soft curves against his hard muscle.

"Jax," I whisper against his mouth.

"It's okay," he says.

I lower my hand to his throbbing cock and suck in a breath.

Fuck, he's huge!

He draws in a shuddering breath, catching my hand.

"Not today, beautiful. I've already taken advantage, I'm not going to allow you any regrets."

"You think I could possibly regret the best orgasm of my life?" I say, pulling back and looking up at him.

He smiles. "I'm hoping not, but Kat, I have great respect for you."

He cups my face in his hand, his forehead returning to mine.

"I would like nothing more than to sink into your silky depths, beautiful."

I open my mouth, but he places a finger over my lips.

"Believe me, my body is begging me to change my mind." He chuckles. "But I'm not going to abuse your trust. I want to take it slow."

My mouth drops open, my eyes wide.

"You want?"

He inclines his head.

"You think I would have touched you if I didn't want more. Kat!"

He sounds cross, his brows furrowing.

I lift a hand and cup his cheek.

"I would love nothing more than to see you again. I just..."

His forehead smooths out, and his lips tilt in a slow smile.

"You would?" he says.

I nod, biting down on my lip. "I really would."

He pulls me onto his chest, resting my head above his heart.

"Good," he says, the sound vibrating under my ear. "Now you go to sleep. In the morning, we'll pack your stuff into Elijah's car and move you to your friends' house."

Jax's phone rings. He jumps up, dragging it out of his back pocket.

"Eli," he says, his eyes darting to mine, his cheeks glowing red.

"No, everything's fine... Yes, I'm with her... There was a problem with her housemate... No, I'm not leaving her alone..." His eyes clash with mine. "Sure, I'll put her on."

Jax holds out the phone, the colour draining from his face.

"Hey," I say quietly.

Eli's voice comes over the phone. "Are you okay? Do you need me to come over?"

"No," I say, maybe a little too sharply.

Jax's eyes are wide. I shake my head.

"Honestly, I'm fine thanks to Jax. He came and got me from the club."

"What the hell happened?"

"Danny, it turns out, is a money hound who is shagging one of my housemates."

"I'll kill him." Elijah seethes, his anger vibrating down the phone.

I roll my eyes. "No, you won't. He's not worth your time, or mine for that matter. I'm certainly not heartbroken. Relieved if anything."

"As long as you're sure. I'm not past making a visit."

I chuckle.

Elijah is six feet six, but one of the biggest pacifists I know.

"It's okay, tough guy, you can stand down. I'm a big girl. Plus, I used one of Doug's manoeuvres when he grabbed my arm. He won't be bothering me again if he knows what's good for him."

"Way to go, little sis." Elijah growls. "Did you say he grabbed your arm?"

I kick myself metaphorically for letting that slip. Jax stares at me, a crease forming between his brows. He looks ready to commit murder himself. He knows about Doug. He's been at the house for Gabe and Caleb's lessons.

"Oh hell, now Jax is going all growly. You both need to calm down." I shoot Jax a glance, which has him returning to the bed. "I'm moving in with some of the other girls I've met." I bite my lip, my eyes roaming over Jax's bare chest. "Is it okay if Jax keeps the car for tonight and helps me move tomorrow? I can't live here any longer."

"Are you sure you're okay?" Elijah asks, his voice quieter, more gentle. "I really can come over."

"No," I say, trying to sound calm. "I promise I'm fine. Jax is here and taking really good care of me."

Jax blanches, and I smirk, placing a hand on his thigh, before sliding it higher.

"Okay, as long as you're sure. But if anything changes."

I roll my eyes. "I'll call, I promise. I love you," I say.

"Put Jax back on the phone. And Kat, I love you more."

I hold the phone away from us before saying, "Jax, Elijah wants to speak to you."

Jax takes the phone, listening carefully to whatever Eli says to him. He flinches as I run a hand up his thigh before cupping his very hard cock.

"No problem. I won't go anywhere, she's in safe hands," he breathes.

He captures my hand in his, but I simply replace it with my other one.

He coughs.

I flick the button on his trousers and lower the zipper slowly, sliding my hand inside, drawing him out.

I lick my lips at the sight of him.

He squeezes his eyes closed and grits his teeth as I lower my head.

"I'll see you tomorrow after Kat's settled."

He disconnects the phone and checks it twice before throwing it away. He captures my face in his hands. I look up, my eyes sparkling. I hold his gaze as I poke out my tongue, licking the moisture pooling on the end of his cock, before trailing it down the side, treating it like my favourite lollypop.

"You're a very naughty woman, Kathryn Frazer... Your brother."

I grin, adding pressure to his hands.

"Oh, believe me, I've only just begun to show you how naughty I want to be... As for my brother, he's not here and has nothing to do with us. We're consenting adults."

I drop my head and place my lips around him, drawing him deep into my mouth. I want Jaxson's thoughts on me alone, far away from my brother.

Jax's fingers sink into my hair, flexing against my scalp, as he lets out a deep moan.

I smile, taking him deeper.

His eyes never leave mine as I slide him in and out of my mouth, circling him with my tongue. I clasp the base of his dick with my hand, moving it up and down, while my mouth torments his crown, letting my body take over.

Jax raises a hand and bites down on his wrist, his eyes rolling back in his head.

My movements become faster until he grabs me around the waist, pulling me off him and crushing me to his chest. His body vibrates, jerking against me. Warm jets hit the bare skin of my stomach.

Jaxson captures my face in his hands, his mouth devouring mine. I kiss him back until both of us pull away, panting. He rests his forehead against mine.

"You're so beautiful, Kathryn Frazer," *he says, his eyes locked on mine.*

"Is that what you say to all the girls, after you come all over their stomach?"

A flush darkens his cheek.

"No, and this is not something I expected, or could have imagined in my wildest dreams."

"You dream about me?" *I ask, my heart beating rapidly in my chest.*

"For years. Since I first met you."

"You never said anything. All the times we've talked."

He brushes hair from my forehead.

"You're my best friend's little sister. He'll kill me if he ever finds out what we've done. You're off limits."

"And now?"

"And now. I'm damned. One taste, and you've hooked me. I'm yours."

I run a hand over his cheek, my fingers tracing his beautiful bone structure. He takes my hand and kisses my palm.

"We better get cleaned up," *Jax says, his eyes dropping to the sticky mess coating us both.*

"This way."

I get up and take his hand, leading him to the en-suite.

My room is one of the only ones with an en-suite, but I pay for it. I'll miss it, but not enough to put up with the shit that goes with living with this group of girls.

I set the water going and strip out of the rest of my clothes.

"I'll wash your back if you wash mine," I say, stepping under the spray.

My heart constricts at Jax's sexy grin.

CHAPTER 24

JAX

My arms slice through the water, my muscles quivering from the abuse, but I'm past caring. Anger bubbles deep inside my chest as my brain whirs.

Kathryn Frazer has once again fucked with my head, something I swore I'd never let happen again, only this time it's not only her.

I turn in the water and head to shore, slowing my pace to let my muscles cool down. Years of training cannot be ignored, despite my racing heart and overactive mind.

I stumble up the beach, dropping onto a sun lounger and closing my eyes.

"That was some swim, young man."

I open my eyes and find Mary, Philip's wife, leaning over me.

My muscles twitch from overexertion.

"I was working through a few things," I say, my breath coming in pants.

"I'd say," she tuts, making me smile. "You know a good conversation works wonders and is far less taxing on the body too."

I harrumph, although it comes out more as a huff.

My chest rises and falls rapidly.

I feel a hand on my wrist and realise she's taking my pulse.

I sit up.

"I'm okay, honestly," I say. "I swim over one hundred laps a day."

She raises an eyebrow.

"Physically, maybe, but I've just watched someone abuse their body to almost breaking point, so I'd say mentally, young man. You're screwed."

"Is that your medical opinion?" I ask, raising an eyebrow.

"Nope, it's one of a seventy-seven-year-old woman. Someone who has lived a lot and seen even more."

Philip appears to be carrying a bottle of water, which he hands to me.

"Here you go, drink that."

"Thanks," I say, taking a deep swig. My hand and arm shake, although not as much as I feared.

"Did you and your lady have a falling out?"

"Mary!" Philip says. "Mind your own business."

I bite my lip to stop myself from laughing.

She turns on her husband. "Poppycock. If someone hadn't spoken to me all those years ago. You and I would never have happened."

She pauses, then turns back, staring me down.

"I'm paying it forward," she says.

"Paying what forward?"

"The advice I was given."

Her hand snakes out and grasps Philip's, entwining their fingers.

Philip shoots me an apologetic look, but stays quiet.

Mary smiles, taking my silence as my willingness to listen.

"You only get one chance in this life, and sometimes you have to take the bull by the horns. Nothing worth its salt comes easy. Things worth fighting for require effort and steely determination. Only you can decide if she's worth it. But looking at what you just put your body through, that level of emotion means something and shouldn't be ignored."

"If only it were that simple," I say, brushing my hair off my face.

"Have you tried talking to her?"

I look up and find her wise, blue eyes staring down at me. She shrugs, and her eyes sparkle.

"It's the best place to start. You don't want to reach my age and have any regrets. Life is not a dress rehearsal. You get one shot. *I wish or I just* moments, those suck, believe me. I've been around enough dying people throughout my career. Those are always the saddest."

Her voice drops, and she places a hand on my shoulder, giving it a quick squeeze.

She turns back to Philip, sharing a silent message.

"Just think about it," she says, before they both turn and walk away, leaving me sitting there, alone.

I rest my elbows on my knees and watch the waves roll up the sand.

I sip the water until it's empty.

My muscles begin to relax, and I stand up, pulling on my t-shirt.

My mind races, searching for answers as I make my way back to the villa.

I know I promised Caleb I wouldn't rock the boat, but bloody hell, I'm tired of all this shit.

When I enter, Kat is sitting on the sofa, curled up with a book and a half-empty glass of wine.

She looks up, her eyes hollow, and I would swear she's been crying.

Something in my chest snaps.

"Hey," she says, returning her bookmark to its page and closing the book. No folding down the page corner for Kathryn Frazer, even the spine of her book looks untouched.

"Hey."

I dump my water bottle into the recycle bin before moving to the end of the bed and sitting down, my elbows resting on my knees.

I pull out the letter and toss it to one side.

Kat's eyes follow the movement, her throat bobbing.

"We need to talk," Kat says, before I can open my mouth.

"We do," I agree. "But first I want to know, why? Why did you let me read it?"

Kat shrugs. "Its contents affect you as much as me, and to be honest, I'm tired of all the lies, the deception. I've spent sixteen years being someone else's puppet, unwillingly dancing to their tune. It's time I take my life back."

"Kat—"

She may call herself *a puppet*, but she went from my bed to his in a short time. My stomach roils as the thought of them together, her crying out his name as her body milked his cock.

I press my thumb and forefinger into my eye sockets, trying to ease the pressure building behind my eyes.

When I look up, Kat has schooled her features.

She opens her mouth, but it's like her voice has lost its power. She closes it again, her posture sinking slightly.

"Kat. I don't know what you want me to say?" I tell her truthfully.

I run a hand through my hair, resting it at the nape of my neck.

"You don't need to say anything. It's me who needs to apologise. To own what happened. I'm sorry I believed them over you. I'm sorry I've treated you the way I have. Blamed you, when you were innocent." She shakes her head. "Not that words can undo any of it. Please don't think I'm making up excuses. I'm not. I'm trying to own it." Her hand goes to her pendant. "I believed them over you, and I'll have to live with that choice for the rest of my life."

I lean forward, resting my forearms on my thighs and glance up.

"The whole thing is a mess," I say with a sigh.

Too many people have had their lives controlled because Zach and Darra were complicit in her old man's scheme.

Mary's words haunt me. *Regrets.*

Kathryn Frazer will always be my biggest regret. Loving her, never. But, our relationship since that day... Caleb and Elijah weren't my only friends in the Frazer household. Kat was that, long before Cal. Losing her nearly broke me. It was why, when Dillon Myers offered me the internship, I went as far away as possible.

"Do you know, when you confronted me, I initially thought it was a joke. How could you believe that of me? Then I began to wonder, did you doubt me because you knew I wasn't good enough for you?"

Kat's stoic expression cracks, and is replaced by one of horror.

"Not good enough? Why on earth would you think that?" she blurts out. "What the hell, Jax! I truly thought you'd slept with Sasha. When did I ever give you the impression you weren't good enough for me?"

Kat jumps up and starts pacing. I can almost hear her brain humming. She spins to face me.

"You were my lover, my best friend. Do you know how lost I was without you?"

My heart pounds at her words.

She clearly has a poor memory of past events.

Heat rushes through my body, my muscles tense.

"Lost? Really? Wow, we have quite a different recollection of past events."

Kat frowns. I stare at her.

Has she really forgotten?

"You were fucking hanging off Zach within a few weeks of us breaking up."

It's my turn to get up and start pacing, although the additional bed makes the space small.

"I came back from my interview in the US, and he was all over you like a rash. It didn't look like you were too lost from where I was standing. It looked like Zach was the perfect replacement. One you later moved in with, need I remind you."

Kat blanches at my words, her cool exterior finally shattering.

She shakes her head, but the adrenaline rushing through my system has taken over. I grit my teeth and inhale deeply before closing my eyes. I pinch the bridge of my nose.

"You've got it all wrong," she whispers. "He was helping me."

I growl.

"Not like that," she snaps. "He was a buffer. After everything that happened, I couldn't face the parties and the social events alone. He offered to be my platonic plus one."

"I'm sure he did," I hiss, having read his fucking *explanation!*

"He said if people saw me with him, they'd leave me alone. I needed space to process, and he was offering as a friend, or so I thought. I was too bruised to argue. It's not like I could talk to Elijah, he was going through enough of his own shit, and you were gone."

"How did Zach know about us? Did you tell him?"

Kat's head shoots up.

"He didn't. Not as far as I was aware."

I shake my head.

"You never questioned how he knew you needed a *buffer?*" I ask sarcastically.

The colour drains from Kat's face.

"I…"

She sinks onto the sofa, her head in her hands.

"After everything Sasha said, I asked Zach about your love life. He told me you had a flock of women chasing you."

"Did you ever mention you and me? That we were together?"

Kat's eyes clash with mine, and she inclines her head as if trying to remember. She bites her lip before shaking her head slowly.

I let out a forceful breath at the sharp tightness in my chest.

"Everything was such a mess. Elijah had just found out about Darra's pregnancy, and my family were in turmoil. Then straight after I confronted you about Sasha, you disappeared off to the US for two weeks."

My body temperature rises, my voice growing thick.

"I didn't have a choice. Did you think I wanted to go after everything that had happened?" I run a hand through my hair and spin to face her. "I was in the hotel that day, because Dillon had offered to meet with me. Your father arranged the interview. For someone like me, it was the chance of a lifetime. Dillon Myers was my hero." I sink onto the edge of the bed. "I didn't even know Sasha was going to be there, not until I turned up and Dillon introduced Emma, his daughter, and Sasha, her close friend. They left almost immediately, and Dillon conducted my first interview. I never gave it another thought. I was as surprised as anyone when he invited me to visit their offices in the US."

Kat frowns, "Someone like you?"

I raise an eyebrow. "Don't be naive, Kat. I wasn't born

with a silver spoon in my mouth. I couldn't turn down opportunities like the one Dillon was offering. It jump-started my career. I'd still be a nobody if I hadn't taken that internship."

"You've got it all wrong. You were never going to be a nobody, Jax. I never blamed you for taking that job."

Her words stab me in the chest. She always had so much faith in me, even before.

"But you didn't tell me about it. The interview," she says.

When Robert approached me, he'd asked me not to tell anyone at Dillon's request. I didn't want to ruin my chances, so I kept it quiet, even from Kat. My first mistake. I should have trusted her.

"No, I didn't," I say, shaking my head. "And that's on me. I was asked to keep it quiet, and when I didn't hear back, I didn't think anything was going to come of it. I should have told you."

"You were my best friend." She sighs. "When I finally found out, I knew what a big deal that interview was to you. My first thought was to ring and congratulate you, but then there was Sasha. Beautiful, gorgeous, confident Sasha and I began to question whether I'd been stupid and naïve. You were always so driven, had your life planned out. Our lives were heading in different directions. Why would you want me holding you back?"

I flinch at her words. According to her parents, Kat never allowed herself to be vulnerable, even as a little girl.

"I never in a million years thought I'd get the position. When I was offered the internship, I wanted to tell you. But then I remembered you hated my guts."

We fall into an awkward silence.

"Do you know, you're one of the few people who would call my brother or me out on our shit when you didn't agree with us. Not many people do that when your last name is Frazer."

I chuckle.

"It's why your brothers' like me," I admit. "I refuse to take any of their shit."

Kat repositions herself on the sofa and laughs quietly. "It's a rarity. It's also something we value, especially when it's genuine and comes from the best place."

My eyes find hers, and a sharp pain stabs through my chest.

"You say this, but you went from my bed straight to his?"

Kat gets up and walks towards me. She pauses before sitting down on the mattress next to me.

She turns her head her haunted gaze meeting mine.

"I didn't," she says with a sigh. "But looking back, I can see how it might have appeared that way."

I pause, waiting for her to continue.

She drops her gaze to her hands which are clasped in her lap.

"Zach and my relationship was purely platonic for a long time. He would accompany me to functions and family events as my plus one. Was an effective barrier to those irritating social climbers and money hounds."

"I haven't heard that phrase in a while."

She chuckles. "He also made me laugh, something I didn't do for a long time after you left."

"But you did begin a relationship with him," I say. The thought is like a knife to my gut. They lived together for seven years.

She drops her chin to her chest, biting down on her bottom lip. Kat closes her eyes for a second, and when she opens them again, they're filled with pain. "It was the day Elijah announced your engagement to Emma."

My lungs constrict, making it difficult to breathe.

"But that was eighteen months later."

Emma was my rebound. Luckily for both of us, I came to my senses in time and called off the wedding.

It sounds like Zach became Kat's.

His words are now beginning to make more sense.

Silence descends.

I drop my head into my hands, resting my elbows on my knees.

I turn my head to face Kat.

"What now?" I ask.

"I'd really like, for us to be friends," Kat says, suddenly sounding tired. "I've spent so many years resenting you. I knew you, should've known they were lying."

"I should have fought harder, made you listen. Realised there was something wrong with the scenario."

She rests a hand on my shoulder, the warmth of her palm burning its way through my t-shirt. "I'm not sure I would have listened. The evidence they presented was pretty compelling."

I catch her gaze.

"You never told your brothers about us," I say, surprised when Kat laughs. She removes her hand, dropping it to her side. I miss it instantly.

"What? Admit to them I'd been duped. That I'd fallen for your sweet-talking charm, that handsome face? Besides, Eli needed you, and whatever happened between us. I'm not that selfish. His needs trumped mine."

It's those words that remind me why I fell in love with Kathryn Frazer, and why no one else has ever come close to replacing her.

CHAPTER 25

KAT

We head out for dinner. The villa has become incredibly claustrophobic since our conversation this afternoon.

Jax has been unusually silent. After we finished talking, he took his book and sat in the shade on the terrace.

Do I blame him?

A lot of wounds were reopened, and the pain is fresh. Our only hope now is that they can heal over time.

I glance over at the man walking next to me.

I know I was right in letting him read Zach's letter. I have no regrets.

I turn away. Zach, Sasha and Darra's lies affected Jax as much as they did me. They started a snowball effect that can't be undone. I just hope we can put the past behind us and move forward. If not as friends, at least in terms of building a strong working relationship.

Jaxson's skills are exactly what the FHG and my project need. Caleb was right. His ideas for the new development are next-level and more than I could have hoped for.

We're shown to our table in the restaurant.

"Mary, Philip," Jax says to the elderly couple sitting next to us.

"Good evening," Mary says. "You're looking better than you were this afternoon."

My eyes dart to Jax, but he's focused on the couple.

"I am, thank you. Can I introduce you to my friend, Kathryn Frazer?"

Mary smiles, her eyes sparkling with delight.

"Ms Frazer, we meet again. I wanted to thank you for the champagne and fruit basket. It was a very kind gesture."

I smile. "You're welcome, Mary. I hope you've both enjoyed your stay with us."

"Most definitely."

Her hand moves to cover her husband's, and he entwines their fingers, before getting up and pulling out her chair.

My heart skips a beat.

Mary stands up.

"This is goodbye," Mary says, turning to face us. "We leave in the morning."

"It's been lovely meeting you both," I say. "Safe flight."

Mary walks up to our table, and we both stand. Philip shakes my hand before Mary comes in for a hug. I bend down as she pulls me in tight, her hug is surprisingly comforting. I squeeze her back, my throat thickening.

Mary smiles before pulling back and patting my cheek. "It is possible to have it all. Remember that."

She approaches Jax, whispering something in his ear. Whatever she says makes him smile.

She turns and winks at me before she slips her arm through Philip's and leaves.

As soon as they're out of sight, curiosity gets the better of me.

"What did she say?"

Jax's cheekbones darken.

"She said. We make a beautiful couple, and I need to convince you of that."

I cough awkwardly, aware of my cheeks burning.

"It's okay, I've told her a million times we're colleagues. But Mary's a romantic."

The word *colleague* sticks in my throat.

After everything that's happened between us, maybe *colleagues* is the safest term.

"I finished a rough draft of the plans today," Jax says, changing the subject.

My heart stutters, then relaxes.

Okay. Safe. Work I can do.

"Excellent," I say, as our waiter appears to take our food order. "We can go through it tomorrow morning. I've met with the staff and sent my recommendations back to Head Office. The next three days, I'm all yours."

It's only after the words have left my mouth that I realise how suggestive they sound. If Jax picked up on it, he shows no signs of it.

"That's great. There are a few ideas I'd like to discuss with you. See what you think."

"How about we meet up after breakfast," I say, wanting to make it official. "Don suggested we work in the guest library. I had a look around earlier, and it appears to be empty."

After today, the last place I want to work is in the villa.

According to Baskin, the library is an underutilised space. It's only used during bad weather, and for clients leaving the island, but as most leave in the morning before checkout, this is rare.

Our food arrives, and we eat in relative silence, both caught up in our own thoughts.

It's been a long, emotional day. My limbs feel heavy, and my eyes scratchy. I want nothing more than to curl up in bed, read my book and reset.

Once we've eaten, we make our way back to the villa.

"Do you want to stop for a nightcap?" Jax asks as we pass the bar.

"I'd love to, but I can barely keep my eyes open. You're welcome to if you want."

"I think I might," he says.

My chest tightens. Part of me wants to be alone, the other wishes for comfort. But Jax is not the man to give it, and I have no right to ask it of him.

"I won't be late."

"Don't rush on my account," I say, offering him a quick smile before we separate.

I pause, watching him enter the bar.

He's immediately greeted by a number of guests. He stops, his shoulders relaxing as he talks. He smiles, they smile.

I sigh and turn away, continuing my journey back to the villa.

Jax has always been popular and has a way of putting people at ease. Everyone seems to like him and gravitate towards him. My family included.

Is that why I was so easily convinced he'd been unfaithful?

I've always been introverted, guarded. Trust has never come easily to me. My inner circle is incredibly small, consisting mainly of family, the odd friend, like Pen, and the girls I went to uni with, who I catch up with once a year.

I enter the villa and stare at the large bed and down at the tiny cot bed.

I throw caution to the wind, rearranging the pillows the same way Jax did last night, and crawl under the covers. I lean across and flick on Jax's bedside light before picking up my book. I stare at the words, re-reading the same page five times, before giving up. I replace my bookmark and turn off my light.

I wriggle down the bed, my body sinking into the mattress. I close my heavy eyelids, expecting to dream, but instead there's nothing, only silence for the first time in a very long time.

* * *

I WAKE UP AND STRETCH. Rolling onto my back before turning my head. The other side of the bed is empty, although I can make out the indent where Jax's head has been.

I sit up and look around. My senses tell me the villa is empty, that Jax is gone. He's probably swimming.

I pick up my phone. Seven thirty.

Grabbing my gym gear, I head to the small guest gym. Another guest is lifting weights in the corner of the room. He looks up, and we exchange pleasantries before concentrating on what we're there for.

I start the running machine. It's not long before my feet are pounding, and my heart rate has increased. I run like the devil is chasing me. Running from the past few months. By the time I'm done, my hair is plastered to my scalp and my clothes are stuck to my skin.

I make my way back to the villa to shower and change.

There's still no sign of Jaxson.

So I head for breakfast, alone.

I miss yesterday's pastries. I knew what he was doing. Jax is a savoury man, pastries have never been his thing.

My heart does a flip at the thought. Maybe there is a chance for us to be friends.

When I'm done, I make my way to the library.

I stop in the doorway, my chest constricting.

Jax is already there.

"Good morning," I say, after taking several deep inhales.

My breath catches when he looks up. His strong jaw and

high cheekbones don't detract from the dark circles under his eyes, as if he didn't sleep.

"Good morning," he says. "Did you enjoy breakfast?"

"I did, although I missed the pastries this morning," I say, before I can stop myself.

"You could have had one," he says, inclining his head.

"I know, but they're never the same off your own plate."

I had a terrible appetite growing up Mum always found I was happiest eating while sat on Dad's knee, thinking I was eating his food instead of my own. A total Daddy's girl.

Jax shakes his head, moving some paper to uncover a plate full of mouthwatering pastries.

"Jax," I say, pulling out a chair, while he grabs a knife and begins cutting them into quarters. The same way he did the morning before.

I chuckle as he pushes the plate towards me, taking a slice for himself.

"Would you like to share mine?"

Our eyes lock.

"Don't mind if I do."

I take a piece and bite down, closing my eyes as the sweet, sugary coating fills my mouth.

I moan, smashing my hand over my mouth in horror.

When I open my eyes, Jax is staring at me, his pupils dilated.

I cough, and he chuckles.

I put the pastry on a napkin, Jax hands me, moving it to one side.

"What did you want to discuss?" I ask when I finally manage to swallow.

CHAPTER 26

JAX

We spend the next few hours deep in discussion. Kat has gone into work mode. It's as if yesterday never occurred.

Her only tell is her pendant sliding first left, then right, then back again, along the chain around her neck. It's something she did when she was lost in thought or anxious.

It was her twenty-first birthday present from her parents, and as far as I know, she's never taken it off.

I stretch up and out, my back cracking from being sat in the same position for too long.

Kat does the same, her hand going over her shoulder to knead a muscle knot. It's something she used to get when she was caught up in her assignments.

I stand and move behind her, pushing her hand out of the way and digging my thumb into the tender spot above her shoulder blade.

Kat moans.

"You always were good at this," she says, moving her head to the side.

I gaze down at her exposed neck. In the past, I would

drop my lips to her exposed skin. A massage like this would end up with my cock buried deep in her body, both of us hot and sweaty, begging for release.

I harden at the memory, and I'm glad for the long t-shirt hanging over my shorts.

The muscle knot gives under my thumb, and I move away. Kat moves her head from side to side.

"Thank you," she says. "That feels much better."

"Why don't you try out the spa? Get a massage," I say, my voice a little rougher than I would like.

"Maybe I will," she says, turning her head and smiling. "We've got a lot done this morning."

"We're definitely close to having a workable proposal."

Kat smiles. She looks refreshed, the dark circles under her eyes have been replaced by the healthy glow of a tan. I was not that lucky.

After dinner, I stayed in the bar as long as I could, escaping into my thoughts, replaying every scene and event over in my mind. By the time I dragged myself back to the villa, it was late, and Kat was sound asleep, her breathing deep and even. I'd got into bed, but sleep evaded me. Instead, I lay watching her for hours, caught in a vicious cycle of what-ifs.

She tilts her head, her gaze connecting with mine. She smiles again, and my heart skips a beat.

"I want to say, thank you," she says. "I know I was ungrateful when you first came on board."

I stay silent, not sure how to reply.

Kat continues.

"You've dug me out of a deep hole." She runs a hand through her hair and gives me a small smile. "I'll admit, these plans are a thousand times better than the original proposal. Your insight into what I'm trying to achieve is amazing. It's like you've been able to read my mind."

"We make a good team," I say at last.

We always did.

But that was a lifetime ago. We're different people now. Why does that feeling leave me cold?

Kat nods, but I don't miss the faraway look in her eyes.

"What's next?"

"What do you mean?"

"What's next for you, Kathryn Frazer?" I ask, collecting my stuff together. "You've taken the FHG to new heights. This project is going to cement you as *queen* of the hotel industry. Quite a feat by the age of thirty-five. What's your next goal?"

Her brows furrow, and she shrugs.

"More of the same. The FHG takes up most of my time. I still run, so I may train to compete in a marathon. I want to renovate the hotel suite where I'm living."

I'd forgotten she'd moved out of her apartment.

"Are you staying put at the hotel?"

She picks up her belongings and stands up. "It's convenient for work. It just needs modernising. I'd like to add an office."

"If you need me, let me know. I can look at the original plans if you want any structural changes. Let you know what's possible."

"Thank you, I may just take you up on that."

She's all smiles today, and my stomach somersaults.

What am I doing?

We leave the library and make our way outside into the sunshine and heat. The rush of warmth is a strict contrast to the air-conditioned library.

Kat removes her cardigan, exposing her shoulders. Yesterday left her with a healthy tan.

"But what else? Apart from a marathon, the rest is all linked to work. You must want more?"

"Like?" Her brows furrow until understanding dawns, her gaze meeting mine. "Oh, you mean a private life?"

Kat throws back her head, her laughter genuine. "I'll leave the marriage and kids to my siblings. I'm more than happy being, Aunty Kat."

This is not the same Kathryn Frazer of old. Sixteen years ago, Kat wanted it all. A career, a husband to come home to, two-point-four children.

My expression must give me away.

"Don't look like that, I'm married to my job these days," she says, her hand coming to rest on my forearm, before she snatches it back. "It's what I love, it fulfils me. I don't need anything else."

But does it?

I'm not convinced.

I focus on where her hand touched my skin, jolts of electricity travelling up into my body.

"That doesn't seem very balanced," I say, trying to concentrate.

"Maybe not to you, but to me. I'm not someone who will be fulfilled staying at home raising kids while my husband goes out to work. The FHG is my child, as it was my father's and grandfather's before me. There's not much room for anything else."

"They had families, a life outside of the office," I say, as we hit the jetty.

She turns her head and smiles, her eyebrow quirked.

"Not to sound sexist, but it was different for them."

"How?"

"Grandpa had Grandma, Dad had Mum. It's the same way, Gabriel has Leah. Their partners were, and are happy to stay at home and raise the kids and for their husbands to go to work."

"Leah still works. Pen says she's going to continue working," I say.

Kat turns her head.

"Leah is working part time until the twins arrive, then she'll have to stop, and I'm happy for her. Being a mum is her dream. As for Pen, Eli is selling Frazer Cyber Security for a career change, which will see him working from home."

"There are child minders, nannies," I say. "Maybe your husband would want to stay at home?"

She frowns.

"Why would I bring a child into the world to never be there for it? I work crazy hours, and I'm always travelling. Any child would end up thinking their nanny is their mother." She pauses. "As I said, my job is my baby. FHG is all-consuming."

"Okay, no kids," I say, realising I've hit a sore point. "But what about a life partner?"

She stops, before turning to stare at me wide-eyed, her eyebrows raised almost to her hairline.

"You seem very interested in my personal life."

I shrug. "I'm trying to understand the woman you've become."

Kat continues walking.

"I have yet to meet a man who can accept or handle my success," she says. "Unless I meet someone who can accept me for who I am, then I'd rather be on my own."

Did Zach have an issue with her success? Has she tried dating other men?

In his letter, he insinuated she was never at home, was married to her job. He used it as part of his excuse as to why he ended up in bed with Darra. There were so many excuses.

You never loved me, it was always him. I'm sorry I ruined that for you.

A sharp pain spears my chest as Zach's words echo around my head.

I remember Pen joking about how men found her success intimidating.

Is Kat the same?

"Aren't you lonely?"

I know I'm entering dangerous territory. How are you going to feel if she tells you she has a string of lovers waiting on the sideline?

We stop on the jetty and look down into the water below. We watch a stingray trying to bury itself in the sand beneath us. Brightly coloured fish are swimming around it.

"Are you?" she asks, turning my question back at me.

"Yes," I admit honestly. Kat raises her eyebrows.

Splitting my life between London and New York has made holding down a long-term relationship difficult, if not impossible.

"I hate the thought of growing old on my own, not having someone to share life's adventures with."

I think back to Mary and Philip, and their fifty years of shared memories.

Kat wraps her arms around her stomach.

"I'm not alone. I have my family, friends, nieces and nephews, my staff."

"That's not the same, and you know it," I say. "What about intimacy? Physical need? You can't get that from those people."

Kat stays silent as we continue our walk back to the villa. She unlocks the door, pushing it open. I follow her inside and watch as she drops her bag onto the cot bed.

"True," she says, turning to face me, her arms folded over her chest. "But with *intimacy* comes trust." She sighs. "If I get it wrong, I might find my face plastered all over the tabloids.

A one-night stand and I'm easy, if I get into a relationship, someone has defrosted the *ice* queen."

Trust.

My stomach constricts.

I'm part of the reason Kat no longer trusts. Zach and me. Even Danny. Every man she's dated has done something to shatter her trust.

Kat sits on the sofa and drops her head against the back before closing her eyes.

"Maybe I could hire myself a male escort," she says suddenly.

"What?" I squeak, my pitch higher than I intend.

"Got you," she says, her head now up, her eyes sparkling with mischief.

"Your brothers would have a fit," I say, dropping into the chair opposite.

"How would they find out? They never found out about you. We were dating and sleeping together for months."

The memory of Kat and me together has blood flowing south, and I shift uncomfortably in my seat. She has a point, and that thought sits badly with me. Kat was very good at keeping her private life private, even from her family.

"I'm going for a swim."

I stand up, suddenly needing to put some distance between us.

"What a great idea. Mind if I join you?"

I stifle a groan.

The last thing I need is Kat in a bikini, or anywhere near me, for that matter.

"It's a free country," I say, walking into the bathroom.

Kat's laughter follows me, and it's then that I realise she's teasing me, something I'm not used to.

I turn to find Kat leaning against the doorframe.

"Sorry, that was cruel," she says, trying to contain her glee.

I scowl.

"Come on." Her smile spreads, her eyes twinkling. "You should have seen the look on your face."

My shoulders relax.

"Ha, Ha, very *un*funny."

"It was just a little bit." She holds up her thumb and forefinger with a tiny gap between them.

I shake my head and grab my swim shorts, heading to the toilet cubicle. In my current state, I don't need to be getting undressed in front of Kat.

I shut the door and lean back, realising this is the first time in a very long time that I've seen or heard Kat let her hair down, and I like it… Maybe just a little too much.

CHAPTER 27

KAT

I watch him disappear into the toilet cubicle, the only place in this villa that offers a semblance of privacy, and I drop the side of my head onto the doorframe.

I sigh.

That was cruel.

But I couldn't help myself. Being around Jaxson is doing strange things to my equilibrium, and his questions were becoming increasingly personal. The more time we spend together, the more I find myself caught up in unwelcome memories. Memories that have left me more than a little hot and bothered, not to mention incredibly horny.

Intimacy. Hell yes, I miss it. But it comes with a price.

Three years with only battery-operated toys to sustain me. I was tempted to track Zach down after Caleb and April's wedding. Thank goodness I refrained.

I close my eyes for a second and inhale. Yes, I miss coming home to someone, the warmth of a hard body pressing me into the bed.

I sigh.

If only I had one.

My nickname *The Ice Queen,* is not for nothing.

Being strong-willed, persistent and extremely industrious in business, has gained me the title of queen of the hotel industry. In my private life, however, I've been deemed as *distant, with an icy exterior.*

It's amazing how the expectation after a single expensive meal and a semi-expensive bottle of wine is full access to my body. It's called stress relief, apparently.

I may be thirty-five, but I still want to feel something for the man I let between my thighs. There's no shame in having one-night stands, they just aren't my thing.

I push off the doorframe and head towards the wardrobe, grabbing my bikini as I go. Jax comes out, his swim shorts in place, his smooth chest is bare. I swallow hard, darting in behind him.

"Won't be a moment," I say.

"No rush. This is a semi-holiday after all, and we've worked hard all morning."

I close my eyes for a second, inhaling deeply.

What the hell is going on?

Forty-eight hours ago, I could quite easily have murdered the man. Now… now I don't know what I want. All I know is I've seen far too much of Jax's naked body recently, and it's playing havoc with my emotional and mental state.

I pull on my bikini and tie a sarong around my waist.

I step out onto the terrace and watch as Jax twists and turns, trying to apply sunscreen to his back and shoulders.

"Here," I say, before I can stop myself.

Old habits die hard, and it's something we all did for one another during those summers. Mum was a stickler. She wanted no burnt teenagers.

I pick up the bottle and add a generous blob to my hand. I pause, suddenly realising what I'm about to do.

I suck in a silent breath and place my hands on his back.

Electricity shoots south, almost knocking me backwards. I stifle a groan as my core contracts violently.

Jax has frozen under my hands.

I rub in the cream carefully, enjoying the feel of his taut skin under my hands. My eyes trace the intricate design of the tattoo that covers his left shoulder and bicep, while my hands enjoy their journey over his broad, smooth shoulders down to his tight, ripped waist.

"All done," I say, rubbing what's left on my hands into my skin.

"Turn around," Jax orders, his voice a little deeper than usual. I can't meet his gaze, instead, I do as I'm told, for once.

When his hands touch my skin, I jump.

"That's cold," I squeak, although it's not the cold and definitely the man who's got my bikini bottoms in a twist.

I bite the inside of my lip as he takes his *sweet* time, applying sun lotion to my skin.

By the time he's finished, I'm nothing more than a soaking wet mess.

I turn in a daze, only to find Jax moving away, although not before I spot the enormous tent he's sporting in his swim shorts.

"See you in the water," he mumbles, practically sprinting for the steps.

"Yeah, see you in there."

I head back inside and grab a drink of water, rubbing the ice-cold bottle against my fevered forehead.

Oh heavens... Come on, Kat, this is Jax. Suck it up!

I put the bottle back on the side and make my way outside. I reach the steps and look down. Jax is nowhere in sight.

"Over here."

I look up to see Jax treading water off the side of the reef.

I turn and climb down the ladder into the water, carefully

navigating my way towards him. When I finally step off and into the deeper water, my breath hitches. The water is warm, but different to the air.

"Your body will get used to it once you start moving."

"I know," I say, following him as he begins a leisurely swim.

"Do you still swim daily?" Jax asks.

"No. I'm more of a runner these days. It's easier to fit in. I can run on the treadmill, or when I was living at the apartment, I would run to work and back. Get showered at either end. How about you?"

"Daily," he says. "Can't break the habit of a lifetime."

"Do you miss it?"

"What?"

"The competitions, the competitive nature?"

He stops for a moment, treading water, as if thinking how to answer.

"I did, when I first moved to the US. I missed training with Eli, Zach and the rest of the team." He pauses after Zach's name. "But then learning from Dillon Myers took over. I shifted my focus. I never lost that competitive drive, just redirected it towards something new."

I can understand where he's coming from.

I played piano to a professional level, was invited to play as a soloist with the London Philharmonic Orchestra. But, like Jax, my focus shifted. It became all about learning how to run the hotels, what I would need to know before I could take over from my father one day. I thought I'd have years of learning alongside him, but that was stolen from us. Then it was down to me to hold it all together.

Jax ups the pace, but not enough to leave me behind. We swim once around the island. My arm muscles are screaming by the time I haul myself out of the water.

I slip, only to have Jax grip my waist, pulling me back against his chest.

"Careful," he cautions, his breath tickling my ear. My nipples pebble, and I bite my lip to stop myself sinking further into his arms. Grabbing the handrail, I pull myself up and forward, using all my leftover strength to haul myself up the ladder and onto the decking.

I make my way over to one of the sun loungers and grab a towel, wrapping it tightly around myself.

Jax joins me, grabbing his own towel, encircling his waist.

"Nothing like sea swimming," he mumbles.

"Invigorating," I say.

"Do you want to use the shower first?"

"It's fine, you can go first. I'll just sit here and watch the water."

Watch the water?

I drop down onto the nearest sun lounger, facing away from the bathroom and stare out to sea.

Jax pauses for a moment, and I wonder if he's about to say something. I look up, but he's already turning away and walking inside.

CHAPTER 28

JAX

I rest my palms against the shower wall and drop my head forward.

What the hell just happened?

My body is still pulsing from the feel of her semi-naked body pressed against mine, not to mention the memory of my hands on her skin, rubbing in the sunscreen, or her hands sliding over my back. My cheek still throbs where I was forced to bite down hard, to stop myself groaning.

I take my time showering, pulling myself back into the here and now, all I can think about is Kat, sitting stretched out on the sun lounger in next to no clothing. Her silky smooth skin, her tight ass, her endless, toned legs.

I moan, sinking my head under the spray.

When I'm done, I turn to the window. She's still sitting with her back to me. I sigh and pull on my clothes.

"All yours," I say through the open door.

She swings her legs onto the floor and stands up. My gaze travels up her legs to perfectly toned thighs. My eyes travel higher over her flat stomach to her pert breasts. I swallow before my eyes meet hers. She's stopped. Her cheeks flushed, her breathing uneven.

"I won't be long," she says, squeezing past me.

"No rush," I say.

She pauses, but obviously thinks better of whatever she's going to say.

"As I said, I won't be long."

I continue into our bedroom. *Our bedroom.*

I've got used to the sound of her gentle breathing over the past couple of nights, how the bed dips when she turns over despite the wall of pillows between us.

Today was a turning point. Something changed between us. What that means going forward, I don't know. But when she talked about hiring a male escort, I stopped myself from growling. A bitter taste rises in my mouth at the thought of someone, anyone touching her.

Kat reappears in record time, her hand at her ear as she clips in her diamond earrings.

"Ready?" I ask

"Absolutely. I'm starving."

She smiles, and I return it with one of my own. She's been smiling a lot more recently.

I move to the door and hold it open for her. She steps through.

I offer her my arm automatically. She catches my gaze, sliding her hand through mine, her touch electrifying.

We continue in silence.

Kat stops, looking down at the reef sharks that frequent the jetty at this time of night.

They twist and turn, swimming over and under one another.

An audience of guests has formed.

Kat turns and watches the sunset behind us.

"It's so peaceful," she says wistfully.

"It is," I agree. "A lot more peaceful than central London or New York."

Kat chuckles. "Anywhere is more peaceful than central London."

She slides her arm back through mine, stepping into my side as we make our way to the outside restaurant.

The head waiter shows us to our table before taking our drink order.

"Penny for your thoughts," I say after a while.

Kat looks up and smiles.

"I was just thinking how different it is here. The hotels in London and the other major cities are full of sightseers and business people. This is somewhere to come and relax, chill out. FHG has so many branches. Corporate and holiday, they cater to very different clientele, but can attract the same. Business guests should be encouraged to take their vacations where they can relax or partake in a sport, we need to give them options."

Kat's eyebrows furrow.

"Why are you laughing?"

"Do you ever stop, slow down or switch off?"

She drops back in her chair and crosses her arms over her chest.

I hold up a hand.

"It's not a criticism, I mean… Don't you ever simply let go and relax?"

She inclines her head.

"I'm not sure I know how to anymore," she admits. "Do you?"

Our eyes lock, and I see sadness in their depth.

"A question with a question," I say. "But that's okay. And to answer your question. No, I didn't know how to." I lean forward. "Until recently, I was exactly like you, all about work, I never delegated, I was involved in every project, no matter how big or small."

"What changed?"

"Dillon got sick, and it forced me to re-evaluate. I realised I was heading for burnout. I was getting less and less sleep, answering calls at all times of the day and night. Flying to the next emergency or meeting."

Kat inclines her head. "I'm guessing there's more."

"I got the flu. Simple as that. It knocked me on my ass. I mean, I was completely bedridden for two weeks, and then needed another week to recover."

Kat's eyes raise.

I smile.

"When I finally came back, three weeks later. I realised the company hadn't crumbled in my absence. The men and women I employ had kept the cogs turning beautifully. All my clients were happy. They even sang the praises of the teams in my absence."

"You just stepped back?" Her tone is incredulous.

I grin. "It wasn't quite that easy."

Kat laughs, the sound warming me from the inside. "I can imagine."

"But I have begun delegating. While I was working on Caleb and April's plans for Lofton House, I handed over the reins."

"And?"

"It still didn't fall apart."

"Is that why you're here?"

"Partly," I admit. "I needed to see if it was a fluke."

"What's the other reason?"

"Your project is fascinating, and I want to be part of it."

Kat's eyes drop to the table.

"I need it to work," she admits. "It was the last proposal I gave Dad before…"

I place a hand over hers, giving it a squeeze.

Her eyes meet mine, and she turns her hand over, squeezing back.

"What we have done over the past few days," she sighs. "The board and our investors are going to love it. Thank you."

A figure appears next to our table.

Kat withdraws her hand, sliding it into her lap.

"Mr Baskin," she says.

"Ms Frazer. I just wanted to let you know that your belongings have all been moved." He places a keycard on the table, and my heart stutters.

"Thank you."

He smiles widely. "Is there anything else I can get you?"

"No, you've been very kind. Please thank the team."

"Of course."

He turns and nods in my direction. "Mr Lockwood."

"Mr Baskin," I say.

When he leaves, I turn to Kat.

"You've moved out?"

"He called earlier, while you were in the shower," she says. Her gaze is not quite meeting mine. "He let me know the villa is ready. That they'd move my belongings while we're at dinner."

"You didn't say anything."

"Does it matter? You're getting your villa back."

Something in my chest squeezes as my stomach drops.

Does it? Matter?

There I was thinking we'd made progress.

Kat straightens her knife and fork. I focus on the movement, so I don't say something I might regret.

Kat looks up, her hand moving to her chain, twisting and sliding her pendant up and down.

She smiles, but it doesn't quite reach her eyes. "You

should be happy. You get the bed and bathroom all to yourself. No more tripping over that damned daybed."

My eyes lock with hers.

I shrug.

"Fine," I say.

Kat leans back and crosses her arms over her chest.

"Is there a problem?"

Not, what the hell is your problem, Jax?

"No problem." I force a smile. "It's just a surprise. I didn't think it was going to be ready quite so soon," I say with a shrug.

Stay cool, calm. Is it a problem?

If she can't see it, then I'm not going to point it out to her.

Something flashes through her eyes. But it's gone before I can decipher it.

Before either of us can say anything else, our waiter appears to take our order.

CHAPTER 29

KAT

*T*he rest of dinner is held in silence.

I would have thought he'd be happy to have his space back.

I know I need it.

Being around Jax is confusing and becoming more so by the day. I came away to clear my head, but instead I've found it filled with memories and unwelcome feelings.

"Good night then," I say, when we've finished.

"I'll walk you back to your villa," he says. "Make sure you can get in okay."

Always the gentleman.

I bite my tongue to tell him I'm more than capable, but stop myself.

"Thank you."

Jax's head shoots up as if my answer surprised him.

I bite my lip.

He holds out a hand to let me lead the way. No arm offered this time.

We walk down the sand roadway to the end of the island, where the villa is situated. The path is lit by solar lights along the sides. Geckos and other creatures run for cover as we pass.

My villa is the furthest away, at the tip of the island.

"This is me," I say, tapping my keycard against the gate lock. It flashes green.

It opens, and we both step through.

Inside the small secluded garden, has been tidied up. The small plunge pool has been cleared of all the debris. Next to it is the round daybed, washed and clean with an enormous umbrella.

I walk towards the villa. It has two bedrooms, one upstairs and one downstairs.

The door light clicks green as I touch the card to it.

"Thank you," I say to Jax, who's stood behind me, his eyes taking in our surroundings.

"You're welcome," he says.

His eyes meet mine, and an awkward silence passes between us. He opens his mouth but closes it again.

"Goodnight, Kat."

He turns and walks away.

I don't move until the gate closes behind him.

As promised, all my belongings have been placed in the walk-in wardrobe. I move into the master bedroom. An enormous double bed sits in the centre of the room. A TV in the corner. A large double glass door looks out over the beach and sea, beyond the hedge.

I move to the bathroom. A large bright space. The walk-in shower overlooks the garden, although it's concealed from view. A double sink unit has pride of place, with a concealed toilet area for privacy.

My toiletries are all on the side waiting for me.

I prepare for bed, the silence deafening.

I pull open the double doors. The sound of the water lapping on the shore is comforting.

Outside on a veranda, a sofa is covered in plush cushions. I take a seat in the dark, drawing my knees up, watching the moonlight shimmer across the water. My mind drifts back to my conversation with Jax before Mr Baskin interrupted, how he was allowing himself to take a step back. How I wanted to open up and share my thoughts and dreams for the project. How I'd shared that dream with only my father before.

I close my eyes and exhale deeply.

Jax has that effect on me, he always has. I shared more with him in the few months we were together than I've ever shared with anyone else, including Zach.

My eyes grow heavy as the sound of the lapping sea soothes my racing mind. I drag myself into bed, dropping onto the mattress and forcing my mind to rest.

* * *

I WAKE up to an eerie silence. In Jax's villa, you could hear people moving around outside, making their way to breakfast, or heading back to their villa. This morning, there's nothing.

I throw back the covers and get ready for breakfast. I head to the main restaurant.

"Has Mr Lockwood been in for breakfast yet?" I ask one of the servers.

"Yes, Mam. He was in earlier. I think he was heading out on one of the boat trips."

I force a smile, a sudden heaviness weighing down my body.

"Of course, thank you."

Damn, I wanted to apologise. I should've told him straight away after Mr Baskin called. Let him know I was moving out. It's not like I had a choice.

Why hadn't I?

I pinch the bridge of my nose to stem the headache that is beginning to form behind my eyes.

Yesterday was the first time I'd felt connected to someone in a long time. We discussed business in the morning, bounced ideas off one another, discussed plans, and then by the afternoon, we were talking... like old friends.

Then, by the end of the evening, we'd taken a thousand steps backwards, and it was all my fault.

Holding people at arm's length, not letting anyone close to me, has been my modus operandi for as long as I can remember. Self-preservation is hard-wired into my DNA. The only person who it's ever changed around, is Jax. All those years ago, he had a knack for getting me to open up and confide in him. It's why it hurt so much when I thought he betrayed me.

With Zach, it was different. We started out as friends, but never truly progressed past that. We were lovers, lived together, but there was never any real connection.

I sit back and pick up my coffee, staring out over the sand. He never questioned or challenged me, demanded anything of me.

I stare down at the dark liquid.

All those years, we simply co-existed. But after Jax, I locked my emotions away. I wasn't capable of giving Zach what he wanted or needed. Is it surprising he turned to Darra? Allowed himself to be manipulated.

What a mess!

I get up and grab a pastry from the pastry counter, returning to my table. Another coffee is waiting for me, along with a bottle of water.

I cut the pastry up into quarters, the same way Jax did, popping the first slice into my mouth. I stifle a groan. These really are good.

Several guests walk by, greeting me. I smile, my perfected CEO smile, before picking up another slice and tucking in.

The flavours explode on my tongue.

The pastry chef is first class.

Mr Baskin arrives at my table, just as I'm about to take another bite.

"Good morning, Ms Frazer, how was your night? I hope everything in the villa was to your liking."

I force a smile. "It was perfect, thank you."

"Do let me know if there's anything else you need. Your return flight is booked for Friday, am I right?"

"Yes," I say.

"Good, good."

He moves to turn away.

"Mr Baskin. I would like to meet the pastry chefs," I say. "Actually, I'd like to meet all the chefs."

He spins around, colour draining from his cheeks.

"Is everything okay? Is there a problem?" His shoulders stiffen.

Crap, am I really that scary?

"Not at all, I wanted to compliment them."

His shoulders relax, and his face brightens.

"Of course, of course." He looks down at his watch. "The kitchen closes in thirty minutes. We can visit them then."

I go to open my mouth and tell him that's not necessary, but he's already disappeared.

I finish my pastry and grab some fruit. The waiters clear up around me until Mr Baskin reappears.

I follow him through the back and into the kitchen. The staff are all standing in a line, hot and flustered. *Damn*, being forced face-to-face with the CEO after a long shift, what was I thinking?

I go down the line and shake each of their hands.

"I just wanted to compliment you all on the job

you're doing," I say. "It's easy for management to only pass on complaints, but I also like to say, congratulations and well done when it's deserved. I've spoken to a lot of guests during my stay, and everyone has said the same thing, and it's all been positive. Keep up the good work."

"Thank you, Mam," one of the chefs says. He's older and looks to be the one in charge. "Would you like a tour?"

"You're welcome, and I'd love one, if it's not too much trouble."

The staff jump into action, their tense muscles relaxing. Mr Baskin stands hovering like an expectant father, and glows as if he's the one being praised.

I spend the next thirty minutes learning the intricacies of running an island kitchen, from orders to supplies.

When I finally leave, I've made copious notes.

"Thank you," I say to Mr Baskin as we part ways.

"Can I get you another coffee, Mam?" one of the waiters from the bar asks.

I look over and smile.

"An iced coffee to go would be lovely," I say.

"Would you like to wait for it outside?"

The waiter points to a seating area under some trees.

"Thank you."

He nods and steps away.

I get up and make my way over to the seats. Several couples have taken up residence around me. Some old, some young, but all clearly together.

A pressure builds inside my chest as I look around. Everyone looks happy, so relaxed and loved up.

Am I capable of love?

I'm a control freak. Past experiences have meant I've built up numerous walls to protect myself.

My coffee arrives.

I get up needing to put space between myself and everyone else.

Jax has been my buffer to all of this, has held my attention. But today he's not here.

Whose fault is that?

I'm back to being alone.

I take my coffee and walk along the beach towards my isolated villa. I enter through the garden and sit on the same sofa I sat on last night.

I pull up my phone and check my emails.

Several queries from various hotels, some reports on business and planned changes. I read through them, but I find my brain is wandering. All work… my family must have decided to leave me alone.

Yesterday, Jax spoke of intimacy, and it's like my brain won't let go.

I've isolated myself.

Shut myself off from everyone.

When Zach proposed, I knew it was wrong. I turned him down, and he left. It should have happened years earlier, but after Dad died, I threw myself into FHG, proving that I was capable of taking over from Dad. It was all-consuming. And at the end of each day, Zach was just there, waiting for me when I got home. I was so tired that I'd eat dinner and fall into bed. There were no couple-type discussions about how our days had gone. It was more like living with a sibling than a lover. Even the physical side had died off by the end.

I draw my knees up to my chest and rest my chin on them.

Gabriel's face flashes up in my mind, his joy when Leah gave birth to Callum, how excited he is about the twins. Caleb's face when he married April. I've never seen my brothers look so content. Now there's Elijah with my best friend. The way he looks at Pen and vice versa.

My heart thuds slowly in my chest, and my head spins.

This was supposed to be a break to help me make sense of the past.

Now I'm starting to question everything. Feel things I thought were long dead.

I get up and grab my laptop.

I log in, open messages from Michael and some of the other board members, then revisit the reports and make notes.

CHAPTER 30

JAX

I enter a silent villa. The hair on the back of my neck is prickling. Something feels off.

The cot bed has been removed. Everything has been freshened up, there's even a fresh bowl of fruit on the sideboard. Kat has been erased, as if she were never here.

I glance at my watch. It's nearly seven.

It was a full-day trip, island hopping, and just what the doctor ordered.

The last five days with Kathryn Frazer have been an emotional rollercoaster, exhilarating yet terrifying. The woman ties me up in knots. All the years I've spent desensitising myself to her have disappeared almost overnight. Yet I haven't felt this alive in sixteen years.

I'm treading on dangerous ground.

I wander out onto the terrace and sit down on one of the sun loungers.

Leaning down, I pick up the paperback Kat was reading.

I smirk when I see the semi-naked man on the cover.

Flicking through the pages, I skim read the story as I go.

Well, well. Kat Frazer, romance reader. Who would've known?

The thought of Kat reading these words and imagining this story makes me instantly hard. I close the book and lean back, inhaling the sea air, trying to get a grip on my emotions.

***

THE SUN HAS SET by the time I make my way across the island. I reach Kat's villa and press the bell next to the gate. It rings, but there's no answer.

Shit, she's probably still at dinner.

I glance down at the book in my hand.

I'd hate to deprive her of her reading material.

I follow the path around the side of the villa and head towards the beach, where a small gate leads into the garden.

Continuing along the path, I reach the main entrance, where I place the book in front of the door.

Behind me, the gate opens and shuts with a bang. I turn in time to see Kat jump at the sight of me, her hand going to her chest.

"Shit, Jax. What the hell? You scared the life out of me."

"Sorry, I came to return this."

I pick up the book.

She raises an eyebrow, and I swear her cheeks darken.

"Oh, er, thanks."

I grin.

"Very informative reading," I say. "I didn't know you were into vampires and shifters. That's some kinky—"

Kat comes over and reaches for the book in my hand.

I hold it out of her reach and above my head.

"How old are you?" she asks scowling.

"I'm nearly thirty-seven," I say.

She rolls her eyes. "That was a rhetorical question," she says, finally grasping the book and pulling it out of my grip.

"I know," I say, grinning. "How was dinner?"

"Good," she says, her tone non-committal. "How was your day trip?"

My heart leaps, and I bite the inside of my cheek to stop my smirk.

She knows I left the island.

"It was good," I say. "Different, seeing how the locals live. We also went manta ray and shark spotting, snorkelling off another reef."

"A full day."

She turns and places the book on the table.

"Thank you for bringing it back. I wondered where it had gone."

"It was under the sun lounger outside."

Kat nods, her gaze not quite meeting mine.

There's a pause before Kat looks up. "Would you like a drink?"

I should probably say no, go back to my room, but now I'm here, with her. I find myself wanting to stay.

"That would be great."

Kat moves past me, and the citrus, and vanilla notes of her Dior perfume invade my senses. I realise now, I missed that smell when I returned to the villa this evening, as I have done over the years.

"Wine?"

I snap myself into the present.

"Please," I say, moving to one side and taking a seat on the edge of the daybed.

"I'll be right back."

Kat disappears inside, returning almost immediately with a bottle of red wine, two glasses and a corkscrew.

She places the glasses down, and I relieve her of the bottle and corkscrew.

I stare down at the label.

"It's one of Tristan's," she says. "He's one of our main suppliers."

Tristan's business has gone from strength to strength. From one wine bar to six across London, he's even looking at opening a club. His distribution business, however, is where he's currently making his money.

"Last time I saw him, he said it was in the pipeline."

I remove the foil from the top of the bottle before using the corkscrew to lever the cork out. It comes with a pop.

I look up to find Kat watching me. She motions to the table and the glasses.

I half fill each before passing one to Kat.

Our fingers brush as she takes it, tingles of electricity snaking up my arm at the connection. Her pupils dilate at the contact, and something inside me shifts.

I'm not the only one affected.

"Thank you."

We clink glasses, and I swirl the wine around the glass.

"This is one of my favourites," I say, raising the glass to my nose and inhaling the bouquet.

"Mine too," Kat says, taking a sip.

There's another pause.

Kat motions to the daybed, and we both sit down.

I take a sip of my wine, allowing the taste to explode on my tongue.

We sit in silence for a moment.

"I know I've apologised a lot this week, but I'm sorry I didn't get you involved from the beginning. Caleb is right, you and your company are the best qualified to work with us on the project."

I stay silent.

"I don't usually let my personal life get in the way of my business decisions, but—"

"Where I'm concerned, you can't help it."

I turn. Kat is watching me over the top of her glass.

"No," she admits, surprising me.

Her lip curls and her nose wrinkles. "I shall have to thank Caleb for making me see sense."

I chuckle. "Leave him to stew. He'll hate not knowing if his meddling was successful."

Kat's eyes widen, and she lets out a bark.

"I still can't believe you *believed* him?"

"I admit, I was a little surprised, but often desperate times."

"When did you realise?"

"After I read the brief. Everything in it told me this was your baby." She turns, her eyes locking on mine. "Michael confirmed my suspicions when I called to speak to someone about my questions. That's when I confronted Caleb, and he confessed to being a little free and easy with the truth."

"Why go to all this trouble? Why follow me here?"

"Your dad spoke to me about it," I admit.

Kat's eyes fly to mine. "What? When?"

"About a year before he died. He told me about your idea for a fully sustainable hotel. Asked my opinion."

Kat inclines her head. "It doesn't surprise me. He was sceptical," she admits.

"He was, but only because he knew the technology was not where it needed to be."

"He was right."

"We talked a lot about possibilities, for when the technology caught up."

"And it has," she says slightly wistfully.

"As it always does. Where there's a need, someone will always find a way."

We sit in silence, drinking our wine and listening to the waves lapping on the shore. A gecko chirps from somewhere nearby. I grab the bottle of wine from the table and top up both our glasses.

Kat sighs. "It's so peaceful here. I can finally think."

She turns her head and chuckles, as if shocked by her own words.

"Is that why you came? To think?" I ask.

"Yes. The past two and a half months have been like being caught in the eye of a storm. Not knowing which way to turn. My brothers have been pussyfooting around me, wanting to know if I'm okay. They've nearly driven me insane. I put it to the back of my mind, and then they call, asking if I'm okay and drag it all up again."

"You've had a lot to deal with."

Her eyes lock with mine.

"Not as much as Elijah. He's been dealing with Darra for years. And as for Zach, I wonder in my heart if he suspected him deep down." She brushes a speck of invisible flint from her dress. "For me, I'm embarrassed. I let myself be manipulated by vindictive individuals, let myself be used, and that's not a nice feeling. Not when I've worked so hard at being in control of my destiny."

"I think you're being a bit hard on yourself. No one could have foreseen this. It's sick and twisted. Zach's letter was hard reading," I admit.

Kat drops her chin to her chest. "I don't think I am. I've been a coward, Jax. I ran away even to read it. It's offered me answers, excuses for the way I've behaved, but most of all, it's left me feeling empty inside."

"I wouldn't say this is running away. You've simply taken yourself out of the eye of the storm. Allowed yourself to regroup. You're not superwoman, Kat. You're allowed to hurt, to feel everything you're trying to process at the moment."

She grunts and downs the rest of her wine before refilling her glass.

"Nope, definitely not superwoman," she says, staring off into the darkness.

It's then that I realise she's serious.

"You're one of the youngest, most successful CEOs in the hotel industry. Since taking over, the FHG has won more awards and been listed as one of the top destination hotels to visit in the world."

Her lips tilt up, but she doesn't turn around.

"You can talk, Mr Entrepreneur. You also pointed out that my life is *sad*. That I have nothing else."

She gets up and moves to the edge of the plunge pool.

"Sorry, this is not meant to be a pity party," she says, scooping up her dress and sitting down, her legs dangling in the water.

She turns and faces me.

"I used to love watching you all in the pool. The camaraderie."

I move to join her. Rolling my shorts above my knees, I drop down next to her. The water is cool, refreshing against the humidity.

"The holidays were fun. Being an only child, I loved spending time with you all. My parents' divorce during my first year meant home was not a happy place. Francesca and Robert offered me an escape. They made me feel welcome."

"Mum enjoyed watching us all grow and develop. You became her adopted child. Dad was happy when she was happy."

Francesca always made us welcome, and we respected and followed her rules. I still visit her if I'm in the area and support her charity. I've even offered internships to the students she supports.

Kat gently swings her legs, sending ripples through the water.

"I'm sorry I didn't trust you," she says, turning her head, her eyes locking on mine.

I open my mouth, but close it again.

"After reading Zach's letter again." She sighs, her gaze returning to the water and her legs. "I'm truly sorry."

I set my glass aside and rest my hands on the edge of the pool, leaning forward slightly and focusing on my legs and the water.

"It hurt," I admit. "That you believed Sasha of all people over me."

I turn to face her. My stomach twists.

"Why, Kat?"

She sighs. "You know I overheard Sasha and saw the tape of you and her at the hotel. She insinuated she was worried there was someone else, someone you were trying to hide your relationship from."

I pinch the bridge of my nose hard as realisation dawns.

"And you thought that someone was you?"

Kat's features remain unchanged, although her eyes darken.

"Shit, you really thought it was a line I was using."

"Well, it would be perfect. Shag who you wanted, but tell them all to remain quiet about it."

"But surely you knew how I felt about you. More importantly, how I felt about Darra and her friends, especially Sasha. I'd told you as much."

Kat drops her chin to her chest and inhales.

"I didn't believe them initially, but then there was more and more evidence. In the end, I couldn't ignore the facts. However much I wanted to."

I rub the back of my neck, trying to ease the growing tension. "You know, Darra probably hoped you'd go running to Elijah, tell him what was going on between us. Mine and Elijah's friendship would have been over. I would have finally been out of the way."

Kat moves her hand to rest against mine. Our little fingers touching. The way we did during our time together, when the others were around. It was our thing.

Kat sighs.

"She did get her wish. You left for the States after you graduated. She isolated Elijah from everyone who cared about him."

We sit in silence, staring at the water.

"You tried to tell me it was a lie, and I wanted to believe you." Kat's voice sounds tired. "But the evidence was stacked against you. Sasha, Zach, the hotel, and then Eli."

"Elijah?"

What the hell?

"When I asked about you and women, he laughed. He told me you had a flock of admirers, that there was always a harem of women following you around… I read it as confirmation. I thought you lied to me because you were afraid of what it'd mean to your relationship with Eli."

I turn, cupping her chin, angling her head to face me.

"If that was the case, why the *fuck* would I have risked sleeping with you in the first place?" I say, inhaling. My gut tightens as I force out my breath. "God, Kat, I was in love with you. Every time we were together, I risked my friendship with Elijah, because I simply couldn't stay away from you. Why would I have jeopardised that with Sasha of all people?"

Kat closes her eyes.

"I can see that now." When she opens them again, her gaze locks on mine. "But at the time…"

"It was my word against theirs, and of course I was going to say I was innocent."

"You were my greatest weakness, Jax. I was in love with you, too. They found out and played me. Took my worst fears and used them against me. Reading Zach's letter reminded me of something my father said years ago. *Never show your true feelings, or they can be used against you.*"

"Against you? I don't—"

"My insecurities. I'd spent two years watching from the sidelines as women threw themselves at you. You were gods on campus. You, Elijah, and Zach. And there I was, socially awkward Kathryn Frazer. Insignificant little sister to the great Elijah Frazer. I couldn't keep a guy interested, even with my Frazer name. Look at Danny, he wasn't even prepared to wait a couple of months before he was off shagging my housemate. You rescued me that night, and I seduced you."

"Insignificant?" I stare at Kat wide-eyed. "You have never in your life and never will be insignificant."

She chuckles, colour riding her cheekbones. "Maybe not now."

"Not ever," I say, giving her chin a gentle shake. "As for seducing me. I beg to differ."

Kat frowns as I laugh.

"Kathryn Frazer. Only you," I say. "Beautiful woman, you could not be further from the truth. I began fantasising about you from the moment I walked in on you playing piano. For two years, I watched you from afar, thinking you would never look at someone like me. When I heard you were dating Danny, I was nearly sick. That night when you called, and I got to play the knight in shining armour—"

I let go of her chin and take her hand in mine, as she raises an eyebrow.

"Dream come true," I say, grinning. "And when we kissed. It took all my willpower to only touch you, not bury myself deep in your body."

Kat inhales sharply, and her pupils dilate. Her pulse beating rapidly at the base of her throat.

I look away as everything in me screams to take her in my arms.

"Later, I began to wonder if you'd been using me. I was your brother's best friend and someone to experiment with safely. You were so far out of my league."

"Out of your league?" she splutters.

I tilt my head, turning it towards her.

"I'm not exactly from the same social or economic background as you."

"And when has that bothered a Frazer?"

"Back then, Elijah was with Darra," I say.

"Ah, but he wanted to be with Pen."

I incline my head. "But he wasn't. Zach made some comment about you being destined to marry a friend of your parents, old money."

Kat's mouth opens and closes as her expression shutters. "He said a lot of things. I think we need to put aside everything he ever said and move on."

CHAPTER 31

KAT

Out of my league?

Hearing Jax put himself down knocks me sideways.

How wrong could he be? But then I've spent years building walls around myself to hide my insecurities and protect myself, enabling me to portray the strong image my position as both CEO and a Frazer entails.

I also can't deny his words, although we both know that if Darra hadn't announced her pregnancy, Eli would have been with Pen.

"I thought maybe you'd come to your senses. After all, I had nothing to offer you but a pile of student debt."

I cover one of his hands, squeezing it.

"You offered me yourself, allowed me to be me. You made me feel beautiful. Were one of the few people who didn't care about my last name, you saw past it."

He lifts his head and stares at me.

"God, Kat, I treated you like that because you were and always have been so much more than your name."

My heart skips a beat.

Manipulation and deceit.

What would have happened between us if Darra hadn't interfered? Would we have stayed together? Still be together?

My stomach repels, as it does every time I think of how Zach manipulated me, how I let him into my body.

I pull away and stand up, water trailing down my legs. I need to put some distance between us. With Jax this close, I can't think straight.

I walk through the gate and towards the sea, my arms wrapped around my waist.

My heart aches, and my throat thickens.

I stop on the shoreline, the sea lapping at my feet. I curl my toes into the sand, grounding myself.

Jax appears beside me.

"We were so young," he says quietly.

"I was young and naïve... gullible," I say eventually.

Jax moves behind me, wrapping his arms around my body, pulling me back against his chest.

"Zach's letter vindicated you of any wrongdoing," I say, turning my head and looking at him. "I'm surprised you're here talking to me after everything I've put you through. Some of the things I've said."

"The letter may have told the truth, but it doesn't make me feel any better." I can feel his heart beating in his chest. "The past is the past. We can't change it, however much we might wish we could. We can only move forward."

I spin in his arms before I realise what I'm doing, my palms flat against his broad chest. His hands are resting against my lower back.

"I'm not that forgiving," I say. "I've been horrible to you. Blamed you for something you didn't do." I rest my forehead against his chest. "I'm a logical thinker, Jax. I don't let my emotions drive me, but where you're concerned. I can't seem to help it."

The words are out before I can stop them. The stress of the last five days, of being in his company, having the past dredged up. I can no longer blame anyone but myself for the choices I've made.

Jax grips my chin and lifts my head. I try to pull away, but he holds me firm.

"Stop it," Jax says firmly. "Darra is a master manipulator. Look at what she did to Elijah, to Pen, to her own daughter. No one could escape her, as we didn't understand the rules. We were nothing more than collateral damage in the sick game she and her father were playing."

My fists clench against Jax's chest, my fingernails biting into my palms. My chest tightens.

The desire to yell, shout, scream wells up, bubbling in the pit of my stomach.

I grit my teeth and close my eyes, slowly releasing my breath.

When I open my eyes, I look up to find Jax watching me.

A fluttering sensation spreads through my chest. I shiver, despite my body growing hot and feverish.

I push up on my toes, brushing my lips against his. Coaxing, tasting.

His hand moves, gripping the back of my head, his fingers tangling in my hair, crushing me to him, deepening the kiss.

I open for him, our tongues dancing, duelling, exploring. Shudders of pleasure wrack my body, and I press my breasts against his chest. My nipples harden against the friction.

I bite down on his bottom lip before sucking it into my mouth, eliciting a moan of pleasure.

He pulls me hard against him, cupping my arse cheek, kneading it with strong fingers. His cock grows hard between us, as I roll my hips against his.

We stand on the sand, our mouths dancing, tongues duelling.

Laughter sounds in the distance, and I rip my mouth away, my breath coming hard and fast, my pounding heart making it impossible to think.

"What are we doing?" I ask, my hands resting on his shoulders, stabilising me.

"What we've both been denying ourselves, for far too long."

I grip his shoulders, loving the feel of the hard muscle beneath my hands, wanting to explore, but knowing I'm playing a dangerous game.

He's right. From the first time we kissed, I knew my life was never going to be the same. It was as if my body recognised his. We had a natural affinity, an immense bond. Nothing in my life had ever felt as right as being in Jaxson's arms. He lit a fire in my belly all those years ago, one that has continued to smoulder unchecked for the past sixteen years, and we just fanned the spark.

My hands curl over his shoulders and behind his neck, finding the short hair there.

He drops his forehead to mine, his dark eyes questioning.

"What do you want, Kat?"

I bite the inside of my mouth. What I *want* is not up for debate.

I withdraw my hands and push away, putting some distance between us, before wrapping my arms around my waist.

Jax stands there, unmoving, watching me.

I drop my head back and look up at the night sky. It's clear, the stars twinkling above us, watching, waiting.

Are we written in the stars?

I inhale, exhale and right myself, my gaze returning to Jax, who still hasn't moved.

For the first time since becoming CEO, I feel lost, vulnerable.

Our eyes lock, and I see a flash of something, but it's gone before I can decipher it.

"There's another day trip tomorrow. Why don't you come with me?"

My brows furrow.

What?

He smiles.

"Spend the day with me. Be a tourist."

I open and close my mouth, focusing on the water caressing my feet.

"Okay," I say, surprising myself. "Why not?"

Jax steps forward, hands squeezing my shoulders. He smiles and steps away, before I've even registered what he's done. I miss the contact instantly.

"I'll see you at breakfast at eight. Our boat leaves at nine."

I nod my head and watch as he backs away. I'm tempted to call him back, my lips and body still throbbing, but what good would it do?

He smiles and turns as if reading my mind. I watch as he disappears around the corner and out of sight.

A day trip with Jax. More hours in his company.

We only have one more day, then it's home time. Back to reality. Maybe a day out is just what the doctor ordered. It's not like I have anything else to do.

I make my way back into the villa and pick up the paperback he returned.

I drop myself onto the daybed and begin reading.

CHAPTER 32

JAX

To say Kat surprised me last night is an understatement.

Walking away from her was the hardest thing I've ever done. It was like leaving part of my soul behind.

The fact that she's agreed to go on this trip amazed me. I was sure she'd shoot me down in flames, or cry work commitments, but here we are, walking through a local market on one of the neighbouring islands, sightseeing together and talking like *old friends*.

We make our way through the stalls and shops.

I raise an eyebrow at the carved wooden puzzle in her hand.

Kat laughs. "Gabe will love it. Besides, table presents are supposed to be something small and fun. I'll write a clue, this should drive him nuts and have him guessing for hours."

She chuckles to herself as she hands over her money, her eyes alight at the thought.

Next is a coffee coaster set for Caleb, and a set of local prints of the sunsets for Elijah.

"Caleb is always complaining about coffee stains on his

desk," she says. "As for Eli, he'll love the colours. He's always moaning about our lack of sunsets in the city."

I admit, they're a practical and well thought out gift for the men who has everything.

Next, she drags me over to a stall, draped in beautiful materials. Sarongs, sundresses, skirts.

She smiles at the woman running it, who joins us instantly.

"These are beautiful," Kat says.

The older woman glows under her praise.

Kat strikes up a conversation with her, learning that she and her daughter make the products.

By the time they've finished talking, Kat has purchased a multitude of skirts, dresses and sarongs, all of which have been folded, wrapped and placed beautifully in a bag.

Kat turns to me. "That's everyone," she says, letting out a deep breath, her eyes alight with happiness.

"Can you help me choose something for Mum?" I ask, not wanting that positive energy to disappear. She's glowing, and I want to keep that for as long as possible.

"Of course. What do you think she'd like?"

I end up purchasing a hand-embroidered sarong-style dress for Mum and some coasters for Peter and Dad.

It's late by the time we make it back to the boat. All the other guests are there, drinking Champagne and eating nibbles.

We take our seats on the open deck, enjoying the last of the day's sunshine.

"Thank you for today," she whispers, her fingers touching mine on the seat. She closes her eyes and drops her head back. "This has been perfect."

"You're welcome," I say quietly. "Thank you for agreeing to spend the day with me."

The boat heads out into open water, and we watch as the

sun begins its descent over the horizon. The sky dims from bright yellow to a deeper gold, then shifts to deeper pinks, purples, and oranges as it finally disappears from view.

When she turns her head, her eyes lock on mine, and I want nothing more than to take her in my arms and kiss her, until we're both breathless with need. But I refrain. Instead, I survive on the flashbacks of last night, her body pressed against mine, our lips fused together.

Kat offers me a slow smile, as if she knows what I'm thinking. I choke down my groan and shift uncomfortably. My body is not getting the memo of time and place.

The boat docks, and I climb onto the jetty and hold out a hand. Kat places hers in mine, the hairs on my arms and nape rising, as she grips it and steps onto the wooden platform.

When she lets go, my fingers ache with the need to reconnect.

We walk in silence past the brightly lit bar, making our way towards the main restaurant.

"Dinner?" I ask.

"I was thinking of ordering room service," she says, her eyes darting towards the bustling space.

My heart drops.

This is it.

Kat stops suddenly, turning to face me. "Would you care to join me?"

I'm slightly ahead, so I turn to face her.

"Join you?"

"With room service. I'm not sure I can face the restaurant."

I get it. She was approached on more than one occasion today by couples who told her what an amazing time they're having. Every time it happened, she neither huffed nor cut anyone off. Instead, she stopped and smiled, asking each of them a question about their trip, where they were from, and how long they were staying. She showed the same amount of interest in the first person as she did the last.

"I'd like that," I say, finding I don't want today to end.

"Excellent," she says, her lips tilting up.

We turn to leave.

"Ms Frazer."

Don Baskin takes that moment to approach, and I stifle a groan.

Her muscles lock, her eyes close briefly.

I want to shout "Leave her alone," but I hold my counsel.

"Ms Frazer," he says again.

Kat opens her eyes, forcing her shoulders to relax as she plasters on a smile, turning to face the man wanting her attention.

"Mr Baskin, Don. What can I help you with?"

CEO Kat is back in place.

He comes to stand next to us. "Mr Lockwood," he says, acknowledging me with a smile before returning his attention to Kat. "How was your trip?"

"It was amazing. I'm glad Jax convinced me to take it. You live in a wonderful part of the world."

His cheeks darken.

"I won't keep you. I just wanted to say, thank you," he says suddenly. "I've just had confirmation that the sea breaks are being rebuilt in the next couple of weeks, which is a minor miracle. I don't know how you managed to pull it off. The new beds are being shipped over and should arrive any day. The wine cellar has been fully stocked. Not to mention having you visit has been a real boost for the staff. They feel they're finally being heard."

Her mouth drops open slightly, a tentative smile building as his words sink in.

"Thank you."

She holds out her hand, which he shakes with enthusiasm. "I'm glad my visit has been productive. Customer and staff satisfaction is something we take very seriously at The Frazer Group."

Mr Baskin inclines his head and smiles. The first genuine smile I think he's offered.

I don't blame the man. It's scary when the big boss comes knocking.

"No, Ms Frazer. This is all you. The industry talks. Your reputation is one of the best. I can see why."

Kat's shoulders relax, the tension leaving her body. She smiles, this one reaching her eyes.

"I try my hardest," she says.

"It means a lot that you, the CEO, visited us. Have taken our concerns and needs seriously. It's not usual. I just wanted you to know everyone here appreciates it."

He inclines his head, offering an almost salute. He holds out a hand to me. "It's been a pleasure meeting you, Mr Lockwood."

I shake his hand.

"You too, Mr Baskin. Don."

"Enjoy the rest of your evening."

I smile.

Resting my hand on the base of Kat's spine, I start us moving again.

Kat looks up and smiles.

"Not what I was expecting."

It's my turn to smile. "Sounds like a productive and successful day, all round."

Kat nods, pulling out her room key and tapping it to the keypad. The light flicks green.

She turns towards me, stepping back through the gateway.

"What do you fancy—"

Her eyes widen as she loses her balance and begins to fall backwards.

I react on instinct and catch her arms, pulling her hard against me.

She lands against my body with a whoosh, as the breath is knocked from her lungs.

Her hands rest against my chest, over my pounding heart.

Dark eyes look up, and I find myself drowning in their depths.

CHAPTER 33

KAT

Jax's heart thunders under my hand, our breathing coming fast and harsh. His arms lock around me.

I stare at his broad chest, my fingers flat against the material of his t-shirt. I raise my eyes, ready to thank him for saving me, but nothing comes out. Instead, I find myself drowning in his dark, smouldering gaze. Seeing my own wants and needs reflected back at me. My breath catches, and I lean in closer to his solid chest and masculine scent, an aphrodisiac to my starving body.

Jax's gaze travels over my face, my body heat rising.

The nerve endings that have been firing all day ignite all at once, pleasure flooding my body, my muscles contracting, my pussy aching with the need to be filled.

I wrap a hand around the back of his head, his grip on me tightening as I pull him forward. He resists for a split second before his lips meet mine.

Last night's kiss was breath-taking. This is something else. All rational thought leaves my body. Only sensations remain.

My back arches, pressing me against his length.

His arms wrap around me, lifting me, as he steps us through the open gate, kicking it shut with his foot. Our mouths continue to feast. Exploring, nipping, sucking... demanding.

Jax continues moving us into the garden. I wrap my legs around his waist, enjoying the feel of his hands as they slide up under my skirt, gripping my thighs. His cock hardens behind his shorts, pressed against my sensitive folds.

I moan into his mouth, deepening our kiss. Sucking his tongue into my mouth, his cock flexes against me, my pussy swelling with the need to be stretched and filled.

It's been too long.

My arse connects with something solid, taking my weight.

Jax rips his mouth away from mine, his lips travelling over my cheek towards my ear and down, finding the spot on my collarbone that makes me melt.

I drop my head back, giving him greater access, my hands sinking into his hair, holding him tightly, encouraging him on.

His hands slide up my thighs, pulling me forward and tight against his very hard cock. When he rocks against me, pushing against my swollen and aching pussy, my head swims, and I see stars. He does it again and again, rocking backwards and forwards, the friction of our clothes against sensitive skin driving my need higher.

I roll my hips, biting down on my lip to stop myself from crying out, begging for release.

My hands slide under his t-shirt, relishing in the feel of his taut, smooth skin against my fingertips. His muscles contract sharply, jumping as I run my fingernails lightly over his defined abs.

I push his top up, pulling it over his head and throwing it to one side.

Our eyes meet for a split second.

Hands and lips are everywhere. There's no thought tonight, only need, a need to be close, to let go and feel.

His hand disappears under my dress, fingers brushing my swollen and pulsating core. Teasing, tormenting, touching and retreating.

He pulls the straps of my dress from my shoulders, freeing my breasts to the warm night air. His mouth latches on, nipping and sucking. It pebbles beneath the onslaught of his mouth, my breath quickening as my body aches and tingles for more. One hand clutches onto his scalp, cradling him against me.

My legs widen, pressing forward into his hand. My soaked panties, moving freely against my skin.

My other hand moves to his shorts, unbuttoning them and pushing them down, allowing his cock to spring free.

His mouth moves to my other breast, as I take his hot, stiff flesh in my hand, using my thumb to smear his pre-cum over the crown. My fingers stretch around him, sliding up and down his engorged flesh, enjoying the feel of his long and pulsating dick in my hand.

He bites down on my nipple, groaning against my skin. My head falls back, making me suck in a breath.

Before I can think, I push forward, shoving my soaked panties to one side before lining him up and sliding myself onto his throbbing cock.

We both freeze.

"Jax, I—" The words splutter out.

He closes his eyes, his forehead touching mine.

My muscles contract around the tip of his cock, making him hiss.

"Kat, are you sure?"

The words are uttered through gritted teeth.

He opens his eyes. I bite my lip and nod.

His lips tilt up, and he inclines his head, brushing them against mine, before sliding his hands under my arse cheeks and thrusting into me.

I suck in a breath at the invasion. His length and girth stretch me to my limit. It's been a long time, but who am I to complain?

Jax freezes, allowing my body to accommodate him. Wave after wave of pleasure floods my system.

Jax grunts as I contract around him, his fingers digging into the skin of my ass. I grip his shoulders as we begin to move. I wrap my legs around his waist, shoving the material of the skirt of my dress out of the way, tilting my hips. Jax's eyes drop to where our bodies join, and mine follow. We watch as he pulls almost all the way out before sliding home again and again. His glistening cock, shines in the dull light, coated in my desire.

When I look up, Jax is watching me, his pupils dilated.

He presses forward, his gaze locked on mine. His thumb finds my swollen clit, pressing down and circling around. My eyes disappear up and into my head as desire rocks my body.

My fingers sink into the bare skin of his shoulders. I lean forward, my mouth and tongue tracing the intricate lines of his tattoo.

He continues to move, picking up pace.

I tighten my hold on him with my heels, spreading my thighs wider, before tilting my hips. His cock hits my g-spot, my heart rate pounding in my chest. A flush forms across my skin as my pelvic muscles begin to contract sharply.

"Fuck—" I shriek, the sound captured by Jax's mouth as it closes over mine.

He speeds up his movements, his thumb still circling my clit as I ride wave after wave, our mouths devouring each other's. He pushes my orgasm further than it has ever gone, spiralling me into a second.

Jax's breathing picks up as he slams home, his body stilling under my hands. He drops his head onto my shoulder, tremors wracking his body, his cock twitching as he comes deep inside me, his cum marking me as his.

I wrap a hand around his head, the other gripping his shoulder as we both struggle to catch our breath.

He lifts up, resting his forehead against mine, his softening cock still buried deep between my legs.

It twitches, and I bite my lip to prevent a moan escaping.

"Shit, Kat, we didn't use anything," he says, his tone apologetic.

"I have an IUD fitted," I admit, years of painful and uncontrollable periods making it a must, although I was too lost in the moment to care with the feeling of his skin, bare against mine. My muscles contract again, making Jax's eyes cross.

"I'm clean," he says. "I'm sorry."

I cup his cheek.

"Sorry for what? Not using a condom?" I tut. "I was right there with you. I could've stopped this at any time."

Jax chuckles, kissing my nose. "Always in control."

It's my turn to laugh, tightening my thighs around his waist to drive the point home. "I beg to differ. I don't think I was in control then, not my mind anyway. That was all lust and want."

Our eyes meet, his gaze tells me it was the same for him.

He steps back, his semi-hard cock glistening in the light as he withdraws from my body. His gaze trails me, pausing between my legs.

I follow his eyes.

He groans quietly at the sight, his body leaning closer. He runs a finger over my entrance, holding up the slick digit.

"Do you know how sexy you look?" he whispers next to my ear, his breath teasing my skin. "Spread out in front of me, my cum dripping out of your body?"

I bite down hard on my lip, unable to take my eyes off him as he returns his finger to my core, adding others, drawing them through the mess we've made, before sliding them up and over the swollen, sensitive lips of my pussy and slit, before pressing them deep into my body.

I suck in a breath, my sensitive muscles clutching greedily at the invasion. I spread my legs wider and lean back, resting my hands on the sink unit behind me, allowing him free access to explore my sensitive flesh. The outside bathroom offering us protection from prying eyes. I watch as his fingers disappear and reappear. He collects more of our lovemaking and pushes it back inside me.

I've never had unprotected sex before, so the feel of his cum on my skin, dripping out of my body, is new. The thought of Jax's cum deep in my body has my muscles clenching hard around his digits.

"You like that?" he asks, his voice deep and husky.

I drop my head forward and groan as he twists them, curling them against my front wall, massaging my G-spot. I spread my legs wider again, opening myself further to his gaze.

A dark flush appears high on Jax's cheekbones as he continues to play and torment my pussy, his cock hardening once more between us.

I bite my lip as my body reignites.

"Maybe we should move this inside," I gasp, my voice catching as another wave of pleasure ricochets through my core.

Jax's eyes darken, his arms sweeping around me, lifting me down. My almost naked body slides down his, and I find myself getting lost once more in the feel of his skin against mine.

Jax bends down, his lips meeting mine.

I don't know how long we stand there, but it's a while before I bend down and grab my purse from the floor, letting us both in.

We have one night before we're forced to return to reality. We need to make the most of it.

CHAPTER 34

JAX

I roll over, my hand reaching out under the covers. The bed next to me is cold and very empty.

I force my eyes open and drop onto my back, staring at the ceiling. My senses are on heightened alert, waiting for a sound, any sound.

Nothing.

Memories of the night before flood my brain, leaving me instantly hard. She's always had the ability to tie me up in knots.

Pushing up onto my elbows, I look and listen.

Silence.

I swing my feet off the bed and grab my shorts and t-shirt from where they were rapidly abandoned. Pulling them on.

I pad to the door, leading outside and open it.

Kat is sitting on the sofa in one of the hotel dressing gowns, her knees drawn up as she stares out over the beach and sea. In her hand, she nurses a steaming mug of something.

Strong coffee.

The smell hits my senses, making my taste buds water.

"Good morning," I say, stepping up next to her.

Her muscles tighten as if my presence has surprised her, and when she looks up, my stomach knots.

"Morning," she says, before inclining her head towards her coffee. "I didn't make you one as you were sleeping."

I drop into one of the cushioned chairs nearby.

"That's okay," I say, my stomach jumping, as a dullness envelops my chest.

An awkward silence settles between us.

"I have a meeting with Don in an hour. After yesterday's trip, there are a few ideas I want to run past him before we leave."

She swings her legs off the sofa, wrapping the gown more tightly around her. "I didn't want to disturb you, but I need to pack."

She turns to walk away. A chill settles in my chest, and I'm suddenly aware I'm probably not going to like what comes next.

"So that's it?" My voice is coming out huskier than I want.

She stops, but doesn't turn. Her eyes close, and she inhales, the image clear in the glass reflection of the doors in front of her.

She turns her head sideways, but her gaze doesn't meet mine.

"I think with the project and —"

"Don't *fucking* say it," I interrupt, trying hard to hold on to my anger. "I'll get out of your hair. I have my own packing to do."

I stand up and move towards the beach entrance. I don't want any of the staff members to see me leaving Kat's villa. Rumours and gossip have a nasty habit of taking hold, and I don't want last night tarnished, even if it meant nothing to Kat.

Kat grips my arm, appearing at my side. I freeze, before turning my head to look at her.

"I'm sorry," she says quietly, her brows furrowed. "I just think getting involved now would be a mistake. Last night was amazing." She pinches the bridge of her nose. "But we're about to embark on a major project together. This. Us… muddies the waters. The board—"

I harrumph. "Don't worry, princess. I get it."

"I don't think you do. I need to be impartial and independent. If not—"

"I said, I get it. Look, you're not the only one who needs to pack. I'll see you at the jetty in a couple of hours."

I gently pull my arm out of her grip and begin walking away. Each step adding additional weight to my already heavy soul.

"Jax," she calls my name.

I spin to face her. "What, Kat? What do you want from me?" I snap.

She drops her chin to her chest, shaking her head. "I want, need you to understand."

"Understand what?" I say sarcastically. "How you can fall apart in my arms one night, but the next day, you expect me to crawl back into my box and act like nothing happened?"

She opens her mouth and closes it again, so I plough on. "Forget that I have bite marks on my shoulders, or scratch marks down my back, or that my cum, even now, is dripping from your body after I filled you with it, over and over again."

Colour floods her cheeks.

"Sorry, princess, I can't turn it on and off like you apparently can."

Last night was magical. Words can't describe what it was like to kiss her lips, sink into her body. I've never felt for anyone what I feel when I'm with Kat, it's like she opens something up inside me, something no one else has been able to reach.

A painful pressure builds in my chest around my heart, as if my ribs are suddenly too tight.

"You think this is easy for me," she chokes out, her voice heavy. "I'd love to be like any other woman, but I'm not. People rely on me... It's not about my happiness."

I sigh, knowing this is one battle I'll never win.

"Keep telling yourself that," I say, my voice having lost all power. "I'm going to go."

Before she can say anything else, I turn around and walk away.

This time, she doesn't call me back.

Staring straight ahead, I exit her villa onto an empty beach, my eyes finding the temporarily repaired breakwater.

I make my way towards the jetty, alone. My eyes track the horizon and I want nothing more than to strip off my clothes, and dive into its crystal blue depths, Where I can swim until my muscles are screaming for me to stop.

I pick up my pace until I'm jogging, realising I've left my shoes at Kat's villa.

Hitting the jetty at pace, I slow only to allow the carts and other guests to pass.

"Good run?" One of the men in the neighbouring villas asks as I pass.

I nod, pausing at my door to retrieve my keycard.

I push the door open, engaging all my willpower to refrain from slamming it shut behind me.

Damn her. I thought we'd finally got somewhere.

Stripping off, I grab my swimming shorts and pull them on, before heading straight for the steps leading down to the water.

I lower myself into the calm sea, the tiny fish darting away from the steps as I descend.

Making my way across the reef, I drop off the edge, diving into the dark, colder water. As I surface, I suck in a breath as the chill cools some of the burning need to return to her villa and demand she give us a chance.

I'm a fool. It's not like she didn't warn me.

I push forward, my arms driving through the slightly stronger waves now that I'm clear of the reef, the saltwater washing away the scent of Kat that clings to me like a second skin.

CHAPTER 35

KAT

I watch Jax walk away, a knot forming in my stomach. Actually, it has been there since I woke up early this morning. I lay for what seemed like forever, watching Jax sleep.

I even reached out to sweep the lock of hair from his forehead, but stopped myself.

My chest tightens as I force more air into my lungs.

This is the right thing to do.

I slide open the door and step into the cool air of the villa, the hum of the air conditioning the only other sound.

I pull out my suitcase and throw it onto the rumpled sheets.

The room smells of us.

Of Jax's spicy cologne, my perfume, our shared desire.

I sink onto the bed and drop my head into my hands.

What the hell was I thinking?

I sit up.

I wasn't, that's the problem.

For the first time in what feels like forever, I was running on pure instinct. An instinct that draws me to Jaxson Lockwood, that has my body responding to his. Last night, my brain checked out, leaving only my pussy and hormones in charge.

I move, aware of the delicious ache between my legs. The sticky evidence coating my thighs. My skin is sensitive, where his touch brought me back to life.

Inevitable.

Yes, Jaxson and I, being together again, was inevitable.

We've spent the week working, practically living together on a remote island, both highly passionate about the work we're doing, surrounded by lovers, honeymooners. The Maldives is advertised as a destination for love, lovers.

The IUD I had fitted years ago means there'll be no unwanted consequences of our night together. When I told Jax there's no room in my life for children, I meant it.

I get up and head into the walk-in wardrobe, grabbing my clothes off their hangers.

I fold them neatly, a habit of moving from one hotel to the next.

Zach's letter falls out of my bag as I empty it of unnecessary weight.

I close my eyes and inhale, shoving it under the stack of clothes before re-straightening the corners. I'll dispose of that when I get home. I don't want to run the risk of it falling into anyone else's hands. That's the last thing my family needs. Another scandal.

I pack in record time, zipping up my case, placing it by the door.

Seeing Don was a ruse, although my mind *is* full of possibilities after yesterday's trip. A market trip, or a local market held on the island once a week. Local entertainment, the possibilities are endless.

I pick up my phone and leave myself a voice note to contact the team when I get back. Get them to talk to him about the possibilities. If I take it on, I'll never let it go, and there are other things that need my attention more.

I stop, my mind racing.

What?

Could some of what Jax has said have begun to sink in?

I laugh.

But you sent him away.

Palpitations form in my chest, my breathing becoming erratic.

I sit down and concentrate on slowing each breath.

"Get a grip, Kathryn Brooke Frazer," I say, holding my pendant to ground me.

There's no future for Jax and me, however much I may wish otherwise. I can't give him what he needs, I'm not sure I ever really could.

He wants love and a family.

I'm not sure I'm capable of that kind of love.

I'm addicted to my job, can't see past the next issue.

Then there are my brothers. He's their best friend. When I mess it up, however much they love Jax, they'll take my side.

The board and investors. I will not jeopardise this project for sex… even amazing, mind-blowing sex.

Starting something with Jax could risk everything, would risk everything. Any relationship between us would overshadow what we're trying to achieve. I just hope, over time, he'll come to see that too.

CHAPTER 36

JAX

We bid the team goodbye and make our way onto the seaplane. The engines make it impossible to talk, not that I have much to say.

As they say, actions speak louder than words, and Kat's actions this morning were pretty clear.

Last night was a one-off, never to be repeated.

I'm taking it she expects professionalism.

Well, Ms Frazer, I can give you that in bucket loads. Professional is my middle name. It's what I've built my reputation on.

We make it to the main airport and are driven to the Frazer jet.

Claudia is waiting to greet us, her smile a welcome sight.

"Ms Kathryn, Mr Jaxson, welcome on board. It's good to see you both. I hope you've enjoyed your trip. Please let me know if there is anything I can get you."

Kat greets her and heads onboard, moving to the back of the plane.

I throw my bag onto one of the chairs near the front, dropping myself down at one of the tables.

I'm too fired up to sit and make polite conversation.

I'm not sure what to say, anyway.

What do you say to the woman who, less than twelve hours ago, was screaming your name as she came hard around your cock, while riding you bareback? To all but ignoring you, hours later.

Shit.

The memory of my cock sliding in and out of Kat uncovered, her desire coating me, glistening in the light. My cum lining the walls of her pussy, dripping out of her.

I choke back the memory to stop myself from moaning.

I drop my chin to my chest and close my eyes, willing away the growing pressure building behind my eyes.

I open them to find Kat with her nose buried in her laptop. Her pendant clasped in her hand.

I exhale quietly.

Time to begin finessing my proposal. It may be two, nearly three weeks away, but I'm sure there are other things that'll need my attention once I return to reality. I've stayed off the grid since coming here, with only upper management having the ability to contact me in case of an emergency.

I check my email, and the download count is going up and up.

My gaze shifts to Kat, but she's still in the same position.

Claudia appears.

"Can I get you anything to drink before takeoff?"

I glance up and smile.

"A beer," I say.

She smiles in her usual manner. "Of course."

If she thinks anything is off, she doesn't let on, instead she moves towards Kat and asks the same question.

Kat turns her head, but her gaze skims over me. I miss what she orders, but Claudia smiles and heads back into her area.

She returns a few minutes later and places a bottle of beer and a glass next to me.

"Thank you," I say.

She moves to Kat, placing what looks to be a fruit juice in the drinks holder.

Kat looks up and smiles.

Claudia says something before she retires.

I place the beer to my lips, taking a long drag on the bottle, returning my focus to the three hundred plus emails I've amassed in my absence.

"Last night—"

"Don't you dare say it was a mistake," I snap, closing my laptop before swivelling to face her.

Kat raises an eyebrow. "I was going to say, it was inevitable. Our sexual chemistry has always been off the scale, even before everything that happened. Add the destination, our situation, our passion for the new project."

"Inevitable?" I repeat the word, seeing how it rolls around my mouth and off the tongue.

There's a definite bitterness.

"We're both passionate people, Jax. We've had a busy few days, yesterday with the trip, playing tourist. I just think it would be a mistake to take it any further. We both have a lot of commitments, things people need from us. I think—"

"Speak for yourself, Kat. Don't make your excuses mine. Fine, if last night was a onetime only fuck, so be it, but own it."

"That's what I'm trying to do," her eyes flash. "Why are you being like this?"

"Pissed?" I ask. "Difficult?"

I sigh.

What's the point?

Telling her I can't simply forget the best sex of my life makes me sound sad and desperate.

"Okay, princess, have it your way," I say. "And before you ask. Yes, I can be professional, and no, I won't tell the board, or your brothers how hard you came around my cock."

"Don't be crude."

"Not crude, factual. As I said. I'm a professional. It's how I've built up my company, made my money. You don't need to worry, I'm not willing to jeopardise that, even for you."

Silence descends between us.

"Now, if you don't mind, I've got several hundred emails to work my way through, and I want to finish the proposal."

There's an indent on Kat's lower lip where she's bitten down on it.

Her gaze locks on mine before she drags it away, returning her attention to her laptop.

I exhale softly and reopen my computer, hoping upon hope, that there's something in my emails that can distract me from the woman sitting only a few seats away.

* * *

I WAKE WITH A START.

"We'll be landing soon, Mr Jaxson."

"Thank you, Claudia," I say, straightening up and running a hand over my face.

I scan the cabin, but Kat is nowhere in sight.

Was my snoring that bad?

The door to the bedroom opens, and Kat appears looking fresh-faced.

"All yours if you want to freshen up. It's about thirty minutes until we land."

I unclip my buckle and drag myself from my seat. I'm not sure how long I've been asleep.

I made it through a chunk of my emails before deciding

I'll head Stateside tomorrow. Play it safe, and put some distance between myself and Kat... for both our sakes.

"Thanks, I will."

I brush my teeth and wash my face. A shower can wait.

I re-enter the cabin and return to my seat. The air pressure is changing as we begin our descent.

"Are you staying with Cal and April?"

"No, I'm going to head back to New York. There are a few issues that require my attention," I lie.

"I thought you were taking a step back?"

"A step back, not totally disengaging. It's still my company. I'm just choosing to get involved in the more urgent and serious matters. Not the mundane."

She nods.

"What about you?"

"I'll head into the office once I've dropped my belongings at the hotel."

"On a Saturday evening?"

"Get ahead of the chaos. December is one of our busiest months. Parties, conferences, people away on shopping trips. Until Christmas Eve, customer turnover is thick and fast. Everything needs to run like clockwork. If not, it can easily fold like a pack of cards."

The seatbelt sign pings on, and the pilot's voice comes over the tannoy.

The wheels hit the ground, and we cruise towards one of the hangars.

I look out of the window and spot Mason waiting for me. Freddy, Francesca's driver, is also there.

When we come to a halt, Claudia reappears.

I stand up, grabbing my things. I want to put as much distance between Kat and me as possible.

"Thank you, Claudia. Have a great Christmas," I say, smiling at her.

"You're welcome. You too."

I move to the door and make my way down the steps. Mason steps forward, reaching out to grab my bag. I hoist it higher on my shoulder, and he shrugs.

"Thanks anyway," I say with a smile.

"Good trip?" he asks, holding open the rear door.

"Informative," I say.

"Thank you." Kat's voice echoes across the tarmac.

I turn to face her.

"You're welcome. I'll see you in a couple of weeks."

I turn and climb into the car, not waiting for a reply. Mason closes the door. The blackout glass allows me to see but not be seen.

Kat stands at the foot of the steps, watching as Mason climbs into the driver's seat. She's still there when we drive off.

I drop my head back against the seat and close my eyes, shutting out the world.

Mason and I would usually talk, but today I'm all talked out.

CHAPTER 37

KAT

The weekend is quiet, despite living in a hotel. It's amazing how quickly you can get used to someone's presence.

Last night, after leaving the airport, I went straight into the office, but found myself unable to settle. For once, the silence was deafening, my mind needing to question, rehash, and replay the disaster of the past twenty-four hours. So, I returned to the hotel and spent the rest of the evening locked in my suite, rechecking my emails and focusing on financial reports until I finally passed out, when the figures blurred.

Now, on a Sunday, I'm sat on a plush sofa, flipping through an article written about me and the FHG. It's factually correct, but I'm starting to realise, Jax is right. When I was questioned about what I like to do outside the office, I struggled to answer. My life really is boring. *I'm boring.*

I throw the magazine to one side and drop my head back against the cushions. It's time to hit the gym, loosen the tightness that's settled in my chest and stomach.

The doorbell to the suite sounds.

I get up, my heart stuttering as I look through the peephole.

Closing my eyes, I huff out a breath.

It's not Jax.

A horrible feeling of not knowing whether to be happy or disappointed floods me.

I really need to get a grip.

Grimacing, I shake my head in an attempt to clear my thoughts of all things Jaxson Lockwood. I inhale and exhale several times before plastering on a smile, and throwing open the door to my best friend.

"We're going out," Pen says, sweeping past me and into the suite. "I'm taking it you haven't eaten yet?"

"Hello to you too," I say. "And we could eat in."

Her eyes lock on the large dining table, my computer, and the piles of paperwork surrounding it.

"Nope, *that* is enough to give anyone indigestion. We're definitely eating out," she says, wrinkling her nose. "Get your things. Robin is holding us a table."

Robin Downsend, owner of Mount Crystals. A high-class restaurant, favoured by celebrities and business people alike. It's known for its discretion. Each table is spaced perfectly to prevent eavesdropping, making it ideal for private conversations.

I know there is no point arguing, and Pen's arrival is the perfect distraction.

"Give me time to get changed."

* * *

WE MAKE it to the restaurant in record time. As promised, Robin has reserved our favourite spot.

"How was the trip?" Pen asks after we take our seats.

"Productive," I say, straightening up my knife and fork.

Silence follows. I look up to find Pen watching me.

"What?" I say.

"You tell me? I know you, Kat Frazer, so don't pretend that I don't."

Pen crosses her arms and leans back in her chair. Her stomach is still flat, no sign of my niece or nephew yet.

My eyes dart around the restaurant. Whatever Pen sees in my expression has her sitting forward.

"Oh. My. God. Did you sleep with him?" she whispers excitedly.

I freeze, my eyes locking on her sparkling ones.

"What the... how on earth did you jump from awkward silence to mind-blowing orgasms?"

"*Mind-blowing* orgasms, eh? That good?" Pen chuckles, and I slap my forehead. I harrumph, making her laugh even harder. "Are you going to deny it?"

I open my mouth and close it again.

Pen smirks. "That, my friend, is how I jumped from silence to *mind-blowing* orgasms."

I growl, making her laugh even harder.

She claps her hands together, holding up a hand in apology when the closest table stares over at us.

"Sorry," she says to them, before returning her attention to me. "You're also off kilter. I don't think I've seen you like this... ever."

I wait until the people next to us return to their conversation.

"Spill," Pen pushes.

"No."

"You're killing me here," she says. "You can't admit to sleeping with Jaxson, having mind-blowing orgasms and then say nothing."

I raise an eyebrow and stare my friend down. "Who's saying I slept with him? You're the one jumping to conclusions."

"Are you going to deny it?"

I could deny it. But this is Pen. I can't lie to my best friend.

Instead, I remain silent as Pen smirks.

"How old are you?" I ask, stopping myself from resetting my cutlery again.

"The same age as you. But what's that got to do with it?"

She drops back in her chair and inclines her head, her hands resting flat on the table.

"Okay, no details. How did you go from wanting to rip his head off, to giving—"

"Do. Not. Say. It."

She shrugs.

"Fine." I huff, knowing I'm not going to get a moment's peace until I at least give her something. "We talked. A lot," I finally admit. "I read Zach's letter."

Pen's eyes widen as she reaches across the table, gripping my hand in hers.

I incline my head. "It was informative."

I purse my lips.

"I hate to say you were right. He was in cahoots with the she-devil, and they played me like a fiddle."

Her hand squeezes mine, her eyes full of sympathy I don't deserve.

She blinks as if realising, and when her eyes return to mine, they're questioning.

"And Jax?"

"Completely innocent of all crimes accused," I admit with a sigh.

I drop my gaze to the table, using my free hand to re-straighten my knife.

Pen flips the hand she's holding over and places it in both of hers.

"Does Jax know?"

I nod.

Pen's face drops.

"It's a good thing the truth has come out," she says eventually.

"It is," I say, my eyes meeting hers. "I let him read the letter."

"Wow. How did he take it?"

"You know Jax." I shrug. "It vindicated him. But I'm not sure I'd want to be Zach the next time he rears his head."

"How do you feel?"

Ah, the crux of the matter, the real reason my friend is here, checking on me.

"I feel like a fool. I allowed myself to be manipulated for years, by someone I thought cared about me."

"You don't think Zach cared?"

"You think he did?" My eyes clash with Pen's. "You don't do what he did to someone you care about."

"No, you're right. But not everything is black and white." She lets go of my hand with a sigh. "But for what it's worth. I think Zach genuinely loved you."

I flatten my hand against the table, my fingers playing with the material of the tablecloth.

"I don't think I ever loved him," I admit. Finally saying the words aloud. I pull my hands into my lap. "I tried to. I really did. But he was never what I wanted, and he knew that."

Pen looks at me, her eyes full of understanding.

"Is Jax what you want?"

I shake my head.

Pen frowns. "Why not? You said yourself, Zach's letter vindicated him. There's clearly still chemistry between you."

I lean forward, resting my elbows on the table, my hands gripping my shoulders.

"Our time has passed, we're different people now," I say. "I broke up with him and moved on with one of his best friends. I'm not sure we can ever get past that, or if I can be what he wants or needs me to be?"

Pen sucks her lip, something she always does when she's thinking, a throwback from when she wore a lip ring.

"What does Jax want you to be?"

I laugh, but it's dry and hollow.

"I don't know."

"Have you asked him?"

Have I asked him?

No. I woke up and panicked, made up a lame excuse about a meeting, then told Jax how it was going to be.

Pen reads into my silence.

"Then how do you know you can't be what he wants and needs?"

Our waitress arrives and takes our order, disappearing as fast as she came.

When we are alone again, I sit back and put my hands in my lap.

"Sex was inevitable." Pen raises an eyebrow and I smirk. "After everything came to light. Us working together on the project. The beautiful environment."

It's Pen's turn to laugh. It's rich and warm. She holds up the palm of her hand.

"Sorry," she says, her eyes wide as she wipes away a tear. "But you. One of the most logical and disciplined people I know is blaming having sex with someone on your environment?"

"Fine." I harrumph, knowing I sound more like Gabriel. "We had a meeting of minds and body. Stick yourself on a beautiful island, surrounded by crystal waters, white sand and honeymooners... a recipe for disaster."

"Or multiple orgasms."

I roll my eyes, my lips twitching as my shoulders relax. "Yes, those too."

Heat floods my cheeks, and Pen gives me a knowing smile.

"Really that good, huh?"

"I'm not discussing this with you."

"Oh, don't be a bore."

"I don't ask for intimate details on your love life."

"Only because I'm sleeping with your brother, and that would be kind of ew!"

"Agreed."

"But, this is Jax."

"And?"

"Come on. You and him. You tell me you had a clandestine romance sixteen years ago, you've barely spoken to one another since and now you announce you slept with him. Or more to the point, didn't sleep! You bumped uglies, performed bedroom rodeo, and planted the parsnip! This woman needs to know. Was it better, the same, awful?"

I shake my head.

"Amazing," I admit, before I can stop myself. "But that's all you're getting."

"What's next?"

"Nothing."

Pen looks confused.

"We have a project to work on. It won't go down well with the board or our investors if they think we're romantically involved. That I'm no longer impartial. I have to remain professional." Pen rolls her eyes at me. "And then there are my brothers."

Pen nods. "Shit, I hadn't thought about the board."

"Welcome to my life."

"As for your brothers. They'll get over it. You have April,

Leah, and me to ensure they do," she says with a wink. "Have you spoken to Jax since you landed?"

"It's only been twenty-four hours," I say.

"So?"

I shrug. "No. He was heading to the US after we landed." My hand moves to my cutlery again, and Pen's eyes follow the movement. I stop. "He has some issues to clear up. I'm not anticipating hearing from him until the board meeting when he presents his proposal."

Pen is silent.

"I'd appreciate it if you didn't mention any of this to Eli," I say.

"My lips are sealed. You're my friend. Despite Eli being my lover and baby daddy, that means a lot to me. I won't break your confidence."

"Thank you."

Pen rolls her eyes. "And don't worry, April and I had words with both Eli and Caleb. They won't be pulling any more stunts."

She has more faith in my brothers than me.

"But know it came from a place of love."

I chuckle. I would have loved to have been a fly on the wall for that conversation.

"I'm used to them trying to protect me. It's ingrained in the Frazer men. My brothers seem to forget I can be a force of nature all by myself."

Pen raises her glass of water and chinks it against mine.

"I keep having to remind Eli I'm not a delicate wallflower, especially with the baby coming. That I run my own multi-million-pound company and have done for years."

"To protective males," I say with a smile.

Pen grins.

There's a long pause.

"To think, you and Jax… I can't believe I never saw it before."

"We were good at covering our tracks, although clearly not good enough. You had more than enough on your plate at the time, with Eli and Darra."

Pen inclines her head, not denying my words. It was a difficult time for everyone.

"I always thought you two would be good together. The way you would sit and talk when you thought no one was looking. How he would always come and support you at your piano recitals."

"Jax was like you, the Frazer name never bothered him. Or at least never appeared to."

"It didn't, he was just happy to be included in the family stuff. His home life wasn't great, as you know. His mum leaving, then getting together with his dad's best friend. No siblings to help him through. Holidays with you and your family were an escape from reality. It was, for all of us. Even Darra."

"Don't mention that woman."

Pen shrugs. "She's Lottie's mum. I can't ignore her. Even if Lottie is refusing to speak to her at the moment."

"Still?"

Pen nods. "She's digging her heels in. If I didn't know better, I'd swear she was Eli's daughter. They both have the same stubborn streak."

"Nurture over nature. He is her father after all," I say. "And Zach, is she speaking to him?"

I almost choke on the words, but I'm proud that I hold it together.

"Not as far as I'm aware. Lottie's keeping her distance from them both. Elijah is trying to support her, but she's still closed-mouthed about it all."

Our food arrives at that moment, so we take a break.

When our waitress leaves, Pen looks up.

"I'm going to say one more thing, and then I'll stop, and we can discuss Christmas presents."

I smile, Christmas is a big thing in the Frazer household. All gifts are well planned and inexpensive, at least for the adults.

"Jax. There's a reason Elijah and Caleb like him. He's a straight talker, and he's not hung up on any of the Frazer bullshit. I've known him for many years and have remained friends with him. He's genuinely one of the good ones."

My hand goes to my pendant. "I know."

Pen doesn't say anything as it sweeps back and forth.

"Christmas presents. I was thinking—"

And just like that, the conversation switches.

CHAPTER 38

JAX

There's a knock on my office door.

"Come in," I say.

Caleb pops his head around with a grin.

"Morning. It's good to have you back." He drops into the chair opposite me. "You were up and out early this morning."

My flight got in from the US late last night, long after Caleb and April had gone to bed.

I motion to the pile of work on my desk. "I wanted to get a head start."

I sit back and rest my elbows on the chair arms.

"And how are *you* doing? Have you recovered from your week away with my sister?"

I force my shoulders to relax as I motion to the final report on my desk.

"Absolutely. We covered a lot."

Caleb smiles, and some of the tension ebbs.

"It looks like you're prepared for tomorrow," he says.

Am I?

It's been almost two and a half weeks since we returned from the Maldives. Since I held her in my arms, the memory alone has my stomach jumping and my breath quickening. Facing her over a boardroom table, surrounded by other people…

I shake myself mentally.

"Did you get a chance to look over the electronic copy I sent you?" I ask, wanting to distract my thoughts.

"I did. I think the board will be impressed. You've really come through. I hope Kat appreciates it."

I inhale and smile. Even hearing her name makes my breath catch. I need to get a grip.

I stretch, wishing I hadn't forgone this morning's swim, but I didn't want to face Caleb over breakfast. The downside of staying with one of my best friends. If I'm spending more time here, I'm going to need to find a place to stay long-term. Caleb and April have been very generous, but I don't want to overstay my welcome.

My grandma always said, "Visitors and fish stink after three days."

Caleb heads to the door, turning as he reaches it.

"I'll leave you alone to catch up, but I wondered what you're doing for Christmas?"

"Mum and Peter have invited Dad and me to spend Christmas with them."

Caleb's eyebrows almost reach his hairline, and he chokes on the air he's just inhaled.

"That's a bit of a change from when they split."

No one was more surprised than me.

"And your dad has agreed?"

"According to him, it's about time they buried the hatchet."

Caleb chuckles. "As long as it's not in each other."

"That's what I'm worried about. All I can say is it's going to be an interesting Christmas."

Although both my parents have mellowed over the past

eighteen years, I'm still on tenterhooks. This will be the first time they've been in the same space for an extended period. The fact that Mum and Peter invited us gives me some hope. The fact that my father didn't turn them down, even more so.

"I wish you luck. You know there's always a spare bed at Mum's if you need to make your escape. She'd love to see you. Especially as Pen and Eli are going to be staying in his cottage this year with Lottie."

I nod, although being that close to Kat, and not being able to touch her, I'd be playing with fire. Kat made it very clear where I stand. I'm not sure I'm ready for that.

"How is Simon doing on the latest development plans?" I ask, wanting to change the subject.

Caleb smiles. "Really well. He's fitted in with the rest of the team. He was a good choice. He's not you, but he's learning and adaptive... a close second, I'd say."

"I'm pleased. I was going to pop down and see him later. I've tried to step back and not crowd him."

"I imagine it's hard when you've always held a tight rein."

"You have no idea, but it's what needs to happen. It's either that, or Lockwood Architects stops expanding, and that's not the aim."

"Keep that in mind when temptation hits," he says, with another grin. "Catch you later."

Caleb leaves, and I sink back into my chair.

Spinning to face the window, I rest my arms on the armrests, steepling my hands in front of my face, my forefingers touching my lips.

I need to get myself under control before I see Kat tomorrow.

The latest report was sent across this morning. Although the ideas in the proposal are as much hers as they are mine, so I'm not sure what I'm hoping for.

She hasn't replied.

I'm not sure what to expect or what rules we're playing by, but I promised her I'd be professional, and I will.

Kathryn Frazer has taken up too much of my emotional headspace for far too long. It's now time to shut it down and get on with living my life.

I pull up my phone directory and scroll through. Most of my exes are either married or in steady relationships.

I smile when I reach one name.

"Michelle," I say, when the phone connects.

"Hey, stranger. It's been a while."

"I'm in town. Do you want to meet for dinner?"

We exchange pleasantries for a while, and I agree to pick her up at eight.

> ME:
>
> Heading out tonight for dinner with an old friend.

> CAL:
>
> Friend or flame?

> ME:
>
> Michelle

> CAL:
>
> Both then. Have fun. We won't wait up.

I sink back into my chair. What would Caleb think if he knew what had gone on with his sister? My stomach churns at the thought of what I'm doing.

I'm playing with fire.

* * *

MICHELLE IS as beautiful as ever. She's a lawyer and someone Caleb and I worked with on one of our initial projects. That was before she moved across into criminal law. She's work-driven but also up for fun.

"I was surprised when you called," she says, waiting while our waiter shakes out her napkin and drapes it over her lap. She looks up and smiles. "Thank you."

He comes around the table and does the same for me.

"Wine?" I ask.

Michelle smiles. "Lovely. You choose."

I scan the menu and order us a bottle of Chablis Cru.

"Good choice," she says. "How have you been?"

"Shouldn't that be my line?"

She grins. "Maybe, but I'm all about equality, you know that. So, how are you?"

"I'm about to start work on a new project. Just got back from the US, having been in the Maldives before that."

"Jet setting. You always did lead a busy life. The Maldives sounds romantic."

It was. I'm beginning to regret bringing it up. Tonight was about forgetting, resetting.

I smile. "Work. How about you?"

Michelle stares at me for a moment but lets it slide. I forgot how good she is at reading people.

She rests her forearms on the arms of the chair, just as our waiter returns with our wine.

We pause while I taste the wine. It's zesty and rich flavour resting perfectly on my tongue. I nod, and we wait while our waiter fills our glasses, placing it in the cooler next to the table.

Michelle lifts hers and holds it forward.

"To old friends."

Our glasses sing as they chink together, and we both take a sip.

"You were going to say?" I say, placing my glass on the table.

Michelle smiles, but it is followed by a scowl.

"My firm is tied up in the Simone Asher case. It seems her murder was the tip of a very large iceberg."

I nod. Sir Leonard Crawley may be dead, but he was not working alone in his sick and twisted world. The files uncovered implicated many unsavoury people involved in numerous nefarious crimes.

"Do you think you can win?"

"You know I can't talk about it."

I shrug.

"I hope you nail the bastards," I say, earning myself a smile.

"Me too."

"So why are we really here?"

I drop back and steeple my fingers.

Michelle grins. "There's only one woman I know of who can send Jaxson Lockwood into a tailspin."

"Am I that obvious?" I say, grimacing. "I'm sorry."

"Don't be." Michelle reaches over and pats my arm. "We're friends first and foremost. Although I never complained about the benefits."

Michelle is one of the few women who know about Kat. I'm beginning to wonder if that's why we're here. When we worked together, Cal left to go home. We carried on drinking, and during that evening shared our pasts, among other things. She doesn't know who, but knows there was a woman. The same way, I know she lost the love of her life.

"Is she back?"

"It's complicated," I mumble.

Michelle laughs, the sound warm and gentle. "When isn't life? It doesn't mean you should give up."

I raise an eyebrow.

"Ah, but my situation is different," she says, with a weary smile.

Michelle fell in love with her ex-fiancé's father. Messy doesn't come close.

"Don't try to distract me. I'm a lawyer, it won't work. What happened?"

I fill her in on some of the details. Michelle's hand comes across the table and pats mine.

"It sounds to me like there's hope, and remember where there's hope—"

I groan. "Don't say it."

"It's true. Don't give up. It sounds like your story is far from over."

A flutter starts low in my stomach, and my breath bottles up in my chest.

Our waiter appears to take our order, offering me a reprieve.

CHAPTER 39

KAT

A new email flashes up.
JLockwood

My heart rate picks up, and a tingling starts in my stomach and chest. It's been over two weeks since we returned. Over two weeks since Jaxson and I were together in the same space. Over two weeks since he reawakened my body.

Tomorrow, we'll come face-to-face in front of a boardroom full of my colleagues.

I inhale, exhale, repeating the process until I steady my breathing.

You've got this!

I can almost hear Dad's voice in my ear.

After my conversation with Pen, I've thrown myself into work. With Christmas on the horizon, it's been the perfect distraction. Work has been crazy. I've barely come up for air, especially after a week away.

I click on the email.

Kat,

I have attached my proposal. Let me know if you have any questions. I've couriered over printouts for you to distribute.
Jaxson Lockwood
(CEO/Owner Lockwood Architects)

No niceties.

No, how've you been?

But what did I expect? I made my position perfectly clear. All he's doing is honouring my wishes.

I can do professional too. It is, after all, what I'm best at, what I asked for.

I open the attachment and read through his proposal. It's good. Everything we discussed has been included, priced up, with some additional nice-to-haves. He really has gone above and beyond.

Did I expect anything else?

This is Jaxson after all. It's clear to see where his passion lies. I'm just glad our little slip-up in the Maldives hasn't jeopardised this.

Remember. Jaxson Lockwood is a win for the FHG, for this project.

There's no doubt, Jaxson Lockwood is a passionate man.

I suck in a breath as memories of him bringing me to orgasm over and over again flood my brain. How he played my body like a finely tuned instrument. I can still recall the feel of his cock deep inside me, sliding in and out, him coming hard, the look of ecstasy on his face. Of him holding me in his arms as we fell asleep.

A rush of desire has my pussy contracting, a throbbing need awakening deep within my core.

Get a grip, Kathryn Frazer! You're in control here, not your base desires!

I pick up the phone.

"Kat," Caleb answers.

"Hey, little bro. Have you had a chance to go through Jaxson's proposal?"

"I have. It looks good. I think the board is going to be happy with it."

He's not wrong. That both excites and disappoints me.

"Me too. It finally looks like we may be able to move on it."

"I'll see you tomorrow for the presentation," he says.

"See you tomorrow."

* * *

I TOSS and turn all night. By the time my alarm clock goes off, I've already been awake for three hours.

Shit!

I get dressed.

Come on, Kat, you've got this. You've been facing Jaxson Lockwood for the past sixteen years. What's one more day?

The only thing is, you hadn't been naked and felt his body moving in and against yours in all that time, his lips sucking and nibbling!

My cheeks heat at the thoughts, moisture pooling between my thighs.

I've found myself in a permanent state of arousal since arriving back.

If it only takes a memory to do this to me, how am I going to withstand a two-hour, face-to-face meeting?

I make it into the office. Michael is ready.

He distributed Jaxson's presentation yesterday after they arrived, giving everyone a chance to read the proposal and come up with questions.

"Mr Lockwood has arrived with your brother," he says.

"Thank you, Michael."

He hovers by the door.

"Is there anything else?"

He looks uncomfortable. "There's been an incident at the New York hotel with several of the hotel guests. Police are involved."

I pinch the bridge of my nose, shaking off the layers of exhaustion. "Who's dealing with it?"

"Marco," Michael says.

"Walk and talk," I say, grabbing my annotated copy of the proposal from my desk and making my way to the door.

Michael jumps into step next to me.

"Apparently, the police raided one of the suites after some of the guests complained."

I stop, almost causing Michael to careen into me. "Er. It was being used to film a porn movie," he says, with a grimace.

I squeeze my eyes shut for a second before opening them and turning to face him.

His cheeks are flushed.

"It's not the first time," I say. "I'm sure it won't be the last."

Which is true. One of my first jobs after joining Dad at the office was dealing with a porn scandal.

"Tell Marco to speak to Darren in Chicago. They had something similar last year. Make sure public relations has been informed in case there's any fallout."

Michael scribbles down some notes.

"Anything else I should know about?"

Michael proceeds to list off a host of other incidents, including deaths, births, and celebrity scandals, that have occurred over the past twenty-four hours at various Frazer Hotels. A headache begins to form behind my eyes. My break, although a working one, seems like a lifetime ago.

I fire off a list of instructions as we head to the boardroom, and Michael takes copious notes.

I think back to what Jax said about taking a step back. Not everything needs to come through me.

I stop and give Michael a list of the teams who should be involved in addressing these issues. We begin walking again, and by the time I'm done, we've arrived at the door to the boardroom.

"Give them a couple of hours and follow up. Any issues, let me know," I say. "Anything else?"

"I think that's it," he says. "I'll get on it now."

I nod, inhaling deeply as I grip the door handle.

Pushing it open, I step inside. The rest of the board is already in place.

"Mr Lockwood," I say, stepping forward and holding out a hand to Jax.

"Ms Frazer."

Our hands touch, and it's like a shot of electricity zings up my arm and into my chest. My heart rate picks up, and I pray the warmth I can feel in my cheeks doesn't show.

Jax shakes my hand briefly before letting it go almost instantly.

"Shall we begin? I know you're a busy man."

Jax inclines his head in acknowledgement as I take my seat.

He begins the presentation. His rich, deep tone has the board hanging off every word. My mind wanders to that same voice whispering how good it felt to be buried deep in my pussy, how my body was weeping for his.

The room goes silent. I look up to find everyone's eyes on me.

"Thank you, Mr Lockwood. I know Michael distributed your proposal yesterday. Does anyone have any questions?"

I sit back as the questions flow. Some directed at Jaxson, others directed at me. We work in tandem answering them all.

"I never thought I'd say this, but Kat, I think we're onto something," Sadie says. "This is impressive."

I bite the inside of my mouth to stop myself from making a scathing reply. The bitch has been against this project from the beginning. Now she's suddenly all for it? It's only when I see the look she's shooting Jaxson that I realise why. My blood begins to boil.

I grip my pendant and slide it up and down my chain, only stopping when I notice Jax's eyes on the movement.

"Great job," Douglas and Lewis say together, the other board members following suit.

A few more questions are thrown around before I draw the meeting to a close.

"Thank you, everyone. I look forward to hearing your thoughts. I'll schedule another meeting to discuss the finer points at the end of the week. If we're all in agreement, it will be full steam ahead in the New Year."

Caleb joins me as the other members of the board filter out.

"That went well."

"It did," I say, watching over his shoulder as Sadie sashays up to Jax, leaning her hip seductively against the boardroom table.

Could she be any more obvious?

Caleb follows my gaze.

"Jax has another fan," he chuckles under his breath.

"Unprofessional," I hiss.

"Only in your world, sis. To the rest of us mere mortals, sex and relationships are par for the course."

"Jaxson is an external consultant. He'll be working closely with us on this project."

Jaxson laughs at something Sadie says, and my hackles rise.

Caleb grips my forearm as I take a step forward.

"Whatever is going on, now is not the time," he hisses against my ear.

He doesn't continue, his warning clear.

I'm the one being unprofessional.

I meet Caleb's questioning gaze.

"It's nothing," I say. "A bad night's sleep, and a host of other issues that require my attention."

There's a knock on the boardroom door. Michael appears, his body practically vibrating.

Here we go.

"Speaking of," I say to Caleb. "I better go. Can you thank Jaxson for me, tell him I'll be in touch."

I turn and leave without waiting for an answer or offering a backward glance.

Caleb's words stick in my mind.

Another fan?

What did he mean?

CHAPTER 40

JAX

I extract myself from Sadie Tripp.

I'm not sure what game she's playing, but her unsubtle flirting is not welcome or trusted. The woman is a snake.

"Looks like you have a fan," Caleb says, when it's only the two of us left in the room.

I grimace, making him chuckle.

"Kat says thank you, she'll speak to you soon," he says. "She got pulled off into yet another Christmas crisis."

I saw Kat leave. I hoped we could talk.

"Doesn't she always?"

"What can I say, my big sister's a workaholic, with delegation issues. She has no off switch, just like Dad." Caleb looks at the door and sighs. "I hoped the break away would help slow her down, but she seems to have come back like a woman possessed. Did she rest at all while you were away?"

Memories of Kat, head thrown back, mouth open as she came hard around my cock, flood my brain. I shift uncomfortably.

"We worked on the project. I know she was in constant contact with the office. She did have some downtime."

"That's good to know. Did you and she…"

My heart thunders in my chest.

"Get to sort out whatever stick has been stuck up her arse where you're concerned?"

I exhale slowly.

"We talked, called a truce," I say vaguely.

If that's what you can call it.

"A lot of the ideas in the proposal are Kat's. She knows her stuff."

Explaining Kat and my past is not something I'm going into, not when it has remained between us for sixteen years. Caleb and Elijah have always fished, but I've simply shrugged, deciding it was up to Kat what she told her brothers.

Caleb sighs as if disappointed.

He looks up. "What time are you heading off to meet your dad?"

I glance down at my watch.

"Three hours, before we catch the Eurostar."

"Fancy grabbing some food before you go?"

"I was actually hoping to catch Kat before I leave."

He smiles and pats my arm, making me frown.

"No problem," he says, his tone a little too chirpy. His expression lets me know he's pleased with my answer.

He hasn't bothered to question me about Michelle. The fact that I was home by ten thirty probably told him all he needed to know.

* * *

I MAKE my way up to Kat's office.

Michael is on guard duty outside.

"Is Kat available?"

He looks up and freezes. "Ms Frazer is on a call," he says.

I smile. "That's okay. I can wait."

He scowls as I take a seat and pick up one of the magazines that have been placed neatly on the table. They all have articles on Frazer Hotels. I open the top one and begin reading their article dedicated to Kat.

Kat's door opens.

"Michael—" she stops instantly the moment she sees me.

"Jax, what are you doing here?"

"I was hoping to catch a few minutes of your time before I leave."

"Michael?"

His ears turn pink, and he visibly swallows.

"You were on the phone," he says quietly, his eyes not meeting Kat's.

She stares at him, a furrow appearing between her brows.

"I was on the phone with Gabriel, my brother, about a Christmas present. Next time, interrupt."

She turns tail and walks back into her office, holding the door.

"Can you get Mr Lockwood and me some coffee, please? Americano for Mr Lockwood and I'll have my usual."

Michael jumps up, clearly not enjoying being reprimanded but also not wanting to piss off his boss.

"Aren't you worried he'll spit in your coffee?" I say after Kat closes the door, my eyes go to the coffee machine that takes up pride of place on her sideboard.

"I doubt he'll be the first, or the last," she sighs. "He knew the conversation with Gabe was not urgent, so he should have interrupted, especially knowing I've just come from a meeting with you. I'll not have him acting as a filter to who is and isn't important."

"Isn't that what a PA does?"

"You're important, Gabe isn't. If he can't see that, then no."

"Important, am I?" I say, grinning.

Kat rolls her eyes and motions for me to take a seat.

"Sorry I missed you at the end of the meeting. I thought it went well. Sadie seemed very impressed."

I bite my tongue to stop myself smiling. If I didn't know better, I'd say she sounded jealous, but that's probably wishful thinking.

Kat continues. "I've already received a number of emails from board members wanting to push on, and for the plans to be drawn up and submitted to the local authority," she says, taking a seat behind her desk.

Watching her in action steals my breath.

This is professional Kat. Her suit is fitted and immaculate, her glossy dark brown hair is tied up, not a wrinkle or stray wisp. The sprinkling of freckles on her nose is covered under a thin layer of perfectly applied makeup. She still holds the glow from our time in the sun, but that's the only similarity to the woman who walked barefoot on the sand and laughed as she walked through the market.

She's back to being perfect Kat. It makes me want to take her in my arms and ruffle her feathers, just a little, or maybe a lot.

She runs on, giving me more and more information. Details on construction, potential amenities.

"Kat, stop," I say eventually.

She pauses and looks up.

I'm surprised she listened.

"Kat I—"

Before I can say anything more, there's a knock at the door, and Michael enters carrying our drinks.

He places them down on the desk, his face a mask.

"Thank you," Kat says. "Can you chase up on those calls you made earlier? Make sure everything is in hand."

His shoulders relax.

"Of course. I'll get on it right away."

He turns and leaves silently.

Kat's hand goes to her chain, but falls into her lap as if she realises what she's about to do.

"How was America? Did you get everything sorted out?"

I lean back in the chair.

Okay, so we can build up to that conversation.

"Yes. It turned out to be nothing major, but it was good to catch up with the team."

"I'm glad to hear it."

"Kat, look, about…"

Her phone goes off, and she closes her eyes briefly before letting out a deep sigh.

"Sorry, I need to take this."

I sigh and stand up.

"Don't worry. I'll see you in the New Year. I'm heading off to France tonight, to stay with Mum, Peter, and Dad."

She raises an eyebrow, but doesn't say anything, instead picking up the phone.

"One moment, Marco."

She places him on hold.

"It was good seeing you," she says, her expression softening as she adds. "I hope you have a peaceful Christmas."

I grimace. "Me too."

I make my way to the door, leaving behind the coffee. "Have fun at your mum's."

"I'm working in the morning, so only going down for lunch," she says.

I open my mouth to speak, but she holds up her hand.

"We can talk when you get back."

I nod, and Kat frowns, motioning to the phone in her hand.

"I'm really sorry, but I do need to take this."

I nod and turn to leave.

"Marco. How the hell did this happen?"

That's all I hear as I close the door behind me.

CHAPTER 41

KAT

*C*hristmas this year is different.

Is it because we now have new family members to replace those we've lost?

Mum has invited everyone to join us. Leah's parents, Di and Julian, April's foster mum and dad, and Louise, Pen's mum. Sarah and Tim, April's biological mother and stepfather, are arriving with their children for New Year's. The idea of shipping all of Lois and Nick's Christmas presents down was too much.

I miss Harper.

My little sister loves Christmas. She'd put on Christmas shows growing up, I'd play the piano, while she'd sing and dance. Not to mention her job as chief present distributor. She'd clamber under the tree in her PJs, handing out all the presents. When she was little, Elijah and I would help her with the name tags.

This year, she's been invited to spend it with Mum's friend and her grumpy son, AKA Harper's boss. It's still too risky for her to come home. We video called earlier when I arrived, and I have to admit, she looks well. Probably better than she has in a while. But then they say *a change is as good as a rest.* In Harper's case, it seems true.

"You're quiet," Mum says, taking a seat on the sofa next to me.

The little body snuggled against my chest wiggles, but settles back down.

"Enjoying the peace and quiet," I say with a smile. "It's been a manic month."

"But productive?"

"Always."

"Your father would be so proud. He loved this time of year at the hotels. Crazy, he'd say, but electric."

Her tone is wistful. I don't know how she does it. She and Dad were a team, but despite losing him in such a tragic way, she's soldiered on, rebuilt her life.

"But he would also say, you need a balance. He would never forgo the holidays. Spending time with the family."

Here it comes.

"You need to create a balance, Kathryn." I turn my head, and she holds up a hand when I open my mouth. "I'm worried about you. After everything that has come out this year. It's like you've buried your feelings. I didn't push you that night. I understand the need to process your feelings better than most. But, my darling, there's more to life than FHG, but you aren't going to uncover it stuck in an office, or the hotel twenty-four-seven."

I turn away and drop a kiss on Callum's sleeping head. He smiles in his sleep and snuggles closer.

He asked to climb on my knee almost as soon as I arrived. My little buddy.

Leah is enormous with the twins, but she's made it to her final trimester, which is a bonus, so I was only too happy to oblige.

"I know this might seem hard to believe, but I'm happy, Mum. I love my job," I say. "As for Zach and his affair…"

I can't bring myself to say Darra's name. It still turns my stomach to think of them together in our space. Not because I loved him. I've realised now that what I felt for Zach wasn't love, it was more sisterly, a companionship. It's more because of the smug feeling Darra would have felt. That it gave her power over me, us.

"People have affairs all the time. I'm not entirely blameless. After Dad passed."

I swallow past the lump in my throat.

Mum must sense it as she places a hand on my arm and squeezes.

Our eyes meet.

"After Dad passed, I was too busy trying to establish myself. I just wanted to prove I was the right person to take the FHG forward and could keep the business running. When I look back, I was never home. Despite when their affair started, Zach would have probably strayed, and I can't blame him for that. By the end, we were more roommates than lovers."

"That's no excuse. Zach should have left if he wanted to carry on with someone else. Been man enough."

"Maybe, but sometimes life isn't as cut and dried as we would like."

She gives my arm another squeeze before letting it go.

"It's a mother's prerogative to worry about her children."

I smile.

"Of course it is. And you have always been an amazing mum."

"I have tried. I know I haven't always got it right."

"Sadly, life doesn't come with a dress rehearsal, it's a one-take only, there are no do-overs. All we can do is use the information that's available to us at the time."

Mum inclines her head.

"Ah, you're talking about Jaxson," I say.

My head turns sharply, shifting my body. Callum grumbles, so I shift him slightly, rubbing soothing circles on his back.

She offers me a sly smile.

"You think I didn't know about you and Jaxson? Oh, Kathryn, I'm your mother, and the feelings you had for one another were plain to anyone who saw you together."

I open and close my mouth. Finally raising my eyebrows.

My brothers had no idea, thank heavens.

Mum's smile widens. "Ah, but they weren't looking," she says, with a knowing smile.

I remain silent, not wanting to incriminate myself.

"I don't know what happened between you," Mum says, patting my arm. "Although I have my suspicions. But take it from me, Jaxson Lockwood is a good man, Kat."

"How do you know that?" I ask, before I can stop myself.

"A mother's intuition. Plus, Jaxson looks at you the same way your father used to look at me, even while you've been fighting." She sighs. "All I'll say is, don't let pride or work overshadow finding true happiness. If losing your father taught me one thing, it's to grasp life and enjoy every moment. All the years I spent with your father, despite the heartbreak of losing him, I would not have chosen a different path, or changed a moment of the time we spent together."

I bite my lip, blinking rapidly.

"Jax and I are different. We're working together now. The board would never go for it. They'd lose respect for me, everything I've worked for."

"Kathryn Brooke Frazer, that's total bull-shit," she says, her face hardening. "Firstly, you've run that company better than any of your predecessors, and secondly, no one should have control over your life but you. It's not like Jaxson's a convicted criminal. He's a highly intelligent, self-made man who runs his own successful business."

I sigh.

"I know you're right, but there's a lot of history between us. I'm not sure we can get past it," I admit.

"Your father and I didn't start off on the best footing. I'm not sure you can when you're forced to marry someone you barely know, but we opened ourselves up to the possibilities offered to us, and you know where that took us. You and Jaxson are no different."

I drop my head onto Mum's shoulder, and she wraps her arms around me, careful not to squash the still sleeping Callum.

"You don't have to always be strong," she whispers against my hair.

"I'm not sure I know how to be anything else. If I let go, what happens if it all comes crashing down and I can't get back up again?" I admit quietly.

"And if it does? So what?" She cups my face, forcing me to meet her gaze. "You have a family who loves you, who'll help pick you up if you need them to." She pats my cheek. "Not that I think your life will crumble. You're so like your father. Industrious, disciplined and oh-so-focused." She smiles at me, her eyes glistening. "He wasn't always the easiest man to love, especially in the beginning. He'd built so many walls around himself, but when he loved, he loved with his whole heart. I think you're the same."

I've never heard my mother speak of Dad in this way.

Her thumb rubs my cheek, and I realise she's wiping away tears.

"But I loved him with my entire being, adored him. Because he was the other half of my soul, as I was his."

"How do you do it? How do you go on?"

She gives me a watery smile.

"Because he gave me all of you. And now." Her eyes drop to Callum. "There is a new generation joining us. I know for a fact, he would've wanted to be here to spoil you all, and his grandchildren. I'd be doing Robert a serious disservice if I didn't appreciate everything I've been given, when it was stolen from him."

I bite my lip and close my eyes, swallowing past the painful lump that has formed in my throat.

The doorbell sounds.

Mum's eyes sparkle, and she runs a finger under each of my eyes.

"Take a minute and think about everything I've said," she says with a smile. "I'm going to greet our extended family."

She gets up, giving my shoulder a squeeze before making her way to the door. She holds the handle and turns.

"Just to let you know, I've invited Jaxson for New Year," she says, before turning on her heel to greet our guests.

I sink back into the sofa, staring down once more at the little boy snuggled in my lap.

CHAPTER 42

JAX

I enter the hallway. The Christmas decorations, glittering lights, take me back eighteen years, to the first New Year's I spent at the Frazer home. Back then, the house was alive with Francesca and Robert's friends and business associates, and a separate party was arranged for the *young adults*. Francesca's wording, not mine.

She confided in me years later that she'd called us that, hoping we'd act like young adults and not the teenagers we were.

I hated to disappoint her, we all did. We got drunk, some people snuck off and had sex. It was a party after all, but no one embarrassed her or Robert.

"Jaxson," Francesca says, walking into the hallway and pulling me down and into a hug. It's hard to believe she's so petite when her sons are all giants.

"It's good to see you. Thank you for inviting me."

She grins and pats my cheek. "Always so polite. As I've told you before, you're one of the family. Part of the furniture. We'd miss you if you weren't here."

I want to disagree with her. I know at least one member

of her family who'd probably prefer I wasn't present. But having survived Christmas with both parents, under the same roof, I was not going to chance New Year, so I got on the Eurostar and headed back, leaving Dad with Mum and Peter.

"How was your journey?"

"It was good, thank you. No delays."

"There you are," Caleb says, coming out of one of the side rooms. "Merry Christmas and Happy New Year." He pulls me in for a man hug and slaps my back. "You survived?" he asks, pulling back and looking me in the face.

"I did," I say with a grin. "They were remarkably civil to one another. I decided to take you up on your invitation and get out of there while I still had a chance."

"And we are glad you did. Everyone is here apart from Kat. She had a few last-minute emergencies to contend with." He rolls his eyes, and the bottom drops out of my stomach. "But she should be here in the next half an hour."

Pen appears behind Caleb and pushes him out of the way.

"Stop hogging. You're not his only friend," she says, pulling me in for a hug.

"You and she need to talk," Pen whispers against my ear.

I pull back and frown at her.

"No frowning old man, it's New Year," Elijah says, stepping up and slapping me on the shoulder, almost causing me to lose my balance.

"Jaxson," Lottie squeals, running from the room they have all just vacated. She throws her arms around my waist and hugs me tight. "I'm so pleased you are here."

"This is quite the welcome," I say, shifting her to my side, my arm resting on her shoulder, as it has done since she was little.

"Will you be on my team?" she begs.

"Team?" I ask shooting Elijah a look.

He shrugs. "Pregnant women and children," he says. "Party games."

A heavily pregnant Leah takes that moment to waddle into the hallway.

"Fair enough. I'm in," I say, shooting her a smile.

She grins. "They are drinking games if I know this lot," she says, "Only it will be juice for Pen, Lottie and me."

Lottie groans. At fifteen, she's growing up fast. It's good to see her smiling again. It was touch-and-go after her birthday, but it looks like Christmas with her family has done the trick.

"I've put you in your usual room," Francesca says. "If you want to go and freshen up before everything starts, feel free."

"Thanks," I say, hoisting my bag onto my shoulder, but noticing my case has already disappeared.

"Lottie, you're with me. Diana needs to be let out."

Diana takes that moment to come bounding into the hallway. She jumps up, her back legs propelling her high into the air. Elijah catches her mid-flight. She's followed by a very excited Nick and Lois, April's half-brother and sister.

"No, you don't, scamp. No mugging the guests."

She licks his face, and his eyes soften.

"Kisses will get you nowhere. Come on."

Lottie grins at her dad and the puppy, who's almost full-sized now, although she looks tiny against Elijah's enormous frame.

"I'll see you all in a bit," I say, making my way up the stairs.

I reach the top, and the front door opens.

"Kat, you made it," Pen says.

"Traffic was pretty good," she says. "Hey, look at your little bump."

I step onto the landing and out of sight, my heart rate picking up at the sound of her voice.

I close my eyes for a second. It's not like I didn't know she was going to be here. This is her family home, and my best friends are her brothers.

"I'll just drop my things upstairs, and I'll be right back."

I move towards my room at record speed, closing the door silently before Kat makes it to the top of the stairs.

Chicken!

I head into the en-suite and jump in the shower. I allow myself a moment to catch my breath and prepare myself for what's coming before washing away the hours of travel that seem to have stuck to my skin.

I get changed into my dinner suit and open the door.

Kat's bedroom door opens at the exact same time. She steps out and pauses.

"Jaxson," she says, in little more than a whisper.

"Kat," I say. "Happy New Year. You look well, beautiful."

You look well, beautiful?

What on earth am I saying?

I frown.

She inclines her head. "Thank you. So do you. I mean, you look handsome, not beautiful." She stutters awkwardly over her words, and I grin. "I'm going to start again," she says with a smile. "Happy New Year to you too, although we officially have another couple of hours to go, I think." She chuckles. "I see you survived Christmas in one piece."

I roll my eyes. "Remarkable, I know," I say as we begin walking down the corridor together. "They were actually civil. I didn't want to jinx it, so I got out of there before the fireworks could start."

"I'm glad it wasn't as you feared."

"Me too."

We reach the top of the stairs and stop, staring at each other in silence. My whole body tingles with awareness.

"Shall we go down?"

Kat startles at my words. "Yes, probably. If not, they'll send out a search party."

She smiles, and my stomach contracts.

I motion for her to lead the way.

She's changed out of her work suit into a long black evening gown with embroidered edges. It hugs her figure, but floats around her legs.

I follow behind, my eyes tracking every movement she makes.

"There you both are," Caleb shouts up the stairs. "The festivities are about to start. You two are partners, by the way. Mum and Louise are together. Lottie is now with Lois and Nick, which leaves you two to battle it out against the rest of us."

"Bring it on," Kat says, her competitive streak rising to the surface before she can stop herself.

She bites her lip before turning to stare at me.

"I'm with you. Let's show your brothers," I say.

Her eyes sparkle, transporting me back in time to when Kat was so much more carefree.

* * *

MIDNIGHT CHIMES, and everyone shares a hug and a kiss. My lips graze Kat's cheek, although they want nothing more than to claim her mouth after watching her sass her brothers all night. Her relationship with her sisters-in-law is something else as well. There's no doubt how hard the Frazer men have fallen for their partners. And that's what they are... partners.

Leah gets up and stretches, leaning back and gripping the back of the sofa. Her stomach protrudes almost abnormally with the twins she's carrying. She rubs a hand over her belly and smiles.

"These two little monkeys need to go to bed, and I know Callum will be up and wanting his breakfast in six hours."

My chest constricts as I look at Gabriel. He now has everything he didn't know he desired. His eyes glow as he takes in Leah, his hand sliding around her waist. We all wish her and Gabriel goodnight as he ushers her towards the door.

"That's me too," Pen says, getting up.

Elijah and Lottie jump to their feet.

"I'm driving," Pen says.

I'd forgotten they were staying at Elijah's house on the property.

"Can Diana come?" Lottie asks.

Diana has been asleep with her head on Lottie's lap for the past two hours, having been worn out by all the children.

"She can," Francesca says, "but make sure you let her out in the morning."

"We'll call it a night, too," Sarah says. "Lois and Nick will no doubt be up at the same time as Callum."

April gets up and kisses her mum and stepfather goodnight.

"I'll take them for a bike ride in the morning," April says. "Give you both a break."

Sarah cups April's cheek. "You don't have to."

"I know. I want to. They're my siblings. It'll be nice spending some time with them."

"Well, if you change your mind."

"If we're getting up early, then I suggest we hit the sack too," Caleb says with a grin and a knowing twinkle in his eye.

April rolls her eyes, but leans forward and places a kiss on his lips, before taking his hand and pulling him to his feet.

Everyone filters out, leaving only Louise, Francesca, Kat, and me.

Louise and Francesca exchange a look. "I'm going to call it a night," they say almost in unison.

"Me too," Kat says quickly.

Francesca's shoulders slump, and she lets out a heavy sigh.

If I didn't know better, I'd think she was disappointed.

Kat shoots her mum a look, but remains silent.

I stand, dropping a kiss on each of the women's cheeks.

"Goodnight, ladies. I'll see you in the morning."

I leave without a backward glance, heading up to my room.

The winter moon hangs low over the trees. It's mild for this time of year, so I decide to do something I haven't done in many moons.

Go for a midnight swim.

CHAPTER 43

KAT

The need to get out and breathe fresh air is intense, despite the late hour.

The house is silent as I make my way downstairs. All my siblings, their partners and guests are tucked away in their rooms.

For me, hours spent partnering with Jax have left me restless. My nerve endings have been firing all evening, knowing he's so close, and yet completely out of reach. All by my own doing.

Pulling on a woollen dress and grabbing my thickest fleece, I head outside. I may be overheating now, but once in the gardens, I know the crisp, cool air will hit me, and I'll need it.

Unlocking the back door, and then relocking it, I pocket the key. Thankful, solar lights illuminate my path. Mum had them added years ago. I know she likes to go for a midnight wander, especially after Dad passed. The garden was their passion outside Dad's work.

I make my way past the orangery and through the walled garden, running a finger over the naked branches. The majority of plants are hibernating, but, like every year, in a couple of months, this place will breathe new life into itself, ready for summer.

I stop, something drawing my attention.

Water. A splash, followed by a splosh, reaches me. Memories of Jax, Eli, and Zach racing one another, their powerful arms cutting through the water.

Who?

I make my way through the garden to the pool, pulling my fleece closer.

Underwater lights reflect off the tiles, giving them an ethereal, blue glow in the darkness. A mist rises above the water where warm meets cold. Strong arms cut, almost silently through the water, the noise coming only from the ripples hitting the side.

I should leave, but I find I'm rooted to the spot. Watching Jax swim is mesmerising. It always has been.

In the sea, I could not see his true form, the gentle tilt and sway of his body, the flexing of his muscles. My skin grows hot despite the coolness of the two AM air.

I drop myself onto one of the sun loungers and watch. Drawing my legs up and under my long dress, protecting them against the chill in the air.

Jax continues up and down. The man is a machine. I don't know how long he's been going, but he shows no sign of stopping. Until he does.

His hands come up and grip the sides, instead of performing another perfect tumble turn.

He drops his head back in the water before ripping off his goggles and placing them on the side.

I sink back against the bed.

"What are you doing here, Kat?" he asks without looking at me.

I lean forward and hug my knees.

"I went for a walk and heard someone in the pool. It's dangerous to swim alone, especially at night after you've been drinking."

He turns his head, water trailing from his hair down his face.

He smiles.

"I had two drinks, as you well know. As for swimming alone, I've been doing this since the beginning."

He rests his palms on the side of the pool and pulls himself out in one swift movement. Most people would be incapable of doing so after the gruelling swim he's just put his muscles through, but there isn't even a wobble.

Smooth skin appears, only snug trunks preserving his dignity.

He steps forward and grabs the towel from the end of the sun lounger next to me.

"Couldn't sleep?" he asks.

I shake my head.

"You?"

He ignores my question, picking up another towel and wiping the droplets running down his face, before towel-drying his hair.

The wind begins to pick up, a sign that a storm might be coming in. The weatherman predicted one was on the way.

The first large drop of rain hits, then another and another. Unlike in the Maldives, this rain is icy cold, enough to steal my breath.

I jump up, grab Jax's clothes and run barefoot towards the summerhouse at the end of the pool. When Eli took up swimming, Mum and Dad had it built so he and his friends could shower and get changed here instead of dripping all over the house.

I grab the key from under the plant pot. After the door got left open last summer, and the glass smashed in the wind,

Mum had a lock installed. Now we are all under strict instructions to lock up after ourselves.

My body tingles as Jax appears at my back. I throw open the door, as the heavens open and the first flash of lightning hits, followed quickly by a roll of thunder.

We step inside. The atmosphere is cool, but at least we're dry. I close the door, ensuring I hear the click as the handle engages.

The sauna and steam room lights glow in the darkness, letting me know they're on. Not surprising, as Elijah and Gabriel have been home all week and swim daily. Little Callum takes after his dad and uncle, and is a total water baby even in the winter months.

"That was close," I say.

Jax laughs. "I'm already wet, so a little bit of rain wasn't going to scare me off."

Another clap of thunder rumbles overhead, and I shiver.

"No, but your clothes were dry. I can throw them back outside if you like."

"That's okay. They can stay. Thank you for rescuing them," he says.

A sudden flush of warmth spreads from my core outward, as I find myself inhaling the scent that's all Jax. I close my eyes before I can stop myself.

Shit!

I place them on the bench and step away, warmth flooding my cheeks.

"I'm going to grab a shower," Jax says suddenly, heading towards the partition that houses the shower unit.

What the hell is wrong with me?

The water starts up, and my breath quickens. The sound changes as he steps beneath the flow. I picture Jax pushing down his trunks, kicking them off. The cap of a bottle clicks as he opens it, visions of him running his hands over taut abs, cupping his beautiful, thick cock have my heart pounding, and my pussy throbbing.

My body grows wet, my clothes suddenly chafing against my sensitive skin.

I rip off my hoodie before sliding my dress up and over my head.

I left my bra off, not expecting to see anyone. I slide my lace panties down my legs, leaving them in a pile with the rest of my clothes.

This is a bad idea.

I round the corner of the shower to find Jax's hands flat against the wall, his head dropped down, water spraying off his back.

His cock stands proud against his stomach.

I suck in a breath.

He must sense me as he turns his head, his eyes opening, water streaming down his face.

He pushes off the wall, turning to face me.

"What are you doing, Kat?" he asks, his voice gruff.

I bite my lip.

"I don't know," I admit.

I take a tentative step forward, only to have his hands reach out and pull me firmly against him.

Our eyes lock before he lowers his head.

His lips touch mine, and I open for him instantly.

A moan fills the air, his or mine, I don't know, but the air is filled with the sound of our pleasure. Jax's mouth leaves mine, travelling across my cheek and down my throat, sucking on the spot where my neck and collarbone meet.

My hips jerk forward, pressing against his aroused cock. I grind my pulsating core against him. Wanting, no needing him with a desperation I've never felt before. Whatever happened in the Maldives has changed me. It's like I'm suffocating without him.

Water continues to cascade over us.

My fingers sink into his hair, clasping him closer as his mouth moves lower. He draws my hardened nipple into his mouth, and I instantly miss the pressure of his cock. My body is alive, it screams for pressure, more friction.

I groan in frustration.

Jax smiles against my skin, his hand moving lower, cupping the area that aches the most. His mouth torments my breasts while his fingers move across my silken, swollen skin.

I throw back my head and let out a groan, spreading my legs wider, angling my core and clit against the object of my desire.

Jax's moan vibrates against my skin as his fingers draw teasing circles over my swollen lips and clit. My hips take on a life of their own, thrusting backwards and forwards, trying to get traction.

"Fuck, Kat."

He moans against my skin before taking my other nipple in his mouth and giving it equal attention. He slides one of his fingers just inside my entrance, teasing the sensitive skin while his thumb torments my clit, circling but not quite touching the hard bud of nerves.

I sink my fingers into the skin on his shoulders, dragging him up and forward, making him stand. Our eyes meet, holding each other's gaze, before our lips once again join.

I wrap one of my legs around his hip, pulling him firmly against me, rubbing my slick centre up and down his rock-hard cock, my desire coating him. His fingers trapped between us, driving me higher.

I bite his bottom lip, earning myself a moan, before drawing it into my mouth and sucking it.

Jax's hips rock forward.

He pulls away sharply and spins me around, pressing my

hands against the wall of the tiles, moving in behind me, his front crowded against my back, his hands resting over mine. He nips at my earlobe, blowing gently. My hips tilt back against him, my arse cheeks cradling his cock. He moves his hands, gripping my hips, and I groan at the feel of his cock sliding down and between my thighs.

I drop my head back against his shoulder as the head of his cock breaches my entrance.

Jax nips my earlobe. "Are you ready?" he says, my pussy contracting sharply at his tone.

I turn my face towards him, biting my lip.

He smirks and presses down on my back, bending me forward before thrusting into my pulsing depths.

I grunt, angling myself forward to take more and more of him. The stretch and burn of his invasion raises my body temperature to fever pitch. The feeling of fullness, the knowledge he's buried deep in my pussy leaves me panting, a desperation sweeping my system.

"Yes."

I mewl, spreading my legs wider, giving him more access.

Jax slides in further, and my body welcomes him. He pauses before pulling out and thrusting back in, then sliding in and back out, repeatedly. I turn my head, his eyes glued on where our bodies are joined.

"I love watching my cock get devoured by your pussy," he says, slamming home before withdrawing slowly. "Your body is sucking me in like it never wants me to leave."

"It doesn't," I admit breathlessly. "It wants you buried in me forever."

I hiss as he changes the angle, his cock hitting my G-spot until I see stars.

"Have. You. Missed. This?"

He pants, thrusting in and out, until we're a panting mess.

"Yes," I shriek, as his hand snakes around, finding my

swollen and throbbing bunch of nerves. I suck in a breath as his fingers begin their torment. The pressure of my orgasm building almost instantly in my lower body.

"Please, Jax," I beg, my lips quivering.

My emotions are riding me as never before.

"Slowly, princess," he whispers against my ear, sliding almost all the way out before slamming back into me. "Feel what you've done to me. How hard I am for you." He rotates his hips, driving his point home. He nips my earlobe again. "When I come, Kat. I'm going to paint the inside of your sweet pussy with so much of my cum, it's going to be dripping out of you for days. You won't be able to forget tonight."

My eyes roll back in my head as he takes his time, driving me almost to the point of no return before pulling back and starting up again, his body truly savouring mine.

His fingers are moving through and around my lips and clit. Stretching my entrance around his cock.

I bite down on the inside of my mouth to stop myself from crying out.

My muscles begin to clench.

Jax withdraws his hands, his cock buried deep inside me. He grips one of my hands that is still against the wall.

"Not yet," he whispers against my throat, his lips moving against my sensitive skin.

One hand leaves mine and cups my breast, tweaking and pulling first one, then my other nipple.

I try to move away from him, but he wraps an arm tight around my waist to stop me.

His hand slides south once again, finding my bud of nerves, his cock in and out, pumping hard and fast. The pressure builds deep in my core, and before I have a chance to think, my muscles are contracting and I'm falling into the abyss. Lights flash behind my eyes as I come harder than I ever have before. Jax continues to move in and out before slamming in deep. I feel his cock pulse, his cum emptying deep inside me, just as he promised. My muscles milk him dry, sending me into another instant orgasm.

By the time Jax's head rests between my shoulder blades, we're both panting hard. His arms wrap tightly around my waist, stopping me from collapsing in a heap on the shower floor.

Jax moves, standing upright, his cock slipping from deep within my pussy.

My muscles contract, wanting to maintain the stretch, the pressure.

A warm liquid trickles down my leg. I look down at the white milky liquid, evidence of what we've just done.

Jax groans, dropping to his knees, his fingers sliding through the white, sticky mess.

"Do you know how sexy this is?" he whispers, pressing his lips against the skin of my lower back.

I turn in his arms, so his mouth is now against my stomach.

He looks up at me, his pupils dilated, his cheeks flushed.

His eyes don't leave mine as his tongue snakes out, lapping at my clit.

Hot water continues to run off us.

His fingers move up my thigh, finding my entrance, pushing the escaping liquid back into my body.

I drop back against the shower wall, the ice-cold tiles steal my breath, but I'm lost in Jaxson and his magical fingers as they continue their torment.

CHAPTER 44

JAX

There's a loud knock on my office door, which flies open before I have a chance to answer.

Caleb appears, almost vibrating with excitement.

"Leah's in labour, the twins are on the way. Gabriel just called." His words come out in a gush, and I grin back at him.

"What are you doing here? You need to go."

I know how devastated Caleb was to have missed Callum's birth. Leah delivered early, and he was stuck in the US with me. The twins may be different in personality, but their bond is undeniable, and when Gabriel finally found love with Leah, Caleb was over the moon. When Callum was born, it was almost like he had a child of his own.

"I have an investor's meeting, they're all waiting in the meeting room," he says.

"I've got this. I take it Simon will be there?"

I already know that he will be. He spent yesterday afternoon running through his part of the presentation with me, to ensure he hadn't missed anything.

Caleb nods.

"I've listened to your spiel more times than I care to think over the years. I can probably repeat it verbatim."

"Are you sure? I know you're trying to get the FHG permits through."

"Go. I've got you covered."

Caleb doesn't need me to say it again, he flies out the door, leaving a whirlwind of excited energy in his wake.

"Send Leah my love," I shout after him with a chuckle.

"Will do," comes a distant reply.

I log onto the server and download a copy of Caleb's presentation. As management, we have a directory set up to cover each other in cases like this, when someone needs to step in.

Once it's downloaded, I head up to the meeting room.

"Ladies, gentlemen, it's good to see you. Caleb has been called away, so I'll be taking you through today's presentation."

I go around the room, shaking the hands of all those present. We've all met before, when I was involved in the initial discussions. Simon nods in my direction. I shoot him a look that lets him know I'm not here to step on his toes. I know he's got this.

The presentation goes well. I really have heard Caleb give it enough times to deliver it myself.

I enter my office and check my phone.

CAL:

Beautiful twin girls.

ME:

Congratulations to everyone.

I smile at the message and click on the photo of a tired-looking Leah, holding two tiny bundles. Gabriel is grinning down at her and their two latest additions, his love shining through. Leah's made it to thirty-seven weeks. Between her mum, Francesca and Kat, I know they've all been helping out after the doctor demanded full bed rest following the New Year.

New Year.

My mind wanders to Kat.

Is she there too?

My body hardens at the memory of us together. The storm kept us trapped within the summerhouse until five AM, not that either of us complained. The time flew by as we enjoyed each other's bodies.

When the storm finally subsided, we'd crept back into the manor like a couple of naughty teenagers, narrowly missing Betsy, who was heading down to the kitchen.

There was not much talking about the future. We discussed our Christmases, my parents, and her siblings. I left her at her bedroom door with one final smouldering kiss, but when I emerged a few hours later, she was gone, a note pushed under my door, explaining that she was being called back to London to deal with an emergency at one of the hotels.

Coincidence?

I sigh.

We've hardly spoken since the New Year. Work and life are pulling us both in different directions. I can't even blame Kat. Two days after I returned to London, I was required to fly to the US for a week, only to have one of our older clients demand my presence at a meeting.

I can't regret the time we spent together. When I opened my eyes in the shower and saw Kat standing there, her bottom lip pulled between her teeth, her body on full display... My cock was already throbbing simply from her proximity. When I pulled her into my arms, there'd been no rational thought, only a driving need to sink into her silky depths until she was screaming and coming around my cock.

I know Kat wants to keep our relationship professional, and I appreciate that. But I also crave the woman, like I've never craved another. The simple thought of her ties me up in knots, has me breaking out in a sweat, my body tingling with need.

I sink into my chair, adjusting myself.

I open my laptop and type out an email, copying in Simon and Caleb, outlining the meeting. Trish, Caleb's PA, took the minutes, but I want to give my take. It's something we've always done after every investor or client meeting. Gut feel. Make sure everyone is on the same page going forward.

My phone pings.

More pictures.

Caleb grinning down at one of the twins nestled in his arms, while Gabriel stands next to him, the other nestled in his. Both brothers are looking proud as punch.

I know Caleb and April are waiting. She's just got her business off the ground, and they now want to ensure Lofton House has been renovated before they think about starting a family. With April being fostered, I know they've even discussed fostering. And knowing how they've both worked closely with the young adults and children in the community, I can see it being a serious possibility.

Children and a family are not something I've thought too much about. Emma and I discussed it, but after our relationship ended, I pushed all thoughts aside. Since then, my relationships have been more friends with benefits than anything stable or long-term. As an only child, from a broken marriage, it's not something that has driven me. Before bringing a child into this world, I want to know I'm in a stable, loving relationship.

This time, when my phone pings, it's pictures of April

holding one of the twins. Francesca grinning down at her latest grandchildren.

Is Kat there?

My mind always wanders to her. Where she is, and what she's doing, it simply can't help itself.

My laptop pings this time with a notification.

PERMITS.

Something I can get my teeth into.

I click on the attachment and begin going through the details, pushing all thoughts of Kathryn Frazer and babies out of my mind.

CHAPTER 45

KAT

"Ant-ie Kat, look," Callum pulls on my skirt, holding up a picture.

It's brightly coloured squiggles from the crayons I gave him at Christmas.

"Wow, little man, that's amazing," I say, dropping down onto one knee to take a closer look.

He scowls at me, looking so like Gabriel and Caleb that it takes my breath away.

"Not ickle."

He pats his chest. "Big bruv-er."

I grin, pulling him in for a hug. "That you are. And big brothers are so important."

He rests a hand on my chest. "You, big sister to Daddy."

"That's right. I'm your daddy's big sister. And uncle Caleb's and Aunty Harper's."

I stand up, picking him up as I go, giving him an enormous squeeze. He squirms, the paper flapping in his hand.

"Big-bruver," he says, patting his chest again proudly.

"I know you are. The best big brother. Daddy was telling me how much you've been helping him and Mummy."

I kiss his cheek as I transfer him to my hip. He's getting so big.

Callum grins. He's growing up fast, and now with the twins, Gabriel and Leah have their hands full.

My brother appears, carrying one of the twins, freshly changed. The tiny bundle looks even smaller against his enormous frame.

I don't think I've ever seen Gabriel look as content as he does surrounded by his family.

Callum squirms in my arms, and I put him down. He takes my hand and pulls me forward.

"Hey Callum, are you showing Aunty Kat your picture?"

Callum nods, holding it out once more.

"Is this for me?" I say, when he pushes it into my free hand.

I drop down and place another kiss on his cheek when he nods.

"Thank you. I'll hang this one up in my office so I can see it every day."

His grin widens, and he wraps his little arms around my neck. I pull him close, my eyes shutting.

Gabriel grins.

"Kat Frazer, crawling around on the floor in her designer suit. The press would have a field day."

I open my eyes and scowl at Gabe, who chuckles.

"The press can…"

I stop myself from saying any more, as Leah walks in and coughs.

"Stop tormenting Kat," she says, walking up with my other niece in her arms.

She looks amazing, given that she has three children under two and only gave birth less than a week ago.

"How do you do it?" I say, standing up and giving her a

side hug so I don't disturb the tiny sleeping bundle in her arms.

She looks over at Gabe, the love shining in her eyes.

"I have a lot of help."

The transformation is unbelievable. My baby brother has gone from an introverted workaholic to a loving husband and father of three in two and a half years.

"Lottie has also been invaluable. She's here every night after school, helping with bath time."

Leah's eyes meet mine. She's been amazing, allowing Lottie somewhere safe to escape as she tries to make sense of the nightmare she uncovered. I incline my head in acknowledgement.

"And who's this?" I ask Leah.

"This is Ava. She was born ten minutes earlier than Isla."

Leah places the sleeping bundle in my arms, her little face scrunching up as her mum releases her, but she remains asleep.

"Hey, Ava," I say, running my finger down her tiny cheek.

Her mouth purses into an almost smile.

Leah bends down and scoops up Callum, who leans over to stare at his baby sister, total adoration in his eyes.

"Baby."

He sighs.

Gabriel walks up.

"And this is Isla. She's the loudest of the two. Lets us know she's here."

"A female version of Cal, then," I say.

Gabriel chuckles.

The doorbell goes, and I raise a brow in question. I didn't know they were expecting anyone. Gabriel hadn't said anything when I called.

"That'll be Jaxson," he says, answering my unasked question.

My heart skips a beat at the mention of his name.

Typical Leah misses nothing.

I give her a weak smile.

"Jax," Callum squeals, throwing himself at the man who's entered the room.

Jax scoops him up and spins him around.

"Hey, scamp, how are you?"

Callum buries his head in Jax's neck. "Goog," he says.

Jax looks up, his eyes meeting mine before going to the baby in my arms. His gaze warms.

"Aunty cuddles?" he says.

"I brought some gifts," I say.

His eyes dart to the twenty bags filled with clothes and toys.

"Kat can't help herself," Gabriel says, laughing. "She was as bad when Callum was born. I think she bought out half the toy and clothing stores."

Jax rolls his lips to stop himself laughing, but his eyes are sparkling. My stomach does a somersault.

I shrug, as I work to control my breathing, aware that my brother and sister-in-law are privy to our interaction.

Jax breaks eye contact as Callum squirms in his arms, asking to be put down. Jax complies and runs off, returning with the large car I bought him as a *big-brother* present.

"Did Aunty Kat get you this?" Jax asks, dropping onto one knee.

Callum nods and grins, holding it out to him.

"Well, it will go perfectly with this."

Jax leans behind him and grabs the bag he was carrying when he entered. He digs around and pulls out a large wrapped box.

Callum lets out another squeal, and his sister grumbles her complaint in my arms. I rock her gently until she resettles.

Callum tears open the wrapping, revealing another matching car to the one I bought.

"Great minds," Gabriel chuckles.

His eyes flash between Jax and me.

"More like we both know what little boys like," I say, dismissing his claim.

"Thank you, both of you. You've spoiled all of them," Leah says.

Ava opens her eyes and lets out a squeak, her mouth moving sideways against my top as she tries to forage for food.

"Looks like someone is hungry," Leah says, scooping Ava out of my arms before she can leave a damp patch on my blouse. "If you'll excuse me, it's a juggling act of feeding one before the other wakes up and demands her share."

"I better go," I say. "Leave you in peace."

"You don't have to," Leah says, a look of guilt passing over her face, as if her words have chased me away.

I give her arm a gentle squeeze.

"I'll pop around on Saturday. Maybe I can take Callum to the P.A.R.K." I spell out. "Give you guys a break."

Leah inclines her head, her eyes welling up. She sniffs.

"Sorry, my hormones are all over the place. That would be wonderful."

I smile and give her arm one final squeeze. "I'll see you then."

I lean in and kiss Leah on the cheek before running a finger down Isla's arm, then turn to Gabriel, looking at the second tiny bundle.

"Fatherhood suits you, baby brother," I say.

"I know," he says with a grin. "Thank you for all the presents."

"Isn't that what aunts are for? Spoiling their nieces and nephews?"

Gabriel walks me to the door.

"Bye, Jax," I say, his proximity playing havoc with my equilibrium.

"Bye, Kat," he says, looking up from the toy cars Callum has him playing with.

I turn to find Gabriel watching me closely.

I smile.

"Right, that's me out of here."

"You work too hard," Gabriel says, opening the door to his and Leah's apartment.

I shrug. "Pot calling kettle, and all that."

"That was the old me, I've—"

"Let me guess, seen the light?"

He chuckles and wraps his free arm around me, pulling me into his side. "Take care, sis."

"You too."

Heading down to the carpark in the elevator, I close my eyes and do breathing exercises to calm my racing heart. Seeing Jax face-to-face was much easier when I thought I hated him, that he was a two-timing snake. Now... the man sets my lady parts on fire, and has my heart racing, and stomach jumping at a mere glance. The Maldives was clearly a bad idea. New Year was even worse. It's woken up my libido, and it appears there's no putting it back in its box. My body is starting to crave Jax's, like it does water after a fierce workout. Jaxson Lockwood has left me insatiable, not only for his body, but I find myself missing our conversations, his company.

Kat Frazer, you're having a pre-midlife crisis. Time to get a grip!

I squirm as I drop into the seat of my McLaren. The vibration of the engine as I fire her up, exciting my already sensitive clit. I groan and close my eyes briefly before putting her in reverse and getting as far away from Jaxson Lockwood as possible.

By the time I make it back to the hotel, I take the elevator straight to my floor, bypassing reception and any staff members who may want my attention. Closing the door to the suite, I lean my head back against it.

Heading to my bedroom, I strip off my suit, hanging it up before stepping into the steaming shower. My sensitive nipples pucker against the spray of water. I bite my lips as my fingers find them, tweaking and pulling as Jaxson did, the last time we were together. I groan in frustration before sliding a hand between my thighs. My pussy is already swollen and wet, pulsing with a need to be filled. I drop my head against the cool tiles, two fingers sliding into my entrance, while my thumb strums my throbbing clit, faster and faster. I close my eyes and picture Jax. His smooth, taut skin, his impressive cock. It's not long before my muscles are clenching around my fingers and I'm groaning into the shower spray.

I turn around and lean against the cold shower wall, cooling my body as I try to cool my libido.

I wash in record time, not wanting to give in to my desires any further.

I bite my lip as I drag my fluffy bathrobe across sensitive skin.

I head for the kitchen, but pause as there's a knock at the suite door.

I move to the peephole.

"You're kidding me."

I throw open the door before I remember I'm in my robe.

"What the hell are you doing here?" I ask, wishing now I'd ignored the knock.

Zach looks at me, his eyes imploring.

"The manager at the apartment building told me you'd

move here. Look, I need to see you. You've refused my calls, left my emails unanswered."

"And that wasn't *pointed* enough?"

I stand in the doorway, blocking his entrance.

He looks around me.

"Can I come in?"

I fold my arms over my chest.

"Why? I don't think we have anything to say to one another."

"Kat, don't be like this, please. I just want to talk."

One of the doors further down the corridor opens, and I remember where we are. The last thing my family needs is for me to be caught airing our dirty laundry in public.

I step back reluctantly and wait as Zach enters. In his defence, he doesn't look smug. If he did, I may have been tempted to knee him in the balls.

He enters, keeping his distance.

"Take a seat and don't touch anything. I'm going to put some clothes on."

There's no way I'm having a conversation with Zach, wrapped in a bathrobe.

I get dressed in record time, pulling on some leggings and a jumper, before scooping my damp hair into a top knot.

Zach is returning to the sofa when I get back.

"I thought I told you not to move," I say.

"I was…" he says, shaking his head. "Never mind."

He runs a hand through his hair.

I fold my arms over my chest.

"Say what you have to say and leave," I snap, my patience running thin.

Him being here, in my space, makes my skin crawl. I left the apartment because of what he did, and I loved that place. Now he's threatening to pollute my new home.

"I just wanted to see if you read my letter."

"I did," I say, my eyes never leaving his. "Quite the set of excuses you gave. Do you take responsibility for any of it?"

"I take responsibility for all of it," he says, more firmly than I anticipate. "I never meant to hurt you, Kat. When you finally agreed to be with me, I was over the moon. When Darra threatened to tell you everything, I didn't know what to do. I had to keep her quiet. She was going to ruin everything."

"Let me get this straight. You kept her quiet by *fucking* her in our bed?"

His eyes almost bulge out of his head.

"Yes, she told me," I snap.

"It wasn't like that."

"What was it like then? Explain how you got naked with my brother's wife, in our bed."

He runs a hand down his face. Dark circles frame his eyes, and his skin holds a greyness it never has before.

"Darra used to bring Lottie over with the nanny, so I could see my daughter. The nanny would take her swimming."

I let out a bark. "So, you and Darra got down and dirty while your daughter went swimming with the nanny? The lousy parent award goes to…"

Zach frowns, and I let out a hollow laugh. "You literally just said, Darra brought Lottie over so you could spend time with her? Get your facts straight, Zach." I stare at the man I once lived with, shared my life with. "Actually, don't bother. The pair of you make me sick. Thank God, Lottie has Elijah."

Stomach acid rises, burning the back of my throat.

Whatever Zach sees on my face hardens him.

"Don't be such a bitch. You act all high and mighty, Kat. But it's not like you were ever around. Once you started working with your dad, there was no time for me. You became obsessed."

"I may have been caught up in my job, but at least I was faithful," I spit.

"In body maybe, but were you ever faithful in your mind? As I said in my letter. It was always him, the perfect Jaxson Lockwood. Did you think I didn't know it was him you were imagining every time you let me fuck you?"

"You're delusional," I hiss.

"Am I? I'd hoped that when you let me be your plus-one, you'd see me as more, but I was only ever the safe option. Admit it. You were married to your job. I was the handy partner who was there to have dinner ready on the table and to keep your bed warm. Not that you ever wanted that."

"I..."

Zach shakes his head sadly. "The thing is, I know you aren't frigid, Kat. I knew that years before we got together. I came home and heard you and Jax going at it, in his bed, when you thought we were all away. It was a risky move by both of you."

He sighs.

"Do you know how hard it is living with someone, and knowing you can't take them to those heights, however hard you try? That every time you try to make love to them, they're wishing it was somebody else moving above them."

I avert my gaze and swallow repeatedly.

"Why?" I ask quietly.

"Why what? Why did I lie? Why did I help Darra?"

"All of it," I say, my eyes finally meeting his.

"Jealousy. I'd fancied you for ages, but Eli warned me off. He and Jax got closer over the years, leaving me on the outside looking in. Both handsome, successful, ready to take on the world, then there was me." He expels a loud breath. "When I found out about you and Jax, I was pissed. How did he get to have you when I was told you were off limits?"

"But Darra? I'm one thing, but your best friend's girlfriend?"

He squeezes his temples as he grimaces. "Darra kind of just happened. I did try to do the right thing by Lottie. As for Darra, she knew how I felt about you and promised to help me if I stayed quiet."

"You overheard what Jax said to me."

It's not a question, as I already know the answer.

"I did. It was perfect."

There's a hint of pride in his voice that makes me want to vomit.

"So, you decided to what? Split us up, take me for yourself?"

He shrugs, and my hands ball into fists.

"It worked, didn't it?"

"Did it?" I hiss. "You just said yourself, I never got over losing Jax."

His shoulders slump, and he becomes unnaturally still.

He inhales before closing and reopening his eyes.

"You're right." His eyes move to his hands. Hands that are clasped together in his lap. "As I said in my letter, you never looked at me the way you looked at him. However much I thought I could step into his shoes, it didn't take me long to realise I was never going to replace Jaxson in your heart."

I pinch the bridge of my nose, pressure building behind my eyes.

"I'm sorry, Kat. If I could change it…"

"Would you?"

He looks up at me, and I see the truth in his eyes.

"No, probably not. I would have always wondered. I'm a selfish bastard. I wanted you, and took you when you were at a weak point, thought that would be enough. I hoped you could and would learn to love me. I've realised, however much you might want it to be different, love can't be forced."

I drop into one of the chairs opposite.

"I'm sorry too. If I'd known how you felt. I would never have asked you to be my plus-one."

Zach gets up.

"But you didn't. You were blind to my feelings. Your head had been completely turned by someone else."

I can't deny his words, so I remain silent.

"I'm going to go." He inclines his head. "I *am* sorry, Kat."

"Me too," I say, the fight having left me.

He moves to the door, his hand resting on the handle.

"Jax was here earlier."

My head shoots up. "When?"

"When you were getting changed."

"And you're only just telling me this now?"

Zach shrugs, and I notice the hardness that has returned to his eyes.

"I'm a selfish bastard, what more can I say?"

"Just go," I say, a wave of exhaustion taking over.

"He doesn't deserve you, you know."

"What are you talking about?"

"Jax, he was never good enough for you. He still isn't."

"But you were? Zach, you really need to leave," I say, trying to maintain some semblance of calm.

"I'm going," he says before turning and staring at me. "He's never going to be able to forget how you fucked and lived with me. It's a man thing. He'll always hate that."

"But it didn't bother you?"

He chuckles. "I won, you chose me."

"That's where you're wrong. I never chose you. You were convenient. As you pointed out, you were there at one of the lowest points in my life. You took advantage of me, manipulated both me and the facts for your own gain. For that, I will *never* forgive you. I may not have loved you the way you wanted, but when you look back, who's to blame? I was supposed to have been able to trust you."

Zach nods. "You're right. But you can't blame me for trying?"

"I can, and I do." I stare him down. "Just go."

He turns and lets himself out without another word.

CHAPTER 46

JAX

I slam the car door shut, hit reverse, pull out of the parking space, then slam it back into drive and re-park. The need to get away is riding me hard, but it's not like I can go back to Caleb and April in my current state. They'll know instantly something's up, and I can't face their questions.

Thumping the steering wheel, I push open the door and climb out.

I head for the hotel bar, taking up a spot at the bar itself.

"Good evening, Mr Lockwood. What can I get you?"

"Malt whiskey on ice, please, Dom. Top shelf," I say.

I've stayed here enough in the past that I know a large portion of the long-term staff. Which is most of them. People seem to love working for the Frazers. For Kat.

My drink appears in seconds, and I take a deep swallow, enjoying the bold, fiery sensation.

Seeing Zach in Kat's suite. The smug look on his face as he opened the door.

What the hell?

I'd reined myself in, even though my hands balled into

tight fists and I wanted to flatten my once close friend. Kat had been nowhere in sight. Was she even there? Had some unsuspecting staff member let him in?

I'm sure there's an explanation, and my head tells me nothing is going on between them, but seeing him there was a reminder of what they shared. The fact that he lived with her for years and slept next to her every night. Was welcomed as her partner at family events. That she chose to be with him, despite all we shared.

I finish my first before motioning for Dom to refill my glass.

Dark eyes clash with mine in the mirror behind the bar.

"You're still here."

"I am," I say, looking at the stool next to me.

"Are you going to join me?"

I push it with my foot.

"Why not?"

Dom appears.

"Evening, Ms Frazer," he says. "What can I get you?"

"I'll have what he's having, Dom, thank you."

I smile. It was all Mai Tais on holiday, now we're back in the real world.

"I have three brothers," she says.

I say nothing, instead turning to face her. She's makeup-free, her damp hair screwed up in a messy top knot.

A designer jumper over— Are those leggings?

A pink flush spreads high over her cheekbones as I take in her appearance.

The bar is almost empty, with only a few guests enjoying post-dinner drinks. All however, are dressed in smart business attire befitting a top-end five-star hotel.

Kat looks around, her shoulders tense as she notices people watching.

She straightens her spine and smiles. Several return her greeting.

Dom places her whiskey down in front of her.

"Charge them to my account," Kat says to Dom.

He nods and moves away.

Silence descends between us.

"Zach?" I say, eventually.

"Turned up unexpectedly."

"Yet he was in your suite?"

Kat flinches at the sarcasm in my tone.

"I had no choice. Was I supposed to have a conversation with him in front of God knows who?"

She has a point, but I still smart at the idea of her being alone with him.

"Big brother is always watching," I say, under my breath.

Something Elijah used to say when we'd go out on the town as students.

"You have no idea," she murmurs, almost too quietly for me to hear.

We nurse our drinks, taking a moment.

Kat takes a sip of hers, the ice clinking against the side. Then she stares at the glass.

"Do you want to come up?" she asks suddenly, turning her head towards me. "I can order us some room service?"

I look at her. Something flashes across her eyes. Defiance? Vulnerability?

A man comes to stand next to us at the bar.

"You have the plans you want me to look over?" I say, suddenly.

Kat shoots me a look, then smiles.

"They arrived this afternoon. I'm sorry I got held up in meetings. We can do this another time if you'd prefer?"

"No, now is fine," I say.

Kat's eyes sparkle as she slips off the stool.

I follow suit. "After you."

We stand at the elevator, it pings open, and I place a hand on her back, sucking in a breath as she looks up at me, her pupils dilating.

We enter, allowing the doors to close behind us.

Kat motions with her head to the camera in the corner, so I keep my hands by my side.

We make it to her floor with no stoppages.

Kat retrieves her key, letting us in.

She's in my arms before the door clicks shut.

CHAPTER 47

KAT

Sleep recedes, and my muscles clench.

My back arches, as lips descend south, over my stomach. I bite my lip to smother my moan.

That tormenting mouth continues south. My hands rise, cupping my breasts, tweaking and pulling on my nipples. Opening my legs, I allow him access, the breadth of his shoulders pushing me wider.

His mouth finds my core, licking me from my weeping hole to my clit. I squirm against the sheets, a heavy arm moving over my pelvic bone holding me in place, while his lips and tongue ruin me.

My hands leave my breasts and cradle the head between my thighs, holding him in place as his lips suckle and torment my clit.

"Jax," I whisper into the air, as a finger finds my opening.

I squeeze my eyes closed as his wicked mouth and fingers drive me higher.

My body should be spent after the night we've shared, but it looks like my body wants one more. I've become insatiable.

Pulling on his head, I draw him up and over my body.

Lips meet mine. Jax deepens the kiss, ensuring I can taste myself on his tongue.

His hard cock finds my entrance. I spread my thighs wider, using my feet as traction on the bed. I rock my hips, encouraging him to slide only the head of his cock into my body. We both pause, enjoying the sensation.

My nails sink into his back as he gently rotates his hips, teasing my opening.

"You have a very wicked cock, Mr Lockwood," I whisper against his neck.

"I'm glad you like it, Ms Frazer," he replies. "It's at your service whenever you want it."

"This could become very addictive," I whisper, lifting my hips so he slides slightly deeper into my wet pussy.

His lips meet mine, and I moan against the mouth and tongue that are now devouring me.

Our hips move, his cock sliding deeper until he's balls deep in my body.

My hands grip his arse cheeks, squeezing and releasing, wanting more.

"Jax, please," I beg.

He slides his hands under my ass, tipping my pelvis up, allowing him to drive in and out. He pounds into me. I meet him stroke for stroke, my body becoming more and more lubricated, the pressure in my pelvis growing tighter.

"Jax, I'm going to come," I hiss against his lips, locking my hip muscles.

"Let go, I've got you."

I know he does. He has all night. As he always has.

The pressure continues to build. I bear down, welcoming the rush of pleasure as my lower body contracts around him, my muscles milking him hard, my body shuddering with desire.

"Yes," I say, pulling him closer, wrapping my legs around his hips.

Jax stills, his cock jerking, his cum emptying deep inside me, coating me. He continues to rock gently before collapsing, his head buried in the side of my neck.

I rub soothing circles over his back, enjoying the masculine weight of him on my body, between my thighs.

"That was one way to wake up," I say, kissing the side of his head.

Jax presses up, his boyish grin something I've missed.

"You always did like an orgasm alarm."

He chuckles.

I raise a hand and run it through his messy hair.

"It's been a long time."

"Too long," he says, kissing my nose before rolling off me.

He flops onto his back before drawing me into his side. Surprising myself, I go willingly, resting my head on his shoulder.

We lie there, together. Our bodies touching, our voices quiet.

My brain is empty. For the first time, in a long time, the incessant noise has stopped.

My phone pings on the bedside table next to me.

I groan.

"No rest for the wicked, isn't that what they say?" Jax says, with a chuckle.

I grab my phone and stare at the screen.

Elijah.

What does he want?

ELIJAH:

Jax is booked into room 350.

The suite next to mine.

Three dots appear, followed by a photo of Jax and me entering the elevator, his hand on my lower back. The picture itself isn't much, but it's the look we're giving each other.

"Shit!" I say, throwing back the covers and standing up.

"What?"

I pass him my phone.

"Kat," he says, his eyes clashing with mine. "I'm sorry."

He drops back, his forefinger and thumb rubbing his eyes.

I stop and draw in a deep breath before sinking back onto the edge of the bed, my hand reaching out, finding Jax's chest.

My brain whirls, unable to focus. My racing heartbeat is all I can concentrate on. Flexing my fingers over Jax's taut skin, I marvel at his beautiful physique, and the fact he's here with me.

Fuck it!

I bite my lip, suddenly trying to suppress a giggle.

My chest lightens, and my head feels slightly dizzy.

Dropping back on my pillow, I stare up at the ceiling. Then turn my head to stare at Jaxson, who's developed a deep groove between his eyebrows.

My lips spread into a grin.

"Fuck it," I say, only this time it's out aloud.

"Kat?" Jax looks at me like I've lost my mind.

I roll onto my side, supporting my head on my arm.

"The cat is out of the bag. My brothers know, the board, our investors, they'll all know. I should be panicking, but I realise, I'm tired of hiding, worrying what everyone else thinks."

Jax opens and closes his mouth. When his phone pings, he drops back with a groan.

Scooting across the bed, I rest my head on his shoulder, looking at his screen.

> **ELIJAH:**
> Pen tells me Kat's a big girl, and to keep my nose out.

I do laugh now as Jax covers his eyes.

I love my friend. Only imagining what Pen said to Elijah when he received that photo.

His phone pings again. This time, it's Caleb.

> **CALEB:**
> Knew it! I'm cupid.
>
> **CALEB:**
> You have a change of clothes waiting in room 350. Mason delivered your case.

It's my turn to groan. All I need is my baby brother thinking he set me up with Jax.

Jax pulls me into his arms, kissing my temple.

"At least they don't want to castrate you," I say.

"But that picture is obviously out there."

"It is. Although Elijah has seen to it, we can deny it."

His muscles tense under my cheek.

I push up and look into his face.

"If we don't, there may be backlash with the board, with investors."

Jax pushes away and stands up.

"Whatever," he says, reaching for his clothes. "I better get back to Cal and April's."

"Jax. Stop."

His hand pauses as he picks up his jumper.

Sitting up, I pull the duvet around my naked breasts.

"What do you want from me, Kat? Am I just a convenient fuck, someone who rescued your project?"

A headache begins to form. I narrow my eyes.

"This is not just about me and what I want," I say, forcing

my jaw to relax. "What do you want, Jax? I'm not presuming anything. I'm merely stating a fact. Whatever we decide, we're in this together."

He drops his chin to his chest, his hand gripping the back of his neck.

When he looks up, I know his answer.

"I want you. I always have."

CHAPTER 48

KAT

Okay, so I missed the memo about how invested the world would be in my love life.

My inbox is filled with emails from the board.

Questions from investors.

Not to mention the press.

I'm getting a whole new insight into how the world sees me. And it's not particularly flattering.

> *Is London's Ice Queen Melting?*
>
> *Kathryn Frazer, CEO of Frazer Hotel Group, has been seen cosying up to Jaxson Lockwood, CEO of Lockwood Architects and a long-term friend and business partner of her brother. The pair were seen together at the FHG Hotel, London, where she currently resides. Mr Lockwood is the principal architect working on FHG's latest development project. The couple were recently spotted together holidaying in the Maldives.*

I groan, and groan again.

All I need now is for Zach or Darra to jump in and add fuel to the fire. My only saving grace is Lottie, and the fact that she's still barely talking to either of them. If they rock the boat, I know my niece. She'll be done with them for good. She already called me to tell me how amazing she thinks Jax and I are as a couple. Oh, to be that young and idealistic.

There's a knock at my office door.

"Come in?" I call, wondering why Michael hasn't announced my visitor.

The door opens, the answer becoming instantly clear.

"Mum, what are you doing here?"

"Can't a mother come and take her daughter out for lunch?"

I look at the time. It's ten thirty.

When she sees where my eyes have gone, she shrugs.

"There wasn't as much traffic as Freddie anticipated," she says.

Freddie being her long-term driver and, I suspect, confidante. He and his wife have lived on the estate for years. He drove my father around before my mother. He has never forgiven himself for being on holiday the night my father was killed in a road traffic accident, and I suspect it is why he insists on driving my mother everywhere she needs to go.

My laptop pings with yet another message.

Sadie.

I grimace.

Remember, Kat, never show your true feelings or insecurities, or they can be used against you.

Never have the words been more prevalent.

"You need a break," Mum says, coming around my desk and taking my arm. "There's nothing here that won't still be here when you get back."

I let her navigate me from behind my desk. We've all learned over the years that arguing with our mother is futile.

She'll always get her own way. *Small, yet feisty*, is how my father described her.

My chest clenches as it always does when I think of him, especially when I feel like I'm losing control.

I may have accepted that I have feelings for Jax, that I want to be with him. I enjoy spending time with him. He lights a fire inside me, one that I thought was out forever.

But now, it's almost like the world is holding its breath. We have neither confirmed nor denied our relationship, and I have no intention of doing so. My private life is exactly that, private.

"You're right," I say, squaring my shoulders and facing Mum. "Let's get out of here."

Mum smiles, her eyes shining with pride.

Michael is sitting at his desk when I open my office door.

"I'm heading out. Please take any messages, I'll reply when I get back."

Michael staggers to his feet when he sees my mother.

"Mrs Frazer," he says.

"Lovely to see you, Michael. I'm taking Kathryn out to lunch. Hold the fort while she's gone."

He almost bows, and I want to laugh. Mum always has that effect on people.

Together, we make our way down in the elevator. Every time I go to open my mouth, she places a hand on my arm and smiles, making me close it again.

We enter the lobby.

Douglas Chapman approaches.

"Francesca, it's been too long."

"Douggie," Mum says, plastering on her society smile.

"What are you doing here?" he asks.

"Can't a mother, and majority shareholder come and visit the CEO, who also happens to be her daughter?"

Her voice is sweetness and light, but there's no missing the underlying edge.

He smiles, but it's a little tight around the edges.

"Of course, of course." He turns to face me. "I was just coming to see you, Kathryn," he says.

Of course he was.

No doubt to lecture me on the dangers of getting involved with someone I work with. Some fatherly advice and all that.

I refrain from rolling my eyes. Instead, I look down at my watch.

"As you can see, I'm a little busy. Speak to Michael, and he'll arrange an appointment."

"We better go, lovely seeing you, Douggie," Mum says, sliding her arm through mine as she manoeuvres us towards the door, leaving him standing there, open-mouthed.

Freddie is at the kerb holding open the car door when we exit the building.

"Thank you, Freddie," I say, smiling at the older man.

"You're welcome, Ms Kathryn. Lovely to see you."

"You too."

Mum and I slide into the back.

"You know he hates you calling him Douggie," I tell her.

"Of course he does, it's why I do it. He's a pompous ass. I don't know why your father liked him so much."

"Dad liked him because he's surprisingly good at his job, he's stable, and he knows the hotel business inside out. The question is, why don't you like him?"

Something crosses Mum's face, but she keeps quiet.

"Ah, you mean the fact he didn't want me becoming CEO after Dad died?"

Mum turns, her mouth dropping open.

I laugh.

"Oh, don't worry, Mum, there's not much I don't know.

Douglas made his feelings very clear from the beginning. Although I think I've proved him wrong."

"I'm sorry," she says.

"For what? You can't blame them. I was relatively green. I'd only been working with Dad for a handful of years. I was still in my twenties."

"They wanted one of your brothers, as if a woman couldn't do it," she huffs. "Brothers who were younger, and who were even less experienced than you. I was not having that."

"Oh, I'm well aware. But I've had the last laugh. Proved them wrong, increased profits, expanded the business. If they had any doubts, they've been made to eat their words."

She smiles, and this time it reaches her eyes.

"You really are so like him."

A lump forms in my throat.

"He was stronger than I'll ever be," I admit quietly.

"Poppycock," Mum says. "You may not believe it, but you're stronger than all of them." I stare at her wide eyes. She shakes her head. "What have you told them in regard to Jaxson?"

"You've heard?"

"Don't change the subject."

"I haven't said anything."

"Why?"

"Because—"

"Why haven't you said anything?" she presses.

"Because it's no one else's business," I say shortly.

"Exactly. It isn't. You're the CEO, it does not give anyone the right to interfere or have a say in your private life."

I drop back against the seat as Mum reaches across and pats my leg.

"Your private life is no one else's business but your own."

"Is that why you're here?"

"Of course. I wanted to get my point across and tell you I couldn't be happier. I love Jaxson like a fourth son."

I laugh, my body warming.

"I'm so pleased he has your parental nod of approval," I add, with a hint of sarcasm. "Is this your way of telling me not to mess it up?"

I raise an eyebrow, and her face crinkles as she lets out a bark.

"No. It means, don't let anyone interfere this time. Including me."

Smiling, I look out of the window.

She taps on the partition between us and Freddie.

"We can head to Claridge's now, Fred," she says when he lowers the partition.

"Very well."

The partition goes back up.

Lunch doesn't open for another hour, I realise, looking at the time.

"Coffee and cake," Mum says, before I can give an excuse.

"Fine," I say.

My mind wanders back to the beautiful pastries Jaxson fed me in the Maldives. When did I develop such a sweet tooth?

"Thank you. I'm looking forward to it."

* * *

COFFEE AND CAKE are just what the doctor ordered. By the time Freddie delivers me back to the office, I'm charged and ready to take on the world.

Michael looks up as I walk past.

"Can you get Elliot up here as soon as he's available?" I tell him.

"Of course."

He jumps up from his desk and follows me.

Here we go.

"There have been a number of calls while you were out—"

He lists off the names, and I nod politely, swallowing the moan that threatens.

Here I was thinking my love life was a boring topic of conversation.

"Thank you, Michael. I'll get back to them all once I've spoken to Elliot."

He nods and leaves, closing the door behind him.

I sink into my chair, picking up my phone.

"How's it going?" Jax says, answering on the second ring.

I groan loudly, making him chuckle.

"I can always use room 350," he says.

"No way. As I said, I'm sick of hiding. We did that once before, and look where that got us."

"I'm with you, Kat, one hundred per cent, all the way."

I drop my head back and close my eyes, letting the warmth of his words wash over me and settle somewhere deep in my chest.

"What's your next move?" he asks.

"I've called Elliot up. He's always been set to head up the new development team. I'm going to step back from the project. That should keep the vultures at bay."

"Are you sure? This is your baby, Kat. I know what this project means to you."

Something in my chest shifts at the concern in his voice.

I smile. "Never more so," I admit. "It's time I take a step back. A wise person told me recently about something called *delegation*. I'm starting to think maybe I should try it."

"Really? I like the sound of this person, they sound very sensible," he says, with a chuckle.

My other line buzzes.

"Michael is trying to contact me."

"I'll see you later? We can look over the plans for your home office."

"I'd like that."

"See you later."

I hang up and connect with Michael.

"Elliot is here to see you."

"Great, send him in."

CHAPTER 49

JAX

"You and Kat, huh?"

I look up at my friend who's standing in the doorway.

"I hope so," I tell him.

If Kat wants to be open and honest, then so will I.

"It was the Maldives, wasn't it? All that romance, the beautiful setting. I knew it. Not even my sister could resist."

Caleb drops into the seat opposite mine.

I don't know yet whether Kat wants her siblings to know about our previous relationship. The current one, they seem fine with, but the fact that Kat has made her dislike for me over the past sixteen years incredibly obvious, maybe letting them know something happened before, is not the best move.

"We talked," I say. "Cleared the air."

There's another knock at the door.

The door opens, this time revealing Elijah's enormous frame.

"Hey," I say, but stop when I see the look on his face.

Oh shit, maybe the cat is already out of the bag.

"You slept with Kat sixteen years ago? I should throw you through the window. I always wondered why my sister hated you so much."

"Come in, and close the door," I say, calmly.

Caleb is sitting in the chair, his head swivelling between his older brother and me.

"You slept with our sister sixteen years ago?" he mutters. "And I sent you to the Maldives with her."

I shake my head.

"Why don't you both take a seat?" I say.

Elijah enters the room, closing the door sharply behind him.

"I'd rather stand," he says, his arms folded over his chest.

The door opens again, this time Pen crashes in.

"Sorry," she says, shooting me a look of apology, as she steps in front of Elijah.

"Slow down, big boy," she says.

"No, Pen, please come in and join the party," I say, with a sigh. "I believe we're just getting warmed up."

Pen turns on Elijah, who unfolds his arms quickly, dropping them to his side.

"What did I say? Stop, and let me explain," she says.

Elijah looks over Pen's shoulder and glares at me.

"I can't believe you knew he slept with her, and didn't say anything."

Pen grips his chin in her hand, re-diverting his gaze.

"How could I?" she says. "Have you forgotten you barely spoke to me for over fifteen of those years? Besides, Kat just told me."

Elijah's arms refold over his chest, the heat of his glare burrowing into me.

"You have some explaining to do— *Friend*."

Running a hand over the back of my neck, I massage the tight muscles, trying to ward off the impending headache.

"Fine," I say.

I fill them in on what happened sixteen years ago, how Darra and Zach conspired against us, and how Lottie's revelation helped clear the air, forcing the guilty parties to admit the truth.

At some point, Elijah has taken a seat on the sofa, Pen next to him. Both her hands enveloped in one of his.

"Do you love her?" his voice is thick and heavy.

"That's between Kat and me," I say.

Not wanting to tell her brothers how I feel, before letting the woman herself know.

He nods as if understanding.

"What I will say is, I'll do everything in my power never to hurt her again. I will fight for us." My eyes move between my friends. "I would rather have you guys on our side than against us."

"You have my backing," Caleb says quickly. "And April's."

Pen shoulder bumps Elijah.

He grunts.

She coughs.

He turns to face Pen.

"What? She's my sister, he's my best friend, or at least was," he growls. "They went behind my back. What about the best friend code?"

"Get over yourself," Pen says. "If you hadn't laid down the law all those years ago, they would not have had to hide their relationship, and Zach and Darra wouldn't have had any ammunition."

Elijah harrumphs and runs a hand through his hair.

Pen looks over at me and winks.

I allow my lips to tilt slightly, although I straighten them as soon as Elijah looks up.

"It was never you I was warning off," he says, his voice suddenly tired. "But she ended up with him anyway. I could never understand why. I think now maybe I do."

My stomach constricts.

"Just, don't hurt her," he says, standing up and pulling Pen into his side.

Elijah steps forward and holds out a hand. I shake it.

Caleb does the same.

Pen steps forward, coming around the desk to wrap her arms around me, whispering against my ear.

"Hurt her, and I'll make these two look like puppies."

She presses a kiss to my cheek before pulling back.

"You and Kat must come around for dinner," she says, returning to Elijah's side.

I incline my head.

"I'll get Kat to call you."

They all leave, and I sink back into my chair.

That went better than expected.

Glancing at the clock, there's half a day until Kat and I can touch base again, or touch in general.

My cock hardens instantly at the thought.

* * *

CALLS from the New York office. Reporters want a statement on my new relationship. I have erected a wall of silence. No one is to speak to the press, or anyone, for that matter.

The London office has been acting as a shield, all calls being directed to a brick wall in the press office.

Thankfully, Caleb arranged for Mason to pick me up and drive me to the hotel.

I check into the room Elijah arranged for me, before knocking on Kat's door.

"Hey," she says, throwing it open.

"Hey, yourself. How was your day?"

"I'd rather not discuss it. Living it was bad enough. Although I did have coffee and cake with Mum. You have her seal of approval," she says, her eyes twinkling.

I wrap my arms around her waist and pull her in for a kiss.

Our lips meet, the passion between us flowing, filling a void inside me.

When we finally come up for air, Kat smiles. "I needed that."

"Me too." I reply, taking her hand and leading her further into the room. "Your brothers paid me a visit today."

"Gabriel?"

"No, he was the only one who didn't."

"Please tell me you told them to mind their own business?"

"Not quite, but in a roundabout way. Pen says we need to have dinner with them."

Kat chuckles. "Is that all she said?"

"She threatened me, that if I hurt you…"

Kat laughs even harder. "Typical Pen. She's a pussy cat, and she loves you."

"Pen is definitely scarier than your brothers, and remember, cats have claws."

I love Pen as we've been friends for years, but her friendship with Kat has survived a lot. Would ours do the same if Kat and I crumble?

"I'll protect you," Kat says, biting her lip to prevent herself from smiling.

I grunt, looking at the table behind her.

"The plans arrived?"

"Dragged them out of the archives myself," she says, winding her arms around my neck. "Do you want to look at the plans, or order dinner first?"

My arms encircle her waist, my forehead resting against hers.

"What I want is to greet the woman I've not stopped thinking about all day. Then we can eat, and if there's time…"

"I can be on board with that," she says, pulling my head down towards hers.

CHAPTER 50

KAT

I roll over, my mind joining the present, and I know instantly that something is wrong. Jax's side of the bed is cold.

Sitting up, I brush my hair to one side.

His clothes are still on the floor where I dropped them. The hotel robe, however, is missing.

Pulling on my own fluffy robe and slippers, I make my way into the main area of the suite. The lights are off, except for the glow coming from under the door of the end room. Currently, it's a spare bedroom, and the place I want to turn into an office.

I smile. He obviously decided to look at the plans, something we didn't get around to last night, having been a little distracted pre and post dinner.

Opening the door, I step into the room. Jax has the plans spread out over the bed, frowning down at them.

"Hey," I say, wrapping my arms around his waist and resting my head on his shoulder. "Couldn't you sleep?"

His hands grip mine as he turns his head and smiles.

"I glanced at the plans last night before we went to bed."

His eyes darken. "Something caught my eye, and I wanted to check it out."

I move to his side, loving how he wraps an arm around my shoulders, pulling me into him.

"What?"

"This room isn't long enough."

I turn my head and frown as my chest suddenly tightens.

"I've measured it out. It's missing a good two metres, and there should be a third window."

My body begins to burn up as my eyes follow the plan.

"It can't be."

Memories flood my system of being here with Dad when I was little. I joined him in the office for *Bring Your Child to Work day*. Elijah wasn't interested. He had a swim meet and the twins were still too young. It had snowed heavily, so Dad and I were forced to stay in London overnight. It was the only time I'd set foot in this suite before I moved in; after trashing the apartment I shared with Zach.

I step back in an almost dreamlike state. I close my eyes and walk towards the far wall.

"I think there used to be a door here," I say, turning to face Jax.

"What do you mean?"

"Dad had an office installed in the suite. It's why I thought of doing the same. Somewhere he could escape when he had an urgent project to get on top of. We never used the family suite here. It was too close to home, although I know Mum and he—"

I pause.

I know Mum would join him here for their date nights out, and even some days. Time away from us children. Time to be a couple, one who was very much in love.

Something twists in my chest. Being here with Jax, having

feelings that strong for someone else. How has she survived without Dad?

I suck in a breath.

"Hey, it's okay," Jax says, coming to stand next to me.

He rubs soothing circles on my back.

"I was only young. Five, when I stayed here, I could be wrong," I say, looking around myself.

I've hardly set foot in this room since I moved in, using the main living space and the master bedroom. I popped my head in and found it was a second bedroom. Thought maybe Dad had changed it back.

"Why would someone close it off?"

"Are you sure it was there? We could step out into the hall and find it is now a cleaning closet."

I catch his gaze.

"Can you remember another door between yours and mine?"

I know he would, he's an architect, the *devil is in the detail* is ingrained in his DNA.

"No, you're right, there's no door."

"So we're missing two metres of a room, and I have vague, albeit childhood memories of there being a door here. I could be imagining it…"

I look at the wall. A beautiful bookcase stands in its place, filled with some of my mother's favourite books. Stories she and Dad loved, talked about. If I didn't know better… I'm being ridiculous.

I step forward and begin lifting the books down, carrying them towards the bed. I place them down in order, knowing how Mum files her books. Jax steps forward to help.

When we've removed a couple of layers, Jax inspects the wall, running his hands over the edges of the bookcase.

"If there was a doorway here, whoever closed it up has done a pretty good job of hiding it."

"But you can see from the plans there's dead space?"

Jax grips my shoulders, turning me to face him.

"These are the original plans. Something could have changed over the years. There may be a reason."

"But I remember. I remember sleeping in here that night. Dad was here, told me he was right next door if I needed him," I say, my breath catching as my heart rate increases.

Jax pulls me tightly against him.

"We can check the outside of the hotel for windows in the morning. There's not much we can do at two AM, without raising serious questions."

I drop my head forward onto his shoulder.

"You're right."

"Of course I am," he says, making me chuckle. "Let's go back to bed."

Making our way back into the bedroom, my eyes drift back to the room we've just left.

"You need a distraction," Jax says as soon as we enter the bedroom. His voice taking on a husky tone.

My nipples harden, chafing against the cotton of my robe, begging to be set free.

"What do you have in mind?"

His gaze darkens. "Do you trust me?"

I bite the inside of my cheek.

Do I?

I nod. Realising he's one of the only people outside my direct family I do trust.

He lifts his chin, his eyes locked on mine.

"Take off your robe."

I open my mouth, but close it instantly at his raised eyebrow.

"If you don't want to do this, we can go to sleep."

"I do," I say, quickly.

Oh, how I do!

I can already feel how wet and ready my body has made itself.

I reach for my belt, untying it and pushing the material off my shoulders.

Jax sits down on the chair in the corner.

"Show me your breasts."

My eyes lock on Jax as I lower it slowly, sliding the material down my body, until it lies in a pool at my feet.

A dark flush appears along Jax's cheekbones, and his tongue snakes out, moistening his lips.

His eyes drop. The cold air puckers my nipples instantly, and Jax sucks in a breath.

My stomach contracts hard at the sound, and I bite the inside of my mouth to prevent myself from moaning.

I stand before him, enjoying the feel of his gaze raking over me.

My fingers go to the band of my panties, and I shimmy them down my legs. They are already wet, and I know he'll be able to see the evidence of my arousal, but I don't care. I'm throbbing, pulsing with the need to be filled.

"Lie on the bed and spread your legs."

I turn my back on the object of my desire and move towards the enormous bed in the centre of the room. I stop at the edge, my heart racing. I place a knee on the mattress and take a deep breath as I crawl up the mattress, my arse in the air, my pussy exposed to Jax's gaze.

Hands clasp my ankles, and I stop.

"Drop your chest to the mattress. Arse in the air."

I do as I'm told. I'm naked and exposed, and so turned on I could cry.

"Time to forget everything but me," he says.

I bite down on my arm to stop myself from crying out as Jax's mouth locks onto my pussy.

He sucks my clit, before moving higher to my opening.

His tongue pierces my entrance as his thumb continues to work its magic on my clit.

He's relentless. I spread my legs wider, my hips undulating under the onslaught.

He smacks my arse cheek when I pull away, the intensity almost too much.

This is a different Jax, this one is dominant, controlling, and I love it.

My body tightens, readying itself for the earth-shattering orgasm I can feel building.

"Roll over," he says, just as I'm about to come.

I groan and earn myself another smack.

I do as I'm told. Jax is standing at the foot of the bed, wrapped in a robe, while I lie here, exposed and vulnerable.

"Open your legs."

Jax moves to my bedside drawer and opens it.

"What are you…"

He holds up one of my toys.

I push up onto my elbows.

"What the?"

He raises an eyebrow. "Are you going to question me, or let me do my job?" he asks. "Open your legs."

I swallow hard. I've never let anyone use one of my toys on me. With Zach, sex was functional.

He switches it on.

Oh hell.

He places my clitoral vibrator against my skin. My hips rise automatically, trying to move it into the correct place.

Jax smirks.

"Patience, kitten."

I let out an impatient sigh.

His fingers move south to my soaking entrance.

"Someone is very needy," he says, drawing his fingers up, smearing my arousal around my swollen clit and lips.

He places the vibrator over my clit, and my hips shoot off the bed, my womb contracting.

"Ahhhh," I say, dropping my head back and closing my eyes.

"That's it," Jax says, his lips kissing my stomach.

My hips rise and fall, my knees falling further apart.

"Yes. Please. Jax," I whisper, biting the inside of my lip as the pressure builds deep in my core.

He finds my entrance, spreading it open with his fingers.

I mewl, slamming my hand over my mouth at the sound.

"That's right, kitten," he says.

"You're so wet, glistening in the light. It's a beautiful sight."

I moan at his words, my body has taken on a life of its own.

The clitoral vibrator continues to work its magic. I can feel my pussy swelling, preparing itself.

"Please," I cry, my head dropping back, my cheeks and body burning up.

"Please, what?"

I can't reply, I'm too far gone.

Jax presses another finger into my pulsing channel. He curls them upwards. My hips jolt as he begins to move them up and down quickly.

He holds the vibrator in place as he continues to play with my G-spot, stimulating me from the inside and out. Pressure builds, almost too much for my body to take. I twist beneath his onslaught, trying to escape, but he's relentless.

I bite down on my arm. My body contracts, muscles clenching as the pressure builds, and I finally let go.

"Oh, oh…"

Jax adds another finger, gently sliding them in and out as my muscles contract violently around him. Shudders wrack my body as I totally let go, my cum squirting out of my body at the onslaught, soaking Jax's hand and the bedsheet beneath us.

"Oh my—" I say, trying to get my brain to restart.

I move to pull away, but Jax places a hand on my stomach, removing the vibrator from my clit. He has dropped his robe and moves between my legs, gently sliding his warm, hard cock into my still contracting body.

"Yes."

I moan at the sensation of him filling me, the warmth of his body adding the missing piece.

I slide my hands to his ass, digging my fingers into the firm muscle. He begins to move, and I join him until we both fly over the edge and into the abyss.

CHAPTER 51

JAX

I awaken to the sound of drilling.
What the?

My eyes go to the clock. Nine thirty. Kat is nowhere in sight, her robe draped over the back of one of the chairs, the chair I sat in last night.

Last night. Wow. I'm not usually one to take control, but I had the feeling Kat needed it if she was going to get any sleep. After we made love, she had all but passed out. I watched her for a while before heading back into the spare room. There's definitely something off. Did her father close off the room for some reason?

The drilling starts again.

I get up, pulling on my abandoned robe.

I make my way towards the incessant sound.

Kat is standing by the wall, drill in hand, pressing the drill bit against the now exposed paintwork.

She must sense my arrival, as she stops and turns to face me.

I look at the back panel of wood, now lying against the side wall.

"It was screwed in place. I found where they covered the screws, dug them out," Kat says, as if this is an everyday occurrence for her.

"And?"

"The plaster work behind it is amateurish and thin. There's definitely something else."

I move closer and run my hand over the plaster. She's right, it's poorly done, even if it was going to be hidden behind a bookcase.

I tap on the wall. It doesn't sound overly hollow, but then, if there's a solid door behind it.

"Are you sure you want to do this?"

"One hundred per cent. If I'm wrong, then I'll call maintenance and tell them I was looking at redecorating."

"Won't they think you're a little strange, tearing apart your room?"

Her brow wrinkles for a moment.

"So, I call Caleb." She shrugs. "Get someone from his team to come in."

"You're really doing this?"

"I'm doing this. Something is off, and I want to know what."

I take the drill out of her hand, tapping the wall in several places. When I find the spot I'm looking for, I drill, making several joined holes next to each other. When the gap is big enough, I push my fingers into the plaster.

There's a definite gap before I hit something solid.

"Last chance," I say, looking up at Kat.

"Do it," she says. "Whatever you're going to do."

I remove my fingers before turning my hand over and reinserting them into the hole. Then I pull.

It takes several tugs before the wood and plaster give way with a loud crack. Several more tugs and the plaster and thin chipboard come away, revealing a space and a wooden door, similar to all the other doors found in the hotel.

Kat drops down next to me. She turns her head, as if sensing I'm watching her.

"I was right," she says quietly. "What the hell? Who blocked up the room and why?"

She grips the wood next to the opening and starts pulling it away frantically.

"Ouch," she says with a hiss.

I grab her hand, turning it over in mine. A small shard of wood has splintered and embedded itself in her palm.

"We need to stop and get some gloves, maybe a crowbar. Nothing is going to change."

She opens her mouth but closes it again.

"Let's get showered and clean this up," I say, motioning to the splinter. "Then we can gather the tools we need. Maybe call Elijah or Caleb to help."

"No," she says sharply. "I'm not involving my brothers. Not just yet. It may be nothing."

She gets up silently, nursing her hand.

I follow suit. "But." I press.

Kat turns to me. "I don't know, it's just a feeling."

I move towards her, pulling her into my arms, and she comes willingly.

"First things first, we need to get that splinter out, and then we can go from there."

"Okay," she says.

Her thoughts are so loud I can almost hear them.

We walk back towards her room.

"Where on earth did you get the drill from?"

"Maintenance."

* * *

I'M apprehensive as we clear the rest of the false wall. There's definitely a door behind it, a locked one at that.

"Shit," Kat says, as she tries the handle.

Someone wanted to keep everyone out of this room.

The question is who?

"Kat."

"Don't say it."

I hold up my hands and back away, sitting on the edge of the bed.

Kat stands with her hands on her hips, closing her eyes.

She stands stock still. When her eyes open, I recognise the glint. She's remembered something.

When she moves out of the room, I follow her into the kitchen.

She pulls open every cupboard until she finds what she's clearly looking for. An old coffee tin.

She grabs a teaspoon and pries up the lid, it gives with a pop.

Tipping it up, she holds up her prize.

"I remember Dad cursing because he'd left his key at the office. Told me he always kept a spare hidden in plain sight. Well, maybe not exactly in plain sight, but where no one would think to look."

I take in the coffee tin that's at least twenty years past production, and chuckle.

Kat grins. "Okay, so maybe his logic was a little flawed, but you have to admit, it's a cool tin."

She leaves before I can answer, returning to the room and placing the key in the lock. She pauses, inhaling and exhaling before she twists her wrist. It sticks.

"Shit," she says, giving it a little wiggle.

She tries again until we eventually hear the telling click.

Kat turns, her teeth embedded in her lip, and we stare at each other.

A fluttery, empty feeling takes hold in my stomach. My heart is pounding as Kat takes hold of the door handle, swinging it open.

"In for a penny, and all that," she says, stepping over what's left of the semi-demolished wall and disappearing inside.

I follow closely behind. Dust particles swirl around us. The musty smell of stale air is almost stifling.

Closed curtains block out the light. Kat moves forward, pulling them open. She coughs as the movement shoots more dust into the air, but floods the space with sunlight.

She spins, taking in the room, covering her mouth with her sleeve.

"Jax, it's exactly as I remember it," she says, her voice so quiet I strain to hear her.

I move to stand next to her.

"So why was it closed up?"

"I don't know. Let's find out."

CHAPTER 52

KAT

Dad's old desk and table are covered in archive boxes. We move forward, pulling the lid off the closest one.

It's full of files and tapes. Picking up one of the files I flick through its contents, sinking slowly into the desk chair, my heart rate accelerating.

Jax picks up the next file, doing the same.

"Is this what I think it is?" he says, picking up another file, and then another.

I hang my head, taking shallow, audible breaths.

Jax drops to his knees before me.

"Hey," he says, cupping my chin with his hand, lifting it up until my eyes meet his.

I pinch my lips together and close my eyes, shaking my head, unable to look at him.

Dad, what did you do?

"Kat?" I can hear the concern in Jax's voice.

"He spied on them," I say, swaying slightly.

I open my eyes and watch as he lowers the folders to the floor, taking my hands in his.

"You don't know it was him," he says.

"Why else would he have these files? Why would they have been hidden in a concealed room?"

"I'm about facts, not jumping to random conclusions. There has to be a logical explanation, Kat."

I love his optimism, but the evidence speaks for itself.

"Someone tried to hide these files, Jax. That's Sir Leonard Crawley. What's the betting these boxes contain information on the rest of the men he's been connected with?"

My brain floods with more and more questions. Did Dad hide the files, or did someone else do it after he died, and if so, why? My chest tightens painfully. Do they have anything to do with Dad's death?

I pull out my phone and dial. I don't wait for the other person to speak.

"Did you know?"

"Kat?"

"Elijah, did you know?"

There's a pause.

"Kat, you may want to back up and explain what the hell you're talking about. Did I know what?" Elijah says.

"Did you know our father was a *bloody* spy?"

"Kat. Slow down, what do you mean, did I know our father was a spy? Where are you?"

"We're in the suite."

"Who?"

"Jax and I."

"Don't leave. I'm on my way. And Kat, have you spoken to anyone else?"

I pause, my body temperature rising.

"Brother, you just answered my question," I say, my tone icy. "I'll see you when you get here, and you better have a bloody good explanation to hand."

Disconnecting the call, I stare at the phone in my hand.

"I'm going to kill him."

"Who? Elijah?" Jax asks, looking confused.

He takes in my tense muscles, pulling me onto the floor and into his lap.

I wrap my arms around his waist before resting my head on his chest. Slowing my breathing to match his steady heartbeat.

"You think Elijah knew?" Jax asks quietly.

"He knows something. He's on his way over. We'll soon find out."

He rubs circles on my back until I begin relaxing in his arms. Dropping my head forward, I allow myself to absorb some of his strength.

When I finally start to feel human again, I lift my head and push myself up. Jax follows suit.

My eyes lock on the piles of boxes, all containing files.

A numbness descends, encasing my body.

Dad, what the hell were you involved in?

My throat thickens, as I know for a fact, it's not going to be anything good.

* * *

THERE'S a knock at the door. I've already cancelled housekeeping, explaining the carnage of the spare room is not something I feel like doing today.

I throw open the door to my elder brother and best friend.

I step aside and let them in. Elijah and I are caught in a staring match.

Pen harrumphs and scoots past Elijah, disappearing into the spare room. Jax follows her.

She reappears a moment later, all colour gone from her face.

"Shit," Elijah says, running a hand down his face. "Are you sure?"

"Ninety-nine point nine," she says.

"Stop," I snap, holding up a hand. "Will someone tell me what the hell is going on. I'm hanging on by a thread and am about to seriously lose my *shit*."

Jax appears behind me, wrapping his arms around my waist. He pulls me back against his chest, his presence soothing some of the irritation bubbling inside me.

"I need to make a call," Pen says.

I'm moving before I can stop myself, grabbing her phone out of her hand, and flinging it onto the sofa. She stops and stares at me, her shoulders tensing.

"Kat," my brother hisses, taking a step towards me.

"No calls," I say. "Not until someone explains what the *bloody hell* is going on."

Jax moves, picking up Pen's phone and passing it to Elijah.

Pen nods slowly, her expression grave.

"Kat, you're going to want to sit down for this one." She turns to Jax. "Can you make some coffee, a herbal tea for me?"

Jax turns, his gaze flicking to me. I nod, earning myself a smile before he disappears into the kitchen area.

I glare at my brother but he doesn't say anything. Instead, he turns and enters the spare room, only to reappear minutes later, his stance is one of defeat.

"You've been busy," he says, brushing a thick line of white paint dust from his jumper.

Pen motions for Elijah to take a seat on the sofa.

"Can you speak in front of Jaxson?" Elijah asks Pen.

Pen shrugs. "He's seen what's here. It will all come out soon enough."

"Stop. What the hell is going on? And why are you asking Pen if she can talk?" I hiss at my brother.

Elijah and Pen clearly know more than either of them has let on. I know they were involved in the capture of Sir Leonard, but that was an accident. Elijah had pissed him off protecting April, and he exacted his revenge. Revenge, our baby sister is paying the price for.

How is Dad tied up in all this? And what does Pen know?

"Pen?" I ask, slightly surprised when she can't meet my gaze.

Jax takes that moment to reappear, carrying a tray full of drinks.

"I can leave," he says, taking in the atmosphere.

"Like hell," I spit.

Elijah chuckles, and I shoot him a look that has him swallowing whatever he's about to say.

Jax sits down next to me, taking my hand in his and squeezing it. A warmth spreads through my body, knowing he's here, by my side.

Pen begins, her voice monotone. She tells me a fantastical tale of how she was caught hacking and, to avoid jail, was recruited by a government agency to use her skills to infiltrate various dark-web groups.

I stare at the woman I've called my best friend for the past eighteen years, and wonder who this stranger is.

"How was Dad involved in all this?" I whisper.

"Your father kept me out of jail. Introduced me to the group I would be working with."

I choke on the lump that has filled my throat.

"How?"

Although I think I already know the answer.

Pen looks to Elijah, who's turned an unhealthy shade of grey.

"Your father was also part of that same government agency."

I lean forward and sink my head into my hands.

"He was recruited to help apprehend a group of men working outside the law. A group who were fastidious in keeping their identities hidden. Your father came across them unexpectedly and agreed to help."

"Why?"

Why would Dad risk everything?

"These were bad people. Involved in people trafficking and drug supply chains. You name it, they had a hand in every aspect of the underworld."

"The files?" I say, locking eyes with Pen.

"Are the files we thought were lost. We assumed they'd been taken."

I sit upright. "Taken?"

She goes to look at Elijah.

"Don't look at him. Look at me. Enough of the half-truths, Pen. When did you assume they were taken?"

Pen's eyes glisten in the light, her throat bobs.

"The night he died."

A tear tracks its way down her cheek, and I follow its path.

Jax squeezes my hand.

"But Dad died in a car accident. A hit and run."

Another tear follows the first. Elijah wraps an arm around Pen's shoulder, pulling her into him.

My eyes flick to my brother. "You think Dad was murdered?"

"Not think, Kat," he says, his voice both low and quiet. "We know he was."

I make it to the en-suite just in time, throwing myself against the toilet bowl as I lose everything I've eaten this morning.

Comforting hands scoop up my hair, holding it out of the way, as my stomach retches until there's nothing left but the pain. I drop my forehead onto the cold toilet seat.

The cool face cloth, placed on the back of my neck, eases the churning in my stomach, but does nothing to help the gaping hole that has been ripped open in my chest.

Dropping sideways, I lean against the wall.

Jax drops down next to me, pulling me into his side, running his fingers through my hair in the way he knows I love.

I rest against him, all my fight gone.

We sit in silence.

My head is buzzing, yet empty. Thoughts appear and disappear, nothing sticks.

Elijah's words replay over and over.

We know he was.

I look up as Elijah appears in the doorway.

"Is she okay?"

"How do you think she is?"

Jax is angry. His arm tightens around my shoulder.

"You just dropped the bombshell that your father was murdered."

Elijah sags against the doorframe.

"How long?"

My voice is hoarse.

"What?" Elijah asks.

"How long have you known?"

I look up. My brother looks drained, as drained as he did the day Lottie went missing.

"Since Crawley died. He mentioned something about Dad. Pen confirmed it much later when I asked her."

"But Pen has known all this time?"

Elijah straightens. "Don't blame Pen, she was doing her job, she was protecting us."

I push up off the floor and move to the sink, washing my face and brushing my teeth, before spinning on my brother.

"Who gave her the right to make that decision?"

Pen appears at Elijah's shoulder, placing a hand on his arm.

"It's okay," she says to him, before turning to me.

"You're right, Kat," she says, her gaze never wavering from mine. "I could have gone against orders and told you all. And don't think for one moment I wasn't tempted." She inclines her head. "You're my family. Robert was the father I never had." Her voice cracks, but she coughs, allowing herself to continue. "What would you have done? The agency I work for couldn't pin it on them. They had covered their tracks, even set up a patsy to take the fall. All you would have done is spent the past seven years living half a life, knowing they were out there, but that there was nothing you could do to stop them."

Her voice catches, and it hits me. That's exactly what she's gone through.

I step forward, pushing Elijah out of the way and pulling my best friend into my arms.

"I'm sorry, Pen. Oh God, I'm so sorry," I whisper against her shoulder. "I'm sorry you had to carry that burden alone."

Pen lets out a sob, and I tighten my arms around her, my floodgates opening.

How long we stand there rocking each other, sharing our grief, I don't know. But we grieve together, for the man we both loved, and who was stolen from us.

It's Elijah who finally breaks through.

"We need to call the files in, Kat," he says. "The case is struggling. They're missing pieces. These might be them."

Pen steps back, her bloodshot eyes locking on mine. Questioning.

"Do what you have to do," I say, my limbs suddenly incredibly heavy.

I leave them standing in my spare bedroom, making my way back into the main area, sinking down onto the sofa and picking up a now cold coffee.

Elijah follows me, dropping into the chair opposite, his large frame filling it.

"I wanted to tell you," he says.

"I know."

"But it wouldn't have done any good."

As I stare around me, a hollow feeling settling in my chest.

"It's over."

"What's over?" Elijah asks, his brows knitting together as he stares at me.

"All this," I say, with a sad smile. "The photos, the tape recordings." He hasn't realised they were all recorded on hotel property. I recognise the photos. I'm sure the video footage is no different.

Elijah shrugs, clearly not understanding the enormity of what I uncovered.

I shake my head.

"Dad used the hotel to spy on our guests, Eli. When it comes out, the FHG is finished. No one of any importance will want to stay here, hold meetings or conferences at our hotels. I'm sure I was working here at the time, so deniability won't work. Everyone will think I was complicit."

There's a knock at the door.

Elijah reaches for me, his eyebrows folding inwards as his nose crinkles.

Pulling away, I shake my head.

He pauses.

I'm holding on by a thread. No more comfort. It is what it is. I only hope the information I'm about to hand over is enough to nail the bastards once and for all. Dad must have felt it was worth it, so I'm trusting him.

"That was fast," I say, knowing Pen must have called ahead after I contacted them.

Elijah averts his gaze.

I get up and open the door. I am faced with a middle-aged woman in a dark pantsuit, her hair tied up in a severe chignon, her makeup flawless.

"Kathryn Frazer," she says. "Pleased to finally meet you."

"And you are?"

She smiles, but it doesn't quite reach her eyes. "An old friend of your father's."

Pen appears next to me, moving me aside, and it's then I realise I'm blocking the doorway. The woman and her two goons enter.

Pen points to the spare room.

"Through there," she says.

The woman nods, her eyes softening as she takes in Pen's dishevelled appearance.

They disappear. Jax has made more coffee, which is now steaming on the table.

I take a seat next to him and wait.

The stranger reappears, her gaze moving to Pen's. She nods, a silent message passing between them.

Pen moves next to me, taking my hand in hers.

"They're the missing files?" I ask, earning myself a surprised look.

The woman walks towards us. I motion for her to take a seat. I can't stand it when people stand when I'm sitting, and right now I'm not sure my legs will hold me up.

"Did you really have no idea what your father was doing?"

I shake my head, meeting her gaze.

"You were working with him closely."

I let out a little huff of air. "I was learning the ropes. I was everywhere. I attended board meetings, had regular check-ins with him, but I was working my way through various departments, learning the business from the ground up. It's the way my grandfather and father started."

She opens her mouth, but I beat her to it. "No, I had no idea my father was spying on guests for you. Not that anyone is going to believe that."

She nods. "Your father wanted to keep you out of it. You have just confirmed he did. Thank you, Ms Frazer."

My hackles rise, but I clamp down on my frustration, masking the way I do best.

"What happens next?"

"I'd like for my team to investigate the contents on-site. Moving this number of boxes will raise questions."

"I'll close off this floor," I tell her. Luckily, being suites, there are only a few up here, and Jax is booked into one. "I'll have the remaining guests moved. That way, your team can come and go unhindered."

"Thank you, that's very much appreciated."

"If you're going to destroy everything he worked for, just make sure you get this right."

She nods. No false promises, that everything will be okay.

My respect for her rises.

"I'll leave you to it," I say.

Pen squeezes my hand again, but I pull it back into my lap.

I need time to breathe, take stock. Work out my next move.

CHAPTER 53

JAX

I run a hand down my face as I stand outside Elijah's door.

"Jax?" he says, throwing open the door. "What—"

"Is Kat here?" I ask, looking past him and into his penthouse.

"No, why would you think she's here?"

Whatever he sees in my expression makes him step back and let me in.

"Come in and explain what has you jumping around like Caleb."

"She's left the hotel, and I haven't been able to get hold of her," I say, running a hand down my face.

"She left the hotel?"

"After your team moved in. It was teeming with people. That woman didn't want to move the files in case word got out they'd been found. All those people... Kat couldn't stay there."

"And she didn't move into your room?"

"She told me she needed some space to process everything. I thought she was going to your mum's."

"And she didn't?"

I begin pacing the floor, Elijah following my movements.

"No. She kissed me goodbye and told me she'd call me. Every time Kat has needed to process anything, she always goes home. She sent me a message to tell me she was okay, but then nothing."

"And you know she's not with Mum?"

"I called your mum this morning. She hasn't heard from Kat in days."

Elijah frowns, his forehead wrinkling.

"Have you spoken to her Pitbull?"

"Michael?"

"Who else? He knows my sister's comings and goings even better than she does. Guards her with the ferocity of a Pitbull."

I think back to the time he kept me waiting outside her office.

"Yes. I've spoken to Michael. He hasn't spoken to her since Monday. He's been covering for her, telling everyone she's sick and working from home."

Elijah's brows draw closer together.

I stop pacing.

"I'm worried," I admit.

"Think, what was the last thing she said to you?"

"That she needed some space to process. Wanted to cry in private... *Fuck*. I should never have agreed to leave her alone."

Elijah rolls his eyes. "As if Kat would have given you a choice. My sister is a law unto herself, as you are no doubt aware. I'm sure she's fine."

He leads me into his living area and points to the sofa, grabbing his laptop as he goes.

He opens it, sitting opposite me, tapping on a few keys. A groove appears between his brows.

"What?" I ask, my heart racing.

He presses a few more keys.

His frown deepens.

"That can't be right."

"Elijah, for the love of—" I say, unable to keep the impatience from my tone.

"Kat's tracker is off," he says, his eyes meeting mine.

"I thought you said that was impossible after you upgraded them?"

Elijah drops his chin to his chest.

"Kat's was never upgraded. Every time I went to do it, she was rushing off to a meeting or needed to be somewhere else."

The front door opens, and Lottie walks in, her eyes lighting up as soon as she sees me.

"Hey, Jax," she says.

"Hey, sunshine. How are you?" I ask, forcing lightness I'm not feeling into my tone.

"I'm good. Busy with school and dancing. I've been spending a lot of time with Aunty Leah helping with Callum and the twins... getting ready for *the baby*." She winks, apparently, Lottie is the only one who knows the sex of her sibling and is arranging all the details for the gender reveal party.

She walks over and kisses Elijah on the cheek. "Hey, Dad."

"Hey, sweetheart." Elijah looks up, his gaze moving to his daughter. "Lottie, did Aunty Kat ask you how you disabled your tracker?"

Lottie's gaze drops to the floor, her toe skimming backwards and forwards on the rug.

"Lottie?"

"It was a while ago. Not long after I got back," she admits, looking at her dad's laptop. "Is Aunty Kat okay?"

"She's playing hide and seek," Elijah says drily.

I only hope he's right and whoever was in those files hasn't uncovered our discovery and found her.

The doorbell chimes, and Lottie runs to the door.

"Granny," she says. "Come in."

"Hello, darling. Is your father in?"

Francesca pulls Lottie in for a hug. Holding her tightly, her eyes closed. When she lets go, Lottie half turns and points towards me.

"In there with Jax," she says.

Francesca grabs her bag and hands Lottie some money.

"Can you go and get some ice cream for your old granny?"

Lottie whoops and makes for the exit. As she reaches the door, she turns. "You're not old," she says before making a sharp exit, clearly happy to get out from under her father's scrutiny.

Francesca walks into the room, her eyes locked on her eldest child.

"What have you done?" she hisses as soon as the door closes.

"Me?"

"Yes, you. Don't play innocent. You involved that bloody woman and have potentially put us all at risk."

Is she talking about Pen?

"Mum," Elijah says. "Calm down. What are you talking about?"

"Your father's office. At the hotel. The files. Don't play dumb, it really doesn't suit you," she says. "The fact that the hotel is quite obviously swarming with government agents."

She sinks down onto the sofa as if all her energy has suddenly gone.

"Mum, what do you know about the files?" Elijah asks cautiously.

Francesca looks up, her eyes swimming.

"That they needed to stay hidden for all our sakes."

The hidden room, the bookcase. Had Kat realised it was her mother as she took the books down, stacked them so carefully?

"It was you. You sealed the room," I say, before I can stop myself.

Elijah turns on me, his gaze questioning.

"Kat mentioned the books were organised on the shelves, the way her mum would. That we had to keep them in a specific order when we took them down," I say.

"Where's Kat?" Francesca asks. "She's not answering her phone."

Francesca looks between us, her eyes growing wide, her breathing becoming quick and shallow.

"Where's my daughter?"

"We don't know. Kat has turned off her tracker," Elijah admits.

He looks to his phone and mouths the word, Pen.

I nod.

"I'll put the kettle on." I move towards the kitchen.

I turn to see Francesca crumple in on herself.

"What have you done?" she mumbles, as she rocks back and forth.

Elijah shoots me a look as he drops into the seat next to hers, pulling her into his arms.

I open my phone and dial.

She answers within two rings.

"Pen, you need to come home."

Something in my tone must garner no argument.

"On my way. See you in fifteen minutes."

I busy myself making tea, before leaving the kitchen and rejoining Elijah and his mum. I place the tray on the table and return quietly to my seat.

The front door opens as Lottie returns. She takes one

look at the situation in front of her and heads for her bedroom with her newly purchased tub of ice cream.

Pen arrives almost directly behind her. She drops to her knees in front of Francesca.

"Franny," she says quietly.

Francesca looks up, her hand cupping Pen's cheek. She gives her a weak smile.

"He loved you so much," she says. "You were like a daughter to him."

Pen covers her hand with one of her own.

"And he was like a father to me," she says, cradling Francesca's hands in hers. "Franny, I need you to tell me what happened?"

"They killed him, Pen. They killed Robert," she says, inclining her head, a fresh line of tears streaming down her face.

Pen's grip tightens, her voice catching.

"I know they did. I wanted to protect you."

"Always such a good girl, putting others before yourself. That's what I did. I had to protect my family. They'd already taken the love of my life. I wasn't letting them have my children, too."

Francesca freezes as she sucks in a shaky breath.

"Who, Franny? Who was going to hurt your children?"

Francesca's head draws back quickly, her arm folding over her stomach.

"I don't know. A man. He called. Told me I needed to give them the files if I wanted to prevent a further accident. He sent me pictures of each of them, showing me exactly how vulnerable they were." She inclines her head. "I couldn't let them get them."

"Of course you couldn't."

"I found the files. All of them. They wanted them desperately."

"But you didn't give them to them."

I can hear awe in Pen's voice.

"Damn right I didn't." She looks up, her eyes locking with Pen's. "I told them I had them. That they were safe, and would never see the light of day unless something happened to someone I loved. Then it would be war. I told him I'd written letters that would be sent to the relevant authorities, releasing their location should anything happen to me or anyone else close to me."

Pen rocks back on her knees.

"Who helped you seal the room?"

Franny smiles.

"Someone I trust with my life, but I'm not divulging their name. This is entirely on me."

She turns to Elijah and places a hand on his shoulder. Her eyes suddenly clear.

"It may have been wrong of me, but I did it to protect you all. It was enough that I lost your father. I was not risking any of you. Handing over the files would have meant I had no leverage. Keeping them was everything."

Elijah scoops Francesca against him.

"I'm sorry," she says.

He mutters something against her hair, but I can't make out what it is.

Pen turns to face me.

"Kat's missing," I say, hoping the complete and unwavering faith I'm about to put in our friend is not unwarranted.

"Shit."

* * *

I sit and stare as Pen does, whatever it is *this Pen* does.

Her fingers fly over the keyboard, perched precariously on her lap.

Who is this woman?

She looks like the same person I've known for eighteen years, but there's something else. Turning to stare at Elijah, he's clearly unfazed by the woman he loves. I draw in a breath. There's a deeper, darker side to the happy-go-lucky woman who turns up at red carpet events in army boots and designer dresses.

"There's no chatter," she says, turning to Elijah.

His shoulders relax a little.

"What does that mean?" Francesca asks before I can.

"It means, if Kat's been taken, then no one is talking about it online. That would be unusual in a kidnapping case. There have also been no ransom demands to date, that we're aware of."

The muscles in my shoulders refuse to relax. Instead, pain begins to radiate up into my head, culminating behind my eyes.

"Is that always the case?" I ask.

Pen turns to me, her hand pinching the skin of her throat, her gaze pained.

"No, not always."

Francesca lets out a mini howl.

Elijah moves to comfort her immediately.

"We'll find her," Pen says, leaning over and gripping Francesca's forearm, before returning her full attention to her keyboard, her fingers flying over the keys once more.

"Where are you, Kat?" I whisper.

CHAPTER 54

KAT

*P*ain.

Rolling onto my side, I draw my knees up to my chest.

Pain.

I stretch out again, my hand clutching my stomach.

I try to sit up, but a wave of dizziness has me dropping back against the damp pillow.

How long have I been here?

Another wave hits. I groan, before rolling onto my side and drawing my knees up to my stomach once again.

My stomach roils, and I wretch into the bucket next to me, only this time there's nothing left. The dry retching sets my stomach on fire.

When did I last eat?

I cough, the pain worsens, and tears leak from my eyes.

I close my eyes.

"Kat?" a voice from my dreams says. "Shit, Pen, she's in here."

Someone turns me, I protest as another wave of pain shoots through my abdomen.

"Jax?" I croak out.

"I'm here, angel."

Hands that soothe follow, running down my face, pushing hair away from my eyes.

I'm dreaming again.

I turn into the hands, but this time they are still there.

I force my eyes open, but they struggle to focus. I bite my lip to stop myself from crying out.

"You're burning up," the voice that sounds like Jax says again.

It can't be him, I sent him away, told him I needed time to think.

"Pen, call an ambulance."

There's a desperation in his tone.

"It's on its way."

Someone grabs my other hand and squeezes it tight.

I'm cocooned in strong arms. Lips brushing my forehead.

"Hang in there, angel. Help is on its way."

* * *

Bright lights flash overhead.

Voices talking in sharp, harsh tones.

Everyone sounds so serious.

Someone presses down on my stomach. Groaning, I try to push their hands away, but they stop me.

"Sorry, I know this hurts," a strange voice says.

Then stop.

I want to scream.

Voices talk in hushed tones around me. Some I recognise, others I don't.

A familiar warmth spreads up my arm, soothing me, and I lean into it as my hand is encased in theirs. Firm lips touch the skin, another hand running through my hair.

A forehead rests against mine. "I love you, Kat," the voice says, before their lips touch the tip of my nose.

I try to smile, let them know I love them, too.

A curtain swishes. Other voices join the mix, speaking too fast for me to follow, as their conversation flies backwards and forwards.

"Scans."

"Ruptured Appendix."

"Potential peritonitis."

"Surgery."

I allow myself to drift off.

I'm so tired.

The pain is finally subsiding, so I switch my focus to the hand gripping mine.

* * *

THE DOOR to my room opens, and I turn my head.

"Hey," Gabriel says, stepping into the room. "You're looking better."

Smiling, I place a finger to my lips, pointing to the corner of the room where Jax has finally succumbed to sleep, although his neck is at an awkward angle.

Gabriel nods, stepping into the room. He drops a kiss on my cheek before placing a punnet of red grapes, my favourite, on the table next to the bed.

"Thank you," I say quietly.

He drops into the chair Mum vacated not that long ago.

"How are you feeling?" he asks, his eyes darting to Jax.

"Is it your turn?" I ask, quirking an eyebrow.

"They are limiting us," he chuckles. "I think the doctors and nurses are sick of us all. We were pacing the corridors for hours while you were in surgery."

I grimace, the Frazer family en masse, in full-blown protective mode... I feel sorry for the doctors and nurses.

Gabriel holds up his hands. "In our defence, we've all written healthy cheques to the hospital. Apparently, they're going to rename the family room they moved us to in our honour."

"What? Pain in the arse relatives' room?"

"Ha ha," he says. "But really, how are you feeling?"

"Like I'm floating. Whatever they've given me is quite something," I say truthfully.

Gabriel catches my gaze. "What the hell happened, Kat?"

I shake my head and shrug. My memory is a little fuzzy on the details.

"I remember going back to the apartment," I say. "I needed somewhere to think, clear my head. I couldn't do that with all those people in the hotel."

"You should have come to us."

I grip the hand he has resting on the bed.

"You know me. When I need to think, I need space. We're no different, you and I."

He takes my hand in his and gives it a squeeze.

I drop my head back against the pillow.

"I was trying to work out how to save the company. If selling the chain would work. So many people rely on us for their living. If FHG goes down—"

"Hey, stop," he says.

Jax stirs in the corner, and I glare at my brother.

He holds up his hands in surrender before lowering his voice.

"You need to focus on getting better. The rest can wait."

I shake my head, and the lump that seems to have taken up permanent residence in my throat presses down. My eyes fill. FHG is my second family, as it was my father's. We've let them down.

"I can't ignore it. I have to update the board and give them a heads-up, at least. I need my laptop. I can video call in, warn them of the shit show that's about to descend."

"There'll be no video calls," he says. "According to Pen, the discovery of the files is currently on a need-to-know basis. The board *don't need to know*."

I open my mouth, but Gabriel interrupts. "Nothing is going to happen yet. If that changes, Mum will arrange a board meeting with Cal and update them if you're still recovering. Until then, everyone has been told to forget what we know."

I struggle to sit up, but groan as pain radiates from my surgical site.

Clearly, everyone in the family is *in the know.*

"Will you stop!" Gabriel hisses, pressing a hand down on my shoulder. "Pen and Elijah filled us in on everything. It's all being taken care of. Concentrate on recovering, will you?"

I drop back, panting against the pain.

"Bloody hell, Kat, I thought I was a workaholic, but you win hands down." He runs a hand through his hair. "You nearly *fucking* died, sis. If Lottie hadn't mentioned your apartment, no one would have thought to look there."

"Lottie?"

"She overheard Pen and Jax talking about the last place you would go. Lottie said your old apartment."

I grimace and offer a weak smile. "It is the perfect place to wallow. Remind me to take her shopping when I'm back on my feet. I'm sure there are some additional art supplies she'd like, or maybe even a new wardrobe. She is a teenager after all."

Gabriel rolls his eyes.

"What happened after you got there?"

"I remember a pain in my stomach when I arrived. I put it

down to the stress of the day, or thought maybe I pulled something when Jax and I dismantled the wall."

Gabriel raises an eyebrow, and I shrug, grimacing as it pulls my stitches.

"Anyway, it lasted a couple of days, and I didn't think anything of it. My mind was a little preoccupied. I went to bed. I woke up in the night, and the pain was worse. I took some painkillers, but then it suddenly subsided, so I went back to sleep."

"Let me guess. By the time you woke up, the pain was a thousand times worse?"

"According to the doctor, that was probably when the appendix ruptured."

"You're lucky you didn't develop sepsis."

I flick the intravenous line, dripping high levels of antibiotics into me.

"It was a close call," Jax's tired voice says from the corner. "The infection was spreading throughout the abdomen. It's going to take her a while to recover, according to the doctors."

I harrumph. "I don't have time to simply lie around. I have a company to run." I say, looking between them both.

It's like they've forgotten what I do.

Sadie will be having a field day with me out of the way.

"Elijah has stepped in as interim CEO. He's handed Frazer Cyber Security to Kris now. He'll hold down the fort while you recover. Cal is by his side, so is Mum."

"Great, so you all want me to simply sit on my hands."

"Yes," they both say together.

"Actually, what we want is for you to give your body time to heal."

I harrumph again, followed by a chuckle from the doorway.

Looking up I find my sister-in-law standing there.

"Leah, please talk some sense into these two."

"I wish I could, Kat, but I'm with them on this one. I want my children's aunty fit and well. You gave us all quite a scare."

The worry lines around her eyes tell me exactly how much.

I cover my eyes with my hands and groan.

"You as well?"

"Afraid so."

She moves towards the bed and drops a kiss on my cheek.

"It's no different from how you would be if it were one of the others. Look at you with Harper."

"Does Harper know?"

The last thing I want is my baby sister worrying about me.

"She's been on the phone every day wanting updates. She was here in the room on a video call while we waited for you to come around after the operation."

Gabriel pulls out his phone.

"Are you with her?" Harper's voice comes over the line.

"I am. Want to speak to her?"

"Duh!"

Gabriel chuckles and hands me the phone.

"Hey, rebel," I say, as my sister's face appears on the screen.

"Don't you *hey, rebel* me." Her voice catches, and she sucks in a breath. "You have scared me half to death." Her eyes begin to fill.

"Rebel," I say quietly.

"I'm not going to cry any more. But don't ever do that to me, us again."

"I'll try not to," I say, placing my hand over my heart in a silent promise, as she has always done since being a little girl.

"I'm holding you to that," she says, making me chuckle and frown.

"Don't laugh," she says. "That's going to hurt. Are they treating you all right, or do I need to come over and kick some butt?"

"I'm okay," I say truthfully. "I'd love to see you, but a lot has gone down."

Her face drops. She closes her eyes, inhaling deeply. My chest constricts, and I want to wrap her in my arms.

"Mum and Pen explained." She stares into the phone. "At least..." she coughs. "At least I know it wasn't my fault."

I close my eyes as my throat thickens.

Despite all the counselling and support she's received, she still blames herself, and I'm not naive enough to think my discovery won't have opened a lot of old wounds.

I open my eyes and smile. "Well, you can stop worrying about me. I'm on the mend and have a lot of people nagging me to behave."

"Good," she says, her fingers reaching out towards the screen. I repeat the action, as if our fingers are touching.

"On a lighter note. How's your job going? Have you won your grumpy boss over yet?"

Harper grunts, making everyone chuckle, but she doesn't quite meet my gaze.

Interesting.

"Oh crap. I've got to go, or I'll be late. I don't need to give the grumpy arse any more ammunition. Love you, sis."

"Love you too, rebel. Take care of yourself and speak soon."

"You too."

She disconnects, and I hand Gabriel back his phone.

Leah disappeared halfway through the call.

"She's gone to get us some decent coffee," Gabriel explains.

My stomach does a somersault.

"Fantastic," I say.

I don't want to sound ungrateful, but the stuff they serve here has no punch, or flavour for that matter.

Jax chuckles. "You're such a Frazer. You and your coffee."

"Fine wine and good coffee, it's what makes the world go around," Gabriel says. "I'm sure that's why Caleb is besties with Tristan. He delivers the best wines."

"He just needs to befriend someone who owns a coffee plantation," I say. "Tristan's now supplying to the hotels you know."

"No work," they say together.

I growl.

"What else is there to talk about?" I say.

"Please, sis, that's just sad," Cal says, bursting into the room. "If the only thing you can talk about is work, you seriously need to get a life!" He turns to his friend in the corner. "Jax, you need to do something."

Jax coughs and Caleb flinches, as he realises what he's just implied. Gabriel chuckles.

Men!

"It's not the only thing," I say defensively.

"Name me one thing then," Caleb says, folding his arms over his chest and lifting his chin.

"Running," I say, mirroring his pose. I grimace as pain shoots through my stomach my hand moving to my stitches.

Caleb frowns.

My mind goes back to this same conversation I had with Jax.

"Oh, running, such an interesting and stimulating topic of conversation," Caleb says with an exaggerated yawn. "Have you been running anywhere interesting lately?"

I throw a grape at him, which he catches with ease before popping it into his mouth.

He grins. "Thanks."

Leah returns with a tray full of rich-smelling coffee. My mouth waters as she hands me the first cup. I cradle the dark liquid in my hands.

"Books," I say. "I like to read."

Jax chokes on the mouthful of coffee he's just taken.

I shoot him a questioning look before remembering the book he caught me reading in the Maldives.

"That was a one-off," I hiss.

"If you say so."

"What am I missing?" Caleb asks his friend.

"Nothing," Jax says, but his smirk speaks a thousand words.

"Was my sister reading a romance book?" Cal's voice sounds incredulous.

"My lips are sealed."

I glare at them both.

"For goodness sake, I picked it up in the hotel library," I lie, shooting Jax a look that tells him not to contradict me. He grins, running a finger over his lips, sealing them shut. I scowl at him. "I couldn't concentrate on the audiobooks I'd downloaded," I add for extra clarity, making the others laugh.

Luckily for me, the doctor takes that moment to arrive, offering me some respite from their teasing.

"Ms Frazer, how are you feeling today?"

"Like I'm being picked on," I say.

The doctor chuckles.

"In terms of your pain levels?"

My siblings take that moment to stand, each kissing my cheek before moving to the door.

"See you later," they all say in unison.

I look at Jax, who hasn't moved. I smile, and he smiles back, my stomach fluttering as my pulse picks up. But gone is the tension, the stress from before.

It's then I realise with Jax I feel safe, whole, for what feels like the first time in forever.

CHAPTER 55

JAX

"Go and stay with Jax. Get away, finish recuperating in peace. The world is not going to end if you leave Elijah and Caleb in charge."

Kat opens her mouth, scowling at her friend.

"I promise to keep an eye on them," Pen says.

Kat closes her mouth, her eyes moving to me. I know she feels we've ganged up on her, but she still has a long way to go before she's fighting fit. Her body has taken quite a battering, and despite being at her mum's, she's not switched off.

The infection has finally gone, but she still has to heal, both physically and mentally, from the trauma.

"Fine, but I'm holding you responsible if either of them messes up," she says, staring her friend down.

Pen salutes her with a grin.

The woman in charge visited Kat at Pen's request. She promised that nothing is going to happen without her prior knowledge. Her specialist team is still working through the files we uncovered, tying them together with the information they found in Sir Leonard's hidden office and building their case. Over the weeks, they've removed the files, bit by bit, to another location. The hotel is now back to being government-free.

I'm not sure Kat trusts her, but thankfully, she still trusts Pen.

But Francesca is concerned that Kat is not switching off. She caught her on the telephone to Michael, despite Elijah being there.

When the family first met to discuss where Kat would recuperate, Francesca wanted Kat with her. No one vetoed this, as Francesca needed her daughter as much as she needed her mother. Although Caleb and Gabriel were sceptical, as it would give Kat too much access to work, and given the ongoing investigation, they may need to question Francesca further about her role in hiding evidence.

The aim has been to allow Kat to recover without any stress, after two weeks in hospital recovering and four weeks at home, her brothers have realised that's an impossibility with her staying at Frazer Manor.

"I don't want to go and recuperate in another hotel," Kat huffs. "No offence," she says, looking at me.

"Maybe we don't have to stay in a hotel," I say.

Her gaze meets mine. "What do you mean?"

"I have a cabin. It's in Yorkshire. I built it a couple of years ago."

"You have a cabin in the UK?"

"You sound surprised?"

"I suppose I am. I always assumed you'd settle down in the US. It has, after all, been your home for the past sixteen years."

I shrug. "I've always intended to come home. Don't get me wrong, I've loved living and working in America, but I've always intended on moving back here, to be near my friends and family."

"So, is it agreed? You'll go and stay with Jax," Pen asks.

"Fine," Kat huffs again. "It appears to be the only way I'll get any peace."

"Excellent," Pen says, making for the door. "I'll let the others know."

Kat's eyes sparkle when she looks at me.

"Some alone time." She sighs.

"Is that what you want?"

"More than anything." She holds out her hand, and I take it in mine. "I love my family, but my mother is like an old mother hen, clucking around me. Caleb, Elijah and Gabriel are so overbearing I'm likely to throw something at one of them the next time they step into the room."

"What about FHG?"

She smirks. "I trust my brothers, not that I'll ever tell them that. It will all still be there when I get back. A wise man once told me that."

I lean forward and press my lips to hers.

"He must be a very wise man," I say against her mouth.

Her hand comes up and grasps the back of my head.

"You have no idea," she says, pulling me down, kissing me with a passion I've missed.

We've spent minimal time alone together since her illness. She's needed to recover. I can't say I'll be sorry to leave my friends behind and have Kat all to myself for a couple of weeks.

A cough sounds behind us.

I pull back, but drop my head against her forehead. Our eyes lock.

"Please, get me out of here!" Kat mouths.

* * *

"Are you sure?" Francesca says, an hour later, as I lift Kat's suitcase into my car.

Pen packed it in record time when she heard where we were heading.

Kat pulls her mum in for a hug. "A change of scenery will do me the world of good," she says. "Just think of all that fresh northern air."

"And a certain man," her mum says drily.

Kat grins, her head turning to mine. "There's that as well."

Francesca walks up to me, pulling me down for a hug. "Good thing I love you, stealing my daughter away," she says, her voice thick as she pulls back and pats my cheek. "Take good care of her."

I pull her in for another hug. "I promise," I say.

She grips me tightly.

Elijah arrives, just as Kat's about to get into the car.

"Hey, sis, go and enjoy yourself. I've got everything covered," he says, walking over and enveloping her in a bear hug.

Kat smiles up at him. "I know you do. I'm sorry you're having to delay starting your new life."

He inclines his head. "It's not a problem. It's giving me a whole new understanding of the life you and Dad live. It's intense."

"Never a dull moment. You never know, maybe you'll want to—"

She doesn't get to finish her words before he slams a finger over her lips.

"I can promise you this, I'll be more than happy to hand it back to you," he says with a smile, his eyes moving to Pen. "My priorities have changed."

He moves away, going to stand next to Francesca. His arm wraps around her shoulder as he pulls her into his side.

"Kat's in good hands," he says, his eyes meeting mine.

"I know, it's just…" she tails off before she finishes.

"I'm only going for a couple of weeks," Kat says. "I promise to call, write, whatever you want."

Pen chuckles. "Let Jax get on the road, or they'll get caught in rush hour traffic."

I shoot her a grateful look.

I open the door so Kat can get in, closing it behind her.

"Ready?" I ask, climbing into the driver's seat.

Kat turns to look at me, her eyes looking heavenward. "About twenty minutes ago," she chuckles.

"Okay then, let's get this show on the road."

I fire up the engine and pull away, watching Kat's family wave us off.

Kat sits in silence, her eyes locked on the scenery outside the window.

The drive north takes four plus hours.

Kat is quiet. Too quiet.

"Are you in pain? We can stop if you are."

"No pain, I promise. If there is, I'll tell you," she says, her voice tired and snappy. She pinches the bridge of her nose. "I'm sorry. I'm not a good patient." She sighs.

"You've been better than I anticipated," I say truthfully.

Kat pushes my arm, and I grin.

"What? I would have thought you'd have found relinquishing control a lot harder."

Her eyes darken, her tongue snaking out to moisten her lips. My cock hardens instantly, my mind wandering back to her relinquishing control to me. How she screamed out, as her orgasm ripped through her.

"There's a time and a place," she says, her eyes suddenly sparkling.

I swallow hard as her hand comes to rest on my thigh.

Interlocking our fingers, I lift them to my lips, catching her smile out of the corner of my eye.

Kat yawns and I recline her seat, putting up the heating to

ensure she's warm enough. It's not long before her breathing deepens and I realise she's gone to sleep.

She's still asleep when I put the car into park in front of a large set of gates.

Kat opens her eyes slowly, turning her head towards me.

"Sorry," she says. "I fell asleep. Great travelling companion, I am."

I chuckle. "I'll forgive you, this time," I say. "We're here."

Kat moves her chair back into an upright position, her eyes taking in the scene before her.

Brick pillars supporting a large double gate, surrounded by twelve-foot laurel hedges, keep unwanted eyes out.

Kat turns to face me. "Wow. Impressive entrance."

I grin. "This was my first big purchase."

I hit a button on my key fob, and the gates open before she can say anything else. We drive in silence. Kat stares out the window, taking in the tree-lined drive to my home and the surrounding woodland.

"Woodland? How did you get planning permission?" Kat asks.

"The land held a derelict house. It still took me quite a few years to get planning permission to rebuild, but the house itself sits on the same footprint as the original, is self-sufficient and is in keeping with its surroundings. I also employ a local team to manage the adjacent land," I say. "It was a win-win."

We pull up outside the large stone cabin, which I call home.

"The house that Jax built," she says under her breath.

I park the car, and Kat is out before I can get around to open her door.

"This is stunning," she says, staring up at the Yorkshire stone building, before turning and taking in the surrounding area.

My chest expands at her words.

I move to stand next to her, my hand resting on her lower back.

She looks up at me, her eyes sparkling.

"Are you going to show me around?"

I drop a kiss on her nose, only to have her tilt her head and claim my mouth.

I return her kiss, although I'm cautious not to hurt her.

Kat growls and pulls me closer.

When we finally come up for air, we're both panting.

"Show me your home."

I take her hand in mine and lead her to the front door. Unlocking it, I push it open, holding my breath as she enters the hallway.

"Oh, Jax," she breathes. "This is beautiful."

CHAPTER 56

KAT

Spinning on the spot, I take in the double-height space and the large wooden staircase that leads to an upstairs balcony, overlooking the entrance hall. Behind the balustrades, I can make out a number of doors that lead off to other rooms.

Jax places a hand on my lower back, my body instantly sparking to life. It's been too long since we were alone together. I really do love my family, but *pussy-blocking* they have down to a fine art.

"I'll show you around," Jax says, leading me towards one of the rooms to our left.

We enter what I can only assume is the main living room. It takes up one side of the house.

A large glass wall spans the length of the room, inviting the outside woodland in.

Comfortable seating is positioned to take in the wooded view. This is the place you would come to unwind.

"Jax, this is… breathtaking."

I move to stand by the window, looking out into the expanse of trees. Two squirrels chase each other up and around one of the oak trees, leaping through the branches. On the ground, a tiny bird is burying itself in leaves, throwing them into the air.

I watch, unable to keep the smile from my face. I sense Jax's eyes on me.

Turning my head, my chest constricts as I take him in. His eyes softening.

"Take a seat and enjoy the view. I'll empty the car."

I open my mouth, but Jax holds up a hand.

"No heavy lifting, doctor's orders remember."

I grunt my disapproval, but have learned there's no point in arguing.

"I hate this," I grumble after him, and watch as he fights a smile before turning to leave.

"Sometimes things are sent to make us slow down. This is yours," he says, moving towards the door. "Now take a seat, and put your feet up."

Jax leaves the room, and I sink down onto one of the sofas. I close my eyes and take in several deep breaths. When I open them, I take in the amazing view. Enjoying the solitude the trees offer, something rare for me.

My fingers encircle my necklace, toying with it.

I notice the weight building in my chest, the moment Jax is out of sight.

When did this happen?

I hear him in the hallway, taking the stairs.

My nerves fire, and the desire to follow him is almost overwhelming, so I force myself to remain seated.

Do as I'm told.

Ha.

The kiss has ignited something deep in my chest. I've missed him. Two weeks in hospital and four weeks with Mum, we've not had a second alone, either one of my family or a member of staff has been present. I put up some resistance to coming here. I'd hate for my family to think they won. But alone time with Jax is what I ordered, not only the doctor, but for very different reasons.

The door opens, and Jax reappears.

"That's everything," he says.

In his hand, he's holding the enormous box of romance books, my brother Caleb bought for me. I'm still thinking of how to exact my revenge.

"Where would you like these?" Jax's lips twitch.

I look around the room. In the corner by the far wall is an L-shaped sofa, perfect for reading.

Jax follows my eyes and smiles. "The perfect spot. Great lighting."

"Designed for reading?" I ask, waggling my eyebrows.

As soon as Jax saw Caleb's present, he started thumbing through them. Purely for research purposes, apparently.

"Everything has been designed for a purpose," he says. "And yes, this corner is my favourite spot for chilling out and reading."

He places the box down and moves towards me until he's standing between my knees. He bends over, his hands resting on the back of the sofa, encasing me between his arms.

"What would you like for lunch?"

I lean back and stare up at him, running a hand down the front of his chest.

"What's on the menu?" I say, biting my lip and raising an eyebrow.

He grins, his eyes sparkling.

"Are you feeling better?"

"Oh, much," I tell him honestly. "Maybe not up for a full-blown run yet, but I'm sure we can think of some other form of exercise."

Jax chuckles, although it turns into a deep inhale as my

hand travels south, cupping his rapidly hardening cock through his jeans. Not the only one who's missed this.

He bends his elbows and drops a kiss on my forehead.

"Food first," he says.

"Party pooper," I say, just as my stomach lets out an embarrassing grumble.

"Don't want you passing out on me from lack of food. Your brothers would never forgive me. I've promised to look after you."

"Depends on what we're doing when I pass out? Certain games, I'm sure they'd rather not know about." My brothers have sex with their partners, but I'm sure the thought of their sister and best friend… how delightful.

"Monopoly? Checkers? Cluedo?" Jax reels off.

I growl.

"It was Kat Frazer, in the living room with a box of romance books," I say, smiling up at him sweetly.

"I'll keep that in mind," he says, pushing back and standing up.

He holds out a hand.

I place mine in his, and he gently pulls me up.

"Let's see what got delivered."

We walk across the hallway hand-in-hand and enter another room. An open-plan kitchen. Once again, a wall of glass allows the outside in.

At one end sits another doorway. To the right, along the opposite wall from the window, is a wall of cabinets and high-end appliances, including a state-of-the-art coffee machine.

I walk over and run a finger over it, making Jax chuckle.

"Newly installed. I didn't want you missing your coffee fix."

"You're spoiling me," I say, my chest constricting, my core tingling.

Jax walks up behind me, wrapping his arms around my waist.

"I want you to relax while you're here."

Turning in his arms, I rest my hands on his shoulders.

"I'm already relaxed," I admit. "I didn't think it was possible. All this peace and quiet, but being here with you…"

Jax pulls me tighter against him.

"It scared me, seeing you like that. I thought I'd found you again, only to lose you."

I drop my forehead to his chest.

"I terrified myself. I dreamed about you coming and rescuing me from the pain. I thought you were another hallucination when you and Pen showed up."

Jax cups my chin and lifts my head.

"I'll always come for you. You should know that by now. Thank God, Pen and Elijah had a set of keys."

I reach up and press my mouth to his.

My stomach growls again, and I pull back.

"Sorry," I say. "Living with Mum for four weeks, it appears my body has got used to regular mealtimes."

"Your wish is my command," he says, dropping a quick kiss on my lips. "Let's see what we have."

I turn and take in the rest of the room, as Jax heads to the enormous fridge.

In the centre of the room is a large island, in front of which and close to the window is a large sofa and an enormous table.

"You enjoy entertaining?" I ask.

"Maybe one day," he says, following my gaze. "I'm never here long enough. I've tried to future-proof it."

I walk around the kitchen as the fridge door pops open.

"What the?" Jax cusses under his breath.

I spin to face him.

"What's wrong?"

"Dad was supposed to have stocked up before we got here."

I look over his shoulder. The fridge is empty apart from a few condiment jars.

"It's okay, I'm sure there's something."

I move to the cupboards and open them. There is literally no food, not even a tin of soup.

"Don't worry, I won't be long," Jax says. "I'll pop to the supermarket, grab us some food and be back. In the meantime, make yourself at home. Maybe start on some of Caleb's reading material," he adds, with a wink.

"I could come with you," I say.

Jax walks over and places his hands on my waist. "You're here incognito, and it's been a long day. Besides, I've much better ways to use up any excess energy you may have, and it's certainly not walking around a supermarket."

My tongue snakes out, moistening my lips.

He groans, his hands tightening on my waist, closing his eyes for a second before letting me go.

"I won't be long," he says, turning around, before doing a U-turn and pulling me in for a breath-stealing kiss.

When he lets me go, my knees go weak as he manoeuvres me to the sofa.

"I won't be long."

His eyes have darkened, and I can make out his erection through his jeans. He follows my gaze and readjusts himself.

"Later," he says with promise.

Jax leaves before he, or I, can change his mind.

"I'm holding you to that," I shout after him.

My body is screaming for release.

Forced abstinence. They say it adds spice. It adds a tear-your-clothes-off form of desperation in my mind.

I hear Jax's car fire up, its throaty roar making me smile.

I leave the sofa and decide to make the most of my time by exploring.

The door at the far end of the kitchen leads to a fully equipped utility room and a downstairs bathroom. I make my way back into the hall, and an office sits beside the front door, and behind the stairs is the last room I expected.

Throwing open the door I walk inside, my eyes bulging as I take in the Steinway Grand Piano sitting in the centre of the room. A large comfortable seating area has been positioned to one-side, perfect for listening, while the windows themselves are framed by large, heavy curtains.

A nearby bookshelf holds folders and books of sheet music.

I approach and run my hand over the volumes. Many of which I recognise. Pieces I've played over the years.

Has Jaxson taken up the piano?

He used to love to watch me play. Said it helped him relax.

I move towards the Steinway, my piano of choice. Running my finger over the highly polished wood. My heart thunders in my chest.

It's been so long.

I lost the passion for playing after Jax and I split. He had become my inspiration, my muse.

I lift the fallboard. The eighty-eight keys beneath are calling to me.

My stomach quivers. I should leave.

I find the middle C and press. The note hits the air, and a breath rushes from my lungs.

Pulling out the bench, I sit down, my heart pounding in my chest.

I place my fingers on the keys as I was taught during my first lesson and close my eyes.

My fingers move of their own accord. I'm stiff, but the notes and music come back to me, flooding my system.

I lose myself.

When I finally stop, I sense I'm no longer alone.

"Please, don't stop on my account," he says. "You play beautifully."

An older man stands in the doorway, leaning against the frame.

"Thank you. That's kind of you. I'm a little rusty. It's been a long time since I last played."

He smiles, and I instantly recognise him. They have the same smile.

"You're Jax's Dad."

He moves towards me. "David," he says, extending a hand. "It's good to finally meet you, Kathryn."

His hand encases mine.

"You know who I am?"

"I've heard a lot about you over the years. Jax told me you were coming to stay."

I suddenly remember Jax mentioning his dad was due to stock the house with food.

"Do you live nearby?"

"Not far. I keep an eye on the place when Jax is away," he says. He looks at the piano again. "Will you play something for me?"

"Of course, any requests?" I say, turning back to the beautiful piano and placing my hands back on the keys.

CHAPTER 57

JAX

My heart stops as I open the front door and enter the house.

Music, and not just any music.

Piano music.

A piece I haven't heard in years.

I move towards the music room, unable to keep the smile from my face.

I pull up short at the doorway.

Dad is sitting next to Kat, and they're laughing. Dad's fingers join Kat's on the keys, and he plays as he did when I was a child.

Kat's eyes come up and meet mine. She's glowing. Something I haven't seen in years.

"Jax."

Her voice is breathless as she says my name.

They've both stopped playing. Dad looks over.

"Hi, Jax," he says. "Sorry the food's late. My car had a flat battery. I had to wait for the recovery people."

I hold up a hand. "It's fine," I say, my eyes still locked on Kat.

She grins at me.

"How is it?" I ask.

"I'm a little rusty, but it's like riding a bike. I can't believe you have a Steinway in your house. Do you play now?"

Dad's gaze burns into me. He knows.

"No, I don't play," I admit.

Kat's brows furrow. Then she turns and smiles at David.

"You play?"

"I do, but this isn't for me," he says quietly, his gaze meeting mine over her head. He places a hand on Kat's forearm. "I better go. I have a million and one jobs that need doing." Dad gets up quickly and moves away. "It was lovely to meet you, Kat. Hopefully we can catch up again while you're here."

"I'd like that," she says. "You can tell me more stories about Jax as a boy."

What?

Dad walks towards me.

"The food is in the kitchen," he says quietly.

The look he shoots my way speaks a thousand words.

Tell her.

"'Bye, Jax. 'Bye, Kat."

He makes the fastest exit I've ever seen.

Kat is watching me closely.

The front door closes.

We both remain silent until Dad's car fires up and the sound of his engine disappears.

Kat closes the fallboard gently before swivelling on the bench.

"I didn't know your dad played?" Kat asks.

"No," I say, moving towards her, unable to stop myself.

It's like she's pulling me into her orbit.

I stalk towards her.

She stays stock still, her pupils dilating as I approach.

She shifts slightly, making my cock harden.

I want her... no, I need her with every ounce of my being.

I drop to my knees in front of her.

"Why is there a Steinway in your house?" she asks breathlessly.

"Why do you think?" I challenge, my eyes never leaving hers.

She inhales a shuddering breath.

"I..."

"Lost for words, princess?"

I spin her on the bench until her back is against the piano. I lock my gaze on hers, taking her hands and placing them behind her on the fallboard.

"Don't move."

Kat opens her mouth, but I place a finger against her lips.

My hands move to her ankles, sliding up the smooth skin of her legs. They disappear beneath her dress, pushing the material aside.

Kat inhales sharply.

"I was going to feed you first," I admit. A tiny glimmer of guilt hits me in the stomach. "But, seeing you here, listening to you play. I've imagined it so many times."

Kat groans as my fingers skim her panties, a damp patch already visible through the material.

I blow gently against her heated flesh.

Her fingers contract against the wood, the tips turning white.

I lean forward, my eyes never leaving hers as I suck on the material covering her beautiful pussy.

I move one of her legs over my shoulder, pushing the material to one side, exposing her to my gaze.

I lick her swollen lips from entrance to clit. My tongue swirling around the pebbled point, before repeating the motion over and over, until she's squirming beneath me.

Kat moans, her eyes never leaving mine.

Her hips rotate, and she leans further back, giving me more access.

I work her hard, using my tongue and teeth, enjoying the salty-sweet taste of the woman who has always rocked my world.

"Jax," she hisses, as I sink a finger just inside her entrance, followed by a second. I scissor them, stretching her as I know she likes. Her hips undulate, her breathing becoming increasingly erratic. I press them further in and twist, vibrating them against her G-spot.

"Jax," she screams as her head drops back, her body milking my fingers as her muscles contract hard around me. I pump them gently in and out, my lips locking onto her clit, extending her pleasure until she sags against the piano.

Kat whimpers.

"Shit, did I hurt you?" I say, sitting up and cupping her face.

She smiles through her tears. "Hurt me? No. Break me? Most probably, but in the best of ways."

I scoop her off the bench and carry her to the sofa, cradling her in my lap.

I wipe her tears with my thumb.

"I'm not a crier," she says. "Doesn't really go with the *ice queen* image."

"As long as they're tears of joy, you can cry as much as you like around me. Your secret is safe."

She rests her head against my shoulder. "They always have. I've always been safe with you," she mutters.

I tighten my arms around her.

She looks up, her hand snaking behind my head, pulling my lips to hers.

It's my turn to moan.

"I can taste myself on your lips," she says, pulling out of

my arms. "I never thought that was sexy before, but with you…"

She stands up, her eyes never leaving mine as she shimmies out of her panties, letting them drop to the floor.

Her knees hit the sofa on either side of my legs.

She leans forward, her fingers working on my trousers, freeing me from their confines. I lift my hips, as she pushes them down, far enough for my cock to spring free.

When her fingers encase me, sliding up and down, my balls tighten.

"I won't last," I say.

Watching her come apart on the bench after weeks of not being able to touch her is more than I can take.

"We can't have that," she says, moving forward and positioning her pussy directly above my pulsing cock.

"Kat, I might hurt you," I say.

She shakes her head. "Doctor said it's fine. As long as I don't try swinging from any chandeliers, and stop if there's any pain. As I haven't seen a chandelier, I'm taking it I'm safe."

Before I can say anything, my cock is sinking into her silky depths.

I let out a sharp breath, her muscles squeezing me as her body stretches around me, welcoming me into its silky warmth.

"You feel so good," she says, her head dropping back as I sink further into her body.

When I'm fully seated, Kat's eyes once again meet mine.

She cups my face, her lips capturing mine. Her dress is spread out around us. "I've missed you. Missed this."

"I need to see you," I say against her lips.

She leans back and pulls her dress over her head, throwing it to one side. Her bra remains, along with a vertical red scar from her operation.

I unclip her bra, allowing her breasts to spill free. I lean forward, drawing one puckered nipple into my mouth.

Kat rocks on my cock. Her hands come up to clasp my head to her chest.

I torment one, before moving to the other.

Moving forward, I turn us until Kat is sitting on the sofa and I'm kneeling between her legs, keeping my weight off her stomach, I slide back between her silky lips, moving backwards and forwards, in and out, twisting my hips. I move slowly and gently. I know the doctor said six weeks, and we're on the borderline.

The last thing I want is for Kat to have complications.

We go slow, savouring each other, each movement.

Pressure builds in my balls.

Kat's muscles contract around me, and she lets out a gasp.

My balls tighten, and I drop my gaze, watching as my cock picks up pace, sliding in and out, glistening in the light, coated in Kat's desire. I continue to move as my body shudders, releasing cum deep into her body.

When my orgasm subsides, I drop my forehead to hers.

"That was..."

My throat is tight.

She runs her fingers through my hair.

I withdraw slowly.

"Did I hurt you?"

"No. That was beautiful and just what I, we needed."

She cups my cheek, and I grab some tissues, cleaning her up.

"I need to get you some food," I say, rocking back on my heels.

She smiles as I hand her her bra, panties, and dress.

As Kat gets changed, I move into the kitchen and begin preparing us some lunch, although it's already mid-afternoon.

"This was the house?"

I turn to find Kat leaning against the doorframe. Her expression is questioning.

When I don't say anything, she pushes off and walks further into the room, looking around herself.

"This was the house we designed in my notebook that weekend."

I smile, my chest feeling lighter than it has in years.

"It is," I say, my heart rate picking up.

She remembered.

Will this freak her out?

It was the weekend everyone was away, or so I'd thought. We spent our days making love, snuggled beneath my duvet, only getting up to eat, before falling back into each other's arms.

We'd discussed plans for our future that weekend. It was when I'd told Kat that once we graduated, we could shout our relationship from the rooftop, but it was too risky beforehand, unsure how Elijah and the rest of her family would take it.

We spent hours planning out our future home. Discussed the must-haves, nice to haves, and definitely nots.

I'd wanted the dressing room and en-suite, and Kat had wanted a music room with her own Steinway.

I watch as her memory kicks in.

CHAPTER 58

KAT

My brows knit together.
Our house. Jax built our house.
What does that mean?

He steps forward and takes my hand, leading me upstairs. At the top of the stairs we turn left. I can see his lines on the paper, as if it were yesterday.

We make our way to the end of the corridor. To our bedroom. Stopping outside the door.

I look up at Jax, his eyes sparkling.

He throws open the door and pulls me gently inside.

I gasp and choke on a sob.

"Yes, this is the house we designed. I had to make a few adjustments to fit with planning stipulations, but as a whole. It's the same."

I step further into the room, my hand clasping my chain.

My eyes pop, my nerves tingling as I take in the sight before me.

An enormous four-poster bed, two doorways, one to the right, the other to the left. I move to the right and throw open the door. A dressing room. I move to the left.

"An en-suite."

I chuckle.

"It was a must. No more sharing. I can walk around butt naked, and no one can see."

"Apart from me… I hope."

I turn to face him.

He moves closer, wrapping his arms around my waist.

"You built my music room," I say, my voice catching, the enormity of what he did sinking in.

"I did. The house would have been missing something if I hadn't."

"You built our house," I whisper. "Why?"

He drops a kiss on my nose.

"There was never another home I could have wanted," he admits.

"But—" confusion hits.

He built a house, including features I wanted when we weren't together. When I was horrible to him. Hated him for what I thought he'd done.

He drops his forehead to mine, our gazes locked.

"I can hear your brain whirring again."

"It does that a lot around you," I say, biting my lip. His thumb comes up and frees it from my teeth. "When did you build this house, Jax?"

He closes his eyes for a moment before reopening them.

"Eight years ago."

I suck in a breath.

"Eight years ago," I repeat.

I was still with Zach then.

He smiles.

"I had faith we would somehow find our way back to one another," he says. "And if we hadn't. There's no one else for me, Kat. I hope you realise that."

My hand covers my mouth as I suck in air, trying to fill my lungs, the enormity of his words hitting me.

Jax moves back, cupping my face in his hands.

"I love you, Kathryn Frazer. I've loved you since I first walked in and saw you lost in the music. I loved you even more when you pulled Pen from the pool and tore us all apart for being idiots. When…"

Jax's voice catches, and I move quickly, cupping his cheeks, before slamming my tear-coated lips against his. He opens for me, our tongues tangling.

"I can't seem to stop crying around you," I admit. "Probably because I love you too," I say, finally pulling my mouth away, tilting my head, and looking up at him. "More than I ever thought possible. I don't think I ever stopped. To think—"

I can't bring myself to say how close we were to losing all this.

He drops another kiss on my lips, wiping my tears with his thumbs, his eyes glistening.

When we finally come up for air.

"No one is going to come between us again," Jax states. "Not your family, or mine, friend or foe. We stand united."

"A promise I'm happy to make," I say, snuggling into his chest, my arms tight around his waist.

When did I become a snuggler? A crier... emotional!

Only with Jax.

I press my lips against his chest, right above his heart. "Without you, Jaxson Lockwood, I realise I'm only half a person. You make me whole. Fire me headfirst out of my comfort zone. Allow me to dream of things, a future, I never thought I wanted."

He kisses my hair, his arms tightening around me, as if he never wants to let me go.

He steps back, his hands gripping mine. Our eyes meet.

He lowers himself to one knee, and I suck in a breath.

"Kathryn Frazer. I know we've not been back together that long." He inhales, making me smile. "But here in the house, we designed so many years ago. Will you agree to marry me? Be my partner, my wife, my love?" he asks.

Tilting my head, I lose myself in his expectant gaze.

He dips his chin and cringes, his fingers tightening around mine.

"Damn, this is not what I envisaged, or how I wanted to ask you."

He lets go of one of my hands and rubs the back of his neck. "Having you here after I found you in that bed, burning up, so ill. I thought I'd lost you again." He sighs. "The thought of losing you nearly broke me."

I place a finger over his lips, my heart racing as goosebumps form all over my body.

"Yes," I say. "I'm savouring the moment." I chuckle at his confused expression. "No proposal could be more perfect, more natural, more... us."

His eyebrows furrow.

"Yes," I say, more playfully. Dropping to my knees in front of him, my arms snaking up and around his neck. "Yes, Jaxson Lockwood, I will marry you. I will be your partner, your wife, your love, as long as you promise to be mine in return... although you will be my husband."

His muscles relax as he pulls me against him.

My chest expands, a giddiness overtaking me.

"There is, however, one request," I say playfully.

He raises an eyebrow, and I grin.

"I don't want a media circus. Minimal drama. I want us to get married in the Maldives, with only our families and a few close friends. It was there we found each other again..."

"It sounds perfect," he says.

Jax throws back his head and laughs, a deep, rich sound

that locks itself onto my soul. A sound I know I want to hear for the rest of my life.

"Minimal drama? You do realise Caleb is going to have a field day with this?"

"True, and we're talking about my family, there's always some form of drama," I say.

Jaxson's face softens as all tension leaves it.

"Well, are you sure we want to include my family then?" he asks. "Christmas was one thing, a wedding…"

He strokes a hand down my cheek, and I turn into it, taking a deep cleansing breath.

"It's definitely what I want. Warring parents or not. We made new memories there. I want to go back."

"You have a deal," he says before leading me back downstairs and finally feeding me lunch.

CHAPTER 59

JAX

The men have the bar, the ladies have the spa.

There are no hotel guests milling around. The island is entirely ours.

Don Baskin called Kat three weeks ago to say there had been a mass cancellation. A movie star and her rockstar fiancé had called it quits earlier in the week. As they had booked the entire island for their nuptials, Kat jumped in. Calling me and asking me my opinion.

As I've wanted to marry the woman for as long as I can physically remember, it was a no-brainer. So here I am, the night before I say *I do*, to the woman who has tied me up in knots for years.

Elijah stands up and taps the side of his glass, our server bringing over a tray of champagne glasses.

"Gentleman," he says.

Caleb chokes on the drink he's holding.

"How come you get to do the speech?" Caleb heckles. "We're only here because of my matchmaking."

Everyone rolls their eyes, and I clasp his shoulder. "Something I'll be eternally grateful for," I say, earning myself a grin.

"Glad I could help. If anyone else is in need of my services—" A drinks coaster comes flying through the air. I'm unsure whether it was Quentin, Tristan or Xander who threw it.

"Don't encourage him," all three groan together.

Elijah taps his glass again, glaring at his younger brother.

"I'm standing here because Jaxson was my best friend at university. I've known him the longest and as Kat's older brother…"

"He's my business partner," Caleb fires back. "I spend more time with him now."

"Can you please just get on with it?" Gabriel says drily. "Cal, you can give a speech after Elijah. Age before beauty, I think the saying is."

It's amazing the pair didn't kill each other while Kat was out of action. Michael all but dropped to his knees at Kat's feet when she finally returned, begging to be rescued.

Elijah glares at Gabriel. I bite the inside of my mouth to stop myself from laughing at the look Caleb shoots Elijah.

Gabriel simply shakes his head and makes a rolling motion with his hand to speed up proceedings.

"Fine," Elijah huffs. "As I was about to say. I'd like to propose a toast."

He takes one of the champagne glasses and encourages everyone else to do the same. Holding it up, he turns to me.

"You're one hell of a brave man taking on our sister, but we know you're up to the job." He smiles, something he does much more these days and especially since baby Amelia arrived. "Like all Frazers, Kat is independent, focused, but most of all, she's loyal to a fault. Loyal is something you've proved to be, time and time again. You've been like a brother to me over the years, always having my back, even when I didn't know or truly appreciate it. Now I get to call you brother for real. Welcome to the family, Jax."

Caleb makes a loud, theatrical sobbing sound, to which Elijah balls up his napkin and throws it at him.

"Well, if you think you can do better, go for it." Elijah harrumphs as he sits down.

Caleb stands up. "This is all down to me," he says, taking a bow. "You can thank me later," he says, shooting me a wink. "If I hadn't arranged for you to stow away on Kat's flight, the two of you may never have found one another again. I take full responsibility, and I couldn't be happier. Just call me Cupid going forward."

"We arranged," Elijah says.

"My idea," Caleb shoots back.

I stand up, holding up my hands.

"Thank you both for your kind words," I say, almost choking on my champagne. "I've been around this family for a long time. I've loved your sister for most of that time. Things have not been easy. No one needs reminding of the trials Kat and I've faced before finally finding one another again."

A cheer goes up.

"And I promise, I'll love her until my dying breath. She's it for me."

Elijah, Caleb, and Gabriel hold up their glasses silently before downing their contents. They're probably the only ones here who will get that statement. They, too, have found their soul mates.

Dad stands up, holding up his glass.

"I'd just like to say how proud I am of you and everything you've achieved." His throat bobs, and he smiles at me. "Congratulations, Jaxson. Kat's a wonderful woman, you're a very lucky man."

"Thanks, Dad," I say.

Peter turns to Dad and smiles. He's joined us this evening, Mum having joined Kat and the other ladies at the spa.

"Speeches done, it's time to drink. This is a celebration," Dad says.

Tonight is family. Tomorrow, a few more of our friends arrive, along with more of Kat's relatives, ready for our evening nuptials. I'm counting down the hours.

CHAPTER 60

KAT

The spa has stayed open for us. Final wedding preparations are in full swing. Nails, massages, facials.

Champagne glasses sit next to us.

It's been a tight turnaround. From the moment Don rang to say there had been a mass cancellation, it's been all systems go.

Chloe, Gabriel's ex-personal shopper and fashion designer, created my wedding dress. Turning my ideas into a stunning reality in record time.

Jax and I arrived a few days ago, and have been working with Don over the final preparations for tomorrow. A security team has been put in place to keep any unwanted visitors and press away. Don ensured that all staff members signed an NDA to prevent them discussing the event in advance.

Now it's here, and I have never felt so calm in my life.

Mum, Leah, April, Lottie, Pen, and Hannah, Jax's mum, are sitting having pedicures in a large room overlooking the ocean. The gentle sound of the waves is the perfect backdrop to our conversation. Louise, Pen's mum, is looking after baby

Amelia for the evening, along with Leah's mum, Louise, and her Dad, who are babysitting Callum, Ava and Isla.

Mum holds up her glass, and the others follow suit.

"Kat," she says, and I drop my chin to my chest.

I hate speeches and being the centre of attention. Business is one thing, personal is a whole different ballgame.

"This is your time. Don't shy away, young lady," she says, making me smile.

"Not so young anymore, Mum," I say.

"Speak for yourself," both Leah and Pen say at the same time.

"I'm not going to waffle on," Mum says. "I just wanted to say how proud I am of you."

She looks at Hannah.

"When Elijah first brought Jaxson home. I knew fate had done so for a reason. When Robert and I saw how they looked at one another, we realised why."

Mum turns to face me, sucking in a breath, her eyes glistening. "Life has tried its hardest to break you both apart, but fate has had other ideas and I couldn't be happier. Love is a gift, hold on to it."

The woman attending my toes stops and I get up, walking over to mum and pulling her in for a hug.

"Your father would be so proud. He loved Jaxson like a son."

Hannah raises her glass. "I'd like to thank you for being there for Jaxson. When his father and I split, it was messy and difficult. Being an only child, he was caught in the middle. Not something I'm proud of." She takes a sip of her champagne before continuing. "When Jax came home that first summer, I must have heard your name a thousand times, Kathryn. That didn't change. For three years, you were all my son could talk about. You and your brothers. When it stopped, I knew something had happened, but he would never tell me. These past six months, my son has come alive again, and it's because of you."

"Well, let's raise a glass, to fate finally getting her shit together," Pen says with a laugh. "For finally untangling the web she wove to get there."

Hannah laughs and raises her glass. "I can drink to that."

I move back to my seat, taking a large sip of my champagne.

My phone rings.

"Hey, rebel," I say. "Where are you? You're missing spa time."

My baby sisters face appears on the screen.

"What's up? You look shocking."

"Food poisoning," she says, with a groan. "A dodgy prawn."

She drops the phone and disappears. I hear her retching in the background.

My heart sinks.

When she returns, she looks even greener, or greyer, it's hard to tell.

"Oh, rebs," I say.

"I'm not going to make it," she says, tears now streaming down her face. "There's no way I can get on a flight… oh, Kat, I'm so sorry."

My eyes begin to fill, a hollow feeling filling my chest.

The Maldives was supposed to be somewhere Harper could come, see us all. Things may have calmed down with the press, but she's stayed in New York, enjoying the anonymity her hidden identity has afforded her. That, and I think she's enjoying her new job, despite her boss. It's probably something I understand more than our brothers.

Pen grabs the phone from my hands.

"Hey, Harps. No tears," she says sternly. "Elijah and I will set you up a live stream for the wedding. You can spend whatever time you can with us from the comfort of your bed. You won't miss a thing... apart from the humidity maybe, I promise."

Harper lets out a wail, sobbing her thank you.

"Now get to a doctor. I don't mean to be rude, but you look terrible."

I take the phone back. We reach our fingers towards the screen. "Feel better. I'll stream you in when I'm getting ready. Make sure you don't miss a second."

"Love you, sis," Harper says.

"Love you more. Now do what Pen says."

I end the call and drop back in my chair.

April looks over and squeezes my arm before grabbing another bottle of champagne, our server taking it off her and popping the cork.

April rolls her eyes. "Will I ever get used to having everything done for me?"

I chuckle. "Probably not, but go with it. It's much easier."

The server steps forward and fills our glasses once more.

"Harper may not be able to join us, but I know what she'd be saying right now." April holds up her glass.

She and Harper have done their fair share of partying in the past.

"Let's get this party started."

CHAPTER 61

JAX

I stand on the white sand under the gazebo.

The sun is beginning to set. Don Baskin stands before me, an ordained officiant.

He smiles. "Congratulations," he says for the millionth time since we arrived.

Elijah and Caleb stand to my right. Gabriel declined, saying two speeches were enough and is sitting with his mother and father-in-law, helping out with the twins. Callum is with Kat and Leah.

Leah and April appear. April grins, blowing Caleb a kiss, which he catches and pockets.

"Just you wait, you and Kat will be as soppy," he grumbles.

"I can only hope," I admit, making him smile.

The music starts, and I draw in a breath as I turn to find Kat making her way across the sand with her mother.

Gabriel leaves his chair to join them. She smiles at him as he offers her his arm. He bends down and kisses both their cheeks, her Mum leaving her and coming to the front. She stops before rushing over and pulling me in for a watery hug.

I return it. "Thank you for letting me marry your daughter," I say.

She smiles and gives my hand a squeeze before moving to her seat.

I look up. Kat is standing where the chairs end, her arm through that of her brother's.

Her gaze finds mine and she smiles.

A smile that hits me in the centre of my chest. There is a pressure, as if something snaps into place. I know I have found my person, the one I will do anything for and I know he will be there for me in return.

Kat walks towards me, stealing my breath.

Elijah places a hand on my shoulder, whispering to Cal. "He's a goner."

I ignore him as I watch the woman who has plagued my dreams for nearly nineteen years make her way towards me, a kitten lace bodice and the loose chiffon material of her skirt floating around her legs.

Gabriel places her hand in mine, shooting me a grin.

My eyes lock on Kat's.

"You look…" I say, suddenly overcome.

I swallow against the lump in my throat.

"So do you."

Kat squeezes my hands, her eyes glistening.

"Shall we do this?"

We turn to Don, who smiles brightly at us both, like a proud father figure.

When Don turns to me, I squeeze Kat's hands in mine, turning to face her, our eyes locking.

"I, Jaxson Lockwood, take you, Kathryn Frazer, to be my lawfully wedded wife." I grin at her, my eyes filling. "You're the love of my life, my soul-mate. Without you I'm only half a man. I stand here today, before our friends and family and choose you, because, beautiful woman, it's only ever been you. You're my best friend, and my heart's partner. My one true love. And with these vows, I promise to love you, cherish you, and support you, every day. For better, for worse, for richer, for poorer, in sickness and in health, until we move on from this life, to the next."

Kat bites her lip, a single tear tracking its way down her cheeks.

"I, Kathryn Frazer, take you, Jaxson Lockwood, to be my lawfully wedded husband." Pen jumps up, placing a tissue in Kat's hand. She takes it wiping her eyes, with a glistening smile. Her eyes lock on mine. "They call me an ice queen, but I think I've well and truly melted, and it's all because of you. I think I fell in love with you the moment you stumbled awkwardly into the room when I was playing piano. People have tried to drive a wedge between us, but love has won out. You are my best friend, my one true love. You are the other half of my soul. I vow to love you, cherish you, support you. For better, for worse, for richer, for poorer, in sickness and in health, until I leave this earth and then I'm going to find you and ensure we do this all over again in another life."

I pull her into my arms, my mouth coming down hard on hers.

A cheer goes up and somewhere in the background I hear Don pronounce us husband and wife.

When I pull back I look down at the woman who is now my wife. A woman who is looking at me with the same awe and wonder in her eyes.

"I love you, Mrs Frazer-Lockwood."

"I love you more, Mr Frazer-Lockwood."

EPILOGUE

HARPER

I sit quietly in the bedroom.

I've missed this, the silence of being in the country, the fresh air, nature. I didn't realise how much until now.

New York is amazing. The shopping, the nightlife... even work. But there's something magical about coming home. Especially here. The peace and quiet. No car horns, no shouting, the roar of the subway. How had I forgotten?

Sneaking into the house wasn't hard, especially when no one is expecting me. Secret passages, hidden door keys. Betsy nearly discovered me, but I managed to hide in the wall panel.

The family is all gathered downstairs. It's not what I was expecting when I came here. Everyone leads such busy lives these days, but I should know. We're Frazers. With all the children, it's the more the merrier. I can't wait to meet the new additions.

My hands drop to my still flat stomach, cradling what I know is nestled and growing deep inside me.

I suck in a shuddering breath. Missing Kat and Jaxson's

wedding was unavoidable, and I'll forever be grateful to Pen for making it possible for me to attend. Seeing everyone laughing and smiling together. Seeing Kat truly happy. Jaxson was always the man for her, even my much younger self could see that. Knew they should be together.

I hear voices approaching in the corridor.

"I love you," I hear Kat say outside the bedroom. "I don't think I'll ever tire of saying those words."

Silence descends, and I cringe.

Kat's going to kill me, talk about baby sister, passion killer.

The door opens and my sister and a man I've loved, like another brother enters. Their arms wrapped around one another, their lips fused.

I click on the bedside light, wanting to stop them before things get too heated. They spring apart, turning sharply.

I get up from the edge of the bed, allowing Kat and Jax to see my face.

"What the... rebel, is that you?" A wide grin lights up her face, as her eyes travel over me, her delight palpable.

She steps forward pulling me into a sisterly bear hug.

"Surprise—" I say, relaxing into her hold and allowing her strength to seep into me, shoving aside the stress of the past couple of months, at least for this one moment. Knowing there's no more hiding and that I'm going to need all my strength for what's to come.

ABOUT THE AUTHOR

Zoe Dod writes emotionally intense billionaire fiction, with complex characters, swoon-worthy romance and a host of plot twists that will leave you guessing until the end. Her books are written in British English.

Prior to becoming a writer, Zoe began her working life as a software development manager in The City of London. In her mid-thirties she retrained as a primary school teacher, and loved teaching children to write and tell stories. She left teaching to spend more time with her family, and it was then she uncovered her love for writing romance.

Zoe lives in The New Forest, Hampshire, England with her husband, two adult children (when they're back from work and uni), her crazy puppy and two rescue cats.

She loves reading and writing. When she's not doing either of those, she's on long walks in The New Forest or attending Zumba classes

Sign up for her monthly Newsletter www.zoedod.com
    You can follow Zoe on
    Instagram: @zoedod_author
    Facebook: Zoe Dod - Author
    Tik Tok: @zoedod_author

ALSO BY ZOE DOD

<u>Forgive Me Series</u>
Always You
Only You
Until You

<u>The Frazer Billionaires</u>
The Donor Billionaire (Gabriel's story)
The Playboy Billionaire (Caleb's story)
The Broken Billionaire (Elijah's story)
The Ice Queen Billionaire (Kat's story)
The Rebel Billionaire (Harper's story)

* * *

Made in the USA
Middletown, DE
04 February 2026